HIGHLAND SINNER

Books by Hannah Howell

ONLY FOR YOU
MY VALIANT KNIGHT
UNCONQUERED
WILD ROSES
A TASTE OF FIRE
HIGHLAND DESTINY
HIGHLAND HONOR
HIGHLAND PROMISE
A STOCKINGFUL OF JOY
HIGHLAND VOW
HIGHLAND KNIGHT
HIGHLAND HEARTS
HIGHLAND BRIDE
HIGHLAND ANGEL
HIGHLAND GROOM
HIGHLAND WARRIOR
RECKLESS
HIGHLAND CONQUEROR
HIGHLAND CHAMPION
HIGHLAND LOVER
HIGHLAND VAMPIRE
CONQUEROR'S KISS
HIGHLAND BARBARIAN
BEAUTY AND THE BEAST
HIGHLAND SAVAGE
HIGHLAND THIRST
HIGHLAND WEDDING
HIGHLAND WOLF
SILVER FLAME
HIGHLAND FIRE
NATURE OF THE BEAST
HIGHLAND CAPTIVE
HIGHLAND SINNER

HIGHLAND SINNER

HANNAH HOWELL

ZEBRA BOOKS
Kensington Publishing Corp.

ZEBRA BOOKS are published by

Kensington Publishing Corp.
850 Third Avenue
New York, NY 10022

Special book excerpts or customized printings can also be created to fit specific needs. For details, write or phone the office of the Kensington Special Sales Manager: Attn. Special Sales Department. Kensington Publishing Corp., 850 Third Avenue, New York, NY 10022.

Zebra and the Z logo Reg. U.S. Pat. & TM Off.

ISBN-13: 978-1-60751-411-4

Printed in the United States of America

HIGHLAND SINNER

The Murray Family Lineage

Iain Murray – m – Jeanne Murray

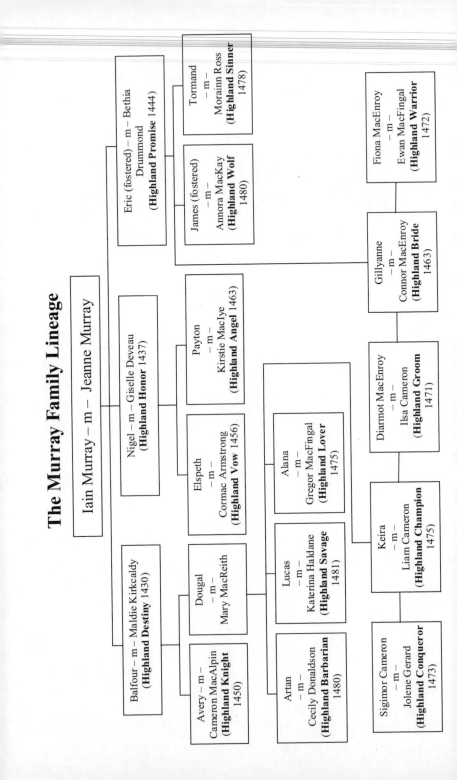

Balfour – m – Maldie Kirkcaldy
(**Highland Destiny** 1430)

Nigel – m – Giselle Deveau
(**Highland Honor** 1437)

Eric (fostered) – m – Bethia Drummond
(**Highland Promise** 1444)

Avery – m – Cameron MacAlpin
(**Highland Knight** 1450)

Dougal – m – Mary MacReith

Elspeth – m – Cormac Armstrong
(**Highland Vow** 1456)

Payton – m – Kirstie MacIye
(**Highland Angel** 1463)

James (fostered) – m – Annora MacKay
(**Highland Wolf** 1480)

Tormand – m – Morainn Ross
(**Highland Sinner** 1478)

Artan – m – Cecily Donaldson
(**Highland Barbarian** 1480)

Lucas – m – Katerina Haldane
(**Highland Savage** 1481)

Alana – m – Gregor MacFingal
(**Highland Lover** 1475)

Sigimor Cameron – m – Jolene Gerard
(**Highland Conqueror** 1473)

Keira – m – Liam Cameron
(**Highland Champion** 1475)

Diarmot MacEnroy – m – Ilsa Cameron
(**Highland Groom** 1471)

Gillyanne – m – Connor MacEnroy
(**Highland Bride** 1463)

Fiona MacEnroy – m – Ewan MacFingal
(**Highland Warrior** 1472)

Chapter 1

Scotland—Early Summer 1478

What was that smell?

Tormand Murray struggled to wake up at least enough to move away from the smell assaulting his nose. He groaned as he started to turn and the ache in his head became a piercing agony. Flopping onto his side, he cautiously ran his hand over his head and found the source of that pain. There was a very tender swelling at the back of his head. The damp matted hair around the spot told him that it had bled, but he could feel no continued blood flow. That indicated that he had been unconscious for more than a few minutes, possibly for even more than a few hours.

As he lay there trying to will away the pain in his head, Tormand tried to open his eyes. A sharp pinch halted his attempt and he cursed. He had definitely been unconscious for quite a while and something beside a knock on the head had been done to him for his eyes were crusted shut. He had a fleeting, hazy memory of something being thrown into his eyes before all went black, but it was not enough to give him any firm idea of what had happened to him. Although he ruefully admitted to himself that it was as much vanity as a reluctance to cause himself pain that made him fear he would tear out his eyelashes if he just forced his eyes open, Tormand proceeded very carefully. He gently brushed aside the crust on his eyes until he could open them, even if only enough to see if there was any water close at hand to wash his eyes with.

And, he hoped, enough water to wash himself, if he proved to be the source of the stench. To his shame there had been a few times he had woken to find himself stinking; drink and a few stumbles into some foul muck upon the street being the cause. He had never been this foul before, he mused, as the smell began to turn his stomach.

Then his whole body tensed as he suddenly recognized the odor. It was death. Beneath the rank odor of an unclean garderobe was the scent of blood—a lot of blood. Far too much to have come from his own head wound.

The very next thing Tormand became aware of was that he was naked. For one brief moment panic seized him. Had he been thrown into some open grave with other bodies? He quickly shook aside that fear. It was not dirt or cold flesh he felt beneath him, but the cool linen of a soft bed. Rousing from unconsciousness to that odor had obviously disordered his mind, he thought, disgusted with himself.

Easing his lids open at last, he grunted in pain as the light stung his eyes and made his head throb even more. Everything was a little blurry, but he could make out enough to see that he was in a rather opulent bedchamber, one that looked vaguely familiar. His blood ran cold and he was suddenly even more reluctant to seek out the source of that smell. It certainly could not be from some battle, if only because the part of the bedchamber he was looking at showed no signs of one.

If there is a dead body in this room, laddie, best ye learn about it quick. Ye might be needing to run, said a voice in his head that sounded remarkably like his squire Walter, and Tormand had to agree with it. He forced down all the reluctance he felt and, since he could see no sign of the dead in the part of the room he studied, turned over to look in the other direction. The sight that greeted his watering eyes had him making a sound that all too closely resembled the one his niece Anna made whenever she saw a spider. Death shared his bed.

He scrambled away from the corpse so quickly he nearly fell out of the bed. Struggling for calm, he eased his way off the bed and then sought out some water to cleanse his eyes so that he could see more clearly. It took several awkward bathings of his eyes before the sting in them eased and the blurring faded. One of the first things he saw after he dried his face was his clothing folded neatly on a chair, as though he had come to this bedchamber as a guest, willingly. Tormand wasted no time in putting on his clothes and searching the room for any other signs of his presence, collecting up his weapons and his cloak.

Knowing he could not avoid looking at the body in

the bed any longer, he stiffened his spine and walked back to the bed. Tormand felt the sting of bile in the back of his throat as he looked upon what had once been a beautiful woman. So mutilated was the body that it took him several moments to realize that he was looking at what was left of Lady Clara Sinclair. The ragged clumps of golden blond hair left upon her head and the wide, staring blue eyes told him that, as did the heart-shaped birthmark above the open wound where her left breast had been. The rest of the woman's face was so badly cut up it would have been difficult for her own mother to recognize her without those few clues.

The cold calm he had sought now filling his body and mind, Tormand was able to look more closely. Despite the mutilation there was an expression visible upon poor Clara's face, one that hinted she had been alive during at least some of the horrors inflicted upon her. A quick glance at her wrists and ankles revealed that she had once been bound and had fought those bindings, adding weight to Tormand's dark suspicion. Either poor Clara had had some information someone had tried to torture out of her or she had met up with someone who hated her with a cold, murderous fury.

And someone who hated him as well, he suddenly thought, and tensed. Tormand knew he would not have come to Clara's bedchamber for a night of sweaty bed play. Clara had once been his lover, but their affair had ended and he never returned to a woman once he had parted from her. He especially did not return to a woman who was now married, and to a man as powerful and jealous as Sir Ranald Sinclair. That meant that someone had brought him here, someone who wanted him to see what had been done to a woman he had once bedded, and, mayhap, take the blame for this butchery.

That thought shook him free of the shock and sorrow he felt. "Poor, foolish Clara," he murmured. "I pray ye didnae suffer this because of me. Ye may have been vain, a wee bit mean of spirit, witless, and lacking morals, but ye still didnae deserve this."

He crossed himself and said a prayer over her. A glance at the windows told him that dawn was fast approaching and he knew he had to leave quickly. "I wish I could tend to ye now, lass, but I believe I am meant to take the blame for your death and I cannae; I willnae. But, I vow, I *will* find out who did this to ye and they will pay dearly for it."

After one last careful check to be certain no sign of his presence remained in the bedchamber, Tormand slipped away. He had to be grateful that whoever had committed this heinous crime had done so in this house, for he knew all the secretive ways in and out of it. His affair with Clara might have been short, but it had been lively and he had slipped in and out of this house many, many times. Tormand doubted if even Sir Ranald, who had claimed the fine house when he had married Clara, knew all of the stealthy approaches to his bride's bedchamber.

Once outside, Tormand swiftly moved into the lingering shadows of early dawn. He leaned against the outside of the rough stone wall surrounding Clara's house and wondered where he should go. A small part of him wanted to just go home to Dubhlinn and forget about it all, but he knew he would never heed it. Even if he had no real affection for Clara, one reason their lively affair had so quickly died, he could not simply forget that the woman had been brutally murdered. If he was right in suspecting that someone had wanted him to be found next to the body and be accused of Clara's murder, then he definitely could not simply forget the whole thing.

Despite that, Tormand decided the first place he would go was his house. He could still smell the stench of death on his clothing. It might be just his imagination, but he knew he needed a bath and clean clothes to help him forget that smell. As he began his stealthy way home Tormand thought it was a real shame that a bath could not also wash away the images of poor Clara's butchered body.

"Are ye certain ye ought to say anything to anybody?"

Tormand nibbled on a thick piece of cheese as he studied his aging companion. Walter Burns had been his squire for twelve years and had no inclination to be anything more than a squire. His utter lack of ambition was why he had been handed over to Tormand by the same man who had knighted him at the tender age of eighteen. It had been a glorious battle and Walter had proven his worth. The man had simply refused to be knighted. Fed up with his squire's lack of interest in the glory, the honors, and the responsibility that went with knighthood Sir MacBain had sent the man to Tormand. Walter had continued to prove his worth, his courage, and his contentment in remaining a lowly squire. At the moment, however, the man was openly upset and his courage was a little weak-kneed.

"I need to find out who did this," Tormand said and then sipped at his ale, hungry and thirsty but partaking of both food and drink cautiously for his stomach was still unsteady.

"Why?" Walter sat down at Tormand's right and poured himself some ale. "Ye got away from it. 'Tis near the middle of the day and no one has come here crying for vengeance, so I be thinking ye got away clean, aye? Why let anyone even ken ye were near the woman? Are ye trying to put a rope about your neck? And, if I recall rightly, ye didnae find much to like about the woman once your lust dimmed, so why fret o'er justice for her?"

"'Tis sadly true that I didnae like her, but she didnae deserve to be butchered like that."

Walter grimaced and idly scratched the ragged scar on his pockmarked left cheek. "True, but I still say if ye let anyone ken ye were there ye are just asking for trouble."

"I would like to think that verra few people would e'er believe I could do that to a woman e'en if I was found lying in her blood, dagger in hand."

"Of course ye wouldnae do such as that, and most folk ken it, but that doesnae always save a mon, does it? Ye dinnae ken everyone who has the power to cry ye a murderer and hang ye and they dinnae ken ye. Then there are the ones who are jealous of ye or your kinsmen and would like naught better than to strike out at one of ye. Aye, look at your brother James. Any fool who kenned the mon would have kenned he couldnae have killed his wife, but he still had to suffer years marked as an outlaw and a woman-killer, aye?"

"I kenned I kept ye about for a reason. Aye, 'twas to raise my spirits when they are low and to embolden me with hope and courage just when I need it the most."

"Wheesht, nay need to slap me with the sharp edge of your tongue. I but speak the truth and one ye would be wise to nay ignore."

Tormand nodded carefully, wary of moving his still aching head too much. "I dinnae intend to ignore it. 'Tis why I have decided to speak only to Simon."

Walter cursed softly and took a deep drink of ale. "Och, a king's mon nay less."

"Aye, and my friend. *And* a mon who worked hard to help James. He is a mon who has a true skill at solving such puzzles and hunting down the guilty. This isnae simply about justice for Clara. Someone wanted me to be blamed for her murder, Walter. I was put beside her body to be found and accused of the crime. And for such a crime I would be hanged—so that means that someone wants me dead."

"That is true enough. Nay just dead, either, but your good name weel blackened."

"Exactly. So I have sent word to Simon asking him to come here, stressing an urgent need to speak with him."

Tormand was pleased that he sounded far more confident of his decision than he felt. It had taken him several hours actually to write and send the request for a meeting to Simon. The voice in his head that told him to just turn his back on the whole matter, the same opinion that Walter offered, had grown almost too loud to ignore. Only the certainty that this had far more to do with him than with Clara had given him the strength to silence that cowardly voice.

He had the feeling that part of his stomach's unsteadiness was due to a growing fear that he was about to suffer as James had. It had taken his foster brother three long years to prove his innocence and wash away the stain to his honor. Three long, lonely years of running and hiding. Tormand dreaded the thought that he might be pulled into the same ugly quagmire. If nothing else, he was deeply concerned about how it would affect his mother, who had already suffered too much grief and worry over her children. First his sister Sorcha had been beaten and raped, then his sister Gillyanne had been kidnapped—twice—the second time leading to a forced marriage, and then there had been the trouble that had sent James running for the shelter of the hills. His mother did not need to suffer through yet another one of her children mired in danger.

"If ye could find something the killer touched we could solve this puzzle right quick," said Walter.

Pulling free of his dark thoughts about the possibility that his family was cursed, Tormand frowned at his squire. "What are ye talking about?"

"Weel, if ye had something the killer touched we could take it to the Ross witch."

Tormand had heard of the Ross witch. The woman lived in a tiny cottage several miles outside of town. Although the townspeople had driven the woman away ten years ago, many still journeyed to her cottage for help, mostly for the herbal concoctions the woman made. Some claimed the woman had visions that had aided them in solving a problem. Despite having grown up surrounded by people who had special gifts like that, he doubted the woman was the miracle worker some claimed her to be. Most of the time such *witches* were simply aging women skilled with herbs and an ability to convince people that they had some great mysterious power.

"And why do ye think she could help if I brought her something touched by the killer?" he asked.

"Because she gets a vision of the truth when she touches something." Walter absently crossed himself, as though he feared he risked his soul by even speaking of the woman. "Old George, the steward for the Gillespie house, told me that Lady Gillespie had some of her jewelry stolen. He said her ladyship took the box that the jewels had been taken from to the Ross witch and the moment the woman held the box she had a vision about what had happened."

When Walter said no more, Tormand asked, "What did the vision tell the woman?"

"That Lady Gillespie's eldest son had taken the jewels. Crept into her ladyship's bedchamber whilst she was at court and helped himself to all the best pieces."

"It doesnae take a witch to ken that. Lady Gillespie's eldest son is weel kenned to spend too much coin on fine clothes, women, and the toss of the dice. Near every mon, woman, and bairn in town kens that." Tormand took a drink of ale to help him resist the urge to grin at the look of annoyance on Walter's homely face. "Now I ken why the fool was banished to his grandfather's keep far from all the temptation here near the court."

"Weel, it wouldnae hurt to try. Seems a lad like ye ought to have more faith in such things."

"Oh, I have ample faith in such things, enough to wish that ye wouldnae call the woman a witch. That is a word that can give some woman blessed with a gift from God a lot of trouble, deadly trouble."

"Ah, aye, aye, true enough. A gift from God, is it?"

"Do ye really think the devil would give a woman the gift to heal or to see the truth or any other gift or skill that can be used to help people?"

"Nay, of course he wouldnae. So why do ye doubt the Ross woman?"

"Because there are too many women who are, at best, a wee bit skilled with herbs yet claim such things as visions or the healing touch in order to empty some fool's purse. They are frauds and oftimes what they do makes life far more difficult for those women who have a true gift."

Walter frowned for a moment, obviously thinking that over, and then grunted his agreement. "So ye will-nae be trying to get any help from Mistress Ross?"

"Nay, I am nay so desperate for such as that."

"Oh, I am nay sure I would refuse any help just now," came a cool, hard voice from the doorway of Tormand's hall.

Tormand looked toward the door and started to smile at Simon. The expression died a swift death. Sir Simon Innes looked every inch the king's man at the moment. His face was pale and cold fury tightened its predatory lines. Tormand got the sinking feeling that

Simon already knew why he had sent for him. Worse, he feared his friend had some suspicions about his guilt. That stung, but Tormand decided to smother his sense of insult until he and Simon had at least talked. The man was his friend and a strong believer in justice. He would listen before he acted.

Nevertheless, Tormand tensed with a growing alarm when Simon strode up to him. Every line of the man's tall, lean body was taut with fury. Out of the corner of his eye, Tormand saw Walter tense and place his hand on his sword, revealing that Tormand was not the only one who sensed danger. It was as he looked back at Simon that Tormand realized the man clutched something in his hand.

A heartbeat later, Simon tossed what he held onto the table in front of Tormand. Tormand stared down at a heavy gold ring embellished with blood-red garnets. Unable to believe what he was seeing, he looked at his hands, his unadorned hands, and then looked back at the ring. His first thought was to wonder how he could have left that room of death and not realized that he was no longer wearing his ring. His second thought was that the point of Simon's sword was dangerously sharp as it rested against his jugular.

"Nay! Dinnae kill him! He is innocent!"

Morainn Ross blinked in surprise as she looked around her. She was at home sitting up in her own bed, not in a great hall watching a man press a sword point against the throat of another man. Ignoring the grumbling of her cats that had been disturbed from their comfortable slumber by her outburst, she flopped back down and stared up at the ceiling. It had only been a dream.

"Nay, no dream," she said after a moment of thought. "A vision."

Thinking about that a little longer she then nodded her head. It had definitely been a vision. The man who had sat there with a sword at his throat was no stranger to her. She had been seeing him in dreams and visions for months now. He had smelled of death, was surrounded by it, yet there had never been any blood upon his hands.

"Morainn? Are ye weel?"

Morainn looked toward the door to her small bed-chamber and smiled at the young boy standing there. Walin was only six but he was rapidly becoming very helpful. He also worried about her a lot, but she supposed that was to be expected. Since she had found him upon her threshold when he was the tender age of two she was really the only parent he had ever known, had given him the only home he had ever known. She just wished it were a better one. He was also old enough now to understand that she was often called a witch, as well as the danger that appellation brought with it. Unfortunately, with his black hair and blue eyes, he looked enough like her to have many believe he was her bastard child and that caused its own problems for both of them.

"I am fine, Walin," she said and began to ease her way out of bed around all the sleeping cats. "It must be verra late in the day."

"'Tis the middle of the day, but ye needed to sleep. Ye were verra late returning from helping at that birthing."

"Weel, set something out on the table for us to eat then, I will join ye in a few minutes."

Dressed and just finishing the braiding of her hair, Morainn joined Walin at the small table set out in the main room of the cottage. Seeing the bread, cheese, and apples upon the table, she smiled at Walin, acknowledging a job well done. She poured them each a tankard of cider and then sat down on the little bench facing his across the scarred wooden table.

"Did ye have a bad dream?" Walin asked as he handed Morainn an apple to cut up for him.

"At first I thought it was a dream, but now I am certain it was a vision, another one about that mon with the mismatched eyes." She carefully set the apple on a wooden plate and sliced it for Walin.

"Ye have a lot about him, dinnae ye."

"It seems so. 'Tis verra odd. I dinnae ken who he is and have ne'er seen such a mon. And, if this vision is true, I dinnae think I e'er will."

"Why?" Walin accepted the plate of sliced apple and immediately began to eat.

"Because this time I saw a verra angry gray-eyed mon holding a sword to his throat."

"But didnae ye say that your visions are of things to come? Mayhap he isnae dead yet. Mayhap ye are supposed to find him and warn him."

Morainn considered that possibility for a moment and then shook her head. "Nay, I think not. Neither heart nor mind urges me to do that. If that were what I was meant to do, I would feel the urge to go out right now and hunt him down. And I would have been given some clue as to where he is."

"Oh. So we will soon see the mon whose eyes dinnae match?"

"Aye, I do believe we will."

"Weel that will be interesting."

She smiled and turned her attention to the need to fill her very empty stomach. If the man with the mismatched eyes showed up at her door, it would indeed be interesting. It could also be dangerous. She could not allow herself to forget that death stalked him. Her visions told her he was innocent of those deaths, but there was some connection between him and them. It was as if each thing he touched died in bleeding agony. She certainly did not wish to become a part of that swirling mass of blood she always saw around his feet. Unfortunately she did not believe that fate would give her any chance to avoid meeting the man. All she could do was pray that when he rapped upon her door he did not still have death seated upon his shoulder.

Chapter 2

"Do ye intend to be my judge and executioner, Simon?"

Tormand watched as Simon struggled to gain some semblance of the calm and sanity he was so well known for. Despite how badly it stung to think that, even for one brief moment, Simon could believe that he could do such a thing to Clara, to any woman, Tormand could understand what prodded the man. Any man of honor would be horrified by what had been done to Clara and would ache to make someone pay for the crime. The brief insanity that could grip a man upon seeing such dark brutality easily explained why finding Tormand's ring clutched in Clara's hand would bring Simon to Tormand's door in a blind fury. The fact that Simon had not immediately killed him told Tormand there was some doubt stirring behind Simon's shock and fury.

"Why was she clutching your ring?" Simon demanded.

"I fear I have no answer for ye," Tormand answered.

"It was undoubtedly put there by the same one, or ones, who placed me in Clara's bed."

Simon stared at Tormand for a moment before sheathing his sword. He sat down, poured himself a tankard of ale, and drank it all down. A shudder went through his tall, almost too lean frame, and then he poured himself another tankard full of ale.

"Ye were there?" Simon finally asked in a much calmer tone of voice.

"Aye."

Tormand drank some ale to prepare himself and told Simon everything he knew. He had not even finished his tale before he began to realize that he actually knew very little. All he could swear to was what he had seen—someone had killed Clara—and what he knew in his heart—that someone was not him. He did not know how he had been captured and taken to the room. He did not even know how Simon had become involved. It could have been simple bad luck, but Tormand's instincts told him that it was much more than that. Although he had no proof of it, he felt certain it was all part of a plan. He just had to figure out what that plan was.

"Why did ye go to see Clara?" he asked Simon. "Did her husband return, find her body, and then send for you?"

"Nay. I received a summons I believed had come from Clara." Simon shrugged. "It told me to arrive at her house with some of my men at a very precise time and to do so as furtively as possible."

"And ye acted on that? Did ye ken Clara weel enough for such a summons to make ye hie to her side?"

"I didnae ken her as weel as ye did," drawled Simon. "But, I did ken her weel enough. She was a cousin of mine." He smiled faintly at the shock Tormand could not hide. "Dinnae fear that I will demand ye meet me at sword point to defend her honor. She had little left to defend. The woman had been lifting her skirts for the lads, any lad with a fair face, since not long after her first flux. She was ne'er sweet, rarely honest, and felt the world owed her homage simply because God had gifted her with a bonnie face. Nay, I did as she asked because I hoped she was about to give me proof of her husband's many crimes, ones I have been look-ing into most carefully for months now. It was a faint hope as she benefited from his dealings, but I could-nae ignore it."

"Do ye think he may have killed her?" Tormand began doubting that possibility even as he asked Simon the question.

"Nay. She was useful to him and, e'en if she had thought to betray him, she was cunning enough to keep him from discovering it, to make sure she could never be connected to that betrayal. As I said, I doubt she would e'er have betrayed the mon, for she fully enjoyed spending the coin he gained from all his crimes and lies. Yet, it can be no surprise that, upon seeing her butchered body, his was the first name that leapt to mind."

"But then ye found my ring in her hand."

"Aye." Simon grimaced and dragged a hand through his thick black hair. "I couldnae believe it of ye and, yet, why was it there? And then I recalled that ye were once her lover. *Jesu*, I feared some madness had seized you and, like some rabid dog, ye needed to be cut down. I think a madness overcame me e'en to briefly consider that ye could do such a thing. 'Tis as if whoever did that to Clara left the stench of their insanity befouling that room and I breathed too deeply of it."

Tormand nodded. "I ken exactly what ye mean. When I realized that Clara must have been alive during some of the horrors inflicted upon her, I did wonder if someone had tortured her because they thought she had some information they needed."

"That is a possibility, although it doesnae explain why such an effort was made to make it look as if ye had committed the crime. There may be some cuckolded husbands who would like to see ye dead, but I cannae see why they would do something like this to strike out at you."

"I dinnae cuckold husbands. Nay knowingly." Tormand hated the defensive note that entered his voice, but forced himself to ignore it. "Yet, I cannae shake the feeling that Clara was killed because of me, because she had once been my lover. It seems vain to think it—"

"Nay. Ye were set there to be blamed for it and thus it must have something to do with you." Simon rested his forearms on the table and stared into his tankard of ale. "Her husband didnae do it and he would have been a good suspect to look to. I ken where he was, ye see, and I ken he couldnae have come home, slaughtered Clara, and then returned to his mistress's house near to ten miles away. As to torturing her for information? Weel, the mon certainly has enemies and many competitors who might think a wife would ken something about her husband's business, something that would make it easier to crush him. But, I doubt Clara would have held fast to any knowledge she had beyond the first threat to her face. After that would have come a swift death, a stab to the heart or a slash across the throat. And in neither instance would ye have been dragged into the matter." He looked at Tormand. "Aye, I think this is about you. The question is why?"

"And who."

"Once we ken the why we can begin to look for the who."

Tormand felt sick. No woman deserved to die as Clara had simply because she had once shared his bed, or he hers. What sort of enemy was it that crept around slaughtering innocents in order to reach the one he truly wished to harm? It made no sense to Tormand. If a man wanted him dead but was too cowardly to do it himself, he could simply hire some other men to do his killing for him. Sadly, there were a lot that would take the job. If the plan was to blacken his name beyond fixing before he died, Tormand was certain that that too could be done without slaughtering a woman. This murder put his enemy at the risk of being caught and hanged, the very fate the man apparently wanted Tormand to suffer. But, then, what had been done to Clara carried the strong taint of madness and who could ever make sense of that?

"My sins come back to haunt me now," Tormand muttered.

"Ye believe ye have sinned, do ye?" asked Simon, a faint smile curling his mouth.

"Gluttony be a sin," said Walter.

"Thank ye, Walter," drawled Tormand. "I believe I am aware of that." He grimaced. "Aye, I have heard it said often enough from my mother, my sisters, my aunts, and near every other female in my clan."

"And, I suspicion, a few of the men." Simon smiled more broadly when Tormand scowled at him. "Weel, ye truly have been a wee bit, er, gluttonous."

"I like frolicking about atween the sheets with a warm woman. What mon doesnae?"

"Most men at least attempt to be somewhat, weel, prudent? Fastidious? Particular in their choices?"

"All the lasses I have bedded have been bonnie and clean." Mostly, he added to himself.

"Your problem has always been too many choices, too much offered too freely."

"Aye," agreed Walter. "The lasses do flock to the rogue."

"And the rogue accepts most of that flock all too readily," said Simon.

"I thought ye were my friend, Simon." Tormand felt an odd mix of hurt and insult.

Simon laughed softly. "Och, I am that, more fool me, but that doesnae mean I must blindly approve of all ye do. Aye, and mayhap I feel the touch of envy now and then. Tell me, Tormand, did ye like Clara even a little bit?"

Tormand sighed. "Nay, but the lusting blinded me for a wee while. She was verra skilled."

"I am nay surprised. As I said, she was but newly turned thirteen when she began her lessons in the art. Oh, I confess that I am nay so verra particular at times, but I do prefer to at least ken the lass I lie down with, to enjoy a wee bit more than her soft skin and womanly heat."

It occurred to Tormand that he could not think of all that many of his lovers who met even Simon's mild standards. He refused to think that he really was what his cousin Maura had once called him—a stallion too stupid to charge coin for his stud services. After all, as far as he knew he had sired no bastards and was not that the sole purpose of a stud? Unfortunately, the longer he considered the matter, the more he began to fear that he had become as mindlessly greedy as Simon implied. Over the last few years it appeared that his qualifications for a bedmate were little more than that she be attractive, relatively clean, and willing. Mostly willing. It was such an unsettling conclusion that he was actually glad to turn his thoughts back to the matter of Clara's brutal murder.

"Did ye find nothing that pointed the finger of guilt at someone besides me?" he asked Simon, ignoring the flash of amusement in Simon's eyes that told him Simon was well aware of his attempt to turn the subject away from his love life.

"Nay," replied Simon. "There was naught but your ring to show that anyone had been in that room with Clara. That and, of course, the simple fact that Clara could not have tied herself to that bed and then cut herself to pieces. Her servants heard and saw nothing."

"How can that be? Clara would have shattered her fine windows with her screams at the first glimpse of a knife."

"True, but I believe she was gagged. I saw the signs of it in what was left of her face."

Tormand forced himself to recall carefully all that he had seen. "Aye, she had to have been. And, I begin to wonder if she was actually tortured elsewhere. Considering all the damage done to her I should have woken up lying in a pool of her blood. There was a lot and I do have the feeling she died in that bed, but now I feel sure it was not where all of that cutting was done."

Simon nodded. "I believe the same. Even with a gag on her, someone should have heard something. It was evident that she violently fought against the bindings on her wrists and ankles. The bed would also have resounded with the struggles she made and yet her servants had not even thought she was home."

"Then her killer knew how to slip in and out of her house without being seen."

"Aye, which means they knew her, e'en if not weel." Simon grimaced. "Considering all the many lovers Clara had, I doubt all the secret ways into her home were e'er really that secret. The servants would never have considered any noises coming from her bedchamber worthy of concern save for some blood-curdling screams. So, they truly heard nothing as they claim. I shall return to Clara's home and see if I can find any blood trail that will confirm that she was brought in after she was tortured." He took another long drink of ale. "In a little while. I sent word to her husband and would rather not be there when he first sees what is left of his wife. He didnae love her and she didnae love him, but he did appreciate her beauty."

"I didnae love her, either, but the sight of her body fair to made me sick."

"And Ranald doesnae have the spine to hold fast as ye did. That isnae why I wish to avoid the mon for a wee while, however. Once he recovers, he will act the great, important laird and demand I find out who killed her. He will also spit out a lot of useless information, as weel as a few threats about what will happen to me if I dinnae find Clara's killer. He always makes me wish to shake the arrogance out of him and, mayhap, take some of the bonnie out of his face."

Tormand smiled briefly, but the seriousness of the situation severely dampened his usual ready sense of humor. It was good that Simon had so quickly accepted his innocence, if only because it revealed that his friend had not fully believed in his guilt despite his rage. It was not good that Simon had not found any clue save what was left for him to find. That meant they had no trail to follow to find the murderer. It left Clara's killer free to kill again. If Tormand was right in thinking he was the real target, the killer would not be gaining what he sought this time. It was very possible that the man would kill again and could well continue to do so until Tormand was hanged.

Pouring himself some more ale, Tormand seriously considered getting blind drunk. It was a temptation he had to ignore and swore to himself that this would be his last drink for quite a while. He needed his wits to remain sharp, for it was a dangerous time. Someone out there wanted him disgraced and dead. The memory of Clara's butchered body was more than enough to remind him of what lengths his enemy was willing to go to achieve that end. Tormand knew he did not deserve the guilt he felt, but it did not lessen it by much. In fact, if he and Simon did not stop this killer, Tormand suspected he could quickly reach the point where he would be willing to take the blame just to make the killing stop.

"I dinnae think Clara will be the only one," Simon said.

Wincing at that echo of his own thoughts, Tormand nodded. "Nay, I fear not. If this was all to bring me to the scaffold then the failure of it to do so will make him try again. I will not be caught off guard as I was this time, however."

"I think it would be verra wise if ye went nowhere alone."

"That could be a problem."

"Why?"

"Weel, there are some places and times where a companion could prove awkward."

Tormand did not need the looks his friends were giving him to know he was being an idiot. It was only good sense, good defense, not to be caught out alone again. He could not allow his enemy to catch him again. Next time he might not be so lucky as to wake up and slip away before someone caught him lying next to a dead woman.

He inwardly winced. That sounded callous, a selfish concern only for his own safety. Unfortunately, he had to be that cold despite his possible culpability in the death of Clara and any other woman who may yet follow her to her grave. If he ended up blamed for Clara's murder or any that may follow, the real killer would slip away unpunished. Tormand was determined to make the man pay for what had been done to Clara and, he prayed, before the beast could do that to any other woman.

There was also a deep need within him to know why. Tormand knew a lot of that need was because of the guilt he could not shake. He might be able to ease some of it if he learned why this man hated him so much. And, Tormand thought, possibly hated the women he had bedded. Clara's beauty had been utterly destroyed; even her lovely hair hacked off. There had been anger and hatred behind that attack, yet that made no sense. Sad to say, he could not think of any man, lover or husband, who had revealed any feelings for Clara that were so deep they would cause such an insane rage.

"Scowling like a stern father willnae change my mind," said Simon. "Ye are nay a fool, Tormand. Ye ken verra weel the need to ne'er be alone until this madmon is caught and hanged."

Yanked free of his thoughts by Simon's words, Tormand sighed. "Aye, I see the wisdom of it, but that doesnae mean I must like it."

"Celibacy willnae kill ye, but this enemy of yours will."

"Celibacy?" Tormand had no intention of admitting that he had been celibate for several months, if only because he did not wish to study the reasons why too closely. "*Jesu*, I think I might prefer hanging."

"Idiot."

"Mayhap, but the need for a guard wasnae really why I was scowling. I suddenly thought that, weel, the way Clara was butchered seemed to reveal a fury, a hatred, and I could think of no one who felt so strongly about her. Sad to say. If the plan was to brand me a killer of women, such butchery wasnae really necessary." When Simon just stared at him for several moments, Tormand actually shifted a little uneasily in his seat. "'Twas just a thought."

"A good thought. One that I should have had myself." Simon muttered a curse. "Aye, there was fury and hatred in that butchery, one that was aimed directly at all that made Clara beautiful and desirable."

"It could still have been torture to gain information," said Walter, although his expression revealed his own doubts about that.

Simon nodded. "It could be, but, truly, Clara would have told him, or them, anything about anyone at the first touch of the knife. Everything she knew would have tumbled from her lips after one lock of her hair was cut off. Clara was vain beyond words. Her beauty was all to her. And, I still believe she was gagged through it all, which just strengthens my belief that this was not done to get information."

"So we still have nothing." Tormand stared into his empty tankard and resisted the urge to fill it up again.

"Nay, we have a murder that someone was determined to blame on you," Simon replied. "That appears to point toward some enemy of yours nay matter how often I study it."

"Could it not also point to some enemy of Ranald's? What could be more humiliating to a mon than to have it so publicly seen that his wife was bedded and then slaughtered in their marriage bed?"

"Clara was too weel kenned as a whore for that to

matter. Aye, and Ranald's mistress is weel kenned. Nay, all were aware that neither wife nor husband honored their vows in that marriage." Simon stood up. "Are ye coming with me to see if we can find a blood trail?"

Tormand reluctantly stood up. Going back to the bloody scene of the crime was the very last thing he wanted to do, but he knew it could help them find at least some of the answers they needed. He just hoped Ranald was not around. Although the man had known that Tormand and Clara had been lovers, Ranald had barely hidden his dislike of Tormand. Tormand could never understand why he was treated so, when half of the men at court had also known Clara intimately. He did not care to see how that dislike might be displayed if he was forced to face Ranald in his own home while Clara's mutilated body was undoubtedly being readied for burial.

"Weel, that was fun," muttered Tormand an hour later, as he followed Simon into one of the tunnels Clara's lovers had slipped through on far too many nights.

Ranald had been nearly as bad as Tormand had feared. It was plain for anyone to see that the man was angry, perhaps even honestly grieving, and that he saw Tormand as a perfect target to aim that fury at. If not for Simon's uncanny ability to interrupt and end such tense confrontations, Tormand suspected that he and Ranald would have been at sword point now, fighting in the great hall of the very house where Clara had died.

"I briefly wondered if he had actually loved Clara, but, nay, I think he but grieves the loss of her influence," Simon said, as he walked along very slowly, holding a bright lantern as he studied the ground in front of him. "Whore she may have been, but she did have some influence. She also gained a lot of useful information from the men she took to her bed, the kind of information that helped Ranald a lot. He must also still suffer from the sight of what was once his beautiful wife. Still, I shall look harder at the possibility that he killed her." Simon suddenly halted. "Aha, look at this," he murmured as he crouched down.

Tormand crouched beside Simon and looked closely at the spot his friend studied so intently. "Blood?"

Simon lightly touched a finger to the spot, licked his finger and, ignoring Tormand's grimace of distaste, nodded. "Definitely blood. We are in luck. The stone floor in this tunnel didnae allow it to sink into the ground and 'tis cool enough down here to keep it from hardening into nay more than a stain." Simon stood up. "I think we have found our trail."

His hope that a quick solution to this mystery might be found rose as Tormand followed Simon. The trail led them out of the passage into the back alley and continued north. It disappeared behind the stables run by the most popular inn in town where the constant traffic of people and horses had wiped it clean. Simon took nearly an hour searching in all directions to see if he could find the trail on his own before he went to get a dog. Tormand stayed close by his side, although his hope for a swift solution was beginning to fade away rapidly.

As soon as Simon's dog Bonegnasher caught the scent they moved quickly and once again Tormand found his hopes rising. The race ended at a deserted hovel at the edge of town. Tormand could smell the blood as he and Simon stepped inside. He did not need Simon's skills to know that they had found the place where Clara had been tortured. The killer had not bothered to clean up after butchering the woman. Tormand felt the sting of bile in the back of his throat, but forced himself to stay with Simon. The way Simon so calmly and carefully looked over the bloody scene made Tormand determined to overcome his own squeamishness.

He did not have the strong gifts so many of the women in his family possessed, especially since his branch of the clan was not actually blood related, but he did have a small skill at sensing emotion, at times almost scenting it in the air. It was not easy here where the air was so thick with the stench of blood, but Tormand closed his eyes and tried to reach out to the echoes of the feelings left behind by those who had been here before him. It was a trick one of his more gifted cousins had shown him and it did allow him to make the most use of his meager talent. The sharp tang of fear was no surprise, but once he pushed beyond that, Tormand sensed other things. Lingering in the air was the anger and hatred he had suspected was behind the mutilation. Those feelings were tainted with something he could only assume was madness.

"Get anything?" asked Simon.

Tormand opened his eyes, realizing that Simon had probably guessed that he had some little gift a long time ago. "Fear, anger, hatred. There is a coldness to the latter two. But, there is also something else. I think it is madness."

"Most certainly."

"Did ye find anything?" Tormand asked, as he followed Simon outside and took a deep breath in the hope of clearing the stench of death from his nose.

"Nay more than that this is where the crime was committed. By the time Clara was carried out of here she was already dying." Simon held out his hand. "I also found this."

Tormand frowned at the small hairpin Simon held. "Clara's?"

"Nay, this is a common bone one. Clara would never wear such a thing." Simon put it in his pocket. "It could have belonged to a woman who once lived here, but I will keep it all the same."

"So we have failed."

"Aye and nay. We havenae found the killer, true enough, but I didnae expect to. Nay, that will take time."

"Another woman could die."

"I fear so, but there is naught we can do about that."

"We must just wait until it happens?"

"We cannae set a guard on every woman in the town, Tormand. Nay, we just keep hunting, my friend. Hunting until we catch and cage this bastard."

And pray I dinnae hang first, Tormand silently added.

Chapter 3

Morainn struggled to ignore the way the shopkeeper crossed himself as she entered the small dim room where he displayed his wares. She was tempted to leave, to not gift him with her business, but she needed some of his sturdy barrels for the cider and mead she made and he was the only cooper in town. She would simply ignore him as she had ignored all the other townspeople who had moved away, crossed themselves, muttered prayers, or made a sign they foolishly thought could ward off evil as she had walked through town. It hurt, but she should be used to that pain, she told herself.

And they were all hypocrites, anyway, she thought as some of her hurt began to spin itself into anger. They came to her quickly enough when they or someone they cared for was hurt or sick and the leech or midwife could do nothing to help. They also sought her out when they needed answers no one else could give them. If she was so evil that they could not even stand to be near her, what did that make them when they came begging at her door for help?

She took a deep, slow breath to quell that anger. It only made her head ache and gained her nothing for the pain. The way the big-bellied cooper paled a little when Morainn looked into his small eyes told her that not all of her anger had been tucked away. The fool probably feared she was about to change him into a newt or something worse, she thought. If she possessed such magic she would not be so kind.

Morainn was just concluding her business with the man when she felt a sharp coldness in the air and she knew it was not from a change in the weather. She quickly smothered the urge to sniff the air like some hound, thanked the man for his reluctant help, and stepped outside. Her barrels would be brought to her home on the morrow and she had no need to linger in the town that had so callously tossed her out years ago. Whatever tainted the air was not her concern, she firmly told herself as she started the long walk home.

Just as she reached the edge of town where lived those with money enough to have a bit of land with their house, a man burst out of a fine home only yards away from her. Morainn could see that he was shaking, his face pale and sweat-soaked as he bellowed for a king's man or the sheriff. She actually took a few steps toward him, thinking to help him, when her good sense abruptly returned. People did not appreciate her efforts to be kind.

From the houses near to his and even from the more crowded center of town, people began to rush toward the man, drawn by his cries. Morainn hastily sought out a place where she could stand apart from the swiftly gathering crowd. She moved to the side of the man's house and into the shade beneath a huge tree that was probably older than the man's house.

Although she knew she could slip around the back of the house and continue on her way home, it was more than curiosity that held her in place. Instinct told her that, for the moment, it might be best simply to remain one of the crowd. The cold she had felt at the cooper's shop was much sharper here and she suddenly knew that someone had died violently. A little voice of caution in her head told her that slipping away home might look a little too much like fleeing to people who would soon be hunting for a killer.

"My wife is dead!" cried the man. "Dead! Butchered in our bed!" He bent over and emptied his stomach, barely missing the fine boots of the two men who were rushing to his side.

She had been right about the bitter taste of that cold, Morainn thought, although she would have preferred to be wrong. One of the two men who had run up to the grieving man's side ran into the house only to run out a few minutes later looking as though he, too, would soon be emptying his belly. Many of the gathering crowd looked as though they dearly wanted to invade the house to see what could so upset two strong men. Morainn could not understand that sort of curiosity. If what was in that house was enough to make two strong men publicly vomit, what sane person would want to see it?

A hush came over the crowd and Morainn watched as people shifted to allow two more men through its ranks. She recognized the tall, black-haired man as Sir

Simon Innes, a king's man rumored to be able to solve any puzzle. When her gaze settled on the man at his side, she nearly gasped aloud.

It was the man from her visions. She could not see if he had mismatched eyes from where she stood, but she had no doubt at all that it was him. Everything else about him was just as she had dreamed, from his long, deep auburn hair to his graceful, broad-shouldered body. Morainn remained within the shadows, but shifted a little closer to the house hoping to catch a name for the man who haunted her dreams.

"Sir Simon!" The distraught man grabbed Sir Simon by the arm. "*Jesu*, but I have need of a mon like ye. Isabella has been killed. She . . . she . . ." The man began to weep.

"Try to calm yourself, Sir William," said Simon, his voice holding a calm that even Morainn felt. "I will find the mon who did this. Ye have my word on that. But, now I must go and see what has happened for myself."

"'Tis a wretched sight," muttered the man who had gone into the house after Sir William had told him what had happened. "I didnae e'en step inside the room. One look was enough."

"Nor did I," said Sir William. "One look was all it took, all I could abide, and no one who sees Isabella can doubt that she is dead. That she has been brutally murdered. I truly didnae need to go farther than the threshold." He suddenly became aware of the man standing by Simon's side. "What is that rogue doing here?"

"Sir Tormand Murray has helped me solve such puzzles before. I wish him to help me now so that I can be sure we put the noose around the right mon's neck."

Morainn thought that was an odd way to speak of the help Sir Tormand might offer.

"How do ye ken he didnae—"

"Careful, Sir William," Simon said in a voice so cold even Morainn shivered. "Dinnae toss out an insult ye can ne'er take back. Ye are good with accounts, but nay so good with a sword, aye? Tormand is verra good, as am I."

Sir William paled a little, showing that he understood the threat. He pressed his lips together tightly and took several deep breaths before saying softly, "He kenned my Isabella ere I married her."

Sir Simon clasped the man by the shoulder. "The words to recall here, m'friend, are *ere I married her.*"

The men were speaking so softly that Morainn edged even closer so that she could catch every word.

"He kenned Lady Clara, as weel, didnae he and three days ago she was murdered." Accusation was clear to hear in Sir William's voice, revealing that he had already forgotten the threat of challenges, but he was wise enough to nearly whisper his words.

"I fear my friend has kenned far too many women," Sir Simon responded, "but that only makes him a rutting fool, nay a killer. Let it go, William. If ye continue to speak so, and do so to others, ye will make my job verra hard. Angry people crying out for the blood of an innocent mon means I must divert my time from finding the real killer in order to protect him."

Sir William nodded, but still scowled at Sir Tormand. Morainn studied Sir Tormand Murray's handsome profile and decided the man probably found it very easy to be a rutting fool. Innocent of murder he might be, but Morainn suspected he was steeped in sin in many another way. She felt surprisingly disappointed by that knowledge.

"Now, allow us to go and see what has been done," said Sir Simon. "The sooner we do what we must, the sooner ye can attend to Isabella. I am sure ye wish to have her cleaned and readied for burial."

"I am nay sure she can be cleaned," Sir William said in a hoarse, unsteady voice. "She was butchered, Sir Simon. Cut to pieces. Was Lady Clara truly done in a like manner?"

The look on Sir Simon's face told Morainn that he did not like how fast word was spreading about these murders. That highborn women were being murdered was enough to stir up anger and fear. That they were being butchered would only make it all worse, bringing those fears to a dangerous height all the more quickly. If Sir William thought as others did, or would, then Sir Tormand Murray was in a great deal of danger. The longer it took to find the killer, the more suspicion would begin to fall upon his shoulders, the more the townspeople would gather together and feed each other's fear and anger. Morainn knew all too well how dangerous that could be.

When the men went inside the house, Morainn debated whether to go or stay. So far luck had been with her and no one in the crowd had yet spotted her. When they did, however, she knew she could find herself in a lot of trouble. Someone who was already called a witch should not be caught so close to a place where a woman had been horribly murdered. Yet, curiosity held her in place. Some of that curiosity was of the morbid kind. Morainn wished to know what the men meant when they said Lady Isabella had been butchered. She sighed and waited for the two men to return, promising herself that she would slip away at the first sign of anyone seeing her or recognizing her.

Tormand looked at what was left of the once beautiful Isabella Redmond and wanted to flee the room. Her thick raven hair had been cut off and was scattered around her body, although he had a strong suspicion that it had not been cut off in this room. If it had been it had probably been done after she was dead. All his instincts told him, however, that it had been brought here along with her body, that a scene had been carefully set. As with Clara, Isabella's face had been destroyed. The big green eyes Isabella had used so well in tempting men to her bed were in a small bowl on a table by the bed. Her soft, bountiful breasts had been slashed to ribbons. The horrendous wounds were too numerous to count and he wondered how many the poor woman had suffered through before death had freed her of the pain.

"This is worse," murmured Simon. "Far worse. Either the killer hated Isabella far more than he hated Clara or he is verra angry that ye escaped his fine trap last time and havenae been hanged yet."

"I but pray that so much wasnae done to her because Isabella took too long to die," said Tormand, as he watched Simon begin to search the room for some sign the killer may have left behind.

"She was with child."

"Ah, *Jesu*, nay. Nay."

"I fear so. I hope William doesnae ken it or that the

women who prepare her body dinnae see it and tell him. I think he would become near rabid with grief and rage."

"And he will aim it all at me. I willnae ask how ye ken that she was with child."

"Best if ye dinnae. Ye are already looking pale."

"Do ye think the killer kenned it, that he might have been even more enraged by that?"

"'Tis possible." Simon frowned at the floor near the window. "They brought her in through here."

Tormand moved to Simon's side and looked outside. An odd array of barrels and wood were piled against the side of the house forming an unsteady stairway. He could see the droplets of blood leading from the window down to the ground.

"So we now look for a strong, agile mon."

"Strong certainly. He doesnae need to be agile, just lucky."

"Do we fetch the hounds again?"

"In a wee while," replied Simon. "As soon as Sir William is too busy to see what we are about."

"Afraid he will want to join us in the hunt?"

"Him and most of the other fools gathered in front of this house."

Tormand grimaced and nodded. The fools would turn it into a loud, crowded hunt. If the killer were anywhere near at hand, he would be warned in plenty of time to flee the area. It was very doubtful that the killer was still around, but if the man was fool enough to want to watch the reactions to his crime, Tormand did not want a crowd screaming for retribution to make him go into hiding.

Just as he was about to ask Simon if he had found anything else in the room, he heard the sounds of the crowd outside begin to grow loud. "What do ye think is stirring them up?"

"I dinnae ken," replied Simon as he started out of the room, "but I doubt it is good."

"Look ye there! Isnae that the Ross witch?"

Morainn was abruptly pulled from her wandering thoughts about Tormand Murray by that sharp cry. She felt a chill flee down her spine as she slowly turned toward the crowd. She saw Old Ide, the midwife, pointing one dirty, gnarled finger her way and her unease began to change to fear. Old Ide hated her, just as she had hated her mother, for she saw her as competition. Whenever she could, the older woman tried to cause trouble for Morainn. This was not a good time or place to meet with her enemy.

"What are ye doing here, witch?"

A soft cry escaped Morainn when Sir William grabbed her by the arm. She inwardly cursed herself as a fool. If she had not been so caught up in her thoughts about Sir Tormand, not all of them particularly chaste, she would have seen Old Ide in the crowd. That would have been enough to make Morainn leave. Ten years ago it had been Ide who had goaded the crowd into turning against Morainn's mother. Now Morainn was trapped and she doubted any of these people were in the mood to listen to or heed her explanations or their own good sense.

"I was but caught up in the crowd," she said, hiding her wince as Sir William tightened his grip.

"She has come because this is a place of death," said Old Ide, as she pushed her way to the front of the crowd to glare at Morainn. "Her kind always comes to where there is death. They can smell it, ye ken."

"Dinnae be even more of a fool than ye already are," snapped Morainn.

"Fool am I? Hah, I say. Hah! I ken what ye are about, witch. Ye have come here to gather up the soul of that poor murdered lassie in there."

Morainn was about to tell the woman that she was an idiot when the murmuring of the crowd caught her attention. Several people were actually nodding in agreement with Old Ide's nonsense. There were not that many, but there were far more than she could ever escape from. If Ide did not shut up, Morainn feared there would soon be even more people ready to heed the woman's lies. Morainn remembered all too well how easily a crowd could be stirred by Ide's words into a dangerous mob. Ignoring the threat of Ide's hatred was what had killed her mother.

"I was but trying to get home," she said in what she prayed was a calm, soothing tone of voice.

"Ye didnae need to stop here. Ye could have slipped around us. But, nay, here ye are, lurking in the shadows. I tell ye," Ide yelled to the crowd, "she is after gathering that poor woman's soul."

She looked at Sir William, hoping to find an ally, but he was looking at her as though he believed she could do exactly as Old Ide claimed she could. "I am nay a witch and I am nay here to catch souls," she said.

"Then why are ye e'en in town?" he demanded. "They banished ye, didnae they?"

"They may have tossed me out, Sir William, but nay one of them complains when I come to heal them or spend what little coin I have in their shops."

"That still doesnae explain why ye were hiding here, lurking about in the shadows near my home."

"And why dinnae ye ask all of them what they are doing here?" She glared at Old Ide. "Aye, why dinnae ye ask why they flock here like corbies, feeding upon your misery?"

Morainn wished the words back even as she said them. The crowd was incensed by them and that gave Ide a fertile crowd in which to sow her lies and their fears. There would be no help from Sir William, either. That man looked as if he expected her to start changing into some soul-stealing demon at any moment. Even as she fruitlessly tried to break free of the man's grip, she attempted to reason with him and the crowd. It was obvious, however, that few of them wished to heed reason. Morainn began to fear that she was about to suffer far worse than banishment this time.

"Silence!"

The bellow that cut straight through all the noise the crowd made startled Morainn so much that she put her foot back down on the ground instead of kicking Sir William as she had planned to. Sir Simon and Sir Tormand stood on the front steps of the house, their hands on their swords, glaring at the now subdued crowd. Morainn prayed that they were going to prove to be the saviors she desperately needed right now.

Nodding once he had the silence he had demanded,

Sir Simon spoke in a quieter but still very firm voice as he asked, "What is going on out here? Have ye forgotten that this is a house of mourning?"

"The witch is here, sir," said Old Ide, pointing at Morainn.

"Aye," said a plump, graying woman who stepped up beside Ide. "Ide says that the witch has come to steal the dead lady's soul."

The look on Sir Simon's face made several of the people in the crowd blush and stare down at their feet. Morainn was glad he was not aiming that look of utter disdain her way. She could not see Sir Tormand's face as clearly, but the taut line of his fine profile told her that his expression was probably just as condemning.

"None of ye should heed such superstitious nonsense," Sir Simon said to the woman and then he looked at Ide. "And ye shouldnae speak it. Nay, nor should ye be stirring up such trouble outside this house. Silence," he hissed when Ide tried to protest. "Only a fool would spit out such idiocy. Aye, or someone who wishes harm to the one she accuses. Do ye fear to lose your place as midwife here, Ide Bruce?"

When that question had several people eyeing Old Ide with anger and suspicion, the woman crossed her arms over her ample chest and said no more. Morainn felt Sir William's grip on her arm ease a little when Sir Simon then looked their way. She glanced up at Sir William and found him flushing beneath Sir Simon's cold, steely gray gaze.

"Is this the woman?" asked Sir Simon.

When Sir William nodded, Sir Simon signaled him

to bring her closer. Morainn stumbled a little as the man dragged her over to the steps. One cold look from Sir Simon had Sir William hastily releasing her. She idly rubbed her arm as she looked up at Sir Simon, fighting the urge to look instead at Sir Tormand Murray, the man who had haunted her dreams for far too long.

"And who are ye, mistress?" Sir Simon asked.

"'Tis the Ross witch," said Sir William.

"This is the woman ye all banished ten years ago?" Sir Simon looked her over and then stared at the crowd. "She would have been nay more than a child and ye tossed her out to fend for herself? That child frightened ye that much, did she?" When most of the crowd was unable to meet his gaze, he nodded and looked at Morainn again. "Your name?"

"Morainn Ross," she replied.

"I dinnae believe what the old woman says." He smiled faintly when Old Ide gasped in outrage. "For 'tis clear that she tries to rid herself of a rival, but, for the sake of those who are seduced by her lies, tell me why ye are here."

"I came to the town to buy some barrels to store the cider and mead I make." Catching a movement out of the corner of her eye, Morainn looked and saw the cooper trying to slip away. "There is the cooper, sir. He can tell ye that I speak the truth."

The cooper stopped and looked at Sir Simon. "Aye, sir, she was doing just that." He scratched his belly. "Truth is, I was surprised she had come this far on her way back home. Must walk fast."

"Mayhap she flew, eh, Ide?" called out one man.

When the crowd snickered, Morainn felt herself relax, her fear seeping away. It would be wondrous if this confrontation made people ignore the lies Old Ide told about her, but Morainn doubted that would happen. For now, however, she was safe.

"I tell ye, she is a witch," snapped Ide, unwilling to give up the battle too quickly.

"Is she?" asked Sir Tormand, his deep voice cold, with a sharp bite to it. "Has she harmed someone then?" There was a murmur of denial in the crowd. "Lied to ye? Cheated ye? Stolen from ye?" Each question brought another muttered denial. "Ah, but she *has* healed some of ye, hasnae she?" This time several nods were his answer.

"But, if she isnae a witch, why was she banished?" asked a young man.

"I suspicion someone stirred up a crowd with lies and superstition. Once it was done, it couldnae be taken back." Tormand smiled faintly when the woman called Ide was glared at by nearly everyone in the crowd, revealing that this was not the first time the woman had played this deadly game. He wondered who had suffered then. "Go home. Ye shame yourselves by carrying on like this before this house of mourning and by listening to a jealous old cow's lies."

Morainn stared at Sir Tormand Murray. Her heart told her that he believed all he was saying, that they were not just words spoken to disburse an unruly crowd. She firmly told herself not to allow that to drag her into some foolish infatuation with the man. He was far too high a reach for one like her and his reputation did not offer any woman hope that he would care for her, or be faithful. Her only responsibility was to try to do what she could to make sure he did not hang for crimes he had not committed.

Tormand watched the crowd meander away and then turned to look at Morainn Ross. He felt his breath catch in his throat as he met her gaze. Wide blue eyes, the color of the sea, stared up at him with surprise and a touch of wariness. Her hair was as black as any he had ever seen, tumbling to her waist in long thick waves. It was impossible to get a good look at her figure beneath her dark cloak, but he caught glimpses of high, full breasts and nicely rounded hips. She was not as small as many of the women in his family, but she was not tall, either. He suspected the top of her head would tuck in just neatly under his chin.

It was her face that fascinated him the most, however. Her dark brows were perfect arches over her beautiful eyes and her lashes were long and thick, accentuating their rich color. Her skin held no blemishes, a true rarity, and was touched with a soft hint of gold. He wondered if that was the color of all her skin and quickly banished the thought when he felt himself begin to grow hard. Her nose was small and straight and the bones of her heart-shaped face were neatly cut from her high cheekbones to her surprisingly firm chin. Her mouth was a little wide and her lips were temptingly full, almost lush. This was not the woman he had expected to see when Walter had spoken of the Ross witch.

"Go home, Mistress Ross," said Simon. "It might be best if ye try to avoid coming here for a while."

"Because Ide might actually get those fools to listen

to her evil lies?" Morainn asked, feeling her anger stir at the unfairness of it all and knowing too well that the answer to her question was a resounding *aye*.

"I fear so. 'Tis unfair, but it would be a bad time to argue that." After Morainn curtsied and left, Simon turned to Sir William. "I am done now. Ye may see to your wife. My deepest condolences."

Sir William nodded, but then looked toward Morainn. "Are ye certain she isnae a witch? The church says—"

"The church says a lot of things few of us heed. She isnae a witch, Sir William. She is a good healer. Nay more."

"They say she has visions."

Simon nodded. "I have heard that but if the visions she has only aid people, then where is the evil in that? Go, Sir William, tend to your wife and let us find this killer."

As Simon and Tormand walked away, Simon quietly said, "They threw out a child."

"Aye." Tormand was a little surprised at the rage he felt over that. "I had expected a woman of at least middle years, if nay some old crone. Mayhap Walter's suggestion has some merit."

"What suggestion?"

"That I take something the killer or the victim touched and see if she has some vision of the who, what, or why."

"Ye just want to see her again."

Tormand just smiled. He would not deny it. What troubled him was the strength of the attraction he felt for her. His interest had never been grasped so quickly, so fiercely. It was worrisome, but he knew that would make no difference in the end. She might not be a witch, but she definitely had some power and Tormand knew that power would soon pull him to her side.

Chapter 4

His eyes were so full of passion's fire she could feel the heat upon her skin as he looked at her. The dual colors of his eyes grew brighter, the blue and the green sharper and clearer as he pulled her into his arms. Morainn purred in welcome as his sinful mouth covered hers. She wrapped her arms around his strong body as he ravished her mouth, his clever tongue stirring a heat within her that she had never felt before.

Eager and ready for more of him, she pulled at his clothes as he pulled at hers until they were both blessedly naked. The sight of him took her breath away. When their flesh touched she moaned with pleasure. He was such a beautiful man, lean and strong, his warm skin smooth beneath her greedy hands. She felt the hard proof of his desire for her press against her and she ached for him. Her breasts felt full, the tips burning for his touch.

He pushed her down onto a wide, soft bed; the fine linen sheets cool against her heated flesh. When he lowered his beautiful body down to hers, she eagerly accepted his weight. The way their bodies fit together so perfectly made her cry out her need for him. His warm, soft lips traveled over her throat, leaving a trail of delicious fire as she ran her hands over his tautly muscled back. When the heat of his mouth touched her breasts she arched against him in silent demand.

Then, abruptly, he was gone, her arms empty. She felt as if a part of her soul had just been torn away. As she began to sit up to look for him, she was pushed back down onto the bed, but this time it was not done gently. Her wrists and ankles were suddenly tightly bound to the bedposts and fear rose up in her so swiftly and fiercely that she felt she could choke on it. The scent of a too rich perfume filled her nose and she coughed. Morainn cried for Tormand to help her, to save her from this unseen threat.

"Your lover is doomed," whispered a soft, icy cold voice. "And so are ye, witch."

Morainn saw a bloodstained knife held in a delicate hand and screamed.

Morainn bolted upright in her bed, startling her cats, and looked around. The sight of her own bedchamber did little to still the hard pounding of heart. This was the third time she had had the dream. It was always the same dream, but each time it became a little more detailed. Morainn was not sure she could go through it again even if it promised some much needed answers to why these poor women were being murdered or who was doing it. No matter how hard she thought over what she had seen in her dreams, she remained certain that they were trying to tell her something about these murders.

"But just what does Sir Tormand Murray have to do with those killings?" she wondered aloud.

She looked out her tiny window, saw that the sky was lightening with the rising of the sun, and softly cursed as she flopped back down on the bed. A small noise by the door drew her attention, making her heart leap with fear. She took a deep breath to calm herself when she saw Walin there watching her with concern. She had obviously woken him up. Again.

"Ye screamed," he said.

"Aye, I suspicion I did," she replied. "These visions are verra troubling ones. I think they are trying to tell me something important, each one just a little different from the one before, but I havenae grasped what the message is yet." None except the one that told her a part of her, a very large part, craved Sir Tormand Murray for a lover. "I am sorry for waking ye, lad, but I fear I cannae promise that it willnae happen again."

"At least this time ye have woken us near the time we must be awake anyway."

"True enough. Go and get ready, dearling, and then we will break our fast as we plan our day."

The moment he was gone, Morainn stared up at her ceiling. These were troubling dreams and not just because they ended with an increasing darkness. She had never had such dreams about a man. Despite the dark ending of this vision, her body still felt heavy with a need she had never felt before. Nor did she fully understand it. She had only seen the man in the flesh once. Despite how he had defended her before an angry crowd, she should not be dreaming of being naked with him. And liking it. Especially when his own friend called him a rutting fool, she thought with a sigh as she got up to wash and clean her teeth.

Two women had been brutally murdered. From what Sir William had said four days ago, Tormand

Murray had *kenned* both women. If any other women were murdered, ones he had also *kenned,* then Sir Tormand was going to be drawing very close to a noose around his neck.

From the few people who did visit or talk to her, Morainn had learned a little about the dead women. Lady Clara and Lady Isabella had each *kenned* a lot of men, although it appeared that Lady Isabella had been faithful to her husband once they were officially wed. Yet, Sir William had cast his suspicions on Sir Tormand and Morainn knew others would as well. Her visions told her he was innocent, as did all of her instincts, but she knew that did not mean he was safe from hanging for murder. Innocent men had been dragged to the gallows before.

Once dressed, she went to join Walin for their morning meal. She had to do something to try to stop Tormand from going to the gallows. It was what her visions were pushing her to do; she was certain of that. Morainn just hoped that she could come up with some useful plan before it was too late.

It was as they weeded her garden that Walin finally spoke about her dreams. "Mayhap ye should go and talk to Sir Tormand. He is the mon with the mismatched eyes, isnae he?"

"Aye, he is," she replied as she sat back on her heels and looked at him. "Yet, what could I say to him, Walin? I have dreams about ye, sir? He may have eloquently defended me before that crowd, but that doesnae mean he will give any weight to my visions. S'truth, he may think I but try to catch his interest."

"Because he is a rutting fool?"

Morainn inwardly grimaced, thinking that it had probably been unwise to say that before Walin. "There is that. But, what could he do even if he did believe in my dreams? He already helps Sir Simon hunt for the killer. He is, I think, nay a mon to flee, either. The dreams that now cause me to scream in the night are trying to tell me who is killing these women, but havenae yet told me enough to help Sir Tormand."

"Mayhap ye are missing something. That can happen when ye get scared."

"True, my wee wise laddie. I shall try to study the ones I have had more intently." Even if they do leave me both terrified and aching with lust, she thought ruefully. "Aye, I must, for I think he is stepping closer to the gallows every day."

"Morainn!" called a woman from somewhere in the front of the cottage.

"Out in the garden, Nora!" Morainn smiled when her oldest and most faithful friend walked into the garden. "'Tis good to see ye. Let me clean up and we can have some cider, mayhap sit in the shade."

"That would suit me," said Nora, as she lightly tousled Walin's thick curls.

It did not take long for Morainn to join Nora in the shade of the huge beech tree near the corner of her cottage. She handed her friend a tankard of cool cider and joined her on the rough bench made of old logs. Sipping at her cider, Morainn watched Walin play with the cats for a moment and then turned to Nora.

"I am verra pleased to see ye, but I didnae really

expect another visit from ye until next week," Morainn said.

Nora just blushed and held out her left hand.

Morainn gaped at the little silver band her friend wore. "James finally asked ye to wed him? Ye are betrothed?" When Nora nodded, Morainn laughed and hugged her. "There is to be a proper wedding, aye?"

"Och, aye. No hand-fasting for the likes of me. I am marrying up, ye ken, and I want nary a one in the town to question the right of the marriage."

The glint of stubbornness in Nora's dark eyes told Morainn the woman meant every word. "James's family accepts ye then?"

"They do. They are good people and I dinnae fault them for trying to get my mon to look higher for a wife. I am nay some swineherd's brat, but I am nay as weel-born as they are. Nor do I bring land to the marriage or even much of a dowry at all. But, they do ken love. James's parents share it, ye see, and they couldnae deny their son the blessing of it." Nora sat up straighter and looked Morainn right in the eye. "I told them that ye will be my attendant."

"Och, nay, Nora," Morainn began to protest.

"Aye, and I am proud to say that they gave me no argument, so ye need nay fret that ye will be unwelcome. The only question they had was, weel, about Walin. Ye ken that near everyone whispers that he is your bastard child."

"I ken it. It stings sometimes and can cause me a wee bit of trouble with men, but I would ne'er give him up."

"And so I told them. I also told them the truth about

how he came to be living with ye. Do ye ken, the fact that ye kept the lad despite the trouble it has caused ye and the harm it has done to your good name—"

"What good name? Ross witch?"

Nora ignored that and continued, "And the fact that ye were still struggling to survive yourself seemed to win them o'er to your side immediately. That and the fact that ye were but thirteen when ye were tossed out to live all on your own. And done verra weel, too. They hadnae realized that ye were so verra young. So, ye will be there for me, aye?"

Morainn had a lot of doubts about the wisdom of joining in Nora's wedding, but she buried them deep inside of herself. Nora and her family had not had the power to stop Morainn's banishment, but their help was one reason she had survived it, even flourished. They never hesitated to argue the ugly rumors that constantly circulated about her, either.

"Aye, I will be there. When?"

"A month from this Sabbath Day. And Walin must come as weel." Before Morainn could think of a good argument for that, Nora continued, "Now, the other reason I have come is because there is news." She sighed and then took a deep drink of cider. "Another woman has been murdered."

"Och, nay." Morainn suddenly knew that was why she had seen the bloody knife in her dream this time.

"Aye. Lady Marie Campbell, married to the laird of Banloch. He is in town to sell the woolens his clan makes and see if he can wrestle a few agreements for trade out of some of the other lairds gathered here. At least this woman wasnae carrying a bairn."

"One of the others was carrying a bairn?"

"Lady Isabella. I grieve for her husband as the bairn couldnae have been his. It seems he had but just returned from a trip to France that had lasted for a six-month. The bairn his wife was carrying was but newly begun."

"Oh, I had heard that she was faithful to her husband, unlike the Lady Clara."

"It appears not. T'isnae weel kenned, mind ye. Naught but a whisper. I suspect her good reputation will be what is most spoken of. Most dinnae like to speak ill of the dead. Weel, at least until she begins to be forgotten. Howbeit, Lady Marie was a good wife, loved her husband and he her. He is utterly desolate. He is readying himself to take her body home. Poor, poor mon. He is a widower now with two young sons."

"What is happening here?" muttered Morainn. "Oh, we have had violent deaths before, but none like these. Nay highborn women and nay so brutal. Usually it is naught but idiot men slashing at each other o'er some imagined insult or a theft, but e'en a death whilst being robbed isnae so verra common."

Nora shook her head, her reddish brown curls bouncing wildly with the movement. "I dinnae ken what is happening, either. Aye, when the court is near as it is now, there can be added troubles, but ne'er anything like this. Ye are quite right about that. And, talk has become quite heated about a mon named Sir Tormand Murray. It appears that he kenned all of these women ere they were married. Some people find that verra suspicious."

"He is innocent. The mon may be a rutting fool, but he isnae a killer."

Nora blinked in surprise. "Do ye ken the mon weel then?"

Morainn grimaced and idly rubbed at her aching temples with her left hand. "Nay. I have but seen him once. Once outside of my dreams, in truth."

"Ye have had a vision of Sir Tormand Murray?"

"I suspicion a lot of women do," drawled Morainn, a little startled by the bite to her words. "I think the mon is steeped in the sins of the flesh, right up to his bonnie eyebrows, but he isnae the one who is killing these women. For the last three nights I have had dreams that have made me wake up screaming and shaking with fear. First Sir Tormand is there and all is weel." She felt herself blush and saw Nora grin, but she ignored it. "The dreams end with me tied hand and foot to a bed, Sir Tormand nowhere in sight, and the stench of danger all round me."

Nora reached over to pat the hand Morainn had clenched into a tight fist on her lap. "'Tis oftimes more of a curse than a gift, isnae it?"

"Aye, and what makes it even more of a curse is that I can tell no one about the dreams. Who would heed me? Weel a few do, but they dinnae really trust in them or me. But these men? If they didnae think I was insane, they would think that I was a witch, would see it all as proof that I am exactly what so many accuse me of being."

"Nay as many as ye think, but continue. Do these visions show ye who the real killer is?"

"I think they are trying verra hard to point the way

for me. Each time I dream there is a little more to see in that final chilling part. I just cannae grasp what that is. I fear I am beginning to scare poor Walin."

"Ye could never frighten him. He fears *for* ye, fears that ye are being hurt in some way. I but hope that ye find the answer ye need in these dreams ere they leave ye too weak, mayhap even ill."

Morainn briefly smiled. "I look that poorly, do I?"

"Nay, my friend. Ye just look verra tired. And, I think one of the things that robs ye of sleep, aside from dark dreams, is that ye ken ye have some hard decisions to make."

"Such as whether or nay to speak to Sir Tormand Murray?"

Nora sighed and nodded. "Ye did say that he defended ye in front of that angry crowd. Isnae that a good sign?"

"It doesnae mean he will believe I am having visions, ones that might actually help him to find a brutal killer. As I told Walin, the mon might just think I am trying a new, clever, and intriguing way to get into his bed." She smiled when Nora laughed, but quickly grew serious again. "I have too little to tell him, Nora. So far all I can say it that I saw a bloodied knife, heard a soft, cold voice, and smelled a heavy scent, rather like some of the scents the ladies at court wear. It isnae enough. I must have more to help him catch this madmon or Sir Tormand is as doomed as the voice in my dream whispered he was."

"The whispers of suspicion are growing louder," said Tormand, as he and Simon trotted after the big hound that had caught the scent of yet another blood trail.

"I ken it, but they are still naught but whispers," replied Simon.

"Dinnae try to soothe me, Simon. The noose is tightening around my neck and we both ken it."

When the hound stopped beside a rough shepherd's hut, Simon paused to look at Tormand. "We both ken it, so what is the purpose of allowing our wee brains to prey upon the matter? We need all our wits and strength to catch this madmon. Marie was a good woman."

"Aye, she was," Tormand agreed, feeling sorrow weight his heart.

"Yet ye bedded her."

"Long ago. She was grieving. Her first husband had been dead for a six-month and the loneliness was eating at her soul. His kinsmen were also trying to steal away all the mon had left her. Barely a day passed when she didnae have a confrontation with them." He met Simon's gaze and said firmly, "It wasnae a seduction; it was a comforting. It was also just the once. Her husband kens all about it for she told him ere they married and he understands."

"That explains why he isnae whispering poison about ye."

"Aye, but some of those around him are. Marie and I remained friends although we ne'er slept together again. I fear that friendship was enough to make many fools believe we were lovers. That is my fault."

Simon grimaced. "I would like to assure ye that it isnae so, but in some ways it is. Ye are the sort of mon who cannae be around any lass without too many thinking that ye are bedding her. T'isnae just because ye do bed so many, but that ye can, and do so easily. Nay doubt some men feel eased by the thought that there is some special trick or e'en magic ye use to get so many lasses into your bed. They dinnae ken that ye are just an ordinary mon who was blessed with the looks a lass likes."

Tormand gave Simon a look of friendly disgust. "Thank ye, Simon. Ye are a great comfort to me."

"My pleasure." Simon sighed heavily. "Weel, we have dallied enough. Let us get this o'er with."

It was as bad as Tormand had feared. Worse in many ways for he had truly liked Marie, had considered her a good friend. He felt the same about her husband, Duncan, who was grieving so hard right now. He stared at the bloodstained pallet, the remains of Marie's clothes, and felt the sting of tears in his eyes. Tormand prayed that Marie had died quickly, that God in His mercy had stopped her generous heart before the pain had become too great.

"I want this mon dead," Tormand said quietly, his voice hard with the aching need for retribution. "And ere he dies, I want him to feel the pain and fear he so callously inflicted upon these women."

"That is a gift I pray for daily," said Simon in a voice equally quiet, equally hard, as he studied the floor of the tiny shepherd's hut.

When Simon picked something up off the floor, Tormand moved closer to the man. "What have ye found?"

"Another hairpin made of bone," Simon replied.

"In a shepherd's shieling?"

"Aye. An odd thing to find here, isnae it? Unfortunately, we ken that a lot of women use them."

"So that means that anyone could have dropped it here, e'en one of two lovers stealing a moment alone."

Simon nodded as he left the hut, not surprised by the fact that Tormand followed close on his heels. "Yet, is it nay strange that we have found one at each of the places where the women were murdered?"

Tormand stared at Simon in shock. "Ye cannae be thinking a woman had something to do with this, can ye? Aye, I ken weel that a woman can be as vicious and as deadly as any mon, but strength was required in these killings, nay only to hold the women but to bring them to where they could be tortured and killed before taking them home."

"I ken it. 'Tis why I dinnae see these hairpins as wee arrows pointing to our killer. 'Tis just a puzzle. Mayhap the mon who is doing this is killing these women because they werenae chaste and he leaves the hairpin of a lass who betrayed him as some sign, as his mark."

"But why choose women I have bedded?"

"That is a verra good question."

Tormand cursed softly as they started the long walk back to town. Each site of the murders was farther away than the last one. He prayed there would be no more murders, but if there were, he decided they would bring horses with them next time.

A shudder went through him. He did not think he could stand over another woman's body. Guilt was robbing him of sleep. Although they had yet to find any hard proof that he was in any way connected to these killings, the fact that all of the dead women had once shared his bed could not be ignored. More and more people were beginning to notice that sad fact and the whispers of suspicion were growing louder every day. He could almost feel the noose tightening around his neck.

By the time they reached his home, Tormand was feeling weary in his body as well as in his heart. One glance at his friend was enough to tell him that Simon fared little better. All Tormand wanted was a hot bath and clean clothes, ones that did not carry the stench of death. He would follow that with a filling meal and a soft bed. He had no doubt that Simon wanted the same things.

Opening the door, Tormand immediately heard voices. Once inside, he shut the door and scowled toward his great hall. He recognized those voices. His family had arrived.

"Ah, there ye are," said Walter, as he strode toward the great hall from the kitchens, a jug of drink in each hand. "Brothers and cousins here. They arenae too happy with you."

Before Tormand could say just how little he cared about that, Walter disappeared into the great hall. He knew Walter would be telling his kinsmen that he was home. Tormand looked at Simon and, without a word, they both bolted up the stairs. Tormand had no intention of enduring the inquisition his family would put him through until he had had a bath and changed his clothes. If nothing else, it would be difficult to convince his kinsmen that all was well if he still stank of blood and death.

It was over an hour before Tormand felt ready to face his family. He had spent most of the time just sitting in his bath until the water grew too cool for comfort, thinking about what he could say and what he should not say. Instinct told him it was foolish to try to hide the truth from his family but he was about to give it his best effort. He did not wish his mother to suffer any more worry and grief. If he had to lie to ease her mind, he would. If his kinsmen wrested the truth out of him and Simon, then he would threaten them into lying.

"Ready?" asked Simon.

A little surprised to see his friend standing in the doorway of his bedchamber as he had not heard the man approaching, Tormand nodded. "Aye, I suppose I am. Troublesome lot," muttered Tormand. "I didnae invite them to come, especially since I ken they are here to badger me with questions." Recalling how his brother had banged on his bedchamber door to demand that he get to the hall the moment he had finished cleaning up, Tormand scowled. "They are here to poke their long noses into my business."

Simon smiled faintly. "Some people would be most grateful for such concern, e'en just for a family."

Tormand gave Simon a narrow-eyed look. He knew the truth of those words, but was in no mood to say so. He also knew that Simon had very little family left and those few cared nothing for the man. Tormand knew very well that he was blessed in his family. There were times, however, when he would be more than willing to toss some of that blessing into someone else's lap.

"What I would like to ken is how did they hear of my troubles?" Tormand asked, as he and Simon headed toward the great hall.

"Are ye certain they are here because of these murders?"

"Aye. They saw me nay so verra long ago, so they couldnae have been struck with a searing need to see my face once more."

The moment Tormand stepped into the great hall, all four of his kinsmen turned to stare at him. His cousins Rory and Harcourt looked amused. His brothers Bennett and Uilliam looked a little wary. They knew their brother did not really want the family getting tangled up in whatever trouble he was in. Tormand's gaze settled on Walter and his eyes narrowed. His squire was looking suspiciously innocent.

"I think I ken who sent word to my kin," Tormand said quietly to Simon.

"Weel, dinnae kill him now," Simon replied, amusement tinting his voice. "I am eager to enjoy my meal."

"Fine. I will kill him later."

Tormand stiffened his backbone and strode to his seat trying to act as though he was not about to face an uncomfortable inquisition.

Chapter 5

"Ye need to leave here," said Bennett the moment Tormand and Simon finished telling them all that had been happening even as they filled their empty bellies. "If ye arenae here then ye cannae be blamed for these murders. All ye need to do is wait until the killers are caught or there is another murder whilst ye are far away and the trouble will be over. They cannae blame ye for something when ye are miles away when it happens."

It was true, but Tormand did not immediately agree with his younger brother. He was torn. If he was the reason the women were being murdered, leaving might well save a few lives. However, the killer could just as easily follow him wherever he went and begin killing women wherever he settled down.

He felt a twinge of embarrassment to realize that there were not that many places where he could find shelter where there were no women he had bedded or had been suspected of bedding. Even the women at his family's home could be in danger if he went there. The few women who worked for him or those who worked for his family within their homes had never been his lovers. He had grown up with the strict rule that the men should leave the women working within their households alone. It was a rule very few of his kinsmen had ever broken. That did not mean whoever was slaughtering the women he had bedded would be aware of that rule or believe he had ever followed it. Few people did.

Also, to leave, to flee the area, was an act that held the foul taste of cowardice. He knew that pride was the bitter downfall of many a man, but he could not ignore how his tightened its grip on him at the mere thought of running away from this trouble. Leaving could also harden the growing suspicion that he was the killer, especially if the killings here ended when he left because the murderer had followed him.

"I dinnae think that would be a good idea," said Simon, relieving Tormand of the chore of explaining why he was about to say nay to what sounded like a very sound plan. "Nay yet. It would look too much like he was fleeing justice for his crimes. There may yet come a time when it would be wise for Tormand to go into hiding. I have even chosen a place for him to go."

Tormand looked at his friend in surprise. "Ye have?"

"Aye. I thought it a wise precaution. With each woman murdered suspicion about ye spreads a little wider."

"I cannae believe that anyone would ever think I could do that to any woman."

"Most dinnae. 'Tis why ye havenae already had to flee an angry mob. But, the fact that ye have been the lover of each woman is slowly eating away at that belief. Such coincidence was easily accepted with the first murder, but now there has been a second and a third. And all of them were your lovers. Since we havenae gotten any closer to the killer I fear there will soon be a fourth. I think we both ken there is a verra good chance that that woman will have been your lover, too."

"But if he wasnae here when that happened," began Uilliam, his green eyes filled with concern for his brother's safety.

"As I said, it could easily look as if he fled because he was guilty," Simon interrupted.

Tormand sighed. "That is what I was thinking."

"Better to be thought guilty for a wee while than to be dragged to the gallows," snapped Bennett, and then he took a deep drink of ale as if he tried to cool the anger heating his blood.

"I willnae allow him to hang," Simon said in the calm voice that had the ability to reach out and soothe those who heard it. "I have his escape carefully planned and, since I ne'er leave his side, I will be able to send him on his way without a moment's hesitation."

"Ah, and here I thought ye were staying so close to me because ye were so fond of me," murmured Tormand.

Ignoring him, Simon continued, "There is also the fact that the killer could follow Tormand if he went somewhere else and then women would begin to die there."

"Are ye so verra certain that this is all connected to him in some way?" asked Harcourt, his amber eyes holding the hard look of a warrior ready to go to battle.

"We have no proof," replied Simon, "but I do believe

it is. There are a few lasses left in this town whom he hasnae bedded." A smile flickered over Simon's mouth when Tormand grunted in annoyance over that remark. "But none of them have been killed. 'Tis why the belief that it is naught but coincidence is fading a little more each day, and with each death. Two of the women's husbands dinnae openly accuse Tormand, but they do naught to quell the growing suspicions, either. The only husband who might have spoken up for him has returned his wife's body to their lands and he will undoubtedly stay there awhile, if only to comfort his wee sons."

"The more ye talk the less there seems we can do to put a stop to this."

"We can only keep hunting. Aye, 'tis maddening that we have gained so little from all our work, but one thing I have learned from all my years of solving such puzzles is that a mistake *will* be made. Something will be found that will lead us closer, mayhap e'en to the killer's door. Someone will see something or hear something that will help us find this beast. Or the killer will become so arrogant that he will no longer take such care not to be found."

"Or we can take something ye found near one of these women to the Ross witch and let her do a seeing," said Walter, shrugging as everyone stared at him.

Simon pulled the bone hairpins he had found out of his purse and studied them. "'Tis a thought, Walter. One I believe Tormand has had, especially since he has seen the witch."

Walter grimaced, making his face even more homely than it usually was. "That may nay be good."

"Ye kenned what she looked like?" Tormand asked his squire.

"But first," Simon said, quickly interrupting what was obviously going to be an argument, and looking at Tormand, "we need ye to make a list of all the women ye have bedded in this town and those living near at hand. Mayhap the ones who travel with the court as weel."

"The women who arenae dead willnae like me telling what they may have kept secret from everyone," said Tormand.

"I fear there has been little secrecy about your many frolics. I believe I could probably make a fairly accurate list myself simply from the gossip I have heard, but a few women may have been discrete. Do ye ken, they treat bedding ye almost as if it is some trophy they have won?"

Tormand felt a blush heat his cheeks and glared at his kinsmen when they all snickered, before turning his glare upon his friend. "Then I will make a list, but nay tonight."

"Nay. Tonight is for resting both our bodies and our wits."

Despite the need for rest, it was late before Tormand finally crawled into bed. Selfish though it was, he had kept his bedchamber to himself, leaving the other men to sort out where they would sleep. With Simon or Walter constantly at his side, Tormand had discovered that he savored this time alone to gather his thoughts and to shake off the frustration of hunting down a killer who was as elusive as smoke.

His gut told him that he would soon have to run

and hide. Simon was good at solving such puzzles, at hunting down the guilty, yet even Simon was finding nothing to lead them to the murderer. There would be another killing, of that Tormand had no doubt, and the killing would continue until he was standing on the gallows, dying for crimes he had not committed.

He flung his arm over his eyes and struggled to force all thought of the murders from his mind. There was no gain in losing sleep over it all. A faint smile curled his mouth as the image of Morainn Ross filled his mind and his body began to harden in interest. It had been a very long time since the mere thought of a woman could stir his need, but Morainn Ross accomplished it. Tormand knew it would be wise to push her from his thoughts as well, but he did not. Dreams of the lush Morainn were far preferable to dreams of blood, death, and grief.

Even as he slipped into sleep his dream of Morainn grew heated. Tormand slowly removed her clothing, kissing each newly revealed inch of her soft golden skin. He savored her sighs of pleasure and the feel of her fingers in his hair. A little cry of surprised delight escaped her lush mouth as he caressed her full breasts, first with his hands and then with his mouth. The heat of her desire turned her eyes into the color of a storm-tossed sea and he felt himself tumble into their mysterious depths, trapped by her beauty and willing to stay there. But, as he readied himself to unite their bodies, to savor her womanly heat surrounding him, everything began to change.

Darkness swirled around their entwined bodies.

The warm, willing woman in his arms became a bloodied corpse. The beautiful eyes that had been shaded with passion for him were gone and he stared in black holes. A soft, cold voice laughingly asked him how he liked his new lover.

Tormand bolted up in bed so fast that he nearly fell out of it. He was soaked in sweat, his breath coming fast and hard. The fact that no one had burst into his bed-chamber told him that he had at least kept silent during what had turned into a chilling nightmare. He stumbled over to a small table near the fireplace and poured himself a tankard of wine. It took all of one tankard full and half of another before he felt his heart-beat slow to normal and his hands ceased to shake.

He took a moment to wash the worst of the sweat from his body before crawling back into bed. If that horror was going to revisit him every time he closed his eyes, he would never sleep again. The first part of the dream was easy to understand. He found Morainn Ross very alluring. It was the end of the dream that troubled him. Was it born of guilt or the horrors he had seen? Or, worse, was it some hint of the future, a warning that if he gave in to his attraction to Morainn she would end up like the others? He prayed that was not true, for he was sorely tempted by Morainn and he was not a man who easily resisted temptation.

Cautiously allowing himself to relax and invite sleep to take him back into its hold, Tormand wondered if the Ross witch really did have visions. Could she truly touch something and see whatever secrets it might hold? If she could, Morainn Ross could well prove to be just what he and Simon needed to find the killer.

They would have to keep her close then, protecting her as she aided them. And with such protection around her, Tormand decided she would be safe enough that he might not have to worry about resisting temptation after all.

Morainn managed to bite back the scream in her throat this time as she sat up in bed so fast she felt dizzy for a moment. She reached for the tankard of cider she had begun to keep at her bedside and took a deep drink, trying to wash the sting of terror out of her throat. It took several moments for her heartbeat to return to a more comfortable pace.

If these dreams did not stop soon she would be too exhausted to do even the simplest of chores. Morainn feared she might start to fight going to sleep at all. That would be an affliction that could easily kill her in the end.

Setting her drink aside, she huddled beneath the blankets and tried to grasp the courage to go back to sleep, to get the rest she needed. Morainn was almost too afraid to close her eyes. The horrific sight of her own body lying there, mutilated, her eyes gone, was not one she could easily forget.

Yet again the horror had come after a lovely heated dream of her and Tormand loving each other. She could almost feel the touch of his mouth still lingering on her breast. The warmth that filled her body at that memory told her that she remembered it all too well. For a virgin, she was having some very vivid, very sinful, dreams about Sir Tormand Murray. It was a blessing that she would not be seeing much of the man or she might find the temptation he offered far too much to resist.

And she would pay dearly if she succumbed to that weakness, she thought as she shuddered. Morainn could not be certain, but she suspected that was what the bloody end of the dream was telling her. If she let Tormand Murray into her bed she would suffer as all the other women had suffered. Then again, she thought ruefully, such ideas could have been put into her head by her talk with Nora today.

Morainn felt her cats curl up against her and welcomed their warmth. She was not sure if she had just had a true vision of what was to come or if it was only a chilling warning to be careful. Since she did not see any reason a man like Tormand Murray would seek her out, she had to wonder why she even needed such a warning.

Because *she* wanted *him*, she thought with a sigh. She could deny the truth to herself all she wanted to, but, in her dreams, that truth came out. Morainn could not believe her own foolishness. Tormand Murray was a man steeped in the sins of the flesh and, if even a few of the rumors about him were true, he made no effort to turn away from any temptation. After years of fighting to cling to her chastity, despite her deep loneliness and the men who tried to steal it from her, she would have to be witless to hand it over to a man like Sir Tormand.

Closing her eyes, Morainn lightly stroked Grigor, her big yellow tom, when it rested its head on her stomach. Its deep, rumbling purr began to ease away the lingering horror of her dream. She felt herself begin to relax, her breathing softening, as she welcomed sleep again. In the morning she would decide if she knew enough yet to risk going to Sir Innes and Sir Murray and telling them about her visions. It was a decision that required a well-rested mind for she knew the danger was not really that he might not believe her. It was that he would and she could easily find herself spending far too much time in the company of a man who sorely tempted her to sin—and do so repeatedly and with great enthusiasm.

A low growl abruptly pulled Morainn's attention from the chickens she was feeding. Her gray tabby William crouched on the low stone wall surrounding the rough chicken coop. The cat's fur was all standing out and its ragged ears were flattened against its head. She looked in the direction it stared, but saw nothing. That did not immediately cause her to relax her guard, however. William might be just a cat, but the animal was never wrong when it sensed, and warned her of, a possible threat.

Morainn had just finished shutting the chickens in the coop when she heard the sound of horsemen approaching and her heart skipped with fear. "Walin," she called to the boy playing with a ball behind her cottage, "get in the house now."

Walin picked up his ball. "Ye wish me to hide?"

"Aye, laddie, at least until I ken what the men riding this way are wanting of me."

"Mayhap ye should hide, too."

"They have already seen me. Go."

The moment the boy disappeared into the cottage, Morainn walked to the front of her home intending to meet her uninvited guests at her front door. A flicker of amusement went through her as her cats gathered around her, her big toms to the front on either side of her. She knew they could do little to help her fight against six men, and that such sights made too many people think of such things as familiars, but she did not order them away. If nothing else, she remembered all too well how often a nicely aimed slash of sharp claws had allowed her to get free of some fool man who thought she would welcome his attentions just because he had a coin or two. William in particular hated men and that had proved helpful from time to time.

When the men were close enough for her to recognize them, Morainn felt her breath catch in her throat. Sir Tormand had come to her and she had to wonder why. Had someone told him that she had visions? Did he seek her help? If so, it would certainly help her to tell him about the visions she had already had. Sir Simon's presence she could understand, but she wondered why the other four men had come. Such a show of force at her door made her uneasy.

"Mistress Ross," Sir Simon said in greeting, as he reined in before her, "we havenae come to cause ye any trouble."

"Nay?" She believed him, but still asked, "Then why the other men?"

Sir Tormand cast a fleeting glare at the other men. "They claimed we needed protectors on the journey here." He looked at her. "But the truth is they are but curious."

"To see the witch?" she asked, glancing at the four very handsome men. "Are ye going to introduce them to me?"

Tormand sighed so heavily that she almost smiled. She remained coolly polite as he introduced his brothers Bennett and Uilliam and then his cousins Harcourt and Rory. They were all a treat for a woman's eyes and Morainn found herself made a little uneasy by that. If nothing else, the gossip such a visitation could stir could prove very difficult to bear. Pushing aside her concern, she invited them all into her cottage, idly wondering if so many tall, strong men would actually fit.

Just as she was about to lead them inside, Tormand paused by William. "That must be one of the biggest and strongest cats I have e'er seen," he said and started to reach down to pat the cat.

"'Ware, sir, William doesnae like men," Morainn cautioned him, and then felt her heart skip in alarm for he was already scratching a strangely placid William behind its ragged ears. "How verra odd," she murmured, praying this was not some sign, as she did not really want to trust Sir Tormand, at least not too much.

"Mayhap it just didnae trust the other men it met with." Tormand kept his tone of voice light and friendly, but inside he found himself wondering just who those other men might be.

He frowned a little as she led them into her small, neat cottage. The thought of her with any man actually gnawed at him, tasting alarmingly like jealousy.

He did not doubt that she was troubled by unwanted attentions from men who felt any woman alone was free for the taking, especially a poor one without any family left, but was there one she wanted?

The fact that he felt eager for an answer to that question even as he almost dreaded it was a little alarming. He did not mind desiring her, but he did not want to feel any more than that. Tormand was not bothered by her birth or circumstances and he certainly did not care what superstitious fools thought she was, but he was just not ready to change his ways. A lover was what he wanted, no more. He was only one and thirty and in no need of an heir. He had a few more years of play left to get through before he started to look for anything more, anything deeper or lasting. He was not playing now simply because every man needed a rest, he told himself.

When the little boy Walin was brought forward and introduced, Tormand had to fight to suppress a frown. With his blue eyes and thick black hair, Walin looked a lot like Morainn, but that was not what troubled him the most. There was something about young Walin that strongly reminded Tormand of someone. Tormand could not grasp the memory that tickled at the edges of his mind, however.

They were soon all crowded around her table, each with a tankard of cider, and a plate of honey-sweetened oatcakes set in the middle of the table. Talk was idle for a few moments and Tormand watched his kinsmen flirt with Morainn. The annoyance he felt over that troubled him so much that he was beginning to think coming to see her had been a very bad idea. Then she fixed her sea-blue eyes on him and he felt his heart skip in welcome.

This was not good, he mused. Not good at all. Unfortunately, he did not have any urge to flee what was beginning to feel too much like a trap too many of his kinsmen had fallen into—the kind that ensnared a man's heart.

"'Tis pleasant to have company to break up the tedium of the day," Morainn said, "but I dinnae think ye rode here just to introduce your kinsmen, Sir Tormand."

"Nay, especially since I didnae invite the fools to ride with me and Simon," Tormand replied, and sent his grinning kinsmen a brief scowl. "They have decided I need to be protected and stick like burrs."

Morainn felt a strong twist of envy in her heart. Even though Tormand was glaring at the others, she knew he cared for them. They were family and she sensed that those bonds were both deep and wide. She had never truly had a family. Once her father had left, shortly after her birth according to her mother, her mother had apparently lost interest in being a true loving mother. She had never harmed Morainn, but the woman had rarely displayed any true affection for her only child. Morainn had spent her growing years being made to feel little more than a burden.

She hastily shook aside the envy and regrets. Her mother had made sure that her child had always had food to eat, clothes to wear, and a roof over her head. She had also taught Morainn everything she knew about the healing arts, the one thing Anna Ross had actually felt passionate about. That knowledge had allowed Morainn to make a life for herself after she had been banished from the town. For that alone, Morainn knew she owed her mother a lot. She may not have had the close, loving family these Murrays obviously did, but she had been gifted with far more than too many others got.

"We heard that ye had visions," said Tormand, thinking it a poor start to the conversation, but not sure how else to broach the subject of why they were there.

Fear of the consequences of admitting such a thing made her hesitate, but then Morainn recalled Sir Tormand's defense of her before the angry crowd. "Aye, sometimes," she replied. "Visions, dreams, call them what ye will."

"They make her scream in the night," said Walin.

"Ah, weel, nay always." Morainn handed Walin an oatcake in the hope that it would keep him silent for a while. "I cannae have a vision just because someone needs one, however. They come to me when *they* wish to. They are nay always clear in what they try to tell me, either."

Hearing the hesitancy in her voice, Tormand said, "Dinnae fear to speak of it to us. The Murray clan is littered with people who have such gifts. Mostly the lassies." He heard his kinsmen murmur their agreement to that claim. "We dinnae think ye are truly a witch simply because ye have these dreams. We Murrays call them gifts for a reason."

It was difficult not to gape at the man. She glanced around at the other men, but saw no sign that Tormand was lying. They all just watched her silently, a hint of compassion in their eyes as though they understood exactly how difficult it was to have such a gift as hers. Morainn knew some people who thought of her gift as God-given, and not of the devil, but she had never met anyone who freely admitted to having such things in their bloodlines. There was even the hint of pride in Sir Tormand's voice as he spoke of it.

"Then, wouldnae ye prefer going to them?" she asked.

"If one of them had seen anything, then I would have been sent word of it. Several of them sensed there was some trouble coming my way, that I could be in danger, but nay more than that. 'Tis why these fools are here."

It was difficult not to press him for more information about his family and the *gifts* he said they had, but Morainn resisted the urge. "If they have sensed that then, why do ye nay leave here?"

"Because that would look too much like fleeing out of guilt and the killer might follow me anyway. I wouldnae be ending the murders, only taking them to a new place, to new victims."

She nodded. "Aye, I have, er, dreamed that ye are connected to this in some way, but that ye arenae the killer. Nay, ye may stand in pools of blood in my dreams, but there is none on your hands. Unfortunately, my telling anyone that willnae be enough to help ye fend off any accusations."

"We ken that, Mistress Ross," said Sir Simon. "We dinnae plan to make ye speak of such things before those who are too quick to see the devil's hand in anything they dinnae understand. We but hoped that ye may be able to help us find this killer. Three women are dead and we have no idea of the who or the why, only supposition. We desperately need some sort of trail to follow."

"Ye want me to tell ye of my dreams? I saw no trail in them, sir. The face of this monster has ne'er appeared to me, if that is what ye are seeking."

"Nay, we come here hoping that ye have a certain gift that many in town say ye have."

"And what would that be?"

"The ability to touch something and see the truth."

Chapter 6

Morainn knew she was staring at the three common hairpins Sir Simon held out to her as if he were holding an adder and asking her to kiss it, but she could not help it. She hated touching anything that had been near death, tragedy, or violence. The visions that came to her when she did were rarely pleasant. If these things were found near the murdered women she dreaded what truths might flow into her mind. The dreams she had been having lately were bad enough.

"Where did ye find these?" she finally asked, although she was already sure of the answer. "They are but common hairpins, nay something any of those fine ladies would have worn." Morainn could tell that was not exactly true, but doubted the men had noticed anything unusual about the hairpins.

Simon watched her closely as he replied, "I found them in the places where the murders were done."

"The women were murdered in their beds, aye?"

"Nay. They were murdered elsewhere and, when they were dead or nearly so, they were carried home and placed in their beds. I found these at the killing sites. They could belong to some woman who once lived in the place, or trysted there with a lover, and have nothing at all to do with the killings."

Morainn was not surprised to see her hand shaking as she reached for the hairpins. Every instinct she had told her touching them was going to be one of those times when she felt her gift was a bitter curse. She was startled when Tormand suddenly put his hand over hers. The look on his face was one of concern, but that was not all that left her feeling breathless. The touch of his elegant long-fingered hand sent such a flare of heat through her body that she barely stopped herself from immediately yanking her hand away from his. A sudden warmth in his unusual, beautiful eyes told her that he had felt it, too. Morainn had to swallow hard before she felt she could speak without her voice revealing how unsettled she was.

"I cannae even try to get a vision unless I touch them," she said, hoping everyone would think the faint but husky tremble in her voice was due to her fear of what she might soon see. That was certainly there, churning away in her belly like a piece of bad beef.

"Ye dinnae have to do this," he said even as he wondered what had possessed him to interfere, for it certainly was not in his best interest to do so.

Tormand needed the answers she might find for them. He had doubted that she could gain any insight simply from touching something, but no more. Her fear was real. It was that which made him reluctant to have her test her gift. And, yet, three women were dead and far too many people were starting to eye him with suspicion. It made no sense to stop her, but he had not been able to sit back when he saw her fear.

"I think I do," she said quietly. "Women are being murdered. They may nay have been innocent of sin, but I dinnae think they deserved what was done to them. And, people begin to suspect you, aye?"

"Aye." He removed his hand with a reluctance that was not fully due to the need to protect her from what she might see or feel. "If these were touched by the killer it willnae be a pleasant vision ye will have."

"Och, I ken it, but three women are dead, arenae they, and more may soon be murdered if this madmon isnae stopped. What sort of person would I be if I didnae at least try to stop it. Is that nay what such a gift is for?" She looked at Sir Simon. "Just one, I think."

Simon placed one of the hairpins in her hand, and Morainn closed her fingers over it. She was just thinking that the concerned looks all six men were giving her were rather touching when she was abruptly pulled into hell. The images came at her so fast and hard she felt as if someone was pummeling her brain. Strong emotions, all of them bad, slammed into her, making her heart pound so fast she feared it would be damaged.

Fear. Pain. Hate. Icy cold fury. Pleasure. The last made Morainn's stomach churn for she knew it came from the ones causing the pain and the fear. There was madness there, too. It swirled around the pair, inflicting such horrors onto another person like some evil spirit. Knives gleamed, and blood flowed. Morainn tried to flee the stench of blood and death but she could not move.

She became aware that her whole body was shaking

violently, but she could not release the hairpin. She struggled to fix her mind's eye on the shadowy figures that moved around in the thick fog of sharp emotion. The victim was easy to find and Morainn did not need to know which person in the fog was doing the screaming that pounded at her mind. She could see the killers bending over the victim, like two carrion birds, who worked to inflict as much pain as possible.

Morainn finally grasped the sense of someone huge, broad-shouldered and bulky with muscle. She also smelled that heavy scent she had smelled in her dreams. It came from a small figure, one nearly lost in the shadow of the larger one, but Morainn could gather no more information than the fact that the figure was slight and female. Then she caught a too vivid sight of a knife aimed at a beautiful green eye, wide open and full of terror in a blood-soaked face, and she knew she could bear no more. A sharp cry escaped Morainn as she finally released the hairpin.

The moment she was no longer touching the hairpin, Morainn felt the contents of her stomach racing up into her throat and she gagged. Suddenly, long, strong arms were wrapped around her and she was vaguely aware of being on the floor on her knees, moaning. A bucket appeared and Morainn violently released all of the poison the dark vision had left boiling inside of her.

By the time she regained control of her stomach, Morainn was too weak to do anything more than slump against the hard body of the man behind her, steadying her. She stared dully at Sir Simon as he knelt down and gently bathed her face with a cool, wet cloth. Someone made her drink a little cider and rinse her mouth with it several times. A small part of her clouded mind was aware of one of the men talking softly, comfortingly to Walin.

As her senses slowly returned they brought intense embarrassment with them. She was sprawled in Sir Tormand's arms like a wanton. The elegant Sir Simon was crouched before her, bathing her face and hands as if she was some helpless child. Morainn caught a movement out of the corner of her eye and saw one of Sir Tormand's handsome kinsmen taking the soiled bucket outside. If she were not so weak, she would run away and hide for a year. The humiliation she felt was almost more than she could bear.

Morainn said nothing as Sir Tormand helped her to her feet. He led her back to the table and she sat down, unable to look at him as he sat beside her and kept a light grip on her arm. She wanted to shrug that steadying hand off, but knew she still needed it. It took a few bites of the lightly buttered bread that magically appeared in front of her and a few cautious drinks of cider before she felt as though she might be able to speak clearly. She stared at the top of the table, however, unable to meet the gazes of the men who had seen her so thoroughly disgrace herself. Morainn placed her elbow on the table and pressed a hand to her aching forehead as she tried to think of a way to tell them what she had seen in a way that would make some sense to them.

"Did one of the women lose her eyes?" she asked softly. "Green eyes?"

"Aye," replied Tormand, shocked by what she

asked, for it implied she had actually seen at least part of the killing of Isabella. "Isabella Redmond."

"*Jesu.*" She shuddered and hastily took a drink of cider. "I ne'er gave much thought to what Sir William meant when he said she had been butchered. Didnae really want to."

"I am sorry ye now have a better idea of what he meant." Tormand glanced at a wide-eyed Walin. "This may nay be something we should speak of in front of the boy."

Cursing herself for forgetting about the child's presence, Morainn lifted her head enough to look at Walin. "Dearling, it might be best if ye go out to play for a while. This is a verra dark thing we must discuss now."

"Are ye feeling better now, Morainn?" Walin asked even as he stood up to leave.

She doubted she would ever feel better after what she had seen, but forced herself to smile gently at the boy. "Aye, and feeling more so with each passing moment. Go play for a wee while, laddie. Ye really dinnae want to hear this." As soon as the boy was gone, she told the men. "At the end I saw a knife aimed at a beautiful green eye set in a face covered in blood from more cuts than I cared to count. Not that any vision would ever let me be so precise. 'Tis why I couldnae stay any longer, why I had to flee what I was seeing." Morainn did not really want to find as much pleasure as she did in the light soothing touch of Tormand's hand against her back.

"Did ye see the killer?" asked Simon.

Finally sitting up straighter, Morainn forced herself

to meet Sir Simon's gaze. She felt the heat of a blush touch her cheeks, but ignored it. There were more important things to worry about at the moment than her own embarrassment. And, in all fairness to herself, she never would have been so sick if she had not touched that hairpin in an attempt to help him find a killer.

"Aye and nay," she replied. "There are two."

"Two men?" Simon frowned. "Aye, I am nay really surprised."

He would be surprised soon, she mused, and said, "Nay, a mon and a woman."

Morainn almost smiled at the look of shock on all the men's faces. She had to admit it had shocked her, too, but not nearly as much as they appeared to be. Did men truly believe that women never fell victim to such a madness, that they could not feel such a murderous hate and anger? If men were so incapable of thinking a woman could be as dangerous, as lethal, as a man, it was no wonder that so many fell victim to the bad ones.

"A woman helped to cut up those women?" asked Tormand, shock still faintly trembling in his deep voice.

"Aye. That hairpin is hers. The others probably are as weel," Morainn replied. "I cannae tell ye if they fell out as she did her evil work or if she left them apurpose, however."

"As a sign, mayhap," murmured Simon.

The man had recovered from his shock quickly, Morainn thought. There was a look in his steel gray eyes that told her he was already working on these new facts, trying to put the puzzle together. She began to doubt that there was much that could shock the man for long. Morainn wished there were more men like Sir Simon Innes. She suspected fewer innocent men would die on the gallows.

"Why would she leave a sign?" asked Harcourt. "And why leave something so common that no one can read whatever message she is trying to send?"

"'Tis nay so common," said Morainn and felt herself blush a little when all the men looked at her. "Common ones are made out of wood or the bones of chickens, mayhap ducks or geese. Sometimes even a sheep. That one is made from the antlers of a stag and it has a wee design carved upon it."

Simon carefully studied the hairpins and then cursed. "I am nay so weel acquainted with such things that I can tell one animal bone from another, but a common hair-pin wouldnae have a fancy design etched into it. That costs money, as does one made of antler horn. 'Tis a rose, I think."

"The perfume," Tormand murmured.

Morainn stared at him in such surprise she barely kept herself from gaping. "Ye ken who it is?"

"Nay, I had a dream last night, a dream about these murders, and I smelled the perfume."

The way he was looking at her and the heat that entered his gaze told Morainn that he had dreamed about more than the killings, but she forced her mind back to the matter of her vision and what it might tell them about the killers. Later she would consider what it meant when a man she was attracted to had a dream the same night she did and, she guessed, one that was probably very similar to hers. It took all of her willpower not to blush when she thought of what had happened in that dream before it had turned into a nightmare.

"Heavy, cloying, almost too strong to tell what it is, for all ye wish to do is pinch your nose shut," she said.

"Exactly like that. Ye have smelled it, too?"

She nodded, forcing herself to think only of the dark parts of her dreams, the ones that had to do with the killings and not the hunger the man stirred within her. "In every dream I have had about these killings. I wondered on it, but then decided it must be the way the vision was trying to tell me that it was a woman being killed. The voice I heard in the dreams wasnae clear enough for me to ken if the one who spoke was a mon or a woman. Yet, in one of those dreams the hand that held the blood-soaked knife was small and delicate."

"But ye have seen no faces?" asked Simon.

Morainn shook her head. "Nay. Weel, nay yet. Each dream gives me a wee bit more. The perfume, then the voice, then the hand. The vision I got from touching the hairpin gave me more." She swallowed hard, fear of what else she might see making her blood run cold, but she could not let that fear stop her from helping in the hunt for this vicious killer. "Mayhap if I hold another one I will see a face or some other thing that will help ye find these killers."

Simon gave her a gentle smile. "Nay, not today. From what I saw, such visions are hard on both body and mind. Rest a day or two and we will try another then. I have put the one ye have already touched aside so that ye will nay have to see its secrets again."

"But another woman could die while we wait."

"Aye, there is that chance, but your gift does us no good if ye use it until ye are ill or broken in heart and mind. Rest. We can return on the morrow if ye think ye will be able to abide touching another one. For now mayhap ye can think long and hard on all the dreams and visions ye have had concerning this matter. There may be some small but verra important thing that ye will remember."

Morainn did not think there would ever come a day when she could abide touching one of those hairpins, but she nodded. She would force herself to do it. To her shame, she admitted to herself that the biggest reason she would do so was for Sir Tormand Murray's sake and not the poor murdered women's. Morainn hated to think that she could be so swayed by a handsome face.

It was only a few minutes later that she stood at her door watching the men leave, her arm around Walin's small shoulders. All the men had given her a very gallant farewell, but it was Tormand's that she knew would linger in her mind. There had been a look in his eyes that had caused her heart to pound with a strange mix of fear and anticipation. If she did not wish to end up as just one more of what was undoubtedly a legion of besotted women, she would have to be on her guard around that man.

* * *

"She has a true gift," Simon said, as he rode beside Tormand.

"Or a curse," Tormand said. "She saw Isabella's murder, saw that they took her eyes."

"Aye, in many ways she did, although she didnae see it too clearly, thank God. I am reluctant to ask her to try again with another one of the hairpins, but we have nothing, have found no trail to follow on our own. Whoever is doing this is verra clever or verra lucky."

"They say madness can oftimes make one more cunning," said Bennett. "I am just finding it difficult to believe a woman would have a part in all this. Och, aye, I ken that they can be as cruel and vicious as any mon, but to actually wield the knife? That is what I find so hard to accept."

"And, yet, it makes a strange kind of sense," said Harcourt, and shrugged when the others looked at him. "From what ye tell me, each woman had her beauty utterly destroyed. A woman could understand how much that meant to the women, mayhap e'en hate that beauty they hold. 'Tis the fact that the women's hair was cut off that makes me inclined to think a woman really is involved. A mon might destroy a woman's face or body in some mad, jealous rage, but I doubt he would realize how important that hair would be to a woman."

"Ah, aye, ye may be right," murmured Simon. "Then again, I believe we can all agree that there is madness behind these murders and who can understand the mind of a mon touched by madness, or a woman's."

Tormand only half-listened as Simon and his kinsmen debated all that Morainn had told them. Most of his thoughts were on the woman they had just left and not on her words. He was certain they had shared a dream last night. Such a thing had never happened to him before, but he knew it meant something, was important in a way that left him very uneasy. It implied some bond had been made between him and Morainn Ross and he did not want any bonds.

There was also what had happened when he had touched her hand to worry about. He did not mind being strongly attracted to a woman. If nothing else, it made the lovemaking richer and more heated, more satisfying. But he had felt a strong lusting for a woman before and had never felt such a wave of heat and longing simply by touching the woman's hand. A large part of him was eager to pursue Morainn, to find out how that fierce heat would feel once he had her naked between the sheets. Another part of him wanted to put the spurs to his horse and ride as far away from Morainn Ross as he could.

"I would appreciate it if ye didnae try to seduce this one."

Simon's voice startled Tormand out of his thoughts about getting Morainn into his bed, which he decided was a good thing because he was growing hard and hungry. Tormand was glad to see that his kinsmen were riding ahead of him and Simon and had not heard the man's words. For a moment, he was angry that Simon would dare to give him such a warning. Then he inwardly sighed, admitting to himself that it was probably deserved. He had been thinking about seducing Morainn. In truth, he had been thinking about riding back to her cottage to get her naked and into a bed as quickly as he could.

"Want her for yourself, do ye?" he asked, and was not really surprised by the tone of possession edging into his voice. Tormand had to accept that he already felt very possessive of Morainn.

"I wouldnae turn her aside if she smiled my way, but that isnae why I am speaking up about this. The lass has enough trouble in her life without ye adding her to your list. Especially now. If we are right in believing all of this is connected to ye, that someone is trying to destroy ye by killing women ye have bedded and pointing the finger of blame toward ye, then bedding Morainn Ross puts far more than her heart and virtue at risk. Aye, and I do mean virtue. I dinnae e'en think that boy is her bastard as so many claim he is."

"Nay, I dinnae believe he is, either."

Tormand was chilled by Simon's words. It was a chill that went far deeper than it should, if all he felt was a simple concern that yet another woman might suffer and die because she had found some pleasure in his arms. Forcing himself to look closely at what he felt, he saw that it was fear, a fear that she would be taken from him before he had ever had a chance to find out what she meant to him.

In some inexplicable way he and Morainn had become connected to each other. He was certain of it. He was also certain that she had shared the dream he had had last night, and he wondered if she had seen them making love. Had she felt the same heated need he had? There was also what he felt when he had touched her hand to consider. It was as though the bond that had begun in that dream, even in the first meeting of their eyes, had been strengthened by that simple touch.

He had the sinking feeling that his days as a man who took what he wanted whenever he wanted it were rapidly drawing to a close. Tormand had always felt that the women of his family had been talking romantic nonsense when they had claimed one just knew when they met their true mate. However, just in case there was some truth in that, he had actually avoided any woman who had stirred anything more than lust in him. The fact that he had liked Marie was one reason he had never tried to return to her bed, had stepped back before that one night of comforting could become anything more. He knew he could not step back from Morainn.

For a moment he nearly convinced himself that that was because her gift was needed to help them find this killer. The lie did not hold firm for any longer than that. Tormand knew he was drawn to Morainn in ways he could not fully understand, at least not yet. Even the fact that she was beautiful and he lusted after her did not explain away what he felt, was feeling.

His unwillingness to look too closely at those feelings was now proving to be more a hindrance than a defense. He knew he was going to have to overcome that unwillingness. Although he was reluctant to change the way he lived, he was not fool enough to push aside or turn away from the woman who might well be his fated match. Then he thought of the list Simon had mentioned and nearly groaned. He might not have to even try to push Morainn away; his past might well do it for him.

"Why dinnae ye believe he is her true child?" asked Simon, cutting into Tormand's rambling thoughts. "He has black hair and blue eyes as she does."

"Nay exactly as she does," Tormand replied, grasping at the change of topic Simon offered like a starving man would clutch at a crust of bread tossed his way. "Aye, 'tis true that children can hold a mix of each parent, e'en look akin to some ancestor many years dead and gone, but ye can still see the kinship if ye look hard enough. I dinnae see it in him. And, he calls her Morainn, doesnae he? Nay *maman*. Why play that game when she holds him close to her side and kens that near all who live round here think the boy is her child?"

"True. I wonder whose child he is?"

"I dinnae ken and yet there was something oddly familiar about him."

"Mayhap ye should check over that list of yours."

"Ah, that list. If ye ken I might try to pull the lass into my sinful clutches, just show her the list I am making. One look at that and any woman with a pinch of wit in her head will stay verra far away from me." Tormand was feeling sorry for himself, but then the import of Simon's suggestion became clear to him and he glared at his friend. "And just what are ye implying by telling me I should check o'er my list?"

"That a mon who spends so much time casting his seed hither and yon will eventually sow something."

"I was always verra careful never to *sow* anything."

"I suspicion many a bairn's father might say the same thing."

Before Tormand could argue that any further, Simon rode ahead a little to speak to Harcourt. Tormand sank back into his thoughts even though it was not a place he wished to be. There was so much turmoil inside of him, he was surprised his stomach had not turned against him. Simon's parting comment had only made it all worse.

He could not believe there was even the smallest chance that Walin was his child. Tormand knew he had always been careful, even when drunk. Most of the women he had bedded, especially those from the court, were well versed in ways to keep a man's seed from taking root as well.

The word *most* suddenly stuck in his mind like a thistle burr to a horse's tail and his heart sank. Cold reason smothered his instinctive refusal to believe he could have sired a child on one of his many lovers and that she would not tell him if he had. Simon was right. Many a new father had probably thought he had been careful, had done all that was needed to insure that there was no bairn produced by his pleasuring a woman. Was it not his own mother who had once said that only celibacy could insure that no child is born? One thing Tormand had never practiced was celibacy. These last few months had been the longest he had been without a woman since the age of fourteen, when Jenna the cooper's daughter had given him his first taste of the pleasures of the flesh.

Tormand cursed. He now had the seed of doubt planted firmly in his mind. There was no returning to a state of blissful ignorance or happy denial. Along with hunting down a brutal killer and trying to keep his neck out of a noose, he was going to have to find out all he could about Walin. If there was even the smallest chance that he was the boy's father, he could not ignore it. He had to find out the truth, one way or another. When he realized that could well prove to be yet another bond he had with Morainn, yet another thing that would keep pulling him back to her side, he cursed again. Fate was obviously playing a May game with him and he was losing.

Chapter 7

Her heart pounding, Morainn opened her eyes. She felt as she did when she had some vision and yet she knew she had not had one. Wearied by the vision that had brought her to her knees as she held the hairpin Sir Simon had given her, she had crawled into her bed early and slept like the dead. Something had startled her awake, however. Something that was making her feel very afraid.

Then she heard a familiar low growl. The moon sent enough light into her bedchamber that she was able to see her cat William crouched low on her bed, its fur all puffed out, making the cat look even bigger than it was. It was glaring at the door and she could swear that its eyes actually glowed. A glance around revealed that her other cats were also tense and staring at her bedchamber door.

And then she heard the floor creak just outside the door. Her heart in her throat, Morainn grasped hold of the large knife she kept beneath her pillow and slowly sat up. There had been a few times when some fool man had crept into her room thinking he could steal what she refused to give him willingly. They had left chastised and bleeding. Instinct told her that this time it was no lust-crazed idiot outside her door.

Even as the door began to open she smelled the cloying scent of too many roses and her heart clenched with fear. Forcing back the rush of panic that threatened to make her scream, she crouched on top of her bed. If her visions were accurate, she was about to face a woman and a very large man who wanted to kill her.

She thought of Walin and, even though her fear increased, she also found a source of cold determination and strength within her. Morainn knew these monsters would kill Walin if he woke up and do so with barely a thought for the innocent life they would end. If she was quick and lucky, she could get past them, grab Walin, and flee. Once out of the cottage she had a dozen places they could hide until these killers gave up the hunt. Morainn prayed she was given a chance to flee, if only for Walin's sake.

The door was suddenly thrust wide open and the voice from her dreams hissed, "Softly, ye fool!"

"Nay need, m'lady," the huge man standing in the doorway said. "She be awake. The lass must have heard us."

Morainn cursed the shadows in her room that kept her from seeing these people clearly as the woman appeared beside the man. His massive size made the woman look tiny and delicate, but Morainn could see the glint of a knife in her elegant little hand. *My knife is bigger,* Morainn thought as she tensed and tried to decide which one of the intruders she should aim for. Her eyes told her to go for the man because he was the one to try to hurt so that she had time to run, but her instincts told her that would be a bad choice. Her instincts told her to go for the woman and the big man would move out of the way to help the murderous bitch, giving Morainn a chance to get out the doorway he now blocked.

William made a choice before she did. To Morainn's surprise, the cat let loose a bloodcurdling yowl and leapt. It did not go for the man as she had expected it to, but lunged straight at the woman. The woman screamed as William landed on her head, a writhing, scratching, and snarling bundle of fury. The man immediately turned to help the woman, who appeared to be stumbling around as if she could run away from the beastie savaging her head and face. Morainn bolted for the door. A large hand reached out at her and she struck out at it with her knife even as she kept running. A loud bellow told her she had succeeded in inflicting a wound.

A sleepy-eyed Walin was standing in the doorway of his small bedchamber. Morainn grabbed him and pushed him toward the stairs, ordering, "Run! Hide!"

The boy did not hesitate to obey, obviously awake enough to know they were in danger from whoever was making all the noise in Morainn's bedchamber. As Morainn followed she felt both pleased and saddened by that. He should obey his elders, but he should not have to live with fear, with the need to run and hide without question.

The hard painful grip of a large, strong hand on

the back of her neck yanked her to a halt. Morainn twisted around on the narrow steps and struck out with her knife again. This time she did not need the bellow of pain to tell her she had cut the huge man a second time; she had felt her knife hesitate slightly as it began to cut across flesh instead of air. The man struck out at her and Morainn went tumbling down the steps nearly taking Walin down with her.

She wanted to lie on the floor and moan over all the aches and bruises she knew she had suffered, but did not give in to that weakness. Leaping to her feet, she followed Walin out of the cottage and ran toward the woods. In there were a lot of places to hide. Morainn had made sure of it.

"Who are they?" asked Walin in a shaky whisper as he huddled deep within the hollow beneath the roots of an old tree.

Settling herself in the small space beside the boy, Morainn fought to catch her breath, and whispered, "They are killers, loving. Hush now for they may come hunting us." This was not the best of the hiding places Morainn had picked out over the years, but they had run about as far as she felt Walin could withstand.

Morainn could not understand why these people had come after her. They obviously intended to do to her as they had done to the other women they had killed, but she had never been Tormand's lover. She had never even met or seen the man, except in her dreams, until the day Isabella Redmond's body was found. They had barely exchanged a word and a look. No one could have known he and the other men would come to see her, either.

Unless the killers were watching Sir Tormand Murray very closely, she thought, and tensed. She shivered, but fought the urge to try to rub some warmth into her arms, afraid of stirring the leaves she was sprawled on. It was the only thing that made any sense. It was also something Sir Tormand needed to know. If she survived this attack Morainn fully intended to tell him about her suspicion.

The sound of voices drifted to her ears and Morainn pressed her body deeper into the hollow. Gently placing her hand on Walin's back was enough to make the child do the same. She heard the slow pace of horses and wondered if they were being walked or ridden. Morainn hoped it was the latter for it would be a lot more difficult for the killers to catch a glimpse of her and Walin from high up on the back of a horse. She felt herself tense so tightly she wondered that she did not snap something as the sounds of approach grew closer, listening carefully for any hint that she and Walin had been discovered.

"Are ye sure that cursed beast is dead?" demanded the woman whose icy cold voice had haunted Morainn's dreams all too often lately.

"Aye, m'lady," answered the man. "I threw it into the wall, didnae I, and it wasnae moving when we left."

Morainn felt her heart skip painfully in her chest, but fought back the grief and rage stirred by William's death. She needed to hear everything these people said. They might let slip some hint as to who they were and, no matter how small it might be, Morainn wanted to catch it. She wanted them found and hanged.

And now she wanted it not just because they were

killers. The bastards had invaded her home, had intended to kill her, had put Walin's life in danger and made him afraid, and they had killed her cat. Morainn did not think she had ever felt such a cold rage and it banished her fear for the moment. Even admitting to herself that part of her rage was because these monsters threatened Sir Tormand Murray did not dim it. Sinner and lecher though he was, he did not deserve what these people were putting him through.

"I want this witch dead!"

"And she will be, m'lady. Soon. But, I am thinking, nay tonight."

The man spoke in a soft, soothing tone despite his deep, rough voice and Morainn suspected he had had a lot of self-training in the ways needed to soothe his companion. They had paused within sight of her and Walin. They were both on their horses and that helped Morainn subdue a sudden flash of panic. As long as the ones hunting her did not dismount and start searching close to the ground, she and Walin would not be found.

"We could fetch the dog," the woman said. "Dunstan would sniff the whore out."

"Aye, the dog has a fine nose, but 'twould be too light for a safe hunt ere we fetched the dog and came back here. And ye need those scratches seen to. I wouldnae mind having me own wounds tended to. The lass had a big knife and was quick with it."

"She cannae live," hissed the woman. "'Tis said that she has the gift, that she can see the truth. That would be our downfall. Innes will use her gift to find us and

I am nay done yet. That rutting bastard Tormand has to pay for all I have suffered, for all my humiliation and shame. I would ne'er have been forced to wed if nay for him and he has to suffer for that. Aye, and for choosing all these whores over me."

"Now, we cannae be sure he has bedded this lass."

The woman's snort of cold laughter echoed through the wood. "Ye saw how he looked at her at the Redmonds'."

"I did, but today was the first time he has visited her and he wasnae alone."

"It doesnae matter. He means to add her to the rolls of his women. He has caught her scent and will soon run her to ground. Innes may only be interested in how she can help him find us, but Tormand wants to lift her skirts. I want her dead ere she lets him into her bed as all the others did, the filthy whores. That would give him pleasure and I dinnae want him to have any. I just want him to be shamed, condemned, and hanged."

In that chilling voice was the tone of a very spoiled child. A spoiled child who had finally been forced to do something she did not want to do, thought Morainn, and the woman blamed it all on Tormand. Whatever ill happened in the woman's marriage would only continue to harden the woman's sense of injury. Morainn did wonder how the woman was able to slip around killing people in the dead of night without her husband at least becoming aware of her absences. Unless, of course, the man had been one of her first victims.

Grimacing, Morainn forced herself not to get too

lost in her own thoughts. She not only needed to listen carefully to every word these killers spoke; she also needed to be alert for the possibility of being discovered.

"M'lady, please, ye are still bleeding," the man said. "And so am I. We are leaving a trail any child could find and follow."

"We have to find the witch!"

"We will. Ye have my word on it. Calm yourself. Where is the good in getting caught hunting for someone we cannae find in these dark woods? We will get ourselves cleaned up, rest a wee bit until our wounds are healed enough nay to draw the eye our way, and then be back on the hunt ere ye ken it."

"I wanted her dead," the woman said, sounding so much like a child denied some treat it made Morainn shiver. "She will tell Innes about us and help him catch us. We cannae let her see us, Small."

Morainn listened to the man continue to soothe the woman as the pair rode off. Even when she could no longer hear them she remained tense and still. For a moment she could not even think clearly. All she could think about was how that woman spoke of killing her, that she did not even know the woman, and that she was marked for death for something she had not done. Sir Tormand had not even kissed her yet. Was Sir Tormand such a lecherous fool that he only had to look at a woman to have the world and its mother believe he would soon have her warming his bed? Morainn knew, deep inside, that what troubled her most was that the woman wanted her to die for far more than what tiny pieces of information

Morainn might get from some vision. *M'lady* wanted to kill her because a man had looked at her with the glint of lust in his eyes and, in Morainn's mind, that only proved the woman's insanity.

"They are gone, Morainn," whispered Walin.

Taking a deep breath to calm herself, Morainn spoke in an equally soft voice. "We shall bide here for a while longer, love. I am nay big enough nor skilled enough with a knife to win in a battle against those two. Giving someone a wee poke with my knife to make them back away so I can run—aye, I can do that. Fighting and beating two people and one of the size of a mountain? Nay."

"Why do they want to kill ye? Ye didnae e'en meet Sir Tormand until today."

"I met him yesterday, briefly. But that doesnae matter to those two. The woman is mad, Walin. Utterly mad. One cannae e'er understand how she thinks."

"How long do we have to stay here?"

"I would feel safest if we could remain hidden until the sun begins to rise. At least then I will be able to see better as we make our way home. If they have hidden in the dark and the shadows as we have, I willnae be able to see them in time for us to flee and hide again."

"What if some beast comes round and thinks we are good eating?"

"First, that beastie will have a difficult time reaching us in here and, second, I have a verra big knife." She smiled when she felt him relax as she pulled him close. "Rest, my bonnie laddie. I will keep ye safe." She prayed she could keep that promise, but knew telling him the truth, that their fate was not always in her hands, would only frighten him.

"Do ye think that mon really killed William?"

Although she could hear the tears choking him and felt strongly inclined to cry herself, Morainn gently rubbed his small back and replied in a calm voice, "I dinnae ken, loving. We will see when we get home. If that mon did kill our William, then our cat died a hero. It attacked that woman and when the mon turned to help her, I was given the chance to flee. I dinnae wish to think on what may have happened to us if William hadnae given me that chance."

"If William is dead, we will bury him in the garden. William loved the garden."

"Aye, it did, and we will give our brave cat a verra fine burial."

"And something to mark his grave."

"Aye. Now, please, rest, laddie. I will keep watch."

"I have to say my prayers first."

She held Walin close as he whispered his prayers, not reminding him that he had already said them once tonight. Morainn was both amused and a little saddened as she listened to him ask God to let William live or at least give the cat a nice garden to romp through in heaven. It was sweet that Walin thought of the cats as his friends, calling them him or her instead of it. What was sad about it was that a cat was Walin's best friend, that he had no other children to play with. No one wanted the witch's bastard near their children. After the first time Walin had cried because a mother had yanked her children away from him as if he carried the plague, Morainn had begun to leave him with Nora when she had to go to town, and there were no small children at the Chisholm house. It was a sad life for a child, but she could think of no way to change it.

Morainn was not surprised when Walin fell asleep the moment he finished his rambling prayer. She dearly wished she could join him in that blissful place of dreams, even if her dreams were sometimes too dark. The fear for his life and her own, as well as the race through the woods to get away from the killers and hide, had badly sapped her strength. She had to keep watch, however, and not only for the very small possibility that some predator might sniff them out. There was always the chance that the woman with the icy voice might yet convince her massive companion to come hunting her and Walin with the dog.

What preyed most on her mind, however, was that her cottage was no longer safe. That murderous pair knew where she lived, knew how to get inside, and the woman desperately wanted *the witch* dead. The only way to be safe again was to leave, to find somewhere to hide until the killers were caught and hanged. Her pride rebelled, wanting her to hold her ground, but she pushed it aside. She had to consider Walin's safety, too.

The problem was—where could she go? Knowing a killer hunted her, she could not go to Nora's or ask help from what few friends she had. That could bring the danger to them and she could not reward their friendship that way. She briefly considered asking the man who rented her the cottage and land, Sir Kerr, for protection and help, but quickly shook that thought aside. He had been kind to her when she was a child thrust out in the cold, but she doubted he would want her and a small boy cluttering up his home. Rumor had it that he was a greater lecher than Tormand.

Mayhap she should ask Sir Tormand and Sir Simon for help, Morainn thought. After all, they wanted hers. It would be a fair enough exchange and that would take away the taint of charity her pride shied away from. Unfortunately, that would put her far too close to a man who stirred her interest in ways it had never been stirred before. He tempted her and temptation was a lot easier to resist when it was kept at a distance. Sir Tormand obviously had very little practice in the resisting of temptation and that would make it all the more difficult to be near him. If he tried to seduce her into his bed, Morainn had the sinking feeling she would soon find herself there. To ask him to keep her safe was to put her virtue at risk, something she had fought hard to cling to. To not ask him could leave her and Walin in danger of their lives.

It was a hard choice that faced her, she decided as she fought a yawn. Morainn told herself that she was simply too weary, still had the bitter taste of fear in her mouth, to make the decision now. She knew she could not put off the decision for long, however. Before night fell again, she and Walin had to be somewhere safe or they could well be dead before the next sunrise.

Tormand rode beside Simon and bit back the urge to continue the argument they had had over their early morning meal. Although he truly felt that it was not right to risk Morainn having another such violent vision barely a day after having the first one, he knew Simon was right to say they had to try. He also knew it was not the only reason he was reluctant to go to Morainn's cottage again. It stung his pride to admit it, but he feared getting too close to her, feared the way she pulled hard at far more than his lust. When he was away from her he could convince himself it was just the hunger of a man who had not had a woman in too long, but when he got near her, looked into her beautiful eyes, he could not play that game with himself. He was all too aware of the fact that it was more and he did not want more.

He knew, deep in his bones, that she was his match, his mate, or whatever else the women in his clan liked to call it. Tormand knew that, if he wanted to keep sampling every fair flower in life's garden, he should be staying as far away from Morainn Ross as possible. He could not, and it was not just the need to find the killer that held him so close to this dire threat to his freedom. Ever since he had first looked into those sea-blue eyes every instinct he had kept pushing him toward her.

It made no sense. Morainn was bonnie, but he had bedded or walked away from women far more beautiful than she was. Despite his own doubt about the truth of it, he could not ignore the fact that many others believed Walin was her bastard child. He had also discovered that she paid Sir Kerr, laird of Dubhstane, a pittance to live in the cottage and work the land around it. Since Sir Kerr of Dubhstane was rumored to be far more of a lecherous rogue than Tormand ever could be, it was only natural to wonder what more there was to that unsavory connection. Strangely enough, that did not make him happily consider her fair game as it would have only a few days ago. It knotted his belly up with something that tasted alarmingly like jealousy. That annoyed him.

"If the lass still looks pale and weary, I willnae press her to touch another hairpin today," said Simon.

Pleased that Simon thought his bad temper was due to their earlier disagreement and not his chaotic thoughts about possible mates who had a legion of lovers to vie with his own, Tormand nodded. "I just cannae think it good for her health or her mind to have such violent visions, to be so upset by them."

Harcourt, hearing those words as he rode up beside Tormand, grunted his agreement. "The lasses arenae as strong as men; they cannae take too much punishment."

Ignoring the derisive hooting of their kinsmen still riding behind them, Tormand looked at his cousin. "I pray ye dinnae mouth such beliefs before any of the lassies in our clan."

Grinning widely, Harcourt shook his head. "I said they were weaker. Ne'er said they couldnae be sneaky or vicious. I fair shudder to think of what they would do to me if they heard me say such things."

"Weel, at least ye have some wit under all that hair. Since I was too busy arguing with Simon when we broke our fast, I forgot to ask if ye heard anything of interest when ye were out roaming the town last night."

"Nay. Would have told ye if we had. Just found a lot of ale and a few willing lassies."

The way Harcourt avoided his gaze as he spoke gave Tormand a very bad feeling. "Harcourt, ye always were a poor liar. What did ye hear?"

Harcourt sighed. "Talk. Nay more than that. Just foolish talk. We set a few fools straight and then had a fine toss or three with those willing lassies. Sweet Jennie sends her best." He winked. "And her best was verra fine indeed."

Tormand bit back a curse. Harcourt did not have to repeat what was being said about him in the taverns and the alehouses. It was all too easy to guess. The whispers that cried him a killer were growing louder and spreading through the town like a plague. Tormand knew many people thought him a sinner, a man unable to resist the temptations of the flesh, but how that could ever make them believe he could be a butcher of women he did not know.

He was about to give in to the urge to ask exactly what was being said when Morainn's cottage came into view. The door was wide open. It could mean nothing more than Morainn forgot to shut it when she went out to do her chores, but a chill of apprehension speared through his body. Without another thought, he spurred his mount into a gallop and raced to the cottage. He heard only a chorus of startled curses from the others and then the sound of them following him.

Dismounting before his horse had even fully stopped, Tormand started to go inside only to come to an abrupt halt at the threshold stone. The smooth flat stone had blood on it. A part of him wanted to race inside calling for Morainn, but a larger part held him firmly in place, terrified of what he would see when he went inside. It was Simon who hurried past him to look through the cottage. Tormand was pleased to see that none of his kinsmen followed Simon, either. It made him look less like the coward he was feeling like.

"She isnae here," said Simon as he returned. "Neither is the boy. There is some blood in the bedchamber, but nay much."

"There wasnae all that much in the other women's bedchambers, either," said Tormand.

"If ye are thinking that the killers have her, I have to say that I just cannae see how that could happen. She isnae your lover, ne'er has been, and ye only met her the other day."

"In front of Isabella's home. In front of the place where Isabella's body was found. Mayhap the killers stood in the crowd watching all of us."

"Possible, but then where is Morainn's body? They take the women at night and return them to their own beds ere the sun rises. We may nay have seen the bastards do it, but I think ye are as sure of that as I am."

"Aye, 'tis the only way they could do it."

"So, my friend, where is the body?"

"Why dinnae ye ask it yourself?" drawled Harcourt and pointed toward the woods.

Tormand looked in the direction Harcourt pointed and saw Walin and Morainn walking toward them, alive and not obviously injured. He felt such a surge of relief he nearly fell to his knees from the strength of it. Then he realized that they were both in their nightclothes, looked again at the blood on the stone, and knew something bad had happened. That certainty was strengthened when he saw that Morainn carried a very large knife.

Afraid of what he would say if he opened his mouth, Tormand waited for someone else to say something. His kinsmen and Simon remained silent. Morainn looked dismayed and a little embarrassed as she walked up to them, but said nothing. It appeared that everyone was waiting for someone else to speak first. The silence began to rub his nerves raw and Tormand wondered who would be the first to break it, praying it would not fall to him. His feelings and thoughts were still so chaotic he did not doubt the first words out of his mouth would have him looking like a complete fool.

Chapter 8

"William!"

The glad cry of the small boy finally broke the increasingly tense silence that had held them all in thrall. Tormand turned to see the big cat limping out onto the threshold just as Walin reached it. Even as Walin gently hugged the cat, Morainn rushed over to the animal as well. She crouched by the cat and began to inspect it gently as though searching for some wound or injury. After listening for several moments as the pair cooed over the cat, calling it brave and a hero, Tormand decided enough was enough. He lost control of his impatient need to know why Morainn was running around in her nightclothes and why there was blood by her door and inside her house.

"What has happened here?" he finally demanded.

Walin looked up at Tormand and continued to hug and stroke the big cat as he answered, "A woman and a huge mon got into the house last night and tried to kill Morainn, but she had her knife under her pillow as always and it is a verra big knife. *And* William attacked the woman and that helped me and Morainn get away and we ran and ran and then hid under a tree but they followed us and got verra close to where we were hiding but they didnae find us. Then they left because they were both bleeding and the big mon thought they needed to fix that. He also said that he threw our William against the wall and killed him because he was scratching and biting the madwoman but ye can see that he isnae dead so we dinnae have to dig a hole in the garden for him. Me and Morainn stayed hiding under the big tree for hours and hours and then we walked home and I was verra scared but Morainn had her big knife so no beastie came to eat me." He looked at Morainn. "I need to give William some cream because he was so verra brave."

Morainn had to bite back a laugh at the stunned looks on the men's faces. She wondered how much they had actually heard and understood of what Walin had just said. The boy had been talking so fast he had barely taken a single breath from beginning to end. She stood up and idly brushed off her nightgown, relieved that she had worn the heavy, linen-lined wool one she had made. Few gowns were as extremely modest as it was.

"Gentlemen, Walin and I have had a verra long night," she said. Much longer than she had planned for, Morainn thought, as she had fallen asleep the moment the sun had risen, the knowledge that she was safe causing her exhaustion to claim her for a few hours. "If ye would give us a wee while to clean up and dress I will be pleased to tell ye all that happened. There is bread, fruit, venison, and cider or ale in the kitchen. Help yourselves. Walin and I shouldnae be long." She grabbed Walin by the hand and started to pull him into the cottage.

"I want to give William some cream," protested Walin.

"And so ye can just as soon as ye have washed up and donned your clothes."

"I am so glad we willnae have to put him in a hole in the garden."

"So am I, dearling."

Tormand stepped inside, watched Morainn and Walin disappear up the steep, narrow stairs to the upper chambers, and then looked to Simon. "Did ye understand all the lad said?"

Simon laughed and started toward the kitchen. "A wee bit. I fear I got distracted waiting for the boy to take a breath. Help me set some food out as I suspicion the two of them will be hungry."

"Did she say she has cold venison?"

"Aye." Simon frowned. "An odd thing for her to have but I cannae see the lass out poaching, so I shall assume that someone gave her some. Considering the fact that I am one of the king's men, a mon sworn to uphold the law, she has wit enough to ken that she shouldnae tell me about any meat she has poached. The laird's cook may have brought her some when she came to collect the mead that is the fee for this home."

"Ah, that is verra possible." The relationship Morainn had with Sir Kerr was not something Tormand really wanted to think of.

"I wonder what the cat did," murmured Harcourt, as he grabbed a jug of ale to place on the table.

Looking at the big cat that sat down on a bench at the table as though it belonged there, Rory said, "It attacked the woman."

"Ye understood all the lad said?"

"Some. I fear I began to get distracted by the need to understand how one can hide under a tree."

While they set food and drink on the table, Tormand's kinsmen fell into a discussion about which parts of Walin's rapidly told tale had grasped their attention, and Tormand looked at Simon. "What caught your attention, aside from the lad's ability to talk fast?"

"A mon and a woman," Simon said, and then frowned. "I truly didnae want to believe a woman was involved in these savage murders. Even doubted Morainn's vision when I thought about it. A mistake I willnae make again. The question is—does the woman participate? Is she the leader or the follower? Obviously they arenae omnipotent or infallible if one wee lass can escape them."

"She had a verra big knife," Tormand drawled.

Simon grinned. "And a ferocious cat." He quickly sobered. "They are watching us. 'Tis the only explanation for why they would go after Mistress Ross so soon after we had visited with her. They are watching every step we make. If I wasnae so absolutely certain of the honor of everyone close to us and this hunt, I would start looking for a traitor."

He was right, and the thought made Tormand's stomach cramp with fear for Morainn. "Then we must convince her to come with us. She cannae stay here alone again; nay until these bastards are dead."

"I agree, even though I am reluctant to place such a bonnie lass right within your home."

Tormand felt as if his friend had just slapped him in the face. *"Jesu,* Simon, I am nay some animal in rut." Afraid of what else he might say, he muttered, "I will see to the horses as I think we will be here for a while."

Simon watched Tormand stride away and winced. He had seen the hurt on the man's face and regretted it, but he could not take the words back. Tormand was a good man but, over the last few years, he had lost his way, in a manner of speaking. The man needed to regain control of his baser needs and urges or he would find himself in trouble. That is, if he survives this one, he mused.

Feeling a presence at his side, Simon turned to look at Harcourt who had quickly and silently moved to his side. "Ye think I was too harsh?"

"Nay. He has acted much like a beast in constant rut for the last few years." Harcourt grinned briefly when his kinsmen snickered. "Howbeit, I am asking ye to step back a wee bit." He spoke quietly so that his words would not be overheard by the woman or child upstairs.

"I dinnae think that bairn is hers nor do I believe she is Sir Kerr's leman." Realizing why Harcourt spoke so quietly, Simon followed his lead. "That would mean she is a virtuous lass and one who has had more than enough trouble in her life. She needs no more, certainly not the sort that an affair with Tormand will bring her."

"Och, I agree, and I ken she isnae the lad's mother,

save in her heart. He was already a lad of two years when some heartless wench or bastard left him on the lass's doorstep. In the dead of winter. In the middle of the night. 'Tis a miracle that the laddie didnae die right there."

"How did ye discover that?"

"I asked. And Sir Kerr ne'er visits the lass, ne'er e'en comes to collect his rent of two wee casks of mead once a year. Sends his cook. Do ye ken that he is a black-haired mon with eyes the color of the sea?"

Simon whistled softly, knowing that very few people actually saw Sir Kerr. "'Tis your bonnie face, isnae it, that gains ye all this information so quickly. S'truth, I wonder why ye e'en sought it."

"Because that lass is Tormand's mate. The lad is just fighting it hard right now."

The wide grins on the faces of the other Murrays told Simon that they all agreed with that strange statement and he frowned at Harcourt. "His *mate*?"

"Aye. Mayhap ye havenae heard that we Murrays believe something that is considered odd by many."

"Only one thing?"

Harcourt ignored that. "We, or most of us, believe that there is such a thing as a perfect match, a mate, that suits each mon and woman in all ways."

"And ye think Morainn Ross is Tormand's? He has only just met her."

"Doesnae matter. It hits some hard and fast, ye ken. My father says he fought it hard, denied it every step of the way e'en though he twisted himself into knots to bring his Gisele to Scotland from France. The lasses in the clan swear to this belief, as ye would expect them to, but most of the men who have married agree to it in private. It has hit our Tormand hard, knocked him right onto his lecherous arse."

Thinking over the way Tormand had been acting since setting eyes on Morainn, Simon thought there might be some truth to what Harcourt was saying. "It could still be naught but a sharp lusting."

"It could be and Tormand is a verra lusty lad, has been since his voice first deepened. But he suffers from more than a fierce lusting. Did ye nay see his face when he saw the blood on the threshold, when he thought Morainn's body might be lying up those stairs? He was terrified that she was dead, bone-deep afraid of it. I wager he hasnae acted like that over the other women. Nay, especially when I dinnae think he has e'en kissed the lass yet."

"Nay, he hasnae done either. Ye are right on that. His vehement arguing this morning was unusual as well. He really didnae want us to come here, so doesnae that disprove your assumption?"

"Of course he wouldnae want to be too close to the lass too often. He has wit enough to ken, or suspect, what she means to his future—an end to rutting his merry way through life. He shows signs of jealousy, nearly flew over this table to catch her when that last vision brought her to her knees, kept hold of her e'en as she recovered, and he looked near to fainting when he saw that blood out there. Och, aye, that laddie is in deep waters and sinking fast."

Simon sighed. "Then I will stand back for now. If he should abuse her trust or her need for his protection, however, dinnae expect me to keep standing back. I will speak out."

"Fair enough, but only after we beat some sense into his wee head."

Looking at the grinning Murrays, Simon laughed and shook his head. He was not sure he really believed in such things as a perfect match or mate or the other half of oneself, but it was a nice thought. It explained why the Murrays never arranged marriages for their children, something considered very strange by most people. When asked why they did not do so, they said they preferred that their children be happy. Since many Murrays had made some very good and advantageous marriages, others believed the clan did make arrangements and treaties with marriages as the binding for them, for how else could they gain so many good alliances. Then again, Simon mused, the clan was also known for its faithful wives and equally faithful husbands.

He had to admit that Tormand had been acting a little odd ever since he had first laid eyes on Morainn Ross. There had been none of the seductive smiles or soft practiced flatteries that pulled the women to Tormand's side and into his bed. There had been, however, a lot of concern for Morainn's health and welfare. Tormand was never unkind to a woman, but Simon suddenly realized that his friend only concerned himself about the woman's health or life when there was some clear sign that she was suffering under the hand of a cruel, brutish man. Thinking back to the moment they had raced to Morainn's door and Tormand had halted his rush into the house so abruptly at the threshold, Simon could clearly recall how terrified Tormand had looked as he had stared at the blood on the threshold stone. Yet, Tormand had never once hesitated to enter the homes of the other murdered women, including that of his friend Marie, not even after he had a full knowledge of what he would find inside.

There was definitely something brewing between Tormand and Morainn Ross. For now, Simon would simply allow it to brew. It could even be amusing to watch his friend, the great lover of far too many women, stumble his way into love and marriage. Simon would just make sure that Morainn did not suffer from Tormand's stumblings or his apparent inability to be faithful to any woman. The woman already had killers stalking her. She did not need any added troubles.

Tormand finished tending to the horses and stepped outside of the very clean stable. It was a surprisingly large and well-kept building for a woman of low birth and no family. As was the cottage, he realized. Laird Sir Adam Kerr had been very generous to an orphaned girl thrust out onto her own by superstitious townspeople. Tormand actually felt grateful for that, but he could not stop himself from wondering why the laird had done it. Very few people had met Sir Kerr and those who had did not talk about him. The gossips said that the man was steeped in sin. It was even whispered that he had a harem like the heathens in the eastern lands. The mere thought that Morainn was one of Sir Kerr's harem had Tormand grinding his teeth in fury.

He took a deep breath and slowly let it out, trying to push out all the chaotic emotion he suffered from with it before starting back to the cottage. Now was not the time to delve into the how and why of Morainn Ross's arrangement with the laird of Dubhstane. Tormand had no doubt that the killers had found Morainn, had tried to butcher her as they had done the other women. For many reasons, some of which he really did not want to examine too closely, it was his responsibility to insure that she was kept safe and out of the killers' hands. If nothing else, Morainn's gift could prove to be a great help to them in their search for the killers.

Pausing at the threshold of the cottage he studied the blood on the stone and recalled the icy fear that had held him frozen in place. He had been unable to face what might lie within the cottage despite having already stood over the butchered bodies of three women without emptying his belly. Just the thought that Morainn might be lying on her bed, her beauty defaced by the killers, her lovely eyes cold and empty of life, had terrified him. Tormand had to face the fact that he was in danger of finding himself enraptured by Morainn, by a witch with eyes the color of the sea on a summer's day. He pushed aside the childish urge to flee what could well be his fate and went inside.

Just as he was about to go and ask what the men in the kitchen were laughing about, Walin came running down the narrow stairs so fast he stumbled on the last step. Tormand moved quickly to catch the boy before he ended up flat on his face on the stone floor. Walin grinned up at him and Tormand felt the oddest pinch in his heart. He could not shake the feeling that there was something very familiar about the boy.

"Thank ye, Sir Tormand," Walin said as Tormand released him.

"Ye should be more careful upon the stairs." Tormand almost cursed at how much he had just sounded like his father.

"I ken it, but I need to give William some cream. He was a verra brave cat."

After a quick glance up the stairs to see if Morainn was coming down, and ignoring the sharp pang of disappointment he felt when he did not see her, Tormand followed Walin into the kitchen. Looking around, Tormand realized that the kitchen was even more proof that the laird of Dubhstane had gifted Morainn with a very fine home. Most people of her birth, the child of a midwife killed by a mob decrying her as a witch, would have one big room with a cook-fire in it and, at best, a small loft for sleeping in.

He watched Walin pour some thick cream into a wooden bowl. There was a thud as the big cat jumped off the bench and went over to enjoy his reward. Like magic the other three cats appeared in the kitchen, but a low, throaty growl from the big tom kept them at a distance. A giggling Walin put some cream in another bowl and set it down for the other three cats to share.

"William is going to become a verra fat cat."

The sound of that sweet, faintly husky voice immediately drew Tormand's gaze to the speaker. Morainn gave him a shy smile that made his whole body go on point like some well-trained hunting dog. Despite the fact that he had not bedded a woman for months, Tormand knew the reaction he had to Morainn was alarmingly strong.

"Thank ye for setting the table," Morainn said, feeling a little uncomfortable beneath the steady gazes of six handsome men. "Walin," she said, turning to smile at the boy, "come sit up at the table, please." She let go a startled squeak when Tormand suddenly grabbed her by the arm. "What is it?"

Tormand moved her thick braid aside to look more closely at the bruise he had caught a glimpse of when she had turned her head to look at Walin. "Where did ye get this? It looks like the print of a hand."

"Ah, that. The mon grabbed me from behind as I fled down the stairs, but I cut him with my knife and he released me." She felt someone move up close behind her and glanced back over her shoulder to find Simon studying the bruising fanning across the back of her neck. "It doesnae feel as bad as it looks." It ached badly, but Morainn knew she could have suffered far worse if she had not gotten away.

"The mon has a verra big hand," murmured Simon.

"Och, aye, he did," said Walin, as he took a seat at the table. "He was as big as a horse. A giant!"

"Sit, Mistress Ross," said Simon, his voice polite yet carrying the hint of command, "and ye can tell us what happened as ye eat. I am certain ye must be hungry."

Morainn took a seat at the table, a little disconcerted when Tormand sat next to her. She was distracted from the way his nearness made her body tingle, as if she had allowed the sun to shine on it for too long, when Harcourt sat down on the other side of her and began to heap food upon her plate. Placed between too men so much bigger than she was, Morainn felt a little overwhelmed, especially when one of those men was the one who could make her body heat and ache. A glance across the table showed her that Walin was seated between Simon and Rory and both men were quietly filling the child's plate. It made her uneasy, for the way the men were taking care of her and Walin felt much too good. Morainn feared it could become something she could grow to crave and she would suffer when she lost it.

"Before ye start your tale," said Rory, his amber eyes glinting with humor, "I really must ken one thing. How do ye hide *under* a tree?"

"Ah, weel, when I first came to live here the memory of how my mother died was still verra sharp," replied Morainn. "Fearing a mob might yet come after me, I sought out hiding places in the woods surrounding me. One big old tree has thick roots that break up through the ground. It required only a little digging to make a hollow in the midst of the roots, giving me a weel-shadowed place to conceal myself in."

"Clever, especially considering ye were little more than a child," said Simon.

"Even the smallest child understands the need to stay alive."

"Verra true. So, mistress, if ye can eat and talk at the same time, I would verra much like to hear what happened to ye."

"I fear your killer is nay one mon, but is most definitely a mon and a woman."

Between bites of food, Morainn told them everything that had happened, carefully leaving out only what the murderous pair had said to each other. She felt sure that the words they had spoken held some hint as to who these people were. They needed to be discussed carefully and not simply stated like some tale told before the fire. There was no doubt in her mind that Simon would want to pick over every word those monsters had said to each other meticulously.

"The mon had verra big feet," said Walin when Morainn came to the end of her story, "and his horse was a huge beastie, too, with one white leg."

Morainn stared at the boy. "Ye were peeking." She fought down a sudden anger she knew was born of fear for Walin. He could easily have been seen and she knew she would not have been able to save him.

Walin blushed with guilt. "Only with one eye, Morainn. I didnae move at all or lift my head e'en a wee bit."

"Which leg on the horse had the white markings?" asked Simon.

"Right foreleg," replied Walin and then looked a little uncertain. "That is what ye call the front ones, aye?"

"Aye, lad. Did ye see anything else with your one eye?"

"Nay. The mon was verra, verra big and sat on a verra big horse and I would have had to move to see him better."

"So they were verra close to where ye were hiding then." Simon looked at Morainn. "Ye said ye could hear them yet ye didnae repeat anything that they said. Did ye nay hear them clearly then?"

"Aye, I heard them clearly." Morainn fiercely controlled the urge to shiver in remembrance of that icy voice, of the insanity threaded through each and every word. "The first thing of importance, I think, is that they were both bleeding. William had to have inflicted a lot of damage to the woman's face. Divine justice in a way," she murmured and then shook herself free of the thoughts of what the killers had done to the other women. "The cat landed on her head and the fleeting glimpse I got showed it slashing and biting her head and face. William has verra long claws so the wounds may be verra deep. The mon also has two cuts although I cannae say how deep they may be. One is on his hand or his arm. The other may be on his body. I have nay doubt at all that I cut him, twice, but I didnae look to see exactly where or how badly. Since he was soon out hunting me they couldnae have been serious. He worried only about her injuries and about the trail of blood they were leaving on the ground. Mayhap a dog could find and follow that trail."

Simon nodded. "Anything else?"

"They are watching Sir Tormand." She glanced at Tormand and then quickly returned her gaze to her nearly empty plate. The steady gaze of his beautiful mismatched eyes made something very womanly and hungry stir inside of her and she wanted her voice to remain calm and steady as she finished telling them what she knew. "They kenned that ye had come to see me and were certain ye were using my *powers* to hunt them down. She badly wishes me dead ere I can help ye find them. She said ye," she fixed her gaze on Simon, "would use my gift to find them and she isnae done yet."

"But why?" asked Tormand, dragging his hand through his hair. "Why are they doing this?"

Morainn took a long drink of her cider, but it did little to ease her fear or wash away the taint of violent insanity that had hung in the air last night. "She wants ye to pay for all she has suffered, Sir Tormand, and for what she claimed was her humiliation and shame. She said she would never have been forced to marry if not for ye and that ye must suffer for it all. She also wants ye to suffer for choosing so many other women over her. Called them all whores." She felt a sudden urge to hug him, to try to comfort him, when she saw how pale and shaken he was, but fiercely beat down that urge.

"So it *is* about me," he finally said, his voice hoarse and unsteady with the lingering effects of his shock. "It is my fault that these women are being murdered."

"Nay," snapped Harcourt. "They are being killed because this bitch has lost her mind and seeks to blame someone for what she thinks are crimes against her. Many a lass has had her heart broken or bruised, or was made to marry some mon she didnae want, but nary a one of them took to slaughtering every woman she saw as her rival. If this woman seeks to blame someone for the misery of her life, why isnae she hunting down her husband or the kinsmen who forced her into the marriage?"

"For all we ken, she already has," said Simon. "And Harcourt is right, Tormand. The woman is mad. Ye cannae blame yourself for what she does." He looked at Morainn. "And now she hunts ye, Morainn Ross. She

fears ye might see her in one of your visions, doesnae she?"

"Aye," replied Morainn. "She doesnae doubt I am a
witch and, as I told ye, she truly feels I will help ye find
her." She blushed faintly. "And because she believes
Sir Tormand is bedding me now."

"I have only just met ye," protested Tormand.

Morainn sincerely doubted length of acquaintance
mattered much to the man when it came to bedding
a woman he wanted. The looks on the faces of the
other men told her they felt the same, but she just
said, "This woman believes ye have, e'en though her
companion did have his doubts. She said ye had
caught my scent and would run me to ground. She
saw ye looking at me when we were at the Redmonds'.
If she cared for ye once, she doesnae anymore. All
she wants for ye is for ye to be shamed, condemned,
and hanged."

"*Jesu,*" whispered Uilliam, the youngest of Tormand's
kinsmen. "Ye have to leave here now, Tormand."

"Nay!" Tormand realized he had come close to
shouting and took a moment to calm himself. "Nay, I
willnae run, nay doubt dragging this mad bitch behind
me. I swear to ye, if Simon tells me 'tis time for me to
hide, then I will, without argument. That is all I will
promise to do." He could see that his young brother
was not happy, but Uilliam just nodded. Tormand
turned to look at Simon. "And, ere ye ask, I have nay
idea who this woman could be. I have ne'er even
hinted at marriage to any lass and avoided all those
who might e'en think of it."

"That doesnae mean some lass still didnae think it

or might have wished it so," Morainn said quietly, wondering why his words stung her heart. Many a bachelor spoke disparagingly of marriage. "This woman also sounded verra much like a spoiled child. If she had decided, in her own mind, that ye should be her husband, it wouldnae have mattered what ye did or didnae do, or say. She may have even done something verra foolish to catch your eye or entrap ye, something ye never e'en kenned about, and that was why she was made to marry a mon she didnae want."

"And so everything she has suffered since then has been my fault? That makes no sense."

"Of course it doesnae, nay to us. She is utterly mad."

"There were no names mentioned?" asked Simon.

"Nay," replied Morainn. "Once she called him Small, but I dinnae think that is his true name. Sounds a wee bit English, doesnae it, and he is definitely one of our own. He only called her m'lady. Oh, and when she suggested that the dog might help to find me she called it Dunstan. Fortunately, the mon told her that it would take too long to fetch the dog and she eventually heeded his pleas that they leave." She smiled faintly. "It isnae much, is it? I am sorry."

"Ye have naught to apologize for. 'Tis far more than we had. If the weather holds, we may be able to get my dog out here and follow that blood trail."

"Ye dinnae sound verra confident that that will work."

Simon grimaced. "Mad or nay, these two are cunning. They havenae left me a sniff of a trail yet. I can follow them to where they did their evil work, but then all scent of them fades away."

"Ye do ken that ye arenae safe here now, dinnae ye?" asked Tormand.

She did, but she was not sure what she could do about it. The fact that the men had been waiting for her at her door when she returned to her home meant that she had not had any time to think about the problem, either. With all the men staring at her, the courage needed to ask for their help faded and the words stuck in her throat. Morainn also felt annoyed that she had to ask men to help her at all. She knew that was foolish, that she had barely escaped with her life last night, but she knew pride often warred with good sense. She had lived ten years without leaning on a man to survive; she did not want to have to do it now.

"I cannae just walk away from here," she said. "I have chickens, cats, and a cow. Then there is my garden."

"We will take ye to my home in town," said Tormand, the tone of his voice indicating he would hear no argument about it.

Morainn gave him one anyway, although she was not really surprised when she lost it. She was also relieved that she had. It stung her pride to admit it, but she was deeply afraid to stay alone in her home with only a knife, a small boy, and an ill-tempered cat for protection.

Her things were collected even as she continued to offer the occasional protest. Even her cats were secured in two small cages she used for taking chickens to market and then secured to the saddles of Rory's and

Simon's horses, much to the animals' loud disgust. Walin made no effort to hide his delight over the chance to go and stay with the men and to ride on a big horse with Harcourt. As Tormand led her toward his horse, Morainn looked at her cottage, her home for the last ten years, and wondered if she would ever return to it.

A soft gasp escaped her when Tormand grabbed her around the waist and swung her up into the saddle. She was struggling to fix her skirts more modestly when he nimbly swung up behind her. Every time the man touched her it felt as if a fire licked at her skin. He wrapped his arms around her, took hold of the reins, and started them on their way.

Morainn felt the warmth of his hard body seep deep into her soul and had to wonder if she was really going to be safe in his home. The killers might not be able to reach her there, but Tormand would, and Morainn was certain that Sir Tormand Murray could be dangerous in his own way. She might walk away alive when this trouble ended, but she feared she might not be taking her whole heart and soul away with her.

Chapter 9

The quiet of the house pulled Morainn's attention away from the tarts she was setting out to cool. She had been in Tormand's home for two days and, although the men went out a lot, it had never been this quiet. Now that she thought about it, the smell of her cooking should have had Walin lurking close at hand and she had not seen the child since they had shared their morning meal together in the great hall, listening to the plans the men made. With so many men keeping a close watch over the boy, Morainn knew Walin had to be safe and yet not seeing Walin for so long suddenly started to make her feel afraid. Deciding she would not cease worrying until she actually saw Walin, she went looking for him.

After searching through the rest of the house the only place she had left to look was the room where Tormand kept his ledgers. Morainn stood in front of the closed door, hesitant to intrude upon the man's private room, but her growing need to know where Walin had gone refused to be ignored. She realized that some of her hesitancy was because Tormand might actually be inside the room.

Since her arrival at his home Morainn had seen Tormand only when they all sat down to their meals. It was as though the man was avoiding her. That hurt, but she knew it was probably for the best. She just wished it was enough to make her stop longing for him. Instead, it was making the longing all the more keen. Shaking her head over her own foolishness, Morainn rapped on the door to see if Tormand was in there. When there was no reply, she called out his name as she slowly opened the door, allowing him more time to reply before she fully intruded upon his work.

Tormand watched the door slowly open and sighed. He had been doing his best to ignore the fact that he and Morainn were alone in the house except for her cats. His best had not been very good, for he had done very little work considering the hours he had spent hiding in his ledger room. Every time he tried to think of another name to add to the list Simon was forcing him to make, his mind began to wander down a path that led straight to a naked Morainn spread out beneath him, crying out his name as he gave her pleasure.

The list, he suddenly thought, and stared at the paper in front of him in horror. Tormand frantically searched for something to put over it to hide it from sight. Even as Morainn took her first step into the room, he put his ledger book on top of the list and opened it just to make sure that the heavy book completely covered the infamous list of lovers.

"Oh, I am sorry," Morainn said. "I knocked and called, but ye made no sound."

He stood up and moved to the front of his desk as he smiled at her. Leaning against the desk, he crossed his arms over his chest and tried not to look as guilty as he felt. Trying to block the sight of a list that was already well covered by his ledger was idiocy, but that did not make Tormand move. As he had worked on that list he had begun to feel less and less like a great lover and more like the rutting fool Simon had called him. In truth, the man appearing in his mind's eye as he wrote down name after name was not one he liked very much. He did not want Morainn to see that part of him, a part he had just decided would now be no more than part of his reckless past.

"I was but slow to answer as I was working on something," he said. "Can I help ye with something?"

"Weel, it feels foolish to e'en ask because I ken that Walin has been weel taken care of and protected, but do ye ken where he is now?"

"Uilliam took him for a ride back to the cottage so that the boy could attend to a few chores. Harcourt is with them."

Morainn was relieved, but also somewhat dismayed. "I must find someone to tend to those things until I can return home. It isnae right that ye, or any of the others, are troubled by the need to take me or Walin to see to what are my duties."

"And ye shouldnae be troubled by doing a housekeeper's work while ye are staying here." A little more relaxed, Tormand was able to move away from his desk and walk to the table near his shelves of books where he kept some wine and small tankards. "Did I e'er apologize for that cursed woman's ignorance and unkindness?" he asked, as he poured them each some wine.

"Aye, as did everyone else. 'Tis no bother," Morainn said. "The work helps me keep my mind off the reason I am hiding here."

"'Tis nay work a guest in my home should have to do." He walked over to her and held out one of the drinks he had poured. "Here. Pause for a wee while in your work, sit, and share some wine with me."

Taking the drink, Morainn allowed him to lead her to a chair set before the fireplace. He took the other chair for himself and turned it slightly so that he could face her across the small table set between them. Morainn took a drink, savoring the smooth rich taste of a wine only those with a full purse could afford to drink.

She felt warmed by his attention, realizing that she had become starved for it, but knew it was not wise to sit there with him as though she were his equal. The craving to see him, to bask in the warmth of his smiles or his gaze, and to let the sound of his deep voice stroke her would have passed after a brief absence. This interlude, fleeting as it had to be, would only work to keep such cravings strong.

"Have ye had any more dreams?" he asked.

"Nay, there have been no more visions about the killers."

Morainn prayed Tormand would think the blush she could feel heating her cheeks was due to a shyness, a maiden's natural unease over being alone with a man, and not press her any harder concerning her dreams. The dreams she had been having lately were not ones she wished to share with the object of them. They were the sort that left her aching with need for him. For a woman who had never had a man, had never even enjoyed a willingly shared kiss, she was astonished at how quickly her mind could fill with images of Tormand naked, of the two of them entwined flesh to flesh. What troubled her most was that she could actually feel the heat of his kiss and the touch of his hands long after the dream had ended. Realizing that just thinking about her dreams was making her feel needy, Morainn hurriedly tried to think of something to say to distract herself.

"I am curious as to why Simon hasnae asked me to hold another hairpin," she said and almost cursed.

She had heard her voice waver a little as she had said the man's name. It still made her uneasy to use the informality they had all insisted upon. Worse, she had just strongly implied that she was anxious to touch another one of those cursed hairpins. Although she truly wanted to help find the killers, she was still reluctant to suffer through another vision of the monsters at their evil work. What she had seen in that vision often slithered through her mind making her feel very afraid.

"I thought I had made it understood that I am willing to help," she forced herself to say.

Tormand wanted desperately to ask her why the talk of dreams made her blush. He had been tormented by heated dreams, ones that made him wake up achingly hard and asweat with a need he had never felt before. However, despite his occasional bouts of jealousy that had him imagining Morainn with a long trail of lovers behind her, all Tormand's instincts told him that she was an innocent. He would be willing to wager his growing fortune that she had very little knowledge of the pleasures a man and a woman could share. Just the thought of being the man to introduce her to those pleasures made his blood race through his veins. Smiling faintly, he allowed her the change of subject.

"Simon was hesitant to inflict another such violent vision upon ye even as we rode to your cottage that day," he said. "Seeing and hearing what had happened to ye in the night made him even more so."

"I cannae say that I wish to suffer through another one, but these killings must stop."

"We are agreed on that."

"The wounds they suffered may cause them to retreat for a wee while, but since the dog lost their trail out of the wood, what I might glean from the hairpins is even more important, isnae it?"

"Aye, it is, although I cannae like it." He grimaced. "And since Magda and her lassies have probably told the whole town that I have brought in the witch to help save myself from hanging, we may as weel try."

Morainn gasped in shock. "Nay, she wouldnae say such things, would she? She worked for ye. She cannae believe ye would butcher women like that."

Tormand shrugged. "I paid her weel, too, but she never liked me. Refused to stay here after dark and watched her lasses as if she expected me to hurl them to the floor and ravish them at any moment. Magda made it verra clear, right from the start, that she thought I was a lecherous swine who was headed straight into hell's fires."

"And ye let her stay? Ye continued to pay her?"

"She was a good cook and she kept the house and my clothing clean. 'Tis all I wanted from the woman and it wasnae so difficult to stay out of her way. I am here to represent my kin at the court and dinnae need to lurk about my home all the day. At least until now."

"Weel, I am certain that will soon end and I dinnae mind the work." She finished the last of her wine and stood up. "'Tis also something I must return to or there will be naught for ye to eat this night."

Tormand also stood up and tried to think of a way to keep her with him for a little while longer. As she started toward the door, he lightly grasped her hand to stop her. Just touching her sent a wave of heat straight to his groin. He knew he was a weak man when it came to women and the pleasure and ease he could find in their soft bodies, but he would wager that the most pious of men would find it a challenge to resist the kind of fire and passion Morainn promised to reward him with. The faint shiver that went through her body and the hint of desire's flush upon her cheeks told Tormand that Morainn felt the same tug of need that he did.

"Are ye verra certain ye can endure another hard vision?" he asked, deciding that revisiting that topic was better than telling her what was really in his mind. Despite his confusion over what he was feeling for this woman, he did know that telling Morainn he ached to get her naked and take her on his desk would not get her to linger in his company.

"Oh, aye, I can endure it. I recovered from the last one."

"Barely."

"A few harsh images do still haunt me, but that cannae be allowed to matter. These people mean to keep on killing and it has to be stopped." Morainn knew she should pull her hand free of his, but her hand did not seem to be inclined to listen to good sense. "My weakness then was born mostly of shock. I hadnae expected the vision to hit me so hard. In truth, I hadnae considered the violence I might see, even though I kenned the hairpin was found in the place where the woman was tortured and killed. But, I havenae had any experience with such things, never e'en thought of them despite the blood I saw when I dreamed. Now I ken weel what I might see and feel and I am prepared for the horror of it all. I will do it because we both ken that I could see something of great importance. Simon need nay worry about me. He but needs to choose a time for me to take hold of the wretched thing."

"Then I will speak to him about it." He slowly tugged her closer to him until their bodies were almost touching. "Now, tell me of your dreams, Morainn."

"I told ye. I have seen naught of the killers or their plans." Morainn was not surprised to hear how soft and breathless her voice was; being so close to Tormand made it impossible to think, let alone speak clearly.

He touched a kiss to her temple, savoring the taste of

her soft skin. "Tell me, Morainn, do ye dream of me? I dream of ye," he whispered before she could answer.

"I dinnae see why ye should."

Pull away, a voice whispered in Morainn's desire-clouded mind, but she lacked the will to obey the warning. She knew she should immediately stop him from placing those feather-soft kisses on her face, each one of which added to the fire spreading through her veins. Instead of pulling away as all her instincts told her to, she moved even closer to him. When he wrapped his arms around her, holding her close to his body, she felt weak in the knees from the waves of desire crashing through her. The man was the greatest threat to her virtue and heart she had ever confronted and yet she could not seem to care.

"Why shouldnae I?" He gave her a gentle kiss, careful not to push her too hard despite how badly his body was screaming out its need for her. "Ye have eyes a mon wants to stare into for hours, as he tries to unearth all of your secrets and mysteries. Ah, and this mouth." He lightly nipped at her full bottom lip. "Warm, sweet honey. Soft as the finest silk and full of fire. In my dreams I have often felt this mouth upon my skin."

Just as she had felt the warmth of his mouth upon hers. Morainn knew this further proof that they had been sharing dreams should alarm her, but then he gently nipped at her earlobe. The light graze of his teeth against that sensitive skin made her cling tightly to his strong body. All the desire that she had dreamed of swept over her now and Morainn felt a faint tickle of fear. The press of Tormand's lips upon hers pushed that fear aside. She opened her mouth to him at the first nudge of his tongue, craving the taste of him.

Tormand was not surprised to hear himself groan as he deepened his kiss. Morainn's taste was intoxicating. His whole body felt painfully taut with need. He wanted to lie her down now and strip the clothes from her lush body. He wanted to taste every inch of her soft golden skin and bury himself so deep inside her that he could not find his way out again.

It was increasingly difficult to keep a tight leash upon his rising desire. There had been too many dreams that had left him aching, hungry and unsatisfied. Tormand struggled hard to grab hold of some control, however, for he could taste the innocence in Morainn's kiss. Even the way she moved into his arms was faintly awkward, even tentative, and told him that she had never had a lover. Yet again the thought that he might be the first to taste her passion slipped into his head and stirred his blood so much he knew he had to pull back a little.

Reluctantly ending the kiss, Tormand turned his attention to her long, graceful neck. He slowly ran his tongue over the rapid pulse in her throat, feeling exultant over that proof that she wanted him as badly as he wanted her. Through the haze of passion clouding his mind came the realization that he had never bedded an innocent before. There was a good reason for that, but he did not care to recall what it was, not if it meant he had to let go of Morainn.

"Ye have had dreams about me, havenae ye, Morainn?" He prayed his assumption was right or he was going to feel like a complete idiot. "Dreams about the two of us doing this, holding each other close, kissing."

"Aye," she whispered. "Sinful dreams."

"Nay, beautiful dreams of fire and need." He slowly stroked his hands over her hips, soaking in her gasp of pleasure at his touch. "Sweet dreams of loving each other, tasting each other's desire."

His voice was pure seduction, Morainn thought. The touch of hungry desire making his deep voice husky only added to the power of it. She felt as if she was on fire and would die unless he quenched the blaze. Even as she thought of how much she needed his hand on her breast, it was there. She pressed herself into his caress, the shock of being touched so intimately swiftly buried beneath her craving for that touch.

Tormand could barely stand he was so full of want for the woman he held in his arms. Even as he looked around for someplace to lie her down and make love to her, he continued to stroke her, kiss her, and keep her beautiful passion running hot and free. Then his gaze settled on the open door and his mind began to push aside desire's demands. Although he wanted to keep her aching and needy for him, he was not sure how he could do it and go shut the door at the same time.

Then, to his utter dismay, the door was pushed all the way open. Morainn leapt back from him at the sound, as if he were a man with a wife and that wife had just come home, armed with a sword and blood in her eye. Tormand watched as her expression changed rapidly from one of desire to one of embarrassment.

Knowing she would now retreat from him, try to pull together all her control and reserve, he silently cursed and looked around for the one who had interrupted them. He was just envisioning all the extremely painful punishments he would inflict upon the one who had ended the fulfillment of his dreams, when he heard a now familiar faint stomping sound. Tormand ceased looking for a man and looked down. William was the intruder and the cat was swaggering toward Tormand's desk as if it was not aware that it was very close to being skinned.

It required several deep breaths to tamp down the hunger gnawing at his insides, but Tormand was finally calm enough to look at Morainn and he almost smiled. Her delicate hands fluttered like nervous sparrows between straightening her skirts and smoothing down some unseen tangles in her thick hair. Now that he was a little calmer, he knew it would have been a mistake to give in to his needs. Morainn should be made love to gently and in a bed, as he was almost certain it would be her first time with a man.

Just as he was about to take her hand in his and say a few sweet words to soothe away the embarrassment she so obviously suffered from, there was the sound of things hitting the floor. He watched as Morainn gasped and raced toward his desk. With a sinking feeling in his belly, Tormand slowly turned to look toward his desk. William sat there on a bare desktop. Everything that had been in the place where the cat now sat calmly watching him was scattered on the floor and a softly scolding Morainn was busy picking it all up.

Tormand had the fleeting thought to race over

there, grab her, and push her out of his ledger room, but he knew he was already too late to save himself. He glared at the cat, briefly nursing the thought that the animal had done this on purpose. The beast certainly looked pleased with itself. Then he heard Morainn gasp and, with an icy cold curling itself around his insides, he turned to look at her. She stood there with a few papers in her hand and, as he watched the color slowly seep from her cheeks, he knew just what she was reading. His mind frantically searched for words he could use to soothe her shock, but found nothing. What could he say to soften the blow of the ugly truth?

Morainn stared at the papers in her hand. She wanted to just set them aside as she had the heavy ledger book, but she could not take her eyes from the top sheet. It had taken only one quick glance at it for her attention to be caught and held. It was a list of names with three names ominously crossed off. For one brief, panic-stricken moment, she feared Tormand really was the killer, but then her senses recovered enough from the shock she was feeling for her to cast aside that mad idea. She had already met the true killers.

This was the list Simon had mentioned once. A list of all of Tormand's lovers, or at least the ones he could remember. And, she realized, the ones living near enough to be in danger from the killers. She read name after name on the list, a list that continued on the back in his elegant handwriting. Unless he was done, he was going to need more paper.

Beneath her shock was a deep, searing pain, but Morainn fought to push it away. She did not want this man to see that he had hurt her. Despite how she had just been melting in his arms like a wanton, she did have her pride. It was all people had left her with and she would cling to it. In a strange way that pride helped to smother at least some of the pain she felt.

Rage came next, cutting sharply through all that pain and the shame she felt for being such a fool. He was trying to use her to fill his bed just as he had so many other women. Despite his talk of dreams and sweet flatteries, she was no more to him than a warm body that happened to be at hand at a time when he was forced to stay close to home.

She had been a fool to think they had truly shared dreams. That was probably just some lie to weaken her resistance to him. She had come here to help him, to try to find the real killers so that he did not find himself with a noose around his neck, and he showed his gratitude by trying to make her one of his whores. At this moment, Morainn was not sure she cared if he did hang. In truth, she rather savored the vision of kicking the block out from beneath his feet. She glared at him. She would hide her pain and the shame she could not seem to shake, but she would let him see her fury.

"Did ye think ye needed a few more names?" she asked, a little astonished by the cold fury in her voice.

"Simon asked me to make a list so that we might ken which women are in danger," he answered truthfully, thinking that she looked glorious in her fury even as it made him fear that he had lost her before he had even had a chance to make her his own.

"Ye would need the king's army to protect all these women."

"I wasnae trying to add ye to a list," he said, but could tell by the look she gave him that he might as well have been spitting into the wind. "I dinnae think of ye as I did those women."

"Nay? Ye didnae whisper sweet words to them? Didnae try to get them into your bed? I have kenned ye but a handful of days and already ye try to seduce me." She tossed the papers onto his desk. "Did ye speak to any of them about dreams? 'Twas a clever thing to do. Ye kenned I hold a strong belief in the importance of dreams."

"Morainn, everything I said to ye was the truth." He reached out toward her, but she nimbly avoided his touch. "What I feel for ye is like nothing I ever felt for any of those women."

She desperately wanted to believe him and that made her afraid. "We are in your ledger room with the door open and ye nearly had me on the floor with my skirts tossed up and ye expect me to believe ye see me as more than a warm body to fill your bed? How do ye expect me to believe I am different from them? Ye are so practiced in soft words and the ways to touch a lass ye could probably seduce a nun. But, Sir Tormand, I willnae be but another name on your list. I have little to claim in name or property, but I do have my pride, and I willnae sacrifice it just so ye can have another woman to play your games with."

Tormand cursed as she strode out of the door. He cursed even more when he heard Simon greet her. Not only had he lost Morainn, but now everyone would know he had and, worse, know how low her opinion of him was. He glared at the cat still sitting on his desk, feeling foolish for blaming an animal for what had happened, but needing some place to throw his anger.

"Morainn, are ye all right?" he heard Simon ask and knew his friend was afraid Tormand had done just what he had tried to do.

"Aye, Simon. I but need to return to my cooking. And I am ready to hold another of those hairpins whenever ye wish to give me one."

"Are ye certain?"

"Verra certain."

"Then we shall try again right after we sup and young Walin is abed."

"Good. We need to stop these killings. And the sooner we do that, the sooner I can return to my home and my life."

Tormand winced as he listened to Morainn walk away. He shrugged when Simon entered the room and looked at him, raising one dark brow in silent question. "She saw the list."

"Ye actually showed it to her?"

The tone of Simon's voice implied he thought Tormand was an idiot and he scowled at the man. "Of course I didnae. I thought it tucked safely beneath my ledgers." He pointed at William. "Then that fool cat came in and neatly pushed everything off the desk and sat down. Morainn rushed over to pick up the mess and saw the list. And, if ye laugh, I must warn ye that I am in the mood to hit something or someone. Verra hard."

"Ye tried to seduce the lass, didnae ye?"

"Aye, mayhap I did, but ye need not make it sound as if I am a leering old fool leading an innocent into sin. I dinnae see her as I have all the other women, nay that she believed me when I told her that."

"Considering how long that list is, I can see why she would doubt your word."

"I havenae lied to her and she kens it."

"Tormand, a lass can trust a mon's word in everything except about his past and his reasons for trying to get her into bed. Unless ye wed with her, she will have doubts about every attempt to bed her. Are ye meaning to wed her?"

"I dinnae ken." Tormand smiled tightly at the look of surprise on Simon's face. "She is different from the others and I think I am a wee bit different now, too. I just dinnae ken how to make her believe that."

"Weel, ye could begin by trying to woo her instead of just trying to seduce her. Ye do recall how to woo a lass, dinnae ye?"

Tormand was about to respond angrily that of course he did, when he realized he could bring forth no memory of a time when he had. Usually all he needed to get a woman into his bed were a few flatteries, a pretty gift, and a kiss or two. None of that could be considered wooing. It was a bit more like hunting. In an attempt to hide his sudden consternation from Simon, he stared at the cat that still watched him closely.

For a brief moment he wondered if he should even try to woo Morainn. With a woman like her wooing would imply he wanted her for his own and intended to be all hers, with a strong possibility of marriage to follow. Oddly enough the idea of marrying Morainn did not frighten him or make him want to flee for the hills. He had seen their children in his last dream and a part of him was anxious to see if those images were true. Even the thought of being faithful to just one woman did not trouble him as he thought it should.

Inwardly shrugging, he decided he would go awooing. "Aye," he said, "I think I can muster a reasonable wooing. If naught else, I want her to ken that she isnae just another woman on a list. So, aye, I will go awooing. How hard can it be?" he muttered as he strode away.

Simon moved to scratch the cat behind the ears, smiling faintly at the loud rumbling purr that came from the animal. "There goes a fool, William. I believe he has a hard road ahead of him and it will do him some good. But he is right about one thing. Morainn Ross isnae just another lass on his list. I begin to think Harcourt kens what he is talking about and isnae that frightening."

Chapter 10

"Are ye certain ye wish to do this?"

Morainn stared up into the surprisingly soft gray eyes of Simon Innes. She was more accustomed to seeing the cold steel gray of a man used to being in command or the slightly murky gray of a man lost in his thoughts as he tried to figure out some puzzle. This look of concern made her realize that Simon Innes was a very handsome man, far more handsome than she had first judged him to be. The fact that he cared about what happened to her, was actually willing to give up a chance to find these monsters even sooner than he might on his own just to save her pain, touched her deeply.

"Aye," she replied. "I am better prepared this time for what I might see and feel. I but pray that I will see something that can be useful to you."

She spoke only the truth, but it was one mixed with a strong dose of hope. She knew just one touch of the hairpin could send her plunging back into that dark world of blood, pain, and madness the killers lived in.

There was no doubt in her mind that, if she had a vision, it would horrify her, but she was determined that it would not terrify her this time. This time she would keep her wits about her and closely study all the images that swirled through her mind. The truth had to be there and she was determined to find it and see those monsters hanged.

There was a slight movement behind her and Morainn did not need to turn around to know that it was Tormand. She knew his scent as well as she knew her own, despite their short acquaintance. She was still furious with him, hurt and jealousy still pounding at her heart, but she could not deny that his presence gave her strength. The temptation to thrust her elbow back as hard as she could and damage that part of him that he had shared so freely with countless women was a little hard to resist, but she did so. No matter what she thought or felt about the man, at this moment she needed the courage he silently gave her. Later, she would think about how he could do that without a word or a touch.

Ignoring the way the rest of the Murrays sat at the table in the great hall watching her, Morainn held out her hand. "Let us get this over with."

"I found this one at . . ." Simon began.

"Nay, dinnae tell me. Such knowledge could easily muddle up the vision or taint how I see whatever it decides to show me. I need to go into the vision totally ignorant."

Simon nodded and placed the hairpin in her hand. Morainn immediately tensed, but quickly forced herself to relax. She would not fight this vision, but let it take her where it chose to. In doing so she hoped to fend off the worst of the effects she had suffered the last time she had held one of the hairpins. Fighting it and allowing the emotions within it to become too great a part of her could be why she was not gaining more of the information they needed.

Minutes passed and Morainn began to think there would be no vision at all this time. She could tell by the frowns growing on the faces of the men that they thought the same. Then it slammed into her mind so hard and fast she gasped, leaving her feeling as if she had just suffered a hard blow to her body. Morainn felt two strong hands grasp her by the shoulders and her strength returned. She faced the vision sweeping over her without quailing before the evil it revealed.

As had happened the last time, the emotions battered her mind first. Pain, fear, hatred, insanity, and an evil pleasure in it all. The emotions were so strong she could almost taste them and she wanted to gag. But this time the vision itself was far more detailed, not just random glimpses of quickly moving images, and Morainn kept her mind's eye fixed firmly on it.

The pain and the fear from the woman staked to a dirt floor of some hovel was just gaining strength, just beginning to infect Morainn despite her efforts to shield herself from it, when it abruptly faded away. The woman was dead. A sense of it being too soon rippled through the fog of evil that swirled around the three figures in the vision. Then anger swelled, a rage so great it made Morainn tremble. The glint of a knife came and went again and again. There was no control, no cold precision in the strikes. The massive dark form that had been crouched on one side of the victim moved to grab the knife. A scream of fury sliced its way through Morainn's head. The pain that caused only grew worse as harsh words pounded into her mind and she fought to cling to each one in case it was important.

"*They must all pay!*"

"*They will, m'lady. They will.*"

Then, suddenly, a woman, her gown splattered with the blood of her victim, looked right at Morainn.

"*And ye, witch, will suffer most of all!*"

Morainn was so shocked she threw the hairpin away from her. Her whole body shook from the strength of her fear. The killer had spoken to her, looked right at her. That had never happened before. There had been the whispers in her mind, but nothing like this. This tasted far too personal, as though the woman knew she was there.

She took a long drink of cider in an attempt to calm herself and put some order into her chaotic thoughts. She could deal with the weakness weighting down her body later. Now, while the vision was still so fresh in her mind, she had to hunt for some of the answers Simon needed to find this murderous couple.

"Did ye find this hairpin before or after ye met me?" she finally asked Simon.

"Before," he replied. "There have been no killings since we first met with ye, only the attack on you."

"True," agreed Tormand, "we didnae ask for her help until after the last killing, but we met her before it. At the Redmonds'. And they have been watching us, havenae they?"

Tormand knew Morainn was still upset with him, but he was pleased that she was not shrugging him aside right now. There was little he could do to help or protect her during one of her visions, but he could at least aid in easing the pain and the fear that came afterward. She was pale and shaking, but this time she had not collapsed or been violently ill. Tormand hated to think she was becoming hardened to what she saw. For that alone he badly wanted to stop this, but he knew she needed to do this. She needed to use the gift she had been given to help find these killers. He lightly rubbed her shoulders, trying to ease some of the tension that still held her in its grip.

"And that hairpin is from the place where the last woman was killed?" Morainn asked.

"Aye," Simon replied and flicked a cautious look toward Tormand. "Lady Marie Campbell was killed there."

Morainn heard Tormand softly curse and wondered if he had actually liked the woman. She hastily shook aside the sharp jealousy that thought brought her. The woman had been cruelly murdered because of some twisted jealousy felt by a madwoman. Morainn did not want to taint the woman's passing with even more ill-feeling. It was her duty to find the monsters committing these murders, not to pass judgment on the victims. Considering how easily Tormand had nearly seduced her, Morainn doubted all of the women he had bedded were true sinners, just a little weak as she was.

"Then, as we now ken, the killers had already seen me. They had seen the incident with the crowd and

Tormand's defense of me and decided I should be their next victim. That explains what I saw." The woman's threat whispered through Morainn's mind again, the icy voice carrying a chill that made Morainn shiver.

"What did ye see?"

"The vision began in the same way the other one did," she replied. "There was a wave of verra dark emotion. Pain, fear, hatred, insanity, and a chilling, evil pleasure. I think the last is the worst of the lot. They enjoy what they do."

"Jesu," muttered Harcourt. "They truly are monsters."

"Och, aye, that is what I would call them." Morainn sighed. "The pain and the fear came from the poor woman they tortured of course, but this time it was ended verra quickly. At first I thought it was because the vision had something else it needed to show me, but, nay, the woman ceased to feel any pain or fear. Whatever wounds she suffered, weel, I would wager most were inflicted after she died." Morainn frowned as she thought hard on that moment in the vision when the pain and fear had so abruptly disappeared and then nodded. "The woman had a weak heart, I think. She kenned weel what was to happen to her, had heard what had happened to the other women, and her fear was great enough that her weak heart couldnae bear the burden of it. It stopped."

After a long moment of silence, Simon said quietly, "I think a letter to her husband telling him of that might ease a little of his grief."

"I will see to it," Tormand said. "I have no doubt that he will believe it for he has long believed in such gifts as Morainn has. And ye are right. It will ease his pain a little. The thought of how Marie must have suffered before she died was tormenting him."

"Once that happened," Morainn continued, "there was anger, a hot searing rage. I saw the knife flash by again and again. It was the woman doing it and the mon finally stopped her. I realized that before there had been a cold precision to the movement of that knife. This time there was only rage. The woman was screaming so many things it is difficult to sort anything useful from the rantings."

Morainn lightly rubbed her forehead. Trying to wade through the cacophony of curses and threats to find anything that might help them find these murderers was making her head ache even more than it usually did after a vision. When Tormand lightly brushed her hand aside and began to rub her temples gently, she did not stop him. It felt too good and helped her think more clearly, something she badly needed to do now.

"Can ye remember any of what she said?"

"Aye, most of it, but it will take me a wee while to sort it all out. A lot of it was cursing and bloodcurdling threats against all those who had destroyed her life. She blames everyone else for her misery, as if she was naught but a poor, innocent victim. She doesnae have the soul of a victim," Morainn said quietly. "I think she was born filled with a rage that just needed a little push to be unleashed."

"And Tormand pushed?" asked Uilliam. "Nay, I cannae believe that. Tormand doesnae hurt women."

Morainn was not about to argue that. She knew

the young man meant physically and she suspected Tormand also had a kindness in him that would not allow him knowingly to be cruel to a woman. The sad thing was he did not even have to know, did not have to realize in even the smallest way, that something he was doing was hurting someone. In truth, Morainn did not really believe this woman's feelings were hurt, only her pride. She had wanted Tormand and she had not gotten him. Since she appeared to be incapable of blaming herself for anything, she would naturally see the other women and Tormand as the ones at fault. It could be as simple and as twisted as that.

"He didnae e'en have to ken who this woman was," Morainn said, after carefully thinking over her words. "The woman is mad. Tormand may never have e'en met her."

"She loved him from afar?"

There was such a tone of cynical disbelief in Uilliam's voice that Morainn almost smiled. "There is no love there. There is pride and possession. She decided he was to be hers. The women were the ones standing in her way."

"Then why does she want Tormand to suffer so?"

"Because he allowed those women to stand in her way; he proved he was naught but a weak mon who thought with what was in his braies and not with what was in his head." She ignored Tormand's muttered annoyance and the wide grins of the other men as she took another drink of cider. Visions always left her thirsty and in need of something sweet. "Remember, this is what I feel, what I draw from the wild swirl of emotions within the vision. Nay more."

Simon nodded. "It makes sense, however. Weel, as much as one can make sense of such madness. It is interesting to ken how the mind of such a killer might work, but I was really hoping for something we could use to find these two ere they kill again."

"I understand," said Morainn. "I feel the same need, but sometimes it takes awhile to pick one's way through all the images to see the truth. These are the first visions where I have e'er heard the voices so clearly."

"Why did ye ask when we found this hairpin?"

"Because of what happened at the end of the vision. Somehow, the woman kenned I was there, watching her. She spoke to me as she has before. Yet another threat of death. But this time she looked right at me as she said it; it wasnae just a whisper in my head."

"Ye saw her face?"

"In a way. I cannae say for certain, but I think she has dark eyes. Her head was covered by a fancy headdress, but there was the hint of dark hair. And she had perfect eyebrows." She had to smile at the looks the men all gave her, looks that said that was a useless piece of information. "They are dark and are perfect arcs over her eyes. Either she was blessed with them at birth or she does something to make them look so precise."

"Then she is of high birth. Some of them are the only ones I have e'er kenned of who shape their brows," said Tormand.

And ye would ken it, wouldnae ye, Morainn thought a little nastily and then shook aside the jealousy she knew would linger in her heart for a while yet. "I think her husband is dead. Aye, and I think she killed him. I fear she didnae call him by name, only referred to him as that fat swine. Aye, she killed him with her own hands. With a knife."

Simon frowned. "I havenae been told of any high-born mon being stabbed to death."

"That is because no one has found him yet," Morainn said.

Little by little the things that had been said were beginning to sort themselves out in her mind, but it was making her head ache even more than it had before. They were all so ugly. Morainn knew she was going to have to take a respite from it all soon. She felt as if all the strength had been bled from her body and, despite Tormand's soothing touch, her head was beginning to ache too much for her to continue to think clearly.

"Ye need to rest," said Simon. "'Tis evident that such visions take a lot of your strength e'en though ye withstood this one better than ye did the last."

"Aye, I fear ye are right. All I heard is slowly sorting itself out in my mind, but my head aches so badly I fear I cannae grasp anything too clearly yet. A good night's sleep may weel end that confusion."

Morainn stood up and felt herself sway. Before she could steady herself, Tormand wrapped his arms around her to help her. She was about to pull away from him when a racket came from the front hall. She could hear voices she recognized arguing with Walter. A moment later three people pushed their way through the doorway. A cross-looking Walter followed Nora and her betrothed into the great hall.

"They wouldnae wait for me to tell ye they were here," grumbled Walter, glaring at Nora.

Nora paid him no heed, her gaze fixed upon Tormand and how he was holding Morainn in his arms. The look of righteous fury on her friend's sweet face fascinated Morainn. She was startled when Nora shook off the grip of her betrothed, who was starting to look uncomfortable, and marched toward her and Tormand. A moment later she was yanked out of Tormand's arms and stumbled into Nora's.

"What have ye done to her?" demanded Nora. "She looks terrible."

"Thank ye, my friend," Morainn murmured, but Nora paid her no heed.

"James, get ye over here and pound this lecherous swine into the mud."

"Ah, Nora, my love," began James.

Nora did not wait to hear his excuses, but kept glaring at Tormand. "Why is she here?"

"Actually, Nora, I was wondering how ye e'en kenned I was here," Morainn said before Tormand or anyone else had a chance to answer the question.

"That fool woman Magda is telling everyone in town that this mon has brought in the witch to help save himself from hanging. Weel, I didnae believe her, so I went out to the cottage. Ye werenae there and neither were your cats. So, I had James bring me here."

"There was no stopping her," said Sir James as he moved closer to the table to accept the tankard of ale Simon silently offered him.

Nora gave her beloved a look that cried him a traitor and then returned to glaring at Tormand. "I still didnae want to believe ye had entered the house of this mon, but when we knocked upon the door and it was opened, I saw William sitting in the hall. That was when I kenned ye really had entered this sinner's house. I have come to rescue ye from him."

"Ah, Nora, I do love ye," said Morainn, "but I dinnae need to be rescued."

"All women need to be rescued from the likes of him."

"There is some truth in that, I suppose. Nora, help me to my bedchamber and I will do my best to explain everything."

Frowning at Morainn in concern, Nora asked, "Are ye sick?"

"Nay, the vision I just had has taken a lot out of me and my head hurts. I need to rest, but I can talk while I am lying abed with a cool cloth on my head. Come, help me up the stairs." She looked at the men even as Nora began to help her out of the great hall. "Gentlemen," she said, ignoring Nora's snort at that appellation, "this is my dear friend Nora Chisholm and I have the feeling ye all ken her betrothed so, if ye will excuse us?" When they all murmured wishes that she would soon recover, she let Nora take her to her room.

The moment the women were gone, Tormand looked at Sir James Grant. "So, Grant, ye intend to marry that woman?"

Sir James grinned and briefly toasted Tormand with his tankard of wine. "I do. She has spirit." He laughed along with the other men, but then grew serious and gave Tormand a hard look. "She loves Morainn like a sister and feels a need to protect her because of all the wrongs done the lass. I may nay have kenned the lass for verra long, but I feel much the same way."

"As do we," said Simon. "Sit, Grant, and we will explain why Morainn is here."

"And tell me what I can and cannae tell others," the younger man said cheerfully as he sat down.

"Of course."

Breathing a sigh of relief as the cool, damp cloth touched with the scent of lavender was placed gently on her aching forehead, Morainn smiled at Nora when her friend sat down on the side of the bed. "Thank ye. I was beginning to fear my head would split apart. The touch of lavender in the water is already working its magic."

"These visions are so hard on ye," murmured Nora. "Why did ye have one here?"

"Because Sir Simon gave me something to hold. Nora, I came here to be safe. I was attacked at the cottage by the same ones who have killed those other women, but was fortunate enough to escape them along with Walin."

"Why? Ye arenae Sir Tormand's lover. Are ye?"

"Nay. The killers fear my gift might lead Sir Innes to them and they wished to make sure I couldnae help him in any way."

"Ye keep saying killers. It isnae just some madmon?"

"'Tis a madmon and a madwoman. Sir Simon found hairpins at each site where the murders were done. I have held two thus far, but have only come up with a few scattered bits of information. I got more by listening to what those monsters said as they hunted for me and Walin in the woods. Still, I have to try. There are also my dreams. Little by little they are also telling me things that might be helpful." She decided now was not a good time to tell Nora what else she dreamed about.

"I suppose that is what your gift is for, helping in such matters, but ye looked so ill."

"'Tis because there is so much evil in the visions I get from the hairpins. The madness that afflicts this pair is also verra hard to bear."

Nora sighed and carefully moved to lie down at Morainn's side. "So they brought ye here to protect ye, as weel as try to find some truth about these killers through your gift."

"Aye. The men downstairs are all staying here. Ye ken who Sir Innes is and Tormand. The others down there were two of Tormand's brothers and two of his cousins. They came because one of the women in their family said Tormand was in danger."

Looking at Morainn in surprise, Nora asked, "Sir Tormand's kin have gifts, too?"

"That is what he told me. He said his clan was riddled with people who have some special gift. Even Sir Innes believes in the dreams now."

"Weel, at least ye can do some real good with your gift this time, instead of just helping some rich woman learn that her son is a thieving bastard."

Morainn laughed. "True."

"Ye could have come to me; I would have helped ye stay safe."

"And I may weel have brought these monsters to

your door. Nay, coming here where I am surrounded by six strong men was better."

"Six strong, verra handsome men."

"One must endure the good with the bad." She smiled when Nora laughed.

"I agree ye are safer here, at least from the killers. But I meant it when I said I dinnae think any woman is safe from Sir Tormand Murray."

"Nay, I dinnae think they are. Howbeit, I do have a verra strong incentive to resist any attempts he may make to seduce me."

Nora frowned at her. "And what would that be?"

"The mon has a list."

"A list of what?"

"His lovers."

"He is keeping a score?" Nora asked in outrage.

"Och, nay. Sir Simon asked him to make up a list of all the lovers he has had in this town and those who travel with the court. He wants to ken how many women are in danger. Weel, I saw the list and I am nay fully joking when I say they would need the entire king's army to protect all the women on that list."

"Oh, my. He must be verra good at it then."

Morainn laughed even though it made her head hurt. "Aye, one must suppose so." She sighed. "I refuse to be just another name on a list. For a moment I was foolish." She saw Nora's look of alarm. "Nay, not that foolish. A kiss only. But I thought the desire was for me, only me, until I saw that list. He but needed a woman and I was near at hand. I willnae be used that way."

"I worry about ye, Morainn."

"Because of Sir Tormand?"

"Somewhat. Ye are a verra strong woman, my friend, but ye have a verra soft and gentle heart. A mon like him could sorely hurt you. But, in truth, I fear for your life more than I fear for your virtue."

Morainn patted her friend's hand. "The men take watch every night. I feel safe here, Nora. And because they need my visions, I dinnae feel as though I am here on their sufferance. Aye, and because that woman Magda deserted Tormand, I also cook and care for the house. And Walin is as happy as I have e'er seen him. The men are verra good to him and I think it does him good to be about men for a while."

"The important thing is that ye are safe."

"Aye, 'tis how I see it. And nay just me. Walin is safe as weel."

"True." Nora stood up and kissed Morainn's cheek. "Rest and if ye cannae abide staying here any longer, but cannae go back to your cottage, please come to me. James will find men to guard us."

"Thank ye, Nora. I doubt I shall need to flee this place, but there is comfort in kenning that I have a place to go. There is one thing ye might do for me. I need someone to care for my animals and mayhap do a little work in the garden."

"Dinnae fret. I have a cousin who will be more than happy to tend to the cottage until ye get back. Now, rest and get your strength back."

The moment Nora was gone, Morainn sighed and closed her eyes. She felt as if she had worked for three days straight without rest. There was one hairpin left, but she was going to have to avoid it for a few days. By then she should be strong enough to try one more time to get something that Simon could use to catch these monsters.

Tormand watched as Nora walked into the hall. She was glaring at him again. It stung and it annoyed him, but he would be courteous. She cared for Morainn and for that alone he would endure her censure without a word. He felt a little uneasy when she marched right up to him, however.

"Ye had best take verra good care of her. She has suffered enough misery in her life and doesnae need a mon like ye bruising her tender heart."

Before he could respond to that, Grant bid everyone farewell and got his spirited betrothed out of the house. Tormand looked at Simon and his kinsmen. The scowl he gave them did nothing to dim the wide grins they wore. Even Walter wore a grin on his usually dour face.

"Grant will have his hands full with that lass," he said.

"I am surprised ye let her speak to ye like that without saying anything," said Uilliam.

Tormand sighed. "She cares for Morainn. I have a reputation." He ignored all the snorting that remark caused. "And she just wishes to be sure that not only Morainn's life is protected while she is here."

"Weel, the lass does give ye some warm looks," said Walter. "I dinnae see why ye should be expected to ignore that."

"I willnae have to ignore warm looks, Walter, because there willnae be any more. She saw the list." He nodded at the looks of horror on the faces of his kinsmen and

Walter. "'Tis verra hard to woo a lass when she has seen proof that the mon wooing her has—as she put it— bedded enough women that he will need a king's army to protect them all."

"Woo? Ye mean to woo the lass?" asked Harcourt.

"Aye, I mean to woo the lass," Tormand answered between gritted teeth.

"Do ye need some help? Ye havenae done much wooing in your life."

"I can woo a lass by myself, thank ye verra much."

"Weel, if ye feel as if ye need a word of advice, just come to me." Harcourt stood up. "Time to wander about the town and see what we can find. Who is with me?"

In minutes the great hall was cleared of everyone except Tormand. He sighed and poured himself some ale. It was going to be a long night. His mind was filled with memories of how sweet Morainn tasted and his body was crying out for more. Even recalling how she had looked at him after seeing that list did not chill the heat inside of him. The angry disdain he had seen there should have frozen any firey thoughts of her that had lit inside of him. He knew only one thing for certain—he had to get her back into his arms.

He needed a plan, he decided. Up until she had seen that list, Morainn had been drawn to him. He had enough experience to recognize when a woman was interested in him, and he had seen that interest in Morainn's fine eyes. Tormand was willing to do what-ever it took to see it there again. In fact, he needed that so badly he would even be willing to ask for advice if what he planned did not work. He just prayed he would not have to, because he knew he would never hear the end of it.

The soft thud of big paws drew his attention and he watched as William hopped up on a chair at the table. The cat stared at him and Tormand scowled at the cat. He still blamed the animal for what had happened, or rather not happened, in his ledger room. If he was a superstitious man, he could easily believe the cat had known what was going on and had come in on purpose to warn Morainn about the man she was kissing.

"Ye can just go and catch mice. I dinnae need a cat tripping me up when I go awooing. And I intend to win your mistress, so ye had best get used to me."

And now I am talking to a cat, he thought. Morainn Ross is definitely turning my life upside down.

Chapter 11

"I think the mon is trying to woo me."

Morainn had to grin at the way Nora rolled her expressive eyes. They sat in the sunlit sewing room of the Chisholm house embroidering linens because Nora was determined to bring as much as she could to her marriage. Since she had no lands and was not rich, she said she would settle for chests full of linens and gowns. Her mother and sister had gone to her aunt's house to work on the gowns, not only for the wedding, but to try to fulfill at least a few of Nora's wants and needs. Pride was behind the flurry of work. The Chisholms were very determined to look as grand as any laird's kinsmen at the wedding.

That left her and Nora blissfully alone in the house, if one ignored the fact that Harcourt and Rory were wandering around guarding them both. Morainn had insisted upon making this visit not only to help Nora, but because she badly needed a friend to talk to and all the men had insisted that she have guards with her. Tormand in particular had not been pleased with the plan, but had eventually given in. She suspected those female relations he often talked about had let him know that sometimes a woman just needed to be with another woman.

In truth, she thought with a smile, she also just needed a woman to talk to for a while. After days surrounded by men, a little boy who had now decided that he was a man too, and cats, just the sound of another woman's voice made her feel better. They were all good men and she loved Walin, but sometimes a woman needed to talk with another woman and this was such a time. She certainly could not talk about what she needed to any of the men.

"And how is he doing that?" asked Nora, a strong thread of contempt in her voice. "With flowers, jewels, and empty flatteries?"

Resisting the sudden urge to defend Tormand, Morainn answered, "Weel, aye, there are flatteries, but I am nay sure they are empty. He compliments the work I do, my cooking, e'en the way the linens feel and smell. Oh, he does slip in a wee word or two about my bonnie smile, my lovely silken hair, and compares my eyes to the sea. Storm-tossed when I am annoyed and sun-kissed when I laugh." She almost sighed as she recalled those pretty words and his deep seductive voice as he said them.

"Oh." Nora sighed in appreciation. "Those are good ones."

"I thought so." Morainn was pleased to see that Nora was also touched by those sweet words, for it made her feel less like she was being an utter fool too easily swayed by pretty words. "And he does give me gifts, but nay flowers or jewels. A wee book of verses, a wooden goblet—"

"Wooden! That mon can afford far better than that. James told me the mon is building a verra impressive fortune, e'en said he needed to talk to the mon to see if there were a few things he could learn from him."

"'Tis a lovely one with wee flowers carved into it, but, aye, he could have easily afforded to give me a silver one." Morainn smiled. "But I would have had to give it back. Such a rich gift would taste too strongly of, weel, a bribe."

Nora frowned and then nodded. "Aye, it would have, wouldnae it. It would feel too much like a payment for your favors. Look what I gave ye, he thinks. Now 'tis time for ye to give me what I want. Cannae think that over such things as a wooden goblet, nay matter how bonnie it is. Clever mon. He is giving ye simple gifts."

"He is indeed. A ribbon he said reminded him of my eyes, a wee journal to write my thoughts in, as weel as the quill and ink to do so." She nodded at Nora's scowl. "Rich for ones like ye and me, but small for a mon like him. 'Tis a verra plain one.

"I think it all started a week ago. I was still so verra angry with the mon, but he stood by me during my vision, helping me find the strength and courage I needed, and he e'en rubbed my forehead to ease the throbbing there after the vision ended."

"Ye like him, dinnae ye? Morainn, the mon just wants to bed ye."

"I ken it, but, mayhap I would like to bed him."

"That doesnae surprise me. He is a handsome mon,

as bonnie as the summer days are long, even with those mismatched eyes. But think on your reputation," Nora began, only to pause and then grimace.

"Exactly. Near everyone in town thinks I have already born a bastard child and they spend far too much of their time trying to guess who the father is e'en after all these years. And they all ken that I now abide in Tormand's house, thanks to Magda and her lasses telling everyone they meet that she saw me arrive, that she had to leave to save her soul. Many truly believe that I am a witch and should like to see me suffer the same fate as my mother did. And let us nay forget how some think I got that cottage from the laird of Dubhstane by warming his bed whenever he wishes it. I have no good name to protect, Nora."

"Ye and those who love ye ken verra weel that ye arenae what the gossips claim ye are."

"I ken it and that knowledge eases the sting of what others say, but it doesnae silence them, does it? I would also like to think that those who love me would still do so e'en if I stepped off the righteous path for a wee while."

"Of course they would, but, Morainn, that mon just wishes to bed ye. Truly. Ye cannae be hoping for more than that from such as him."

"Most of the time I dinnae, but there is a wee foolish part of me that does, I fear."

"A mon like that isnae sincere. He but plays a game with women. Leaping from one bed to another like some demented toad." Nora grinned when Morainn laughed. "Ye deserve far better than that and weel ye ken it."

"I do, but I doubt I shall ever have it."

"And why not? Ye are bonnie and smart. Ye have a fine cottage and lands with it."

"Which a lot of people think I spread my legs for."

Ignoring that, Nora doggedly continued, "Ye work hard, sew a neat stitch, do beautiful needlework, and cook better than I could ever hope to, which is why I am so pleased James has a cook."

Before her friend could continue with her list of Morainn's fine points, which was already embarrassing her, Morainn said, "And a wee boy everyone thinks is my bastard son."

"Idiots. 'Tis no secret that the lad arrived at your door when he was already two years of age. Did they think ye hid him away under a bramble bush until then? 'Tis just their own guilt that makes them say such things, for one of them is guilty of leaving that child there, others ken who it might be, and none of them told ye, nor did anyone offer to take in the child."

"And so ye tell them whenever ye get the chance, but it has never made any difference, has it, and it willnae. People will believe what they wish and what makes them feel better. Because of such gossip the only men who have called on me are ones who think they can buy my favors or steal them."

"Fools."

"Ye will get no argument from me on that. Too many men also fear my gift. Tormand doesnae, Nora. He told me that his clan is riddled with people who have such gifts. 'Tis verra pleasing to be with people who dinnae see what I can do as sorcery or a gift from the devil that might taint them with the evil it came from; people who believe what I tell them when I see or feel something and dinnae just cross themselves. Tormand not only doesnae flinch, he helps me when I fall weak from the vision or my head aches as it so often does after one."

Nora set her needlework down and reached out to take Morainn's hand in hers. "He will hurt ye, break your tender heart in twain and stomp on the pieces."

Morainn smiled fleetingly. "He would ne'er be so unkind as to stomp on the pieces. There is no cruelty in the mon. Trust me in that. Ye ken weel that I would feel it if there was. And, aye, he may weel break my heart, but I will walk away with some verra fine memories to cling to when I am alone again. I believe Tormand will be a generous and skillful lover. Considering how many times the fool has bedded women, he must have learned something." She laughed along with Nora.

"Ye truly want to do this, dinnae ye? Do ye love the fool then?"

"I think I might. I was still fighting it, fighting his allure, but I heard a few things in the last two days that have begun to take the fight right out of me. I heard his kinsmen teasing him about his stumbling attempts to woo me. They made it clear that he has ne'er attempted a wooing before. He said he had ne'er needed to, which brought forth a lot of derision from his loving family. But, he also said that he had ne'er wanted to, either."

"Arrogant, but probably the truth." Nora grimaced as she picked up her needlework again. "I confess, if I was in your place I would also see that as promising."

Morainn felt relieved for she had feared she was grasping for any reason, no matter how weak and perhaps false, to stop fighting Tormand. "Then I over-heard him speaking with Simon last evening. Tor-mand confessed to having an epiphany. He said he grew more and more uneasy as he added name after name to that accursed list of his, that he had begun to see a mon he didnae like verra much. Suddenly the things his kinsmen had said, and more especially his kinswomen, were no longer just annoyances to be ig-nored, but carried the bitter taste of a hard truth. He also confessed to something that obviously startled Simon. It seems that Tormand Murray, the great lover, has been celibate for four months." She nodded when Nora gasped in shock. "He thinks his disgust with his own behavior had already begun to settle into his heart and mind. My reaction to that list and what I said to him in my anger and hurt also struck him hard. He didnae like the mon I was seeing in him."

"Oh, my. That sounds e'en more promising. Yet, are ye certain ye wish to wager your heart and virtue on what might just be a passing mood for the mon?"

Morainn slowly nodded. "I think I do. I dream of him, Nora. Every night, and for a lot longer than I have kenned him, although the dreams I have had since I first set eyes on the mon are, weel, more de-tailed. I wake up feeling needy yet empty. He pulls at everything inside of me. At first my dreams were only of being bedded by a mon with mismatched eyes, cloudy romantic foolishness. They are so much deeper now and not just concerning the lovemaking. I dream of him smiling at me over a meal or of him returning to me after a day at court full of talk about all he has seen and done. And, Nora, I dream of holding his bairns."

Nora cursed. "Ye love the rutting fool."

"I just said that I thought I might."

"Nay. Ye do. There is nay *might* about it. 'Tis the dream of bairns that tells me that. I wager they all look like him."

"Aye, but that dream could be born of the fact that I am three and twenty and have never been wooed. Grabbed, wrestled with, offered a coin or two or e'en a rabbit for stewing, and e'en attacked in my own home, but never wooed."

"Mayhap when this is all done and people ken that ye helped catch these monsters that will change. Ye will have saved so many other women from a like fate."

Morainn smiled slightly for she could hear the doubt in her friend's voice. What she did not hear, had not heard throughout the conversation, was disgust or condemnation. Nora was only concerned that Morainn would be hurt. It was a very great possibility that she would be, but that would not stop her.

"Nay, it willnae change. If naught else, my help in this matter will only confirm people's opinion that I am a witch."

"Ye are going to do it, arenae ye?"

"I believe I am. E'en if it is only a fleeting, tempestuous thing, I want it. E'en if all the mon can give me is his passion and a sweet, fond fare-thee-weel when it is done, I want it. Then again, he may give me more, maybe the mon my dreams tell me he is. If he is my future, would I nay be a fool not to try and grab hold of it?"

"Could ye nay do that without bedding him?"

"Mayhap, but this is Tormand Murray we speak of. I think he is the sort of mon who willnae last long through an innocent wooing, sharing naught but a few kisses. They say that the way to a mon's heart is through his stomach, but I am thinking that, in Tormand's case, it may be a wee bit lower. Aye, if I give that mon but a hint that I am ready and willing to be his lover, that will settle the matter there and then. But who can say, mayhap in the heat of passion, in the soft afterward, that is where I might wriggle my way into his heart.

"And, to be blunt, I have no wish to die a virgin. Also, too many men think I am free for the taking and the knife I keep beneath my pillow may nay save me the next time some bastard comes acreeping into my bedchamber in the dead of night. Or one who catches me alone somewhere. I would rather give it away to a mon of my choosing, a mon I might be able to make a future with, than to have it ripped away by someone else."

"I think I would do the same and I wish ye luck." She laughed when Morainn leapt to her feet and hugged her. "Get to work, woman. My wedding draws nigh and I mean to have a chest or two full of fine linens." As soon as Morainn sat down again, Nora said, "Now, tell me how the hunt for these killers fares."

The sun was going down by the time Morainn left Nora's home. Her friend walked beside her with Harcourt and Rory ambling along behind them. Nora's aunt lived along the route to Tormand's house and Nora was to meet her family there for the evening meal. Morainn was just trying to think of what she could set out for a meal when she felt a cold chill swirl around her and stopped.

"What is it?" asked Nora. "Did ye see someone ye wish to speak to?"

"Ye cannae feel the cold, can ye?" she asked Nora, as she felt Harcourt and Rory step up beside them.

"Nay, there is no cold, Morainn," replied Nora, looking confused. "'Tis a warm night."

"Is it the cold ye feel in the visions, lass?" asked Harcourt.

Morainn looked at him in gratitude. She doubted she would ever be able to explain how good it felt to have people around her who truly understood her visions. "Aye, exactly like that. They are watching us." She felt Nora clutch her hand. "I just cannae see them," she muttered as she looked around.

She started to move, like a hunter stalking a deer she began following the cold she felt, and dragging Nora with her. Harcourt and Rory stayed close and alert and that gave her courage. It was as she walked by a deeply shadowed alley that she stopped. The cold she was feeling grew sharper and Morainn shivered. She could also feel eyes on her, feel the evil intent of the watcher. He was furious that she had found him.

Quickly turning, she stared into the alley. A huge shadowy form stood there and she could almost see his eyes. Morainn knew it was one of the killers. She had seen the huge man in her dreams too often to be mistaken. The way he stood there staring at her made her want to run back to Tormand's and hide under the covers.

"He is in there," she whispered, her voice so soft and shaky that she feared neither Harcourt nor Rory would hear her, but they moved quickly. When Rory hesitated just a little, obviously thinking that someone should stay with her, Morainn shook her head. "Go. We will stand here where we are seen and can be heard by many people." Even as she watched him follow Harcourt she knew they would fail to catch the man who had already disappeared deeper into the shadows.

"Was it one of the killers?" Nora whispered, her voice shaking with fear.

"Aye, but dinnae fret. We stand in the light with dozens of people close at hand." Morainn smiled a little coldly. "And I have a verra big knife tucked in a sheath just inside my skirt."

"Oh. Can ye reach it quickly?"

"Aye. I reach it through a wee slit just beneath my waist and my hand rests upon it e'en now."

"They arenae going to catch him, are they?"

"Nay, I dinnae think so. It will make them verra cross."

"It would make me verra afraid and yet ye seem so calm."

Morainn nearly laughed. Inside she was tight with fear. The proof that the killers were watching her so closely terrified her. She could still feel those eyes on her and she wanted to wash the feel of them away. For a brief moment, as she had stared at that shadowy form, she had smelled the blood on his hands, had heard the screams of the murdered women in her mind.

"Nora, I want ye to ask James to make sure that ye and yours are never alone."

"But none of us has ever had anything to do with Sir Tormand and ye said it was his women the monsters were after." Nora stared at Morainn, her eyes widening with fright. "*Jesu*, and ye intend to become one of them."

"Weel, actually, my intention is to try verra hard to be the last name on that list, but, remember, the killers were already after me. That madwoman believes I am already in his bed. She wouldnae believe me if I told her that was nay so and she is just as concerned about Sir Simon using my gift to find her, as she is about what I may or may not be doing with Tormand. But, since they are after me, I worry that they may try to pull me into a trap by using those I care about. Being my friend could be verra dangerous now. So, please, ask James to have ye and yours weel guarded and ne'er go anywhere alone."

"I promise." Nora shook her head. "I ne'er really thought of the danger ye are in. The murders horrified me, but I didnae think myself or anyone I kenned was in danger and so went merrily about my business. But, as ye say, these people are mad, and they dinnae have to make sense in their choices of victim."

"Nay, and, worse, they like the killing. There is a pleasure in it for them."

"I really wish ye hadnae told me that," Nora muttered. "Now I am truly terrified."

"Good. Until these beasts are caged and then

hanged, I believe everyone round here ought to be terrified. The woman who is doing this kills anyone she feels has hurt or wronged her and those injuries are usually all in her twisted mind. I believe she has already killed her husband, and, considering the way her illness makes her think, she may have already buried some of her own kinsmen."

"And, curse it, your guards havenae found the one ye saw and so the danger remains," Nora said softly, as Harcourt and Rory returned, both men looking furious.

"The mon disappeared like smoke upon the wind," said Harcourt, his anger making his voice hard and cold. "'Twas like trying to chase a shadow."

"I feared that would be the way of it," said Morainn, as they started to walk toward Nora's aunt's home again. "I have told Nora she should get James to see that she and her family are guarded."

"Good idea," said Harcourt. "I begin to fear that these killers are growing bolder and have gained a taste for what they do, mayhap e'en begin to need to feed that sick hunger more often."

Nora groaned. "I didnae need to hear that, either. Shouldnae ye be telling everyone ye can that there are monsters out there who may be growing ever more monstrous?"

"'Tis no secret," said Harcourt. "Nay matter what we say they willnae think they could possibly be in danger. In their eyes this is all Tormand's trouble and they think themselves safe if they have naught to do with him."

Pausing in front of Nora's aunt's home, Nora briefly

hugged Morainn. "Be verra careful, my friend," she whispered into Morainn's ear. "Ye have picked a verra dangerous mon and a dangerous time to fall in love."

Morainn watched Nora disappear into her aunt's house, sighed, and started walking toward Tormand's home. "Mayhap I paused too long to think what that feeling of cold meant," she said, speaking more to herself than to her companions.

"Nay," said Rory. "The mon was watching all of us. He moved as soon as we did. It would have been the same nay matter when ye had mentioned the cold ye felt. It wasnae another vision though, was it?"

She shook her head. "Just a feeling. I get them sometimes. Yet, I begin to fear that some strange bond has developed between me and the killers. 'Tis nay just feeling when they are close; 'tis that I hear their voices in my dreams and visions. Aye, and 'tis the way that woman actually speaks to me when she slithers into my dreams or visions. I wish it gone and yet I also wish it was stronger for it might weel lead us to them."

"Nay, lass," said Harcourt. "Ye dinnae want to be bonded to that pair in any way, nay matter how much it might help us. I ken ye cannae catch insanity, but is that true when 'tis a vision or a dream? If they have grasped hold of your mind, just what can they do?"

Shivering with the thought that such evil was in her head even when she had not called it there, Morainn wrapped her arms around herself as they entered Tormand's house. "I dinnae ken. I only ken that I am terrified whenever I hear that icy voice in my head." She hastily shook herself free of that fear. "I need to wash up and then I will get us all something to eat. I ken weel that ye are all going to be out hunting tonight and ye need a full belly ere ye go."

Everything moved quickly after that until the time working with Nora felt like a nap. Morainn set out a rough but filling meal, all the while answering questions about what she had felt and seen on the walk home from Nora's. She then put Walin to bed, smiling at how weary the boy was. The Murrays were very good at tiring out an active boy.

By the time she had cleaned up the kitchen and returned to the great hall all the men had disappeared, leaving only Tormand staring a little morosely into the fire. She helped herself to a tankard of ale and went to sit beside him on the small wooden settee placed before the fireplace. The small, gently burning fire took some of the damp out of the air and spread a soft flickering light over Tormand. She sipped her ale and thought about how handsome he was, the kind of handsomeness that made a lass lose the capability to breathe. Even when he was looking a bit like Walin did when he was denied something he really wanted.

Tormand knew he was in a morose mood when even the fact that Morainn sitting beside him without being asked only lightened his dark humor a little. "I should be out there with them, helping them hunt down these bastards."

"They would have to guard ye every step of the way and that would hinder their search," Morainn said. "The talk and the mood of the townspeople grow more dangerous every day."

"I dinnae understand how they could believe I am the one doing this. I have ne'er hurt a woman. I am ne'er unkind to the poor and e'en helped a friend of mine set up a verra fine home for the children left to fend for themselves, either because they were tossed aside or they were orphaned and had no kin that could or would take them in."

"That was verra good of ye."

He smiled faintly. "I can be good on occasion."

"I am verra certain that ye can."

Tormand stared at her in some surprise. He knew he had a habit of reading things into her words and smiles that might not be there, hope making him foolish and wishful, but those words had a sultry tone to them that stirred his blood. He leaned back in his seat and idly slipped his arm around her shoulders, feeling a little too much like a green boy trying to steal a kiss. Morainn was not looking at him, but there was the hint of a blush on her face that made him think he had not heard her wrong. She had not been speaking of his charitable deeds. Deciding it would be wise not to admit openly he had heard the tease in her voice, he sought for something they could talk of.

"I but begin to feel like some maiden in a tale who is locked in her tower."

Morainn laughed. "Nay, Tormand, that is something ye will ne'er be. They need to be free to find these people and, whether ye need protecting or nay, they would feel it necessary to watch ye. Be honest, even ye would be hard put to win out over an angry crowd."

"I ken it. That and the knowledge that Simon or my

family could be hurt as they try to help me is all that keeps me here." He cautiously leaned closer and gently nuzzled her hair. "Of course, there is one good thing about being held captive in my own home."

"And what is that?" she asked, not surprised to hear the husky sound of a rising desire in her voice for his warmth, even his scent was stirring her passion and her need for him.

"I have a bonnie lass for company."

"Weel, ye shall have to send her home for I am here."

He laughed. "Wretch."

He touched a kiss to her temple, subtly inhaling her soft scent of clean skin and lightly scented soap. Lavender, he mused. He would probably never be able to smell it again without thinking of her.

Morainn waited for him to do more than idly touch her or place fleetingly soft kisses on her temple. Her mouth actually ached for his kiss, her lips tingling in anticipation, yet he was behaving like the most complete gentleman. She thought it was just her bad luck that when she wanted him to misbehave so that she could just follow him down the road of sin, he was behaving as properly as if some aged, ill-tempered female from her family was lurking in the corner ready to scold him for doing anything inappropriate. It was obvious that she was going to have to give him a stronger hint that his wooing had been successful.

She set down her drink and turned her head—and found her mouth only inches from his. "Are ye still wooing me, Tormand?"

"Trying to."

"Ye have been doing a verra good job."

"Have I?" He dared to brush a kiss over her soft mouth and felt her lips cling to his in welcome invitation. "Morainn? I am all asea here."

"Treading a new path, are ye, and afraid ye are about to step wrong?"

"Aye, that says it weel." He kissed her again and felt the same welcome, watching the way her mouth briefly followed his as he lifted his head. "I ache to kiss ye, Morainn. I have tasted the kiss we shared on my mouth for days and am starved for it."

"Cannae let ye starve, can we?" she said and placed her mouth over his.

His kiss was fierce with the hunger he could not hide. Morainn reveled in it, returned his demand for more as best as she was able. When he ended the kiss he rested his forehead against her and she could feel him shaking faintly. That such a man would feel so in need of her was a heady thing. It might not be any more than a fierce passion, but she was tired of turning it aside. She stroked the back of his neck with her fingers and heard him groan softly.

"Ah, sweet witch, I am nay good at this."

"Oh, I thought ye were verra good."

Tormand grinned briefly and then sighed. "I feel the need too strongly to just sit here and trade a few chaste kisses. I have tried, but the hunger rules me. If ye dinnae want to find yourself in my bed verra soon, ye had best go to your bedchamber." He grimaced. "Mayhap ye should e'en lock the door."

Morainn hesitated but only for a moment. This was the moment when she made her choice. "I believe I will stay right here unless ye take me elsewhere."

He moved so fast, she barely had time to catch her breath. Tormand picked her up in his arms and nearly ran from the great hall. Instead of being frightened by his eagerness to get her into his bedchamber and his bed, she felt exhilarated. What would begin tonight could easily end with her crying a great deal in the night while alone in her own bedchamber at the cottage, but she would chance it. For once in her life she was going to take a risk, reach out and grab what she wanted more than she did her next breath, and just hope it stayed in her grasp.

Chapter 12

Morainn caught a fleeting glimpse of Tormand's bedchamber before she found herself sprawled on top of his large bed. There were signs of wealth everywhere she looked. Rugs upon the floor, tapestries upon the wall, and candleholders made of finely crafted silver all spoke of a man with coin enough to enjoy the best life had to offer. Morainn felt suddenly intimidated by it all, for it was a blatant display of how very far above her touch this man was. He not only had family who loved him, and a title, he had wealth enough to choose a fine highbred woman for a wife.

Then Tormand lowered his lean strong body down onto hers. Despite her promise to herself not to think about his past, to put it firmly out of her mind, the thought of all his past lovers slipped inside her mind. She wondered how many of those women on his list had shared this bed with him and then tensed even as he pulled her into his arms. Morainn tried to banish those thoughts from her mind and relax before he noticed the change in her, but she knew she had failed when he frowned down at her.

"Did I mishear ye? Or have ye changed your mind?" he asked, praying that she had not, for he knew he had never been so desperate to make love to a woman as he was to make love to Morainn.

"Nay," she said and put her arms around him, silently cursing the fact that even that small move revealed the tension she could not shake free of.

Tormand studied her for a moment and then sighed as he guessed what had made Morainn change from soft and welcoming to tense and almost cold. She was thinking of him and his other women, women he might have shared this bed with. He could see the truth of his assumption by the way she refused to meet his eyes, but kept glancing at the bed. After all, was he not Tormand the great lover, Tormand the sinner, or, as one of his female cousins had said, Tormand the man whose braies unlaced at the mere sway of a petticoat. He had sworn to himself that he would always be truthful with Morainn even though he anticipated many uncomfortable moments. This time, however, he could tell her the truth with ease.

"I have ne'er brought a woman here," he said and watched her eyes widen with surprise. "I swear to ye that ye are the verra first woman to share this bed with me."

"But why wouldnae ye bring one of them here?"

"Would ye believe me if I told ye it was to keep Magda quiet?"

"Nay, if only because the woman was ne'er here at night to see if ye brought a woman here or nay. Oh, did ye fear that their scent might linger here long after ye were done with them?"

He blinked in surprise as he realized that that was a very good reason to keep the sort of lovers he had had out of his house. "I ne'er thought of that but, nay, that wasnae the reason. I have a few kinsmen who were, shall we say, much sought after, including my own father. One once told me that the wisest thing to do is to keep your own home free of the women ye use just for pleasure or to scratch an itch. He said a mon should never soil his own nest."

Before she could ask him exactly what that meant, he kissed her. With one stroke of his tongue in her mouth, she lost all concern about other women, well-used beds, and steeped-in-sin kinsmen who spoke of soiling nests. The fire that had briefly cooled inside her flared into full life again. She tentatively touched her tongue to his and heard him sharply catch his breath. That sign that he liked her to give as well as take caused her to feel almost bold and she was soon giving as much as she was taking despite her inexperience.

Tormand struggled to keep control of his raging desire. Despite how quickly she was learning to kiss in a way that had him panting like a hard run dog, he knew she was an innocent. Giving full rein to the passion that was racing through his body could easily be enough to frighten her away and that was the very last thing he wanted to do.

When she slid her small soft hands beneath his shirt, he groaned with the force of the pleasure that rolled over him. If he had been standing up he felt sure he would have been sinking to his knees. He yanked off his shirt and threw it aside, frustrated by the cloth that kept her tormenting hands from moving freely over his skin. He could feel the power of her shy caress all the way to the soles of his feet.

Kissing her again, starved for the taste of her, he began to unlace her gown. Tormand felt that if he did not soon feel their bodies touch, flesh to flesh, he could go mad. The anticipation of that first touch had him shaking. All the skills he had gathered in all those beds he had skipped through were slipping through his fingers with each touch of her hands, each kiss they shared.

Morainn felt shyness try to creep over her and cool her desire as Tormand removed her gown and began to unlace her shift. She had never been naked before a man. She did not think she had been naked before anyone since she had been a small child. Thinking of all the very beautiful women he had bedded made her fear that she could never compare favorably to them. Every fault she had ever seen in her own body suddenly leapt to mind. She forced herself to remember her dreams and how good it had felt to be skin to skin with Tormand. Slowly, she began to feel her shyness and unease ebb away. The feel of his warm flesh beneath her hands helped her to push aside all concern about how she would soon be naked before this breathtakingly handsome man, a man who had known so many women yet felt a strong desire for her. Instead she thought about how soon he might be as naked as she was, shedding his clothes so that she could see and feel all of his fine strong body.

The moment Tormand removed the last of Morainn's clothes, he sat up and began to tear off his own with none of the care and practiced movements he had always used before. He did not want to play any flirtatious or seductive games; he just wanted to be naked with her as soon as he could. He could teach her the pleasure to be found in such games later.

He stared at her as he rapidly undressed. She was slim, but had beautifully full breasts and well-rounded hips. She was soft in all the places a woman should be. Her nipples were a soft rose color, hard, inviting, and temptingly long. Her unblemished skin was a soft golden color all over, just as he had dreamed it would be. Between her surprisingly long, shapely legs was a small arrowhead-shaped nest of dark curls pointing the way to paradise. He fought the urge to lift her legs up, drape them over his shoulders, and kiss that sweet spot for he knew that, for her first time with a man, he had to move slowly.

He saw how she studied his body, the warm look of appreciation in her eyes enough to make him want to preen just a little. Then her gaze settled on his groin where his manhood stood tall and proud. When her eyes widened and he saw the hint of fear steal some of the warmth and interest from her eyes, he quickly returned to her arms and kissed her. The feel of her soft, warm skin brushing up against his in every place where their bodies touched made him tremble like some untried youth. Tormand did not think there was anything in his life that had felt this good. He knew that ought to alarm him, but all he could do was revel in it.

A soft gasp of pleasure escaped Morainn when Tormand's hand slid down from her neck and lightly stroked her breast. Until he touched the hard tip of her breast with his finger she would never have believed they could ache any more than they already did, but now the ache was so deep and fierce it was almost painful. He began to torment her other breast in the same manner, stroking and gently pinching the tips with his long, clever fingers as he spread kisses all round. She arched into his touch, needing more but not sure how to ask, or even what that more was. Then he took one aching tip deep into the moist heat of his mouth and suckled her and she knew.

Morainn felt a wildness seize her. She tried to touch Tormand everywhere, tried to pull him closer and rubbed her body against his in a way that the still sane part of her mind knew revealed her desperate need. The hard proof of his desire rubbed against her womanhood and she was soon aching there as well. Then, suddenly, his hand was there. Morainn flinched once in shock over such a deeply intimate touch, but her shock died quickly beneath the waves of delight caused by his caress. By the time he slid one long finger inside of her she did not care what he did so long as it eased the hunger that was nearly tearing her apart.

Tormand groaned at the feel of her wet heat surrounding his finger and knew he could wait no longer to possess her. Every soft cry of pleasure Morainn made, every inviting shift of her lithe body against his, snapped one more thread of the control he fought for. He knew he could easily spill his seed on the linen if he did not take her soon and that was an embarrassment he did not want to suffer. Moving his hand to her soft thigh, he settled himself between her thighs and slowly began to enter her, sweat sliding down his back at the effort it took to move as gently as he felt she needed him to.

When Morainn felt something a great deal larger than a finger start to push its way inside of her, she tensed despite all of her efforts not to. Her mind was suddenly crowded with every horror story women had told her about bedding a man, especially for the first time, and as a midwife helping with the results of those beddings she had heard a lot. Common sense told her that it could not be as bad as those tales implied or so many women would not do it repeatedly. As she felt herself stretched to accommodate Tormand's invasion of her body, however, the voice of common sense began to be drowned out by the voice of fear.

"Hush, bonnie Morainn, my own," Tormand whispered against her mouth as he felt her tense. "Hold fast and kiss me, sweet. Dinnae think of anything but how good we feel together."

She did and the searing heat of his kiss began to burn away her fear.

"Now, wrap those beautiful legs around me. Ah, *Jesu*, aye. That is the way. Ah, 'tis as I thought. This will be your first time with a mon."

There was a tone to his voice that slipped through the fog of the desire clouding her mind. It sounded very much like male pride and satisfaction, the voice of a conqueror. Morainn had a sudden ridiculous image of him strutting around like a proud rooster among the hens. Her wild thoughts abruptly ended when he suddenly pushed hard inside of her and a sharp pain cooled the heat in her blood like a bucket of icy water.

"Hush, loving," he whispered as he brushed his mouth over hers when she cried out in pain. "It will pass."

"How can ye ken that for sure?" she asked, both concerned by the stinging pain and fascinated by the way their bodies were joined. "Have ye bedded a lot of virgins?"

The very last thing Tormand wanted to talk about when he was finally seated deep inside a woman he had craved for what felt like years was the other women he had known. Then he recalled his vow to be truthful with her no matter how uncomfortable it might be. He knew it was the only way he could gain her trust and he had to accept that her trust was very important to him. Some would say he already had her trust or they would not be naked together, but Tormand knew passion could push aside a lot of doubts and concerns, if only for a little while.

"Nay," he replied as he gently stroked her body, trying to restore the desire that had warmed him before he had ended her innocence. "I ne'er took a woman's innocence before. Ye are my first."

Morainn badly wanted to ask him why he had suddenly broken his own rules, but the fog of desire was filling her head again. As his kisses and caresses reawakened that wildness inside of her, she clutched his body tight against hers and began to shift against him in need. She knew he could give her what her body was again crying out for. When he drew away, she cried out in protest and then he pushed back inside of her and she cried out again in delight. This was what she needed. This was what her dreams had promised her.

Tormand tried hard to keep his movements slow and gentle, not wishing to hurt her any more than he already had, but Morainn was having none of it. She clung to him and began to meet his thrusts and parry them with a greed that he could not resist. Groaning as he succumbed to his need, he began to drive them both toward the release they needed so badly without worrying anymore about how tender she might be after her breeching.

When her body tightened around his and he felt her inner heat clench rhythmically around him, he cried out from the force of his own release as he drove home one last time. The laugh that escaped him when she drummed her small heels on his back as her release tore through her was a sound of pure exultance. The way her body greedily accepted his seed robbed him of all thought and strength and as the last shudder of his release went through him he collapsed upon her. He retained just enough of his senses to fall slightly to the side so that he did not crush her.

Awareness came to Tormand slowly, and he eased himself off the soft body sprawled beneath him. Morainn lay on her back, her arms falling to her side as he rose and dislodged their limp grasp on him. She looked asleep and a closer inspection revealed that she was. He grinned as he climbed out of bed and fetched a cool damp cloth to clean them both off. When she just scowled in her sleep as he washed her clean of all signs of her lost innocence and their lovemaking he had to bite his lip to keep from laughing aloud. Then he yawned, tossed the cloth aside and crawled back into bed. Tugging her warm body up against his, Tormand decided that a short rest was a good idea. Neither of them had been getting the sleep they needed.

A scream shattered his sleep and Tormand bolted upright in his bed. He was just reaching for his sword when he realized there was someone in the bed with him and that someone was thrashing and moaning. A heartbeat later his sleep-dulled mind cleared enough for him to remember what had happened before he had closed his eyes for a short rest. He turned to reach for Morainn even as his door was kicked open. Ignoring the men who rushed into his bedchamber, Tormand turned all of his attention to pulling Morainn free of her nightmare.

Hastily pulling the blanket up around Morainn even as he struggled to still her thrashing, Tormand called to her, "Morainn! 'Tis but a dream. Wake, lass. Wake up now. Come, open your eyes." At the sound of his voice she ceased fighting his hold enough that he was able to gently shake her and speak quietly to her until her eyes opened.

Morainn stared at Tormand for several moments before she realized he was not part of some dream. She still shook from the terror of what she had seen and pressed herself up against him, seeking his warmth. Just as she was beginning to breathe a little easier, she felt someone watching her and her fear returned. She instinctively reached for the knife under her pillow only to realize that she was not in her own bed.

A candle was lit and Morainn looked around. All the Murrays and Simon were standing around the bed in various states of undress. Walter lurked in the doorway and a frightened Walin clung to the man's leg. They were all looking at her in bed with Tormand, naked. Morainn almost wished it was the enemy in her dream she faced. It would be dangerous, but at least she would not feel so painfully embarrassed. Then she recalled what she had been dreaming about and hastily shook aside her humiliation. What she had seen in her dream was of far more importance than her shame over being caught in bed with Tormand.

"She hasnae buried her husband," Morainn said, shivering as she saw the sight of the bloody, mutilated man hanging from chains. "She has only just finished killing him. I had thought she already had, but nay, she just considered him as good as dead. He is dead now."

"Did ye get a name?" asked Simon.

"Only part of it. Edward. She called him Fat Edward and in the vision I saw him hanging in chains and he is verra fat. Or was." Morainn closed her eyes as she struggled to hold the horrible image of the dead man in her mind's eye. "Red hair and nay a pretty red, either. Freckles everywhere." She shivered again and Tormand pulled her a little closer to him. "I am nay sure what he may have done to her, but I get no sense of true cruelty or evil in the mon. Yet, she killed him verra slowly and he suffered in great pain for a verra long time."

"Did ye see where? Did ye see anything that might

tell ye where and when this may have happened? I ken several men named Edward and none of them are small men. If I had a hint of where the body is, it could save me a great deal of searching."

"All I saw was the room where he was hanging in chains. A dungeon, I think, for it was all damp stone and the light flickered as though it was coming only from a fire or torches." She rubbed at her forehead, hating the need to try to remember clearly such a bloody dream, but she tried and then tensed. "A large door with a snarling dog, nay, wolf on it."

"I ken where that is. 'Tis where Edward MacLean lives. He calls his home Wolf Hallow. 'Tis but a short ride north of town."

"This time I am coming with ye," shouted Tormand, as the men ran out of the room, Walter hastily taking Walin back to his bed.

When Tormand leapt out of bed, Morainn flopped back down onto the soft feather mattress and groaned. He turned to frown at her in concern, studying her carefully even as he continued to get dressed. She was looking a little pale, but he could see no sign that she had suffered with this dream as badly as she had suffered with her visions.

"Are ye weel, Morainn?" he asked.

Morainn groaned again and pulled the blanket over her head. "I have just been found in your bed by everyone in this house, even Walin. And I was found here naked."

He forced himself to bite back an urge to laugh. "I got the blanket around ye before they saw anything."

She sat up and glared at him. "They saw me." Then

she paled and put a hand over her mouth. "And how can I be so cold of heart, so verra selfish? There is some poor mon hanging dead in his own home, a mon who suffered all the torments of hell at the hands of his own wife and I am fretting because your friends and family now ken that I have shared your bed."

Tormand sat down on the bed, pulled her into his arms and stroked her back. "Ye arenae cold or selfish. This has all happened so quickly, ye have had no time to e'en think it all through. One moment ye are having a nightmare and the next ye are sitting in bed with six half-dressed and weel-armed men standing around. And ye cannae take on the weight of these murders, loving. It will crush ye. As for those fools seeing ye in my bed, dinnae fret over it. And Walin? His only interest was to see that ye were nay hurt." He gave her a kiss and then got up to finish dressing and arming himself.

"Mayhap ye shouldnae go," she said quietly. "What if it is a trap or the ones who think ye guilty are out there and looking for a fight?"

"I will be with five armed men who have blooded themselves in battle. I will be fine." He gave her another kiss and ran out the door, calling back, "Walter will stay here to watch over ye and Walin."

Morainn cursed and fell back in the bed again. At least while the men were gone she would have time alone to conquer her embarrassment. Discovery had been inevitable, she told herself. It would have been impossible to keep the fact that she was sharing a bed with Tormand a secret in such a crowded house. She prayed Walin was too young to understand fully what her place in Tormand's bed meant and she really did not wish to answer questions posed by a curious little boy.

She leapt out of bed, snuffed the candle someone had lit, and then collected up her clothing, donning her shift for modesty's sake. There were still a few hours before dawn and she needed to get some sleep. Holding her clothes against her chest, she slipped out of Tormand's room and went back to her own. Morainn suspected Tormand expected her to stay in his bed, but she would not do so until he said so plainly.

Once huddled beneath the covers of her bed with her cats curled all around her she began to feel calmer, certain that she would be able to go back to sleep. The sound of Walter's distinct tread only added to her growing sense of calm, for she knew, just as Tormand had told her, she and Walin had not been left unprotected. There were a few things she had seen in her dream that she had not had time to tell the men, but there would be time on the morrow. Telling them that the evil woman had smiled at her in the dream as Morainn had screamed would only worry them.

"That is a sight I could have happily lived a long life without ever seeing," murmured Harcourt.

Tormand was pleased to see that his cousin was looking a little pale. The remains of poor Edward MacLean had caused his own stomach to revolt strongly and he had only barely controlled the urge to empty his belly on the bloodstained floor of the dungeon. The smell of blood and death was so strong they were enough to gag a man. The killers must have tortured Edward for a very long time. The once very large man was only a shadow of the food-loving man he had once been. They had nearly skinned the man alive, broken all his fingers and toes, and castrated him. Tormand was sure there were other injuries, but the man was so filthy and so covered in blood he could not see what they might be and did not want to. He also suspected it was mostly the castration of the man that had drained all the blood from their faces and left them all so pale.

"I cannae think of anything this mon may have done to his wife that would have earned him this death," said Simon, as he began his ritual of carefully searching the area around the dangling body of Edward. "He was an irritant, boastful, somewhat of a pig, and none too bright, but I ne'er saw him lift a heavy hand to anyone or e'en speak unkindly about anyone. He was, in truth, quite jovial in the manner of a not particularly intelligent fellow who found his own humor very amusing."

"Did ye e'er meet his wife?" asked Tormand.

"Once," replied Simon. "A shadow of a woman, quiet and easily forgotten. I would ne'er have thought her capable of such brutality."

"Mayhap that is how she has gotten away with it for so long."

"But where were his people?" asked Rory. "With a house of this size there should be a maid or two, a cook, and such as that. No one came to the door and I saw no one as we made our way down here."

"She could have sent them away," said Simon. "E'en if she didnae do it right away, I doubt anyone would have heard the poor man down here. I think she and her hulking great companion are also long gone."

"Aye, they are too cunning to stay so close to a murder. She would ken that, as soon as we saw Edward, we could guess who she is. Do ye ken her name, Simon?"

"Nay. As I said—she was utterly forgettable. I will find someone who kens who she is though."

"And then what?"

"First I will see if she has any kin near at hand or, more important, any kin that have recently been murdered. As soon as I gather as much information as I can on this mon's wife, we return to our hunting. What I am truly hoping for is that someone can give us a good description of who her large companion might be."

"The huge shadow that can move about silently in the darkness and disappear like mist on a sunny morning?" asked Harcourt.

"Aye, that one." Simon started to walk out of the dungeon. "He cannae have remained in the shadows all of his life. Someone has had to have seen him. Let us search the rest of this house and see if we can find anything that will help us."

"What about that poor old fool Edward? Do we just leave him hanging there?"

"For now."

After several hours of fruitless searching, Tormand rode beside Simon as they headed back home. It bothered him to leave poor Edward MacLean hanging in the dungeon, but Simon wanted to come back with a few of his men and deal with the body then. He hoped Simon gave the men some warning of what they were about to see before they went down those dark steps into that blood-soaked room of torture and death. Tormand had hoped they would find some trail to follow, but he was getting used to disappointment in this hunt. If the mad pair they hunted suffered from a blood lust of some sort, he hoped it was well fed for now.

"So ye have seduced Morainn," said Simon.

Abruptly dragged from his dark thoughts, Tormand needed a moment to comprehend what Simon had just said and he sighed. "Leave it be, Simon. I will but say that she is nay just another warm body to me. Let that be enough."

"Are ye planning to marry the lass?"

"I dinnae ken. I dinnae ken what I feel for her or want from her. Weel, save for the fact that she makes my blood run hotter than any woman ever has. I could nay more keep away from her than I could cease breathing. 'Tis that simple and that complicated. Deciding what will happen next is hard when, for all I ken, I may yet be dragged up on the gallows."

"Oh, nay, we willnae let that happen."

He looked closely at his friend. "Did ye find something that makes ye believe we will soon capture these bastards?"

"I ken who she is now, dinnae I? It will help. It is also far more than we have had erenow. She may have been nay more than a wee shadow to me the one time I met her, but there has to be someone out there who kens who she is and what she looks like. I wager there is someone who also kens who her huge companion is. As I said, a mon as big as this one appears to be cannae walk around unnoticed, no matter how weel he can slip about in the shadows."

"I had hoped for more."

"To catch them with the bloodied knives in their hands?"

"Aye, and to end this. I need to end this and nay just because they are killing women, for all that makes me sound like a hard bastard. I just cannae shake the feeling that I am soon to be running and hiding like James was."

"Nay, we would never let ye suffer like that for three years."

Tormand nodded, then realized that Simon had not given him any assurances that he would not find himself running and hiding soon. He turned to ask his friend about that only to find Simon riding beside Harcourt. Tormand softly cursed and then told himself that running and hiding for a short while was still far better than hanging for crimes he had not committed. He hoped he could make himself believe that, when and if the time came that he had to use the bolt-hole Simon had already found for him.

Chapter 13

"There be a mon here to see ye, Sir Simon," said Walter, as he stood in the doorway of the great hall looking uneasy and his hand on his sword. "He isnae looking verra weel. I think it be bad news."

Morainn felt her heart skip with alarm. She glanced around at the men and saw that they shared her fear. They just expressed it by scowling at the door. Unable to stop herself she reached out to clasp Tormand's hand in hers and had the sinking feeling that it was a good thing Walin had already had his meal and gone to bed. She thought about how they had all gathered together to discuss what else she had seen in her dream two nights ago, the warning of yet another senseless death soon to come. The men had been trying to find something, anything, that would tell them who it might be ever since she had told them, but had had no luck. They had failed to find any sign or gather any useful information about the late Edward MacLean's wife and companion as well. Bad news now could mean that they were too late to halt yet another gruesome murder.

Morainn heartily cursed her visions for giving her only a confused array of the smallest bits of information and never quite enough to put a swift stop to the murders.

"Best show him in then, Walter," said Tormand.

The moment the man stepped into the great hall, Tormand silently cursed. It was the plump, genial Sir John Hay. Tormand felt both grief and a blind rage fill him for the look on the man's face told him that poor Lady Katherine had been the victim in the murder they had tried so hard to stop.

Sir John started toward them, but when he swayed, Tormand rushed to his side to steady him. "Easy, John," he murmured as he led the man to a seat at the table where a full tankard of strong wine already waited for him.

After a long drink that did little to steady the shaking in the man's hands, Sir John announced, "My Kat has been cruelly murdered, just like those other women were. My poor angel is dead."

When the man began to weep, all the other men just stared at him, concern mixed with discomfort on their faces. Morainn did not wait for them to get over that discomfort. She hurried to the man's side and put her arms around him. As she whispered soothing words, he sobbed against her chest for several moments before he was able to regain control of himself. When he finally sat up, she handed him a square of linen to wipe his face with and smiled gently at him in the hope of easing the embarrassment he so obviously felt despite his deep grief.

"Ye are the one they call the witch, arenae ye?" he said in a voice still hoarse from his weeping. "They say ye are trying to help find the bastards who are doing the killing."

"I am trying to, sir," she said, "as are all of these good men." Feeling that the man had control of himself now, Morainn returned to her seat by Tormand's side.

"Please, if ye can, tell what ye may ken or what ye saw, nay matter how little ye may think it is worth," said Simon.

Sir John took a deep breath. "I was late returning home from my cousin's. Kat had had too much to do to go with me. I left young Geordie MacBain there to watch over her. Found him on the ground just below the bedchamber window with his neck broken. And, my Kat, she," he shuddered and his eyes glazed with grief and pain, "I think she had been dead for a while, but I was too sick at the sight of what had been done to her that I cannae say for certain." He looked at Simon. "I recalled ye complaining in the past about people nay leaving things as they were when they first discovered some crime, so I left my angel there when I came looking for ye. I but pulled a blanket over her. I couldnae help myself. She was naked, ye ken, and I didnae want her seen that way. She wouldnae have wanted to be seen that way."

As Simon gently asked a few questions, pausing when Sir John needed a moment to compose himself, Morainn studied the men. It had taken her awhile to gather the courage to face them after having been caught in Tormand's bed, but the need to tell them the whole of the dream, especially about the warning of another murder being planned, had given her the strength. Not one of them had looked at her with contempt or even mentioned where they had last seen her. Everything had been just as it had been before. Nor did they say anything about where she had spent the nights since—wrapped securely in Tormand's arms. Even Walin had said nothing and she wondered if the men had seen to it that he did not pester her about the matter. She would have put up with any and all embarrassment and humiliation, however, if she could have stopped this murder.

She could see the sorrow for the death of Sir John's wife in their expressions. She also saw disappointment over the fact that they had not been able to prevent it despite many hours spent talking about the dream and searching the town for the killers or anyone who might know who they were. It was evident that they thought they had failed the dead woman, failed the grieving Sir John, and Morainn doubted anything she could say would ease that guilt they felt.

Morainn turned her attention to Tormand. He was grieving and she felt an all too familiar pinch of jealousy, but pushed it aside. She had once met Lady Katherine, shortly after Walin had been left at her door, and had found the older woman to be a kind and generous soul. The woman had been honestly upset when she had not been able to find out who Walin's father or mother was. The few things she had heard about the woman since then had all implied that she was indeed a generous soul, a woman ready to help anyone who needed it. Morainn also did not recall seeing Lady Katherine's name on Tormand's list and she knew he had been ruthlessly honest in compiling it. This time the monsters had killed a completely innocent woman.

She knew the others had not deserved what had happened to them, either, but poor Lady Katherine had not even committed the sin the killer felt the others had to pay for.

When the men all stood up to return with Sir John to his home, Tormand moved to join them. Sir John suddenly turned and grabbed Tormand by the arm. "Nay, my friend," he said.

Tormand looked so hurt that Morainn moved to his side, taking his clenched fist in her hands as Tormand asked, "Ye cannae think I had anything to do with this, John."

"Och, nay, laddie. Ne'er. And I havenae believed for one blessed moment that ye hurt those other women, either. I ask ye to stay here because an angry crowd was gathering in front of my home when I left to come here. Word had already reached them about my Kat's death. One of the maids most likely, as I didnae do anything to calm them or keep them in my home.

"The crowd wants someone punished for these murders and, from what little I heard said, they think that someone should be ye. Let Simon do what he is so good at while ye remain here, safe behind these walls. I fear that, with the mood the crowd is in, ye could be in verra grave danger if ye came with us."

"As ye wish," Tormand said in a tight voice. "I offer my deepest condolences, John."

"Thank ye, lad. I ken they are heartfelt. But I would like it more," Sir John replied, including Morainn in the suddenly fierce look he gave Tormand, "if ye would find the bastard who did this. I want to see him dancing at the end of a rope and then I shall spit upon his grave. Get him for me, Tormand."

"I will. I swear it."

The moment the men were gone, Tormand sat down at the table, put his head in his hands, and gave into his grief. Morainn sat by his side, wrapped her arms around him, and held him as close to her as she could. The sadness in the great hall, that which Sir John had left behind and that which Tormand felt so weighted down with, filled the air and Morainn was not surprised to feel her own eyes sting with tears.

This killing made no sense, despite knowing that they dealt with insanity, and that deeply troubled Morainn. She also felt a growing sense of dread. This could be the murder that turned all those whispers snaking through town about Tormand's possible guilt, into shouts and demands for retribution. She held him a little tighter in her arms and reminded herself that Simon had found them a bolt-hole if that should happen.

Simon entered the great hall of the Hays' elegant home and saw Sir John standing by the surprisingly large window, staring out at the street in front of his home. The large, damp square of linen the man clutched tightly in his hand told Simon that Sir John had been weeping again and he felt a surge of pity for the man who had adored his wife. This time Simon felt not only a need for justice, a need to end the senseless killings and punish the ones committing them, but also a deep need for revenge. Lady Katherine had been a good woman, one who had been kind and generous to a fault. Sir John was the same and a very good friend. This heartless murder had made the hunt for the killers very personal. He stepped up behind Sir John and placed a hand on the man's shoulder even though he knew there would be no way truly to comfort his friend.

"I am done now, John," he said quietly. "Old Mary and Young Mary have gone to your wife. They said they will prepare her."

"I should help them," John said, but he made no move to leave his place by the window.

"Nay, my friend. Let the women tend to her. Ye dinnae need to see that again."

"'Tis a sight I will never be able to banish from my mind, Simon."

"Try to dull its sting with memories of all that was good in your marriage."

"Aye, I will. Some day." Sir John frowned as he continued to study the crowd. "The crowd grows larger and its tone grows uglier. There are a lot of people who think Tormand is the killer and they speak their opinions loudly and quite often. My Kat was weel loved for her generous heart and aid to the poor. These people have lost a gracious friend and they want someone to pay dearly for that."

"Ye mean they want Tormand to pay."

Sir John slowly nodded. "Him and the Ross witch as they call the poor lass. Get them away from here."

"Tormand?" Simon studied the crowd. "Ye think the danger to him has become that great?"

"Aye, I do. To him and to that bonnie wee lass. It was all whispering to start with and then it became talking openly of the suspicions so many held, and now this.

Ere I left for my cousin's, my Kat expressed concern for his safety and she kenned far more about the townspeople than I ever did. I think there is also someone behind them, prodding them all on. Mayhap even the killers. Aye, get him and that bonnie lass away to someplace safe."

"He willnae like it."

"At least he will be alive to complain about it. And, I think I would do it now. There are a few in that angry mob suggesting they all go and find the killer and hang him and we both ken that Tormand is the mon they most suspect. I assume ye already have a bolt-hole readied for him."

"I do," Simon said, even as he started to stride away.

"Get them out of here. Aye, e'en if ye have to bind and gag that fool Tormand to do so."

"They will be gone within the hour."

Morainn frowned and lightly placed her hand over Tormand's mouth. They had been talking about Lady Katherine. She knew it helped him deal with his grief for the loss of a good friend. And that was all the woman was, Morainn thought. She had not needed long to decide that. Tormand spoke of Lady Katherine as if she were some dear aunt or cousin, not as a man would speak of a lover he still had a fondness for.

"Did ye hear that?" she asked.

"Hear what?"

Tormand lightly licked her palm and then grinned when she both flushed with a hint of pleasure and squeaked as she tugged her hand away. There was an ache in his heart for his old friend Lady Katherine, but he suddenly had an idea of how he might soothe it just a little. Morainn's passion had warmed his nights and he was always hungry for her. There was also the wish to avoid the men when they returned with news of Lady Katherine's murder. He knew what they had seen and he knew that, at best, there would just be another hairpin. No trail, no witnesses. They were getting closer but, sadly, not close enough to save poor Kat. He wanted to wash the bitter tastes of grief and defeat from his mouth with the hot, sweet taste of Morainn. He was just about to pull her onto his lap when he heard a noise and Morainn started toward the window.

"Ye must have heard that," she said.

"Aye, I did," he said, as he hurried to the window and gently but firmly put his body in front of hers. "I think someone is coming to visit us and not to offer condolences on the loss of a good friend."

Even as he spoke she heard a sound that was chillingly familiar. It was the sound of a crowd full of anger and eager to do something to the ones they were angry with. When they had come after her mother it had been fear that had driven them, but she knew the results would be the same. Her mind filled with memories of the horrible day they had come and taken her mother; their fear, and the anger and hatred it filled them with, driving them to kill her. Morainn had barely escaped with her own life that night and by the time the sun had come up she had found herself with no kin and driven out of her home into the woods. Once calmed, their blood thirst slaked by the death of her mother, the ones who had caught her at her home in the early hours of dawn had simply driven her off like a stray dog and warned her never to return.

She started shaking, possessed by all the fear and grief the young girl she had been had suffered. Tormand put his arm around her shoulders and held her close to him. His warmth and unspoken concern helped her regain some control over the fear that was swamping her.

"Dinnae be afraid, Morainn," he said quietly and kissed her cheek. "They willnae get us."

"Nay, they willnae."

Tormand jumped in surprise and felt Morainn do the same as Simon suddenly appeared at their side. "*Jesu*, Simon," he muttered. "I think we need to put a bell on ye. How did ye get in without us seeing ye? We have been looking out the window and should have seen ye ride up."

"There is more than one way to get into your house, Tormand." Glancing out the window, Simon then looked at Tormand. "Ye have to leave here. Now."

Tormand eyed the small crowd beginning to gather in front of his home. "There arenae verra many of them."

"There will soon be a lot more."

"Weel, with my kin and mayhap a few of your men, we could—"

"Fight them? I really dinnae wish to kill off a lot of the townspeople, idiots though they are right now. This time it is far more than whispers of suspicion, mayhap a few threats and insults, Tormand. Katherine was weel loved and these people are thirsting for blood—yours." He nodded at Morainn. "And hers."

"Morainn? Why should they be calling for her

blood? No one thinks she is the killer, unless there is something ye havenae told me."

"They want me because I am the Ross witch. Just as they wanted my mother," she whispered.

Simon cursed softly. "They want ye because they think ye are helping him either to kill these women or to keep him from hanging for what he has done."

"Of course," she muttered. "It doesnae matter that I ne'er e'en saw him until after the second murder."

"Magda is behind this."

"Weel, she certainly hasnae helped, but I dinnae think she is the one driving this crowd up the street. Now, pack what ye think ye will need for a wee stay in the hiding place I am about to take ye to." Seeing the taut, stubborn look on Tormand's face, Simon knew an argument was coming and there was no time for one. "Sir John also said ye must leave. Ye and Morainn. He said Katherine had warned him about the mood of the people and that she thought it was being poisoned by others."

"The killers?" asked Morainn.

"Mayhap, but it could be any fool with a way to stir up other fools. I—"

Whatever Simon was about to say was lost as a rock sailed through the window they all stood in front of. Tormand shielded Morainn with his body and winced as shards of glass pricked his skin through his shirt. A quick glance out the hole the rock had made in his expensive glass window, and Tormand could see that there would be even more rocks and the crowd would follow them into his house soon.

"Go." He pushed Morainn toward the door. "Grab a few things and then we leave."

"Walin," she began, as she stumbled toward the door.

"Will be safer here with my kin, Simon, and Walter. Hurry," he ordered.

The moment she was gone, Tormand looked at Simon. "Can ye get us out of here?"

"Aye. I can hear your brothers and cousins arriving. Get yourself a few things and then I will take ye to the hiding place I have found. As we flee here, your brothers will face the crowd and try to drive them back to their homes."

Cursing viciously, Tormand ran to his bedchamber and stuffed a few clothes into a bag. He donned his sword and tucked his sheathed knives wherever he could. Although he ached to stand his ground he knew that was pride talking. There was little a man could do against a crowd determined to see him dead. Even four armed Murrays would not be enough to hold the crowd back for long. There was also Morainn to consider. He could not keep her safe here any longer.

Even as they slipped out of the house through a back way where three horses waited for them, saddled and packed with supplies, Tormand could hear his kinsmen yelling at the crowd. He prayed they would not be injured in the bid to give him and Morainn a chance to escape. Simon looked as though he wanted to go join them, sword in hand, but he silently led them through the darkening streets away from the danger.

Simon took them on a long and winding route through the town and out on the west road. Tormand kept a close watch on Morainn, and not because she was not an experienced rider. An angry crowd was frightening, especially when you were the one they were after, but she still looked terrified no matter how much distance they put between them and that crowd. He suddenly recalled her whispering something about her mother and winced. It had been an angry crowd that had made her an orphan and then an outcast. He did not even want to think of the dark memories this had to be stirring up in her mind.

He was just about to ask Simon exactly how far away he was taking them, when a ruined tower house came into view. Tormand frowned as they rode closer, for it looked as though there would be no protection from the weather in such a ruin. Although he had lived rough a time or two he was not fond of doing so, but most of his concern was for Morainn. It was not until they halted and he dismounted that he realized that some very subtle repairs had been made.

"This is it," said Simon, as Tormand helped Morainn out of the saddle.

"Rough," Tormand murmured as he slipped an arm around Morainn's shoulders, politely ignoring the fact that she was unsteady after what many would consider a short ride.

"A wee bit, but nay as bad as it looks. Come inside."

Feeling that Morainn was steadier, Tormand took her by the hand and followed Simon. At first it looked just as great a ruin inside as it did on the outside, but then they turned a corner and Tormand silently sighed in relief. Behind the thick door Simon opened was a sizable living space divided into a cooking area, a sleeping area, and even a tall wooden screen blocking one corner that he assumed was where they could be private if either of them needed to be. A wide bed was up against one wall and there were kegs of drink and other supplies stacked against another. Tormand was both pleased and dismayed. He welcomed the attempt to make his retreat comfortable, but it also looked a little too much like a gentle prison where he would have to hide for a long time.

Morainn wandered around the wide room, astonished by how clean and well supplied it was. After pressing her hand briefly on the bed, she realized there was even a feather mattress. Tormand and she would be hiding away like outlaws, but they would do so comfortably.

"When did ye arrange this?" she asked Simon, as she set her small bag of belongings down next to a chest at the foot of the bed.

"I began preparing it the moment I heard the first whisper of blame placed at Tormand's feet. I have seen too many innocent men die because a judgment of guilt was made too quickly." He shrugged. "Wherever I am, I make certain I ken where there are hiding places, places where one can wait safely until the truth is found and they can return home without fear. Although, some have returned home only to pack up and leave, for they cannae bear living among those who would think so poorly of them, would be willing to see them die for crimes they had not committed."

"One's peace and trust are all gone," said Morainn. "Ye can never fully shake the fear that those people will turn against ye again and the next time ye willnae be able to escape."

"Exactly. Now, I shall take the horses to a safe place not far from here. The small crofter's hut where the dogs made so much noise?" He looked at Tormand.

"Aye, I recall it. They hushed quickly. Do ye think the ones who live there can be trusted to hold fast to a secret?" Tormand asked.

"Oh, aye," Simon replied, conviction heavy in his voice. "They have a son in my service and think I am a great mon for giving the lad such a fine chance to better himself." He smiled faintly. "They dinnae heed me when I tell them I gave their son a place in my service because he is big, skilled with a blade, and verra clever."

"I suspect there are far too many poor lads who are much akin to him and yet ne'er get a chance to live any other way but the hard life in a wee crofter's hut."

"Mayhap. But this one saved my life."

"A coin or two would have been thanks enough in many people's eyes." Tormand looked around the room. "This is a good place to hide. I but pray we willnae be hiding here for too long. How are we to let ye ken if Morainn sees anything of importance in her dreams or has some vision?"

"I will be returning to my own wee home at the edge of town. I believe ye can slip in and out of it with little danger of being caught."

"Who will care for Walin?" Morainn asked. "I slipped into his room to tell him I would be leaving for a wee while, but, in truth, I am nay sure he was fully awake e'en though he answered me. I just need to ken that he will be safe."

"He will be watched as carefully as he has been all the while ye have been at Tormand's house," said Simon. "If that proves unwise, we will bring him to my home. May do so anyway, although I dinnae have the room to house all those hulking Murrays as Tormand does. Dinnae worry over the boy, Morainn. He will be fine. In truth, without ye around, I dinnae think anyone will give him a thought save us, not e'en the killers." He looked back at Tormand. "I would like ye to make a list of all the women ye are friendly with. There is quill, ink, and something to write on in that small chest." He pointed to a plain little box set near a table and chair in a far corner of the room.

"Ye think Kat was killed because of me?" asked Tormand, fearing that himself, and not liking the fact that Simon had also considered the possibility. He had just begun to convince himself that her friendship with him could not have been the cause of her death. "I would have thought everyone would ken she was ne'er my lover."

"I dinnae ken, Tormand. 'Tis possible but, coming so close on the heels of finding out that those murderers had killed Edward MacLean, I have to wonder if there was some other reason they went after poor Kat. Something that has nothing to do with ye. I am going to look into some of Kat's dealings and see if there is something there that may explain this. Howbeit, a list would help me if only so I could warn any of the women who are near at hand."

Morainn watched the two men wander off after Simon said a polite farewell to her and reassured her that Walin would be cared for. She then turned her attention to unpacking the things she and Tormand had brought with them. The hiding place Simon had made for them was far better than what she had expected, but she heartily wished it had not been necessary to use it.

As soon as she finished the chore of unpacking, she stepped behind the privacy screen to wash up and prepare for bed. The fright at Tormand's house and her first lengthy ride on a horse had left her aching and tired. She had never contemplated all the danger she might put herself in when she had first helped Tormand and Simon, but she knew she would not have changed her course even if she had.

At least she was not alone, she thought as she heard Tormand return. She had been through just such a fright ten years ago and never wished to suffer through another time of being alone and frightened, expecting death around every corner. As she stepped out from behind the screen, she smiled at Tormand, who stood there wearing only his braies and holding out a small tankard of wine for her.

"I am sorry ye have been dragged into this," he said.

"Nay, dinnae be sorry," she said, and lightly kissed his cheek. "It has done me good to use my gift in this way. S'truth, I can now actually call it a gift without wincing. I just wish it had been of more help. Do ye think that is why Simon hasnae had me hold another hairpin?"

"I think that if ye hadnae had that dream about poor Edward MacLean, Simon may weel have had ye try to have another vision. Now, however, he has a trail to follow and he will do it in his usual way. If he finds that isnae working fast enough, he may weel have ye hold another."

"He is verra precise in gathering information, and so much of it."

"As he said, he has seen too many innocent men die. Simon has a verra strong sense of justice and, if naught else, he is deeply offended when the wrong person is made to pay for a crime. That means the guilty one gets away, doesnae it?"

"Ah, aye, I suppose it does. Ye dinnae like this, do ye? This hiding bothers you."

Taking her empty cup from her hand, he began to lead her to the bed. "It does. Pride is all it is. And, right now, listening to the voice of pride could get me hanged. I just have a fear that I may end up suffering as my brother James did." Seeing her curiosity, he told her all about James's trials as a man falsely accused of killing his wife, even as he pushed her down onto the bed and settled himself in her arms.

"I dinnae think ye will be here for three long years, Tormand."

"Nay? Is that a prophecy or just a hope?"

"It is a verra strong feeling that this will soon end, that those monsters who are taking such delight in murdering people will soon be found and punished."

"I believe I will accept it as a prophecy." He tugged her nightgown over her head and tossed it aside, enjoying the blush that covered her face. "I will also count my blessings."

"Which are?"

"I have a comfortable place to hide and a soft woman sharing it with me. Two things my poor brother didnae have."

"Lucky you."

"Verra lucky me," he murmured, as he shed his clothes and returned to her welcoming arms. "Verra lucky me, indeed."

Morainn was just about to tell him that she was not just another soft woman like so many others he had known, when he kissed her, smothering her scolding words. She was soon swept up in the passion he could so easily stir inside of her and forgot her complaint. The heat of desire burned away all the dark memories the sight of an angry crowd had brought into her mind. His lovemaking soothed her fears, desire pushing it away as her body and heart gave itself over to the magic of his kisses and caresses.

Sated and drowsy, Tormand held Morainn close to his side. She had fallen asleep right after their lovemaking had ended in sweet satisfaction for both of them. The fact that he still hungered for her, that that hunger grew instead of diminished, told him a lot about how he felt about her; he was just not sure he wanted to listen.

Once the killers were caught and hanged, he would look more closely at what he felt and needed from Morainn, he promised himself. There was time after their troubles were over to delve into such things as emotions and needs. He closed his eyes and smiled a little. For now he would just enjoy the bone-deep pleasure he found in her arms and savor the feeling of having his every need and hunger satisfied as they had never been satisfied before. It was the one thing that would make hiding from his enemies instead of fighting them more a gift than a penance.

Chapter 14

Tormand bolted upright in bed as a scream shattered the peace of the night. A small foot kicked him hard in the leg and he turned toward Morainn. She was thrashing around on the bed as if she was fighting someone, or someone was hurting her. As he reached for her, tensed for the battle he was about to enter, Tormand thought of yet another reason they had to catch the murderers as quickly as possible. Morainn needed a peaceful night's sleep, one where nightmares did not have her seeing butchered women or fighting unseen demons in her dreams. He hated to see her so tormented. She should be doing no more at night than making love to him or sleeping sweetly in his arms.

"Wake now, loving," he said, as he tried to wrestle her down onto the bed and pin her there with his body before she hurt herself or him. "'Tis naught but a dream, Morainn. Only a dream. No one is hurting ye. No need is there to fight. Come back to me, sweet witch. Come back."

As before, the sound of his voice calmed her and she went still beneath him. Tormand eased his grip on her just a little and watched as her eyes slowly fluttered open. For a brief moment there was only confusion in her eyes, and then she recognized who held her down. Her smile was true and sweet and he felt the power of it deep in his soul. He had the fleeting thought that he would be willing to see that smile every day for the rest of his life, but quickly shook it away.

The smile did not last long. Memories of the horrors she had seen in her dream quickly leeched all the color from her skin and put the glint of fear in her eyes. It had obviously been a very bad dream this time and he moved quickly to fetch her a tankard of cool cider.

Morainn took a deep drink of the cider Tormand served her, as he crawled back into bed at her side. She supposed she should count herself lucky. Four nights had passed since she had had a dream about the killers they could not seem to catch. Unfortunately, this one had been so much worse than the last one, she had to wonder if a respite from the dreams was a good thing or not. Rest only seemed to make the dreams stronger and more frightening.

There were also things she had seen and heard in this dream that she felt it would be wise to keep to herself. Tormand was determined to protect her, to keep her safe from the ones hunting her simply because she was helping him. If he knew she had just dreamed of her own death he would probably lock her up somewhere and encircle her prison with big well-armed men. He would also put himself at risk in his attempts to keep her out of danger and that she could not allow.

"It was bad one," she said finally, giving in to the need to tell him something as he sat there so patiently watching her.

"Aye, I could see that clear enough." He put his arm around her and held her close against his side. "Ye looked as if ye were fighting pain or an enemy. Nay just thrashing about as ye did before, but actually struggling against something or someone."

She dared not look him in the eye for she was certain he would see the truth in hers. He had guessed part of what she had endured while caught in the dream all too correctly and she doubted she could fully hide the shock she felt over that. Morainn could still feel the bindings on her wrists and ankles. The only thing that kept her from curling up beneath the blanket and screaming in terror was the knowledge that her dream did not have to be an accurate foretelling. As for Tormand's insight into what she may have been dreaming about, she suspected that he gained it from living in a family that had a lot of people with gifts. At the moment she would almost prefer that he did not believe in her gift at all, even scorned her claims of dreams and visions.

"I dreamed there would be another killing verra soon," she said quietly, hoping she could tell him all the things she had seen that might help them catch those monsters, without telling him exactly who those monsters planned to kill next. She was going to have to dance around the truth very carefully or his suspicions would be raised and he would start pressing her for answers she did not wish to give him. "'Tis as though the madwoman is in a frenzy, as if she has gained a taste for blood, for the pain she can cause, for the power she wields as she decides who will live and who will die."

"Simon expressed a concern about that happening and I have to believe it might be possible. I fear the mon has seen more than his share of madness and evil, so what he says carries a lot of weight." Taking her empty tankard from her hand and setting it aside, he wrapped his other arm around her and held her close to his chest. "Such evil must be a torment for ye to see, especially in your dreams. Dreams should be of bonnie things, nay blood and death."

"Until this stops, I fear mine will all be of the latter kind. And it is a torment to see it, and e'en worse to feel it. But what troubles me most is that it seems as if this woman kens that I am there with her, seeing it all." She shivered despite being held close to his warmth. "'Tis as if she has somehow climbed into my head."

"*Jesu*, do ye think she has some gift as weel?"

"It would certainly explain why she is so elusive. I dinnae ken. Mayhap she does or mayhap my dreams themselves are pulling her in. It has ne'er happened before. I have ne'er heard voices so clearly before than I have since the dreams and visions about this murderous couple began."

"Mayhap it is the violence, the killing, that makes it so. The emotions ye speak of having felt when ye have seen something are all verra strong ones."

"True. That might explain why the dreams slowly

grow more vivid, but nay how she speaks directly to me, looks right at me, e'en gives me one of her cold, adder's smiles as she speaks her threats."

"Ye never told me the bitch had smiled right at ye in a vision."

"What does it matter? She has threatened me almost from the beginning. I did tell ye of that. The fact that she does so is of no help in finding her. I look for things or something said that will tell us where the killing will occur, who she and her huge companion are, and mayhap even some small hint of where they might be hiding or who they might try to kill next. Those are the things that are important."

She was right, but Tormand still felt somewhat stung that she had obviously hidden something from him. He sighed and tried again to push aside the fear he felt for her, but was not very successful. The attack on Morainn that had led to her being at his side had shown them that the blood-soaked pair they chased wanted her dead. It served no good purpose to keep repeating that or allowing it to prey too heavily on his mind. All he could do was keep her out of their reach and pray that was good enough.

"So, tell me, were ye shown any faces this time, or told any names, or, e'en better, shown where this next killing will happen and when?"

"Her name is Ada or Anna. Once she spoke it aloud, as if she spoke of someone else, yet it was clear that she was talking about something she had done. I think her madness worsens, although having seen what she does I cannae see how that is possible. Mayhap she is just losing control over it. 'Tis no longer a cold, icy insanity, but has become wild and unfettered. The mon is struggling harder to keep her under control.

"I did see him a wee bit more clearly this time. It was as though the shadows he has always been surrounded by slowly receded for a moment, like clouds parting just a little to let the sun shine through. He *is* verra, verra big. Tall and bulky with thick muscles. He is still just Small to her though."

"I am thinking that is but a name to distinguish him from another with the same Christian name, like Young Mary and Old Mary."

Morainn nodded, idly thinking about how good he smelled. He tasted good, too, she thought, and felt herself blush slightly. They had not been lovers for even a full sennight yet, but she was rapidly turning into a complete wanton. She was always hungry for him.

For a moment she was tempted to try to lure him away from the subject of her dream by seducing him. Then she had to swallow a laugh hastily. She was no seductress, did not have the experience or knowledge even to try to be. It was also wrong to try to divert him in such a way. They were hunting cold, brutal killers. Now was no time to play such games.

"Did ye not see anything to tell ye where the killing might take place or who the victim will be?"

"That was the odd thing," she murmured, giving in to the urge to stroke his taut stomach as she fixed her mind's eye on all she had seen in her dream. "This time there was a great deal to be seen as concerns the where. I saw sheep."

"Sheep? Dearling, Scotland is full of sheep."

"I ken it." She rubbed her fingers up and down the soft line of hair that started at his belly hole and led down to his manhood. "There were sheep huddled close to the side of a small house made of stone with a mix of slate and thatch for a roof. It was a rough place with a dirt floor and the cooking fire set in the middle of the floor and a hole in the roof to let the smoke out." Her wrists burned faintly again as she spoke of the place where her dream-self had been pinned to the floor, her arms and legs tied tightly to stakes driven into the dirt.

"A shieling mayhap, although it sounds a wee bit too large. Mayhap a crofter's cottage. There are a lot of them about, but only the ones closest to town are important. They need to stay where they can take their victims aside, murder them, and then still get them home and tucked up in their beds ere the sun rises. That would lessen the number we would need to search. And what of the victim? Did ye see anything of her?"

"Ye ken weel that I dinnae ken many people in town, and certainly none of the higher born. E'en if the dreams allowed me a verra clear view of the poor woman I probably wouldnae ken who she was. All I saw was that she wasnae a verra big woman and she had dark hair." She felt guilty about the lie and even more guilty about how easily she told it.

Tormand nodded as he tried and failed to ignore the way she was touching him. As her long, slender fingers stroked the line of hair on his lower belly, his manhood rose up hard and begging for her to stroke it. She would only have to glance down quickly to see just how eager he was. The blanket draped over his hips did nothing to hide his arousal. Part of him was a little embarrassed by his lack of control around Morainn, while another part just wanted her to see his need and satisfy it.

"I just wish I couldnae hear that icy voice of hers," Morainn mumbled, distracted by the sight of the large bump in the blanket she could see out of the corner of her eye.

He was aroused by her touch and that made her start to feel that hunger she could never completely shake free of. She told herself to look away, that it was not even dawn yet, but her gaze seem nailed to that rise in the blanket. Morainn thought it strange how her hand almost itched to touch what was shaping the blanket so interestingly. She had yet to touch him there, despite the fact that he touched her everywhere he could.

Morainn watched her hand pause at the edge of the blanket as if it had taken on a life of its own. Thoughts of how she liked looking at that part of him when it was all arrogant and demanding crowded her mind and she most certainly liked the way it made her feel when it was inside of her. Mayhap she would like how it felt. Mayhap Tormand would like to be stroked as intimately as he stroked her.

She blushed at her own thoughts. They demanded a boldness of her that she did not think she had. Even as she wondered if she could be so daring, she slid her hand beneath the blanket and lightly touched him. He was all silky warm hardness, she thought as she curled her hand around his thick erection. The shock she felt at what she was doing faded abruptly when he hissed in breath between his teeth. She recognized that sound. Tormand liked her touch.

Tormand did not dare speak. He was afraid that anything he said might make Morainn cease her caress and that was the last thing he wanted. Since they were new lovers and she had been a virgin, he had not pressed her to do anything more than let him pleasure her. It appeared that she was learning fast, discovering her womanly powers. He certainly hoped so because he spent a lot of time thinking about all the things he wanted to do to her sweet body once her shyness and uncertainty eased.

Her soft, gentle touch began to drive him mad with need. The silence that hung over both of them as he lay there savoring her touch only added to the hunger. It carried the delicious taste of doing something furtive, something one did not want to be caught doing. He did wonder just how long he could hold still and not do something himself.

His control fled in a heartbeat when her small hand slid between his legs and ever so gently squeezed his sack. With a low growl he pulled her into his arms and rolled over so that she was sprawled beneath him. The blush on her cheeks and the uncertainty darkening her eyes would have troubled him if he had not seen the telltale signs that touching him had stirred her passion as well as his.

"I should go and tell Simon what ye have seen," he said, even as he kissed the soft curves of her breasts.

"There are still a few hours before dawn," she said, crying out softly in delight when he licked at her hardened nipples with an obvious greed.

"That is good for I am nay leaving until I have loved ye so hard ye cannae move."

"Ye will weaken ere I do."

Tormand grinned at her as he dragged his tongue over the warm soft skin between her breasts. "I do love a challenge."

Tormand forced himself to sit up from where he had been lying boneless and sated at Morainn's side. He had to be the first to move so that he could claim victory. Although he had always done his best to give his partners pleasure, he had never worked so hard at keeping them teetering on the precipice of delight as he just had with Morainn. While he did still savor her wild cries of pleasure as he had finally given her the release her body screamed for, he had also been nearly blind with the need for release himself. It had been an exercise in control that had sapped his strength.

He glanced at Morainn who was sprawled on her stomach, her face still flushed from the pleasure they had shared and her eyes closed. The only move she had made since they had both shuddered with the force of their climaxes had been to roll over onto her stomach. He was the first to move, but he would be gracious and not loudly declare himself the victor.

It was not until he was buckling on his sword that he sensed her looking at him. He turned to catch her watching him with the one eye that was not pressed against the pillow. She looked like a very well satisfied woman and he felt an urge to preen.

"Ye are leaving now?" she asked in a husky voice that almost had him crawling back into bed with her.

"Aye," he replied. "I dinnae like how I have to leave ye alone here, but Simon needs to ken what ye saw in the dream."

"I ken it and I will be fine."

"Ye ken to hide yourself away if someone wanders too close, aye?"

"Aye, I learned that trick ten years ago. Dinnae worry over me. Go and tell Simon what I saw."

He opened his mouth to say that he could not help but worry about leaving her alone and unprotected, but the words stuck in his throat. Tormand suddenly realized that he had trained himself to be wary of what he said to a lover, weighing each word carefully so that there was no chance a woman could read a promise or even a hint of caring in his words. He also realized that he did not want to be so guarded around Morainn, but it was going to take time to shake free of that training.

Tormand bent down and kissed her before he started toward the door. "Rest, my sweet. Ye have worked hard and are verra weak. Ye need rest to regain your strength."

"Hah! I but conceded so that your poor wee male pride wasnae bruised."

He laughed and hurried away to collect his horse.

Morainn sighed and rolled over onto her back to stare up at the rough board ceiling Simon had had built for this bolt-hole. Her body still thrummed with the pleasure he had given her and she doubted she would be moving from the bed for quite a while. Tormand certainly deserved the claims that he was a great lover. She just wished she could ignore the knowledge of just how he had gained such accolades.

She loved the rutting fool. Nora was right. Morainn had thought that saying she *thought* she *might* would somehow shield her heart from the pain she knew would come when he set her aside. It had been a foolish plan. Her heart knew the truth, and that was that it was held firmly in his elegant hand.

Memories, she reminded herself. She would have memories, beautiful pleasure-filled memories. She sighed and closed her eyes. The memories would probably only make her heart hurt more in the end for she would still be all alone.

Tormand looked up when Simon entered the great hall in his modest home looking like he should go back to bed and get some more sleep. Tormand had been sitting in the hall for two hours, reluctant to wake the man too soon. It had given him a lot of time to think and he was not sure he liked the conclusions he had come to. Impatient to talk though he was, he waited patiently as the food was set out for them. To his surprise his equally sleepy-looking kinsmen began to wander in and sit down.

"Have ye all been staying here then?" he asked.

"Nay, just last night as it was verra late and Simon's was the first house we came to," said Harcourt, as he began to fill his plate with food. "We all decided we didnae want to ride another yard."

"Out hunting then?" Tormand heartily wished he could be riding with them on that hunt, instead of hiding away, but he bit back the complaint.

"That and keeping a close watch for anyone trying to creep back to a house with a body."

"Why are ye here?" asked Simon. "Has something happened?"

"Morainn had another dream," Tormand replied between bites of food. "She says they grow more vivid."

"Ah, so she has seen something that might help us."

Tormand told them all Morainn had told him. Repeating it all aloud instead of just in his head made him feel even more certain of what he had come to believe while sitting in the hall on his own. When he felt anger stir inside of him he firmly told himself that she had not lied to him. She had simply not told him everything and probably because she did not want to worry him. That did not ease his anger by much.

Harcourt groaned. "So it will be back on the horses so that we can ride about looking at shielings and cottages."

"One with sheep and a roof that is part slate and part thatch," said Tormand.

"Och, aye, that certainly limits the number," drawled Bennett.

"I could—" began Tormand.

"Nay," said Simon. "Ye run enough risk in just coming here. There is also the chance that the killers watch us now, trying to find out where ye have gone. Ye could lead them to Morainn. They badly want her dead."

"I ken it. The woman tells her so in her dreams. Morainn feels as if the bitch has somehow gotten inside her head."

"Mayhap she has. We ken little about such gifts. Ye far more than I, but I wager ye dinnae ken everything about them simply because ye dinnae have one. Weel, nay one that gives ye prophetic dreams and visions."

"Ye really think I have a gift?"

"Oh, aye, ye do. Ye can sense the emotions in a room. Nay always, but it has certainly helped now and again. 'Tis as if ye can smell them in the air."

Tormand thought about that for a moment, felt a strange urge to deny it despite having displayed the skill before Simon on occasion, and then slowly nodded. "I suspicion I do. I just ne'er thought of it as a true gift. Mostly I thought that my cousin telling me how to strengthen my sense, shall we say, just made a natural skill sharper than most men's."

"Nay, 'tis a gift. 'Tis a small one like my father has," said Harcourt. "He kens when danger approaches. Says it has kept him alive. I can sometimes feel it drawing near as weel. A useful wee gift. Nay as strong a one as the lasses have, but useful."

"And here I thought ye dragged me along with ye because I was a clever lad," drawled Tormand, as he grinned at Simon.

Simon grinned back. "Ye are, although I hate to stroke your already considerable vanity by saying so. Ye have a way of looking at things that can also be verra helpful."

"Nay as helpful as Morainn's dreams and visions

though. She was wondering why ye havenae given her another hairpin."

"I had thought on it, but then we discovered Edward MacLean and that gave me a trail. It is slowly leading me toward the killers and so I didnae wish to inflict another vision on the lass. Now that I have the name—Ada or Anna—I have an e'en clearer trail. I believe it is Ada, although I cannae quite grasp what memory makes me believe that. I find it difficult to understand how she could have been wed to Edward and yet so few people e'er saw her and I have yet to find one who can recall her name or appearance." He frowned. "E'en me, and I have always taken great pride in my ability to see clearly, to see everything nay matter how small or apparently insignificant."

"No one can see everything. Mayhap the fact that no one saw her only fed her madness."

"Possible. At least we can be fair sure that her huge companion is named Small Ian. The one who told me has always been an accurate source of information. I just wish that Morainn had gotten more information on who will be killed. It is hard to stop a killing when ye dinnae ken who the victim might be."

Tormand took a deep drink of ale and then said, "I think the victim she saw this time is herself." He nodded at the shocked looks on the faces of his companions, a shock he fully shared. "She didnae say so, but as I sat here waiting for ye, Simon, I gave a lot of thought to what she did say and how she answered my questions about who the victim was."

"Evasive was she?"

"Verra much so. After a long explanation about how

few people she knew and how she wouldnae recognize the victims e'en if she saw them clearly, what she finally said was that the woman wasnae verra big and she had dark hair."

Bennett cursed. "It sounds verra much as if she was hiding something. I am surprised ye didnae ken it as ye have always been good at sniffing out a lie."

"I got distracted." He ignored the derisive snorts of the men. "She may e'en have done that apurpose, although I cannae really believe that."

"Nay, nor can I," said Uilliam. "She isnae a woman who kens how to be so, weel, so—"

"Sneaky?" Tormand said.

"Aye, 'tis as good a word as any. She probably just felt she had given ye the answer ye needed to stop pressing her on the matter and got, er, distracted herself."

"Being distracted sounds a lot more enjoyable than being stuck on the back of a horse all day," muttered Rory, and replied to his kinsmen's derisive remarks with a tart skill that equaled theirs.

It was almost the middle of the afternoon before Tormand was able to leave. Morainn's dream had been gone over so many times he began to feel he was the one who had had it. Each time he repeated what she had seen and heard details of the other dreams and visions she had suffered through, he realized that Morainn was a very strong woman. She had to be to endure such things. What he wanted, however, was to make sure that these killers were removed from her dreams as soon as possible. Simon's increasing collection of information had begun to make him feel a hint of hope, but he was still discouraged at the slow

pace of their progress. Now that he felt Morainn had
dreamed of her own death, he was even more so.

"We *will* capture them," Simon said, as he watched
Tormand get ready to ride back to the ruined tower
house. "We now ken who they are."

"A big dark mon named Small Ian and a woman no
one recalls?"

"A woman and a mon who nay longer have a house
to hide in. And, aye, we dinnae have their precise
names and dinnae ken exactly what they look like, but
we ken enough to recognize them when we see them."

"Mayhap it would be safer for Morainn if she came
back here. More armed men to surround her."

"She has become your partner in this, Tormand. In
the people's eyes she is the one that has helped ye kill
without being seen and keeps ye from the justice ye
deserve. It would be as hard to keep her completely
safe here as it would be if ye came back."

"Why do I think someone is using the people's fury
and fear about these murders to get rid of Morainn?"

"Because that is what is happening." He nodded at
Tormand's look of surprise. "Fair or nay, we can see
why the people look at ye with suspicion. Ye kenned
every one of the women killed. Even the news of
Edward MacLean's death didnae ease that. The fact
that the wife no one recalls is also gone is attributed
to ye killing her. Each time the murmurs quiet a little,
someone stirs it back up again and Morainn's name is
mentioned more and more. There have e'en been a
few whispers about how this is all connected to her
being a witch, to some dark magic she is brewing."

Tormand cursed. "'Tis all idiocy."

"Aye, but people can become witless when they are afraid and a lot of people are verra afraid right now." He frowned. "I would like to tell ye that ye are wrong to think she dreamed of her own death, but the more I think on all ye told me, the more I think ye might be right. E'en so, she is safer where she is."

"At least there she only has to worry about two people wanting her dead instead of a whole cursed town."

"Exactly. Are ye going to confront her with what ye believe?"

"I dinnae ken. Part of me wishes to, but another part doesnae see any gain in it. She thinks she is protecting me in some way." He shrugged. "I will see how I feel about it all when I get back to the tower house."

"Tell me, have ye decided what ye are going to do about Morainn once this is all over?"

"Ye mean if the fool woman is still alive?" He hated to even say the words and the look of knowing amusement that flickered across Simon's face irritated him. The man knew him too well. "Nay, I havenae. About all I can think of right now is how I should like to spank her fair backside for nay telling me all that she saw."

"That could prove interesting," drawled Simon.

Tormand was surprised he could, since his emotions were so tangled and few of those emotions were good or calm ones, but he laughed. Nodding a farewell to Simon, he began his stealthy way out of town, keeping a close watch for anyone following him. The end of this trial was drawing near; he could feel it. He just prayed Morainn would be there to celebrate with him.

Chapter 15

Standing in the doorway to the room he and Morainn shared, Tormand fought to calm himself. He had warred with himself for the whole journey back to her side, going from angry with her to understanding why she had not told him the whole truth. It would do no good to rush in now and demand she tell him everything she saw in her dream. Such a confrontation would serve no purpose except, perhaps, to allow him to ease some of the anger that still swam in his veins. He could not even claim that she had lied to him; she simply had not told him everything. He still had the feeling that she felt she was protecting him in some way. He wondered if it was fair to deprive her of that.

She moved around the room gracefully and efficiently as she made them something to eat. The scent of a rich rabbit stew filled the air and tugged at his stomach. He had not taken the time to eat anything while he was at Simon's except for a small meal to break his fast. Once he had realized that Morainn had dreamed of her own death he had not felt very hungry anyway.

Tormand knew that the depth of the fear he felt for her meant that his other feelings for her also ran deep. It certainly explained why he was so angry, even a little hurt, that she had not told him the full truth. He could not keep ignoring the fact that he was getting more entangled with Morainn Ross with every hour he spent in her company, with every moment that they spent in each other's arms. He no longer felt the need to flee from that or from her, either.

"Ah, ye have come back and just in time," she said and smiled at him. "I am cooking the rabbit ye caught for us yesterday."

"It smells good," he said as he walked into the room and sat in a chair near the rough stone fireplace. Taking a deep breath, he added, "Verra good indeed. Simon obviously supplied us verra weel."

"Och, aye, he did."

She poured him a tankard of ale and handed it to him. He murmured his thanks and gave her a small smile. It felt good to cook his meal for him and to greet him this way when he returned to their shelter. Morainn could see the danger in that, however. She was settling into the ways of a wife more than just a lover and Tormand Murray did not want a wife. Even if he did, he would not choose the bastard daughter of a witch burned by the townspeople and one who was thought to be a witch as well. A man like Tormand could reach very high indeed when he finally felt like marrying and begetting a child or two.

At the thought of Tormand giving some other

woman a child, Morainn felt such a pain in her heart she was surprised she did not cry out. Instead, she quickly turned her attention back to her cooking so that he could not see that pain in her eyes and wonder on it. The stew did not really need close watching, but she hoped that Tormand, like most men, did not know a great deal about cooking.

By the time she got her emotions back under control, Morainn started to feel that the silence in the room was not a companionable one. There was a tension to it that troubled her. She looked at Tormand only to find him staring morosely at the wall. Something was bothering the man, but Morainn was a little afraid to ask what it was. Her mind was rapidly filling her head with all sorts of possible reasons for his strange behavior and none of them were good. It could be that he brooded over their failure to catch the killers, but it could also be that he brooded over the fact that he was stuck in a ruined tower house with a woman he was already tiring of.

Even though she was curious about what Simon had said concerning her dream and about what was happening concerning the hunt for Ada and Small, she did not ask. Morainn decided it might be safer, if only for her poor misguided heart, just to wait until he felt like talking again. She forced all of her attention and thoughts on the work she had set out for herself. Stitching flowers onto linens for Nora's dowry chests would keep her busy and she was heartily pleased that she had had some brought to her to work on. The tedious chore would help keep her from worrying about all the reasons Tormand had become so strangely quiet.

It was not until long after they had eaten and Morainn had returned to her needlework that Tormand was finally able to shake off his dark mood. He was not a man given to brooding much, but he had obviously learned the way of it. After a while, however, it had begun to feel too much like self-pity.

He looked at Morainn busily stitching pretty flowers onto what looked like a cover for a pillow and grimaced. She had been slipping around the room like a ghost, obviously sensing his bad humor. His anger over how she had not told him that she had seen herself as the next victim had finally left him. He actually found it oddly touching that this tiny woman who had been unwillingly pulled into this tangle because she had a gift, would try to protect him in any way.

He would let her keep her secret. He would also not tell her how hard everyone was working to find the cottage she had described, of how desperate they were to find it before she did become the next victim of the killers. His inability to join the other men in that hunt was one reason he had fallen into such a black mood. Morainn was his woman and he should be the one out there hunting down the ones who meant to do her harm.

His woman. Tormand decided he liked the sound of that. Possessiveness was not something he had ever suffered from before, but he definitely felt possessive about Morainn.

"Your friend means to take a lot of linens to her

marriage, doesnae she?" he said, smiling at her when she gave him a startled look.

Morainn could see no signs of the strange mood that had possessed Tormand when he had first arrived and she inwardly sighed with relief. She had been thinking she ought to go to bed as it was very late, but she had been hesitant to bed down with Tormand when he was in such a bad humor. Now she felt alert, sure he would soon give her an explanation for his long, silent study of the walls.

"She has no lands or money, but she wishes to bring some things of value to her marriage," Morainn replied. "All the women of her family are sewing and doing needlework night and day. I am glad that your brother Uilliam was able to bring me this work to do."

"If all the work is as fine as yours, James's kin will be verra impressed." He sighed. "I apologize for being such poor company these last few hours. I fear I succumbed to self-pity."

"Self-pity? Over what?"

"This trouble we are mired in, these murders so many wish to blame on me, and the fact that I must hide away here whilst Simon, my brothers, and my cousins hunt down *my* enemies."

"Aye, I suspicion such things would be a sharp pinch to the pride of any mon."

He laughed softly. "Ye dinnae sound verra sympathetic to my woes, love."

"Oh, I am. But—"

"Aha, the infamous *but*."

She ignored his teasing. "Ye have a verra good life awaiting ye when this is all over. Yet, if ye joined the hunt now ye could lose all of that; ye could lose your life. To give in to pride and go out ahunting these monsters with the others would put yourself right back in harm's way. Others could be hurt or killed, as weel for the crowd, if stirred into a frenzy as they were the night they surrounded your home, might try to attack ye e'en if ye have a half dozen armed men riding with ye. Or more. In their fear and anger they would fight with the ones trying to keep ye alive and find the real killers. In the eyes of the mob, the ones protecting ye would also be seen as the enemy." Once finished she was a little afraid that she had far overstepped her bounds, but he did not appear angry.

"I ken that," he said quietly. "'Tis why I didnae fight coming here to hide. I trusted Simon to ken when it was time for me to find a bolt-hole. I but find it verra difficult to accept that from time to time."

She slowly nodded and asked, "Are they closing in on these mad dogs?"

"The noose is finally tightening around their necks, aye."

"Good, for that is what is truly important." She shook her head. "'Tis a shame that the ones who were heaving rocks at your house couldnae be made to see the truth. Then ye could have used some of them to help ye find the killers and ye wouldnae be held prisoner here any longer."

"Weel, 'tis a verra fine prison. And ye are right. I would be naught but a hindrance, either because my presence would stir up a mob again, and that could put everyone in danger, or because we would all have to be so verra careful that I wasnae seen by anyone, there would be little hunting going on. As Simon said—he wouldst rather catch the real killers *before* I hang."

"Simon Innes has a rather dark sense of humor."

"He does, but some of that may come from the fact that he deals with a lot of verra dark things. Simon has seen nearly every evil one mon, or woman, can do to another. Sometimes I worry that such work is slowly eating away at his soul."

"Or his heart," she murmured. "Was anything I saw in my dream of help to him?"

Tormand nodded. "It was and he is already putting it to use."

"Did the name of the woman help? I was not sure which it was—Ada or Anna—but I find I am already calling her Ada in my mind."

"I think Simon believes it is Ada, too, although he hasnae been able to get any real information on MacLean's wife, and his own memory of meeting her is too faint to trust it. He cannae find any of the servants who worked for the MacLeans, which is verra strange."

"I hope that is because they fled the place and nay because they are also dead. These two are filling far too many graves."

Tormand stood up and held out his hand. "Come to bed, Morainn. Let us talk no more of monsters and death."

She blushed, but set aside her needlework and put her hand in his. He tugged her toward the bed, stopped just at the edge of it and kissed her with such gentle passion she was feeling dazed when he stopped. Tormand then moved to bank the fire and snuff all the candles save for the one next to the bed. Morainn felt a little less shy as the light in the room dimmed to a soft glow. It was foolish considering how often they had made love, but she was still shy about him seeing her naked.

Kissing the blush upon her cheeks, Tormand slowly undressed her. He took his time, savoring each new patch of skin that he uncovered. It pleased him that she looked dazed with desire by the time he settled her down on the bed. He knew he had stirred passion in other women, but it made him feel far more satisfied to do so in Morainn. It also stirred his blood in a way that no other woman's look of desire ever had. The desire of those other women had always been simply a means to be sure his need was satisfied. With Morainn, he wanted her to feel all the passion she was capable of, and his own needs were no longer all important to him.

He removed his clothes swiftly, tossing them to the floor, and then crawled into bed with her. Tormand's own hunger for her prompted his speed, but so did the knowledge that Morainn was still uneasy about being naked with him, about him seeing her body. He did not want that shyness to intrude and cool her ardor now. Tonight he was going to love her as he had never made love to another woman.

Morainn eagerly welcomed him into her arms. She could see his desire for her blazing in his eyes and that look always eased the fears she had about risking her heart with this man. The feel of his warm skin against hers made her sigh with pleasure. Morainn did not think she could ever grow tired of that feeling.

Although she quickly grew eager for him to possess her fully, he took his time. Morainn tried to control her rising desire, for she loved the way he made her feel with his touch and his kisses, and she wanted to savor it for as long as she could. She no longer flinched in shock when he kissed and caressed her breasts, but arched up, welcoming every touch of his hand and the warmth of his mouth.

"Ah, love, ye are so beautiful, so warm," he murmured against the soft skin of her flat belly. "Ye taste like the finest mead and I can get drunk on you."

She wanted to return his flattery, but the way his clever fingers were stroking her womanhood made it hard to put two coherent words together. Morainn did not know how he could talk while making love. When she was in his arms like this she did not doubt his desire for her, felt certain it ran as hot and fierce as her own, and yet he could talk. She could barely say his name.

Then, suddenly her eyes widened with shock, and she felt her hunger waver. He was kissing her *there*. Sure it was a sin she not allow him to commit, she tried to push him away, but he held fast to her hips and licked her. Shock quickly gave way to a rapidly rising passion that had her arching into his intimate kiss, allowing him to move her legs so that he could be even bolder in his attentions. Morainn was not sure she would survive this sort of lovemaking for she ached with need even as she felt as if fire was racing through her veins. He kept murmuring something, soothing words and flatteries, but she was too blind with her own need to understand what he was saying.

When she felt her body tightening in the way it always did before the pleasure she felt crashed over, she grabbed him by the shoulders and tried to pull him up into her arms. She needed him inside of her, but she did not know how to make such a demand. Then he began to kiss his way back up her body. When he reached her mouth, he kissed her hungrily, almost fiercely, at the same time that he buried himself deep inside of her. Morainn cried out in welcome and wrapped her legs tightly around his body. His thrusts were hard and deep and she met them eagerly. Just as she shattered and fell into that state of utter bliss he always sent her to, she heard him bellow out her name as he joined her there.

Tormand had already cleaned them both off by the time Morainn had regained her senses enough to start to feel embarrassed. She tensed in his arms and buried her face against his neck. She was the worst sort of wanton, she decided. Embarrassed though she was, and shocked that she had allowed him to do that, she realized very quickly that she wanted him to do it again. That only made her feel even more embarrassed.

Feeling the tension seep into her body, Tormand lightly stroked her slim back and grinned into her tousled hair. She was going to be embarrassed, but he decided she would have to get over it. He had never loved another woman in that way, but he decided he liked the taste of his little witch. She was clean, sweet and tart, and she had never known any man but him.

Tormand would not allow her to shy away from such loving now.

"Cease fretting over it, dearling," he said and turned her very red face up to his to brush a kiss over her lips.

"But, ye shouldnae be kissing me *there*," she muttered, unable to meet his gaze.

"Why not? I like to kiss ye there. Ye taste good," he added and laughed when she groaned and buried her face back in the crook of his neck. "Ye liked it, too."

"That doesnae make it right."

"Aye, it does."

Before she could argue that, he tensed and then suddenly leapt out of bed. A moment later, she heard what he had. Someone was approaching the tower house on horseback. Several someones. Morainn quickly got out of bed and threw her clothes back on. Tormand was fully dressed and armed before she was done, moving with the speed and efficiency of a man who had known danger and battle. With one jerk of his head, he ordered her to slip away through the little bolt-hole in the wall. She wanted to stand at his side, hated fleeing without knowing what he might face, but he had made her promise that she would run when he told her to, so she started toward the small bolt-hole that would lead her out into the woods.

"Be at ease, Tormand," called a familiar voice. "We have news."

Morainn hastily ran back to the bed to pull the covers back over it and was just moving to fetch some tankards and ale when Simon and the Murrays banged on the door. She was not quite sure how many Murrays were on the other side of the door, but she set out six tankards anyway. When Tormand unbolted the door and the men came in she was glad of it. The fact that all of them had come to the tower house in the dead of night did worry her, however. She prayed it was good news as she poured out the ale. It had taken Tormand a long time to shake free of his black mood. News of another murder that he would blame himself for could easily have him brooding for days instead of a few hours.

"Do ye fools never sleep?" Tormand asked, as he grabbed one of the tankards Morainn had filled, and sat at the foot of the bed.

"Not when ye work with Simon," muttered Harcourt, as he picked up a tankard of ale and gulped it down as if he had not had anything to drink for a very long time.

"Nay tonight. Tonight we go ahunting," said Simon, ignoring Harcourt as he also grabbed a tankard of ale and sent Morainn a brief smile of gratitude. "Someone has finally sent word about the people we are looking for."

It was difficult for Tormand to hide his rising excitement as he pulled Morainn down to sit beside him. Could it really be all over? That would mean that he and Morainn could return to his home and he could finally have time to study what he felt for her and decide what he would do about it.

"Ye ken where the bastards are?" he asked.

"That was what the message we got implied. I had thought to just ride over there myself, but then thought that ye may be displeased if we didnae include ye in this."

"Oh, aye, verra displeased. But are ye confident this is true, that this person who sent word can be trusted?"

"As much as anyone else. I have never kenned the mon to be other than honest."

Tormand looked at Morainn. "Will ye be all right if I leave ye here alone?"

"Of course," she replied. "Ye have left me here alone before."

"Nay at night."

"There is a verra thick door with a sturdy bolt and I ken to run and hide if I must."

"I wouldnae ask ye to come if I didnae think she would be safe," said Simon. "No one kens ye are here and, if this proves to be all it promises to be, the threat will be o'er by morning."

Morainn watched as the men left and bolted the door securely behind them. She hoped they would find the killers and either cage them for a hanging or kill them. For what those monsters had done, they deserved no less. She also knew that Tormand needed this to be over.

As she returned to bed, she huddled beneath the covers. She missed Tormand's big, warm body curled around her, but told herself she had better get used to sleeping alone again. It brought tears to her eyes even to think about it, but if the monsters were killed tonight, she would be sent home to her cottage to live with just a memory of love, and an unrequited one at that.

She grimaced as the tears slid down her cheeks despite her efforts to hold them back. She was the only one who loved in this relationship. Tormand lusted. He might be kinder to her than he had ever been with his other women, but he had never even hinted at any feelings stronger than desire. Nor had he hinted that there would be any future for the two of them. She would go back to her garden, her orchards, and her beehives, and he would go back to his women. It hurt, but Morainn suspected she had better get used to that as well. When she had to walk away from Tormand she was going to be leaving her heart behind.

"How did ye get word of this?" asked Tormand after they had ridden for an hour.

"A boy came and gave me a missive. Badly written but understandable. Old Geordie said he had seen the ones we were looking for. Said they were lurking around a deserted crofter's cottage not far from him."

"It will take us at least another two hours to get to Old Geordie's since it is so dark we must ride slowly and carefully. Isnae that a little far away for the murderers? I thought they would be closer to town where they can find more victims easily."

"They dinnae have a house anymore, do they? Mayhap this was the easiest place to hide away in. I suspicion that those two are more concerned about survival now, than about who they can kill next."

Tormand wrapped his plaid more tightly around himself as the chill, damp night air cut deep into his bones. He did not feel right about this, but was not sure why. It could be that after so long and hard a search, so many deaths, this all seemed too easy.

"Wouldnae killers like these make verra sure no one could see them?" he finally asked Simon.

"Do ye have a bad feeling about this?"

"It just all seems too easy, too quickly and neatly settled."

"Ye expected a fight?"

"Mayhap, or mayhap I wanted one. It doesnae appear as if I will be granted that wish."

By the time they reached Old Geordie's hovel, Tormand knew he would not be getting back to the tower house any time before the sun rose, and that would only happen if he turned around right now and started back. He was sorely tempted to do so and take the others with him. His instincts were crying out that this was a trap.

When a sleepy-eyed Old Geordie opened his door after several wood-shaking pounds of Simon's fist, Tormand felt his unease begin to change to alarm. The man did not look as though he had expected Simon's visit. Tormand heard his kinsmen behind him ease their swords out of their sheaths. One look at the frown on Simon's face told him that his friend was now very suspicious as well. Tormand could not see, hear, or even smell anyone around and it would be impossible for an angry mob to hide away anywhere on the rocky grazing land surrounding Geordie's home.

Then he realized that the trap had not been set for him or the men with him, but for the one they left behind. Tormand fought back the urge to leap on his horse and race back to the tower house. He could not be sure that it was a trap for Morainn, or he could be succumbing to the fear he had suffered from ever since this trial began. It would help to at least find out why they were at Geordie's house when he obviously had not expected them and who might have written the note to draw them there.

"Is something wrong, lad?" the graying Geordie asked Simon.

"I thought ye were going to tell me about that," said Simon. "Did ye nay send me a message asking me to meet ye here?"

"Why would I be doing that?"

"Your missive said ye kenned where the killers I have been hunting have gone to ground."

"Missive? Laddie, ye must ken that I can barely write me own name. I wouldnae have written ye a missive. Sent one of me lads to speak to ye, aye, but nay write anything." Simon started to show Geordie the scrawled letter, but the man shook his head. "Come in and let me light a few candles. Cannae see anything here in the dark."

Tormand followed Simon inside, glancing back to see that his kinsmen had placed themselves around the cottage as guards just in case there was a trap yet to be sprung. He also noticed that Geordie had set a huge knife down on a table and realized the man had not answered his door unarmed. The inside of the cottage revealed that it was a lot larger than one would suspect from the outside. Geordie was not exactly some poor shepherd. The moment the candles were lit, Simon handed Geordie the message that had supposedly come from him. As he tensely waited to hear what the man would say, Tormand idly wondered who the man was to Simon, for few men called Sir Simon Innes laddie.

"As I said, lad, I cannae write," Geordie finally said as he handed the note back to Simon. "Cannae read verra weel, either. Nay enough to send ye something like this."

"Do ye have any idea who would have written this?"

"Looks like me cousin's scrawl. The old bitch taught herself to write so that she could keep records of her medicines and salves and all."

"Where is your cousin?"

"Right here, sad to say. She came round last evening and said she had been off to deliver a child and it was too dark for her to go home, so could she bed down here. Couldnae say nay could I, but I am nay sure why she has stayed another night." He scowled at a small, narrow set of stairs that led up to the next level of the house. "She says she wanted to look over my lands for some herbs. Nay sure I believe her." He looked back at Simon. "Just what does it say?"

"That ye had some information on the killers I have been trying to catch, that ye ken where they are hiding."

"Nay, dinnae ken anything about that, but if Ide wrote that note, she might ken. I will fetch her."

The name Ide made Tormand tense. That was the woman that had been trying to stir up the crowd in front of the Redmond home. It was also the woman that had helped lead the crowd in the murder of Morainn's mother and in Morainn's banishment when she had been too young to be left on her own. Now Tormand was certain that this was a trap and that it had been set for Morainn. Even as he turned toward the door, Simon grabbed him by the arm.

"Steady, Tormand," Simon urged. "We need to ken what is happening."

"That old bitch is trying to get someone else to kill her rival for her," snapped Tormand.

"I think ye may be right, but think. Calm yourself and but think for a moment. That would mean that the old bitch kens the killers and may even ken where they are hiding. Mayhap she was the one who tended to the wounds Morainn and her cat left them with."

The truth of what Simon said was all that kept Tormand standing where he was and not rushing back to the tower house to make certain that Morainn was safe. It was also all that kept him from grabbing Old Ide, as Geordie led the woman down the stairs, and shaking the truth out of her. The moment the woman stood in front of them, Tormand knew she was behind all of this, and that she had done it to get Morainn killed. There was a nasty look of triumph, of gloating, in her eyes.

"This is your work?" Simon demanded as he showed Ide the letter.

"Aye," she replied and crossed her arms over her chest. "Nay sure why ye are trying so hard to catch them. Ye should be chaining up the real killer." She scowled at Tormand. "Him and his witch are the ones causing all the trouble."

"Ye are nay only mean of spirit, ye are a fool."

Ide looked at Simon in astonishment and then glared at him. "Ye have nay right to speak to me that way. I am just doing what ye ought to be doing, trying to see that the evil visiting our town is banished from it for good."

Tormand was stunned when Simon grabbed the older woman by the arms and slammed her up against the wall. He did not think he had ever seen the man so furious. For Simon to manhandle a woman, especially an older one, implied that his control was lost or was teetering on a very narrow ledge. Tormand could understand that. With every word the woman had said, Tormand had been fighting the urge to slap her. He noticed that Geordie had just crossed his burly arms over his wide chest and was watching, doing nothing to stop Simon.

"Geordie," the woman cried as she tried to wriggle free of Simon's hold.

"Tell him everything, Ide," said Geordie, "and I would do so honestly and quickly if I were ye. I have never liked ye much, but getting yourself hanged for having a part in these killings will shame my name, and so I will ask that if ye are honest and helpful now, Sir Simon doesnae send ye to the gallows with the others, doesnae tie our name to that filth."

After a frantic look at all three hard-faced men, Ide began to talk.

Chapter 16

A soft rustle in the low-growing bushes to her right made Morainn's heart stop and then stutter into such a fast pace that she felt a little breathless. She never should have come outside no matter how much the sunny morning had tempted her. Simon and the others may have said that they would soon have the killers chained and headed for the gallows, or dead, but they could just have been trying to raise her spirits or even their own. They could also just be wrong and had ridden off on yet another fruitless chase. Morainn wondered if she could get to safety fast enough to avoid capture.

When a black and brown dog suddenly appeared and sat down only a foot away from her, she frowned. It was panting and its tail was wagging so fiercely it was clearing the ground beneath it. She started to relax, for the dog was obviously no threat and then she recognized the animal. It was the one Simon used to follow a trail. Had the dog gotten loose from his pen and followed Simon's scent to her door?

"Bonegnasher?" she said and the dog yipped happily at the sound of his name, one that she had bluntly told Simon was a ridiculous name to give such a friendly dog.

There was another rustle in the bushes, but Morainn did not immediately panic this time. The dog showed no sign of scenting any threat. And, once she had controlled her fears, she had realized that Ada and Small would not be lurking around in the brambles and bushes at the break of day. If nothing else, Small was far too large to hide in such things.

Her first look at the person who did scramble out of the bushes, however, shocked her so much that she could not say a word for a moment, just stare. "Walin," she finally choked out, her thoughts too chaotic for her to think of anything else to say.

"I had to find ye, Morainn," the boy said, tugging hard on his dirty shirt until it pulled free of the grasp of the brambles with a soft ripping sound. "They just kept telling me that ye were safe and that I didnae need to worry and that ye would be back soon, but they wouldnae tell me where ye were. I ken ye have to hide from the bad people, but they could have told me where ye were hiding. I wouldnae have told anybody."

Morainn sighed, releasing the last of her shock. The men had not handled the boy well, but she could not really blame them. They were hunting killers. They undoubtedly thought Walin knew all he needed to know and, afraid of looking too much like the small boy he really was, Walin probably had not bothered them much with his growing worries and fears.

She should have taken the time to warn the men that Walin had a deep, abiding fear of losing her, something she had felt would ease as he grew older. The attack that had forced them to leave the cottage, the only home the boy had ever really known, and hearing the woman speaking of how she wanted the witch dead had undoubtedly sharpened that fear. She could not be too sympathetic, however. Walin had done a dangerous thing traveling alone at night and he had to learn that he could not endanger himself so foolishly again.

"How did ye find me?" she asked, crossing her arms over her chest and trying to look stern. It was not as easy as it should have been because she had sorely missed him and ached to hug him.

"I followed Simon and the others," he answered, beginning to look guilty and uncertain when he got no smile or hug from Morainn.

"They were on horses, Walin, and I doubt they were traveling at a slow pace. Ye havenae stolen a horse, have ye?"

"Nay. I cannae ride, can I, and they werenae riding verra fast because it was dark and all, but I still lost them. Nay, I took Bonegnasher though. He caught the scent and we followed it here. I kenned the men had stopped here because Bonegnasher did that wee circling thing he does when he is trying to find the new trail. Then I saw ye walking about over here. What are ye looking for? Can I help?"

"Dinnae try to distract me from the scolding ye ken verra weel ye deserve."

His small shoulders slumped and Morainn did

not think she had ever seen a child look so woeful.
Walin had become a master of the look at an early
age, however. "I just wanted to see ye and they wouldnae let me, wouldnae bring me to visit ye."

"And did ye nay stop to think that there was a good
reason for that? Ye need to be safe, love. I left ye there
with all those big, weel-armed men so that ye would
be safe. Did ye think I would leave ye for any other
reason?"

"Nay. Are ye going to send me back there now?"

Morainn almost smiled. The child really was good
at looking so sad one just wanted to take him into
one's arms and soothe away all his hurts and fears
until his bright smile returned. If she had not had the
raising of him for the past four years she knew she
would be doing just that. She also knew it would be a
very big mistake. He was probably a little hurt and a
little sad, maybe even a little afraid. He was also peeking at her from beneath his ridiculously long lashes to
see if she was falling for his little game of poor, poor
me.

"I cannae, can I?" she said and pretended she did
not see the brief flash of happiness he could not hide.
"I must stay here."

"Then I can stay here with ye?"

"Aye, and ye will sit still for the scolding ye so richly
deserve."

He sighed and followed her into the tower house,
the dog trotting along behind him. Walin was shuf-
fling his feet along sounding very much like some
condemned man headed for the gallows, but Morainn ignored him. She knew she would not scold him

very much. Despite all his plays for her sympathy, Walin knew he had done something very foolish and wrong. She did not need to belabor the matter.

Once inside the tower house, Morainn gently pointed out all Walin had done wrong, all the various ways he had put himself in danger, as she cleaned him up. The dog collapsed on the floor in front of the fireplace and actually began snoring. She then warmed some of the rabbit stew for both the boy and the dog that woke up quickly when she set a bowl of food in front of him. It was nice to have Walin with her, but Morainn did not let him know that. She also made it very clear to him that he would return to Tormand's house with the other men when they came back and do so without a single complaint.

Her thoughts turned to Tormand and she hoped he was safe. She also hoped the men found the killers as they had thought they would. Part of her did not want this to end because it would mean that she would lose Tormand and she was ashamed of her own selfishness. Ada and Small were vicious, cold-blooded killers. A bruise or two to her heart was nothing compared to the crimes they would continue to commit if they remained free.

"When do ye think the men will come back, Morainn?" asked Walin, as he sat down near the dog that had fallen asleep right after licking the bowl clean.

"I have no idea, love," she replied. "They may be back soon if all goes weel, but they could be gone for hours yet."

"Och, weel, I want them to catch those murdering

bastards, but I also would like to stay with ye for a nice long visit."

A little stunned by his language, Morainn had missed the chance to scold him about saying *murdering bastards*, especially in front of a woman. She decided that Walin was obviously learning a few things from the men that she had rather he did not. For now she would let him mimic his heroes, as she knew all those big, handsome men had become in the boy's eyes, but when they were home at the cottage once again, there might be a few things she had to make him unlearn.

"If they catch these killers, Walin, then ye and I will be together at the cottage again." She was a little puzzled that that news did not immediately make the little boy happy. "Dinnae ye want to go home?"

"Och, aye, I do, but I will miss the men. They have been teaching me all sorts of interesting things."

Like how to curse, she thought. "Oh, dear. Dare I ask what they have been teaching you?"

"All about knives and how to throw them and how to wield my wooden sword like a true warrior and how to ride and care for a horse, although I havenae had much chance to learn to ride as the men are always going out hunting for those people. Simon is teaching me a wee bit about how to solve puzzles, too. He says I am a verra clever lad."

"That ye are. The most clever lad I have ever kenned e'en when ye do foolish things like ye just did. Do ye like solving puzzles?"

"Aye, but if they think I am clever then why didnae they listen to me?"

"About what?"

"When Sir Simon was getting ready to go after the killers last evening I said I didnae think it was a verra good idea."

Morainn decided that the men had definitely succeeded in making the little boy feel comfortable as well as safe, or Walin would never have spoken up so boldly. "What did Simon say?"

"He said he couldnae ignore such a clear trail. I was going to tell him that it wasnae verra clear to me and that I kenned something he didnae, but he didnae have time to speak to me again." Walin frowned. "Or he forgot."

"What did ye ken that ye think he didnae?"

"That it was all a lie."

That icy voice Morainn hated spoke from behind her just as Bonegnasher started to growl. The dog was standing now, his head lowered and his body tensed. Morainn wished she had a full pack of Bonegnashers as she slowly turned to face her worst nightmare. She also wished she had remembered to bolt the door.

Ada and Small stood just inside the door, just inside what had been Morainn's bolt-hole, her shelter. Small towered over the too thin, plain woman as he shielded her back from any possible attack. Morainn realized right then that it had all been a trap, and, worse, Walin had been caught in it alongside her.

The way the woman smiled at her suddenly made Morainn very angry. It was the knowledge that this woman found the idea of killing Morainn amusing, even something to look forward to, that made the rage swell up inside of Morainn. She would like this woman to find out for herself that pain and death were nothing to smile about.

"Who did ye get to help ye set this trap?" she asked, pleased with how calm she sounded. "Simon is no fool and for him to be led astray ye must have gained a verra good ally."

"Old Ide," the woman replied, obviously more than willing to boast.

"Simon wouldnae listen to Old Ide about anything."

"Nay, but he trusts her cousin, and Ide helped us fool Simon into believing a message had come from his old friend and clansmon."

"Please tell me that ye did what seems to be your custom and killed the bitch."

The laugh that came out of the woman's mouth was as cold as her voice. "Nay, we didnae kill her. Nay yet. If Simon discovers what she has done, he may do it for us, although I will be sorry to miss the chance to do it myself. A terrible old woman, full of spite and hate and jealousy. She has no sense of honor."

And ye do? Morainn asked silently, knowing it would not be wise to say such a thing aloud. Nor did she think she would get any hint of where Simon and the others had been sent, something that could tell her just how good or bad her chances of a timely rescue were. There was only one other thing she was concerned about.

"There is nay need to hurt the boy," she said.

"I would ne'er hurt a child."

Morainn did not know how such a cold-blooded killer could look so offended. Did she really think that binding and torturing to death helpless women was honorable? With a man like Small standing at her side, those poor women who had been killed had not had any chance to escape or fight for their lives. She knew the women had been grabbed and made prisoners by the hulking Small, may even have been lured into danger by this plain, coldly smiling woman. Then the woman gave her what could only be called a smirk, even though it held that same cold madness her other smiles had held.

"I especially wouldnae hurt Tormand's child."

So deep was Morainn's shock that she could only stare at the woman for a moment. She fought to regain her senses, knowing she needed to be alert for any chance to escape, or to allow Walin a chance to get away. Staring into the woman's hard, soul-empty dark eyes, Morainn could see no evidence that the woman was lying, but perhaps it was impossible to tell that when a person was utterly insane. They could even believe the lies they told.

"Ye think that Walin is Tormand's child?" she asked, imbuing her voice with a hint of amusement. "He would have claimed Walin if he had thought he had a child."

"Of course he would. The mon can display some honor, though nay much. He didnae ken about the boy. Margaret Macauley was a stupid little whore. I think she believed he would marry her when he found out she carried his child. Sad to say there was no chance that he could be told so that he might believe it or doubt it, for she was sent to a nunnery shortly after she bedded the bastard. Her family realized at last that she had the soul of a whore and sent her to get purified by the power of the church. I was there at the time and she told me all about her great love for Tormand."

There was a bitter tone to the woman's voice with a hint of a growing temper. "Why didnae she send word to him?" Morainn asked. "He would have helped."

"She did send word to him, but all those sweet love letters telling him how she was carrying his child beneath her heart, a heart that beat only for him, ne'er made it to him."

"Because she trusted ye to see that he got them."

"Ye are a verra clever lass, arenae ye?" Ada did not look as if she appreciated that. "But, alas, the poor lass died shortly after bearing a son. Bled to death. Happens at a birth, ye ken."

Especially when aided by an insane woman, Morainn thought. She glanced toward Walin to see him staring at the woman with wide eyes, his little face pale. This had to be hurting him. Walin was a very clever boy and Morainn was sure that he understood everything this woman said, probably understood all she was not saying directly as well. She prayed that he would have the courage to speak to Tormand if Morainn did not escape this trap.

Walin's parentage was of no consequence at the moment, nor was the sad and tragic fate of his mother. All that she should be thinking of was how to get Walin out of the reach of these two insane people. She could not openly order the boy to run, for Morainn was sure the hulking great Small would catch Walin before he could get away, even if Walin knew how to get out without going to the door. She had not had the time to point out where the bolt-hole was. She was going to have to depend on the cleverness of the boy to figure out when to run and where to go, and Morainn was sure that was a lot to ask of a little boy.

"How did Walin end up at my doorstep then?" Morainn asked, honestly curious even if most of her questions were simply intended to keep the woman talking as Morainn tried to think of some way to free Walin.

"Weel, I thought having a bairn would get Tormand to notice me so I took it home with me." She shrugged, but there was a tightness to the gesture that told Morainn the woman was getting angry just remembering that time. "I didnae like the nunnery anyway. My parents thought the bairn was mine and they were ready to confront Tormand, to make him marry me. Then my father decided that it was best to be sure I wasnae lying and he had a midwife determine my virginity. Of course I hadnae thought of that and my ruse was revealed. They took the baby and gave him to one of the servant women to raise. They then made me marry that fat pig."

The woman's temper was rising rapidly and Morainn could almost smell a wildness in the air, the sharp scent of uncontrolled emotion. Morainn wanted to hear the whole sordid tale, but she began to think it might have been unwise to urge the woman to tell the rest of the story. She felt as if she had just prodded a snake.

"Weel, they have all paid. All of them. And that fat pig my father made me marry isnae so verra fat anymore, is he? And the servant woman who took the bairn and ruined my chance to claim Tormand as my own paid too. That is when the lad was brought here. I would have come and gotten him after I rid myself of the traitor who took the bairn away, but I was forced to marry that fat pig."

Just the way the woman said *all of them* told Morainn that Ada's parents had paid dearly for making their child do what she did not wish to do. Ada seemed to be implying that she had also killed the maid, mayhap her own mother and father, and someone who had supposedly betrayed her by bringing Walin to Morainn's doorstep. Morainn did not know what to do in the presence of such madness. A quick glance at Small told her that, although Ada appeared to be lost in her memories of all the wrongs done her, he was alert and watching her.

"What was the betrayal?" she felt compelled to ask.

"Weel, the fool was to kill the boy and leave him at Tormand's door. I had written a verra eloquent note to tell Tormand that his son lost his life because of Tormand's own sins. I felt sure that would hurt the fool. He may be a cruel bastard to women, caring nothing for them except for bedding them, but I kenned that he loved the bairns. But, nay, the mon ruined my idea and it was a good one. 'Tis unfair that I must always be surrounded by fools, save my wonderful Small who has never let me down."

"Enough, m'lady," the man said in his deep rumbling voice. "It is time for us to leave this place."

"Oh, those fools willnae be back any time soon. The witch wishes to ken a few things ere she dies. 'Tis only courteous to tell her what she needs to know." She reached up to pat his chest. "We will leave soon, Small. I ken that ye are eager to make the witch pay for our injuries." Ada looked at Morainn and smiled. "Old Ide healed our injuries verra nicely and I discovered that she hates ye. That is what I used to make her help us. She truly thinks ye are the one behind all these murders, although I think she just convinces herself of that so that she may get ye hanged. She wants ye dead, witch. The old fool was willing to do anything we wanted just so that would happen."

A woman who killed people over imagined slights mocking another woman who imagined an enemy where there was none? A woman who wanted to kill an innocent child just to hurt someone and then killed the person who could not bring himself to obey her order finding Ide's need to kill a rival something to disdain? Morainn felt all that was as great a proof of the woman's insanity as anything. She also should not be so surprised that Old Ide would do anything to see her dead, for she had done the same with Morainn's mother. It was beginning to look as though the woman would be victorious again.

Small moved to reach out and grab Morainn. She took one step back, frantically wondering where she could go and how she could take Walin with her, when Bonegnasher suddenly leapt in to help her. Small howled when the dog latched onto his arm. Morainn started to run toward Walin only to be leapt on by Ada. The woman acted very much like William had when the cat had leapt on Ada. It took all of Morainn's attention just to save her eyes from the woman's long nails.

A yelp caught her attention. As Morainn turned, intending to slam the slightly smaller woman against the wall, she caught a brief look at Bonegnasher lying limply against the wall a few feet away. When she finally managed to slam the woman against the wall, Ada screeched so loud Morainn's ears started to hurt. A high cry of anger came from Morainn's right as she shook free of the dazed woman's hold and Morainn saw Walin racing over to Small. She cried out in alarm and moved toward Walin to stop him. Small swung out with his arm, the blood dripping from it making a gruesome arc, as he hit Walin.

Morainn watched in horror as Walin's little body seemed to fly through the air. He landed on the bed, but before a sense of relief had even begun to grow in her, Walin bounced a few times and fell off the other side with a sickening thump. She started to go to him only to be yanked to a halt by Small's thick, calloused hand grabbing her by the arm. He twisted it up behind her back until even breathing caused her a searing pain in her arm. Morainn watched as Ada shook herself and then walked over to glare at her.

"I will so enjoy killing ye, witch," Ada said.

"M'lady, we really should get out of here," Small said. "The men could be back and they might be able to stop ye from getting what ye want."

"As ye wish." Ada started toward the door.

"Walin," Morainn said, wanting to ask if she could see to the boy and yet knowing there would be no mercy shown by either of these people.

"Ye come along quietly and I willnae have Small come back and cut the lad's throat."

There was no other choice but to nod and allow herself to be dragged along by Small as the man and his mistress discussed the best way to get to whatever hovel they planned to kill her in. As Small started to pull her out of the room she called back to Walin, "I love ye, Walin. Tell Tormand that I will ne'er stop dreaming of him."

Small slapped her on the side of the head so hard, her ears rang and Morainn began to pray as she was dragged away. She prayed that Walin had not been badly hurt. She also prayed that Tormand and the others would return soon so that they could help the boy. She prayed her lover would understand the message she had been sending him and also prayed that little Walin had been conscious enough to hear it. They stepped outside into a sunny day and she prayed that it would not rain so that there might be a trail the men could follow to come to save her. She then began to pray for herself as Small threw her over his saddle, knocking all the breath from her body.

"Who is Geordie?" Tormand asked Simon.

Tormand needed to talk; he needed to be distracted so that he could stop thinking of what might be happening to Morainn. Everything within him was screaming that he had to get to her, yet there he stood while the horses were watered and allowed to cool down a bit. He knew the stop in his mad race back to the tower house was a necessary one. It would help no one if the horses were injured or killed because they had been pushed too hard. He knew he needed his horse because he could not run or fly to the tower house. That did not make standing there while Morainn was in danger any easier to bear.

"He was my father's second," replied Simon.

"Second? Ye are the son of a laird then, are ye?" Tormand decided he must look as crazed with worry as he felt, for Simon never spoke of his past or his family, except in the most vague terms, and was obviously doing so now just to distract him.

"Second son. My older brother Henry is the laird now. Geordie left shortly after I did. My three younger brothers are," Simon paused and then shrugged, "somewhere. My two sisters were married off shortly after their first flux, but they seem to have fared weel enough. I e'en hear from them now and then. Henry is a mon ye dinnae wish to linger with. Brutal, especially with women. I ken at least two he probably killed with his *affections*. I believe he killed our father, too, and some day I will prove it."

"*Jesu*, Simon," Tormand muttered, sure he looked as shocked as his kinsmen did. "'Tis nay wonder that ye never speak of your kin."

Simon smiled faintly. "Old memories. I havenae been back there since I was ten years old. I went to visit the family at Michaelmas that year. I should have stayed with the family that was fostering me as they had asked me to. When I returned to them after the visit, the only time I left them after that and went home was to see my father buried three years later."

"And ye really think Henry killed the mon?" asked Harcourt.

"I am as sure as I can be of anything that is recalled

from a time when I was more boy than mon. I think the fact that Henry has blood on his hands, our father's and that of several women, is why I work so hard to punish those who break our laws, nay matter if they are the ones of the church or the king. I suspicion Henry hasnae changed much over the years since I last saw him. When Geordie found me one day he told me why he had left the only home he had ever kenned. Henry grew more obviously brutal once my father's restraining hand was off the reins. Geordie refused to make his oath to a mon like Henry and so he left."

"He is a good mon," Simon said, as he looked around at the Murrays and Walter. "He had no part in this."

"I ken it," said Tormand. "'Twas that bitch Old Ide. She deserves a far harsher punishment than being scared nigh unto death by ye. I just cannae think of what that might be, seeing as ye promised Old Geordie that ye wouldnae hang her."

"I did, didnae I?" Simon smiled faintly. "I didnae, however, promise nay to punish her in some way. Ye see, Ide has good reason to fear that Morainn will take her place as midwife and healer here. Ide is nay verra good at her craft. In truth, she has killed a few people with her clumsy, ignorant methods, and, I believe, her utter disdain for the healing that can be done with a good use of soap and water."

"Are ye going to try and have her charged with the murder of those people?"

"Nay, for that will get her hanged and I promised Geordie I wouldnae do that, didnae I? That doesnae mean that I cannae make verra certain that, slowly, whisper by whisper, it becomes verra clear to a lot of people that ye will be risking life and limb if ye call upon Old Ide to come and heal ye or bring your bairn into this world."

Tormand shook his head in admiration. "Sneaky. I like it." He could not stop himself from glancing in the direction of the tower house again.

"The horses have rested enough," Simon said and immediately mounted his. "A steady, even pace and we will be there soon."

Simon had barely finished speaking before Tormand was in the saddle and riding toward the tower house. He felt such a need to reach Morainn that it was hard to follow Simon's advice about keeping a steady, even gait. He ached to spur his horse into a gallop, demanding that the beast go as fast as it could. Every instinct he had told him that they would be too late, that the trap Ide had helped set for Morainn had already closed around his love.

His love. The words hit Tormand so hard he nearly fell out of the saddle. He loved Morainn. It was so clear to him now that the words had entered his head. They had been in his heart from the moment he had first seen her, first looked into her beautiful sea-blue eyes. Tormand had to wonder why he had fought against it so hard, especially since he knew he did not want to return to his heedless bouncing from bed to bed, being intimate with women he quickly forgot. He wanted Morainn and only Morainn.

Then Tormand thought of his past and of the list Morainn had seen, a list that made it very clear what sort of life he had led before meeting her. He just prayed he would have the chance to tell her that.

Chapter 17

Tormand slowed his rush to find Morainn the moment he saw the open door to the room they had shared. This time he forced himself to go forward, fighting the cold fear that gripped him and tried to hold him in place. He breathed a huge sigh of relief when he saw no sign of a body or even much blood. He did see a few signs of a struggle, from the knocked over table and the disordered rushes on the floor to a little blood near the door that he quickly looked away from, refusing to allow the sight to stir his fear for Morainn into a useless panic.

A soft moan had him rushing to the far side of the bed, where he found Walin struggling to sit up, blood trailing down his pale cheek from a cut on his head. He could not understand how or why the boy was here as he bent to help Walin up. The others joined him and he soon had Walin bandaged and sitting in a chair sipping at a small tankard of cider.

Simon was crouched by his slowly rousing dog. Tormand could not hear what the man was saying, but the tone of Simon's voice told him the man was trying to coax the dog into getting up. Seeing how pale and shaken the boy was, Tormand put aside the gnawing need to rush out and hunt for Morainn.

"Lad," asked Simon, as he stepped up next to Tormand, "how did ye and Bonegnasher come to be here?"

"I wanted to see Morainn," the boy replied, as tears slowly trickled down his cheeks. "I missed her and no one would let me go to visit her e'en for just a wee while."

"What happened here, Walin?"

"Those bad people came here just like they came to our cottage," Walin said, crying so hard that his voice cracked and shook, making what he said a little difficult to understand. "The woman said a lot of awful things and then the mon said they had to leave so they werenae caught here when all of ye returned. He tried to grab Morainn, but Bonegnasher leapt over and bit him on the arm." Walin looked at the dog that sat by Simon's side, leaning up against the man as though it was still a little stunned.

"Calm yourself, lad," Tormand said gently. "We need ye to speak more clearly and tell us what happened step by step."

"When ye left, I let Bonegnasher free and followed ye. Morainn gave me a verra long lecture. I just wanted to see her. We had something to eat and then the bad people came and the woman and Morainn talked about a lot of things and then when the mon reached for Morainn, Bonegnasher leapt right up and bit the mon on the arm. He threw the dog against the wall just like he did to William, and then I tried to fight him but he threw me, too. Is Bonegnasher going to be all right?"

"Aye." Simon scratched the dog's ears. "I think ye will be too. That means we only have to find Morainn and bring her back."

"They are going to hurt her and kill her," Walin said. "That lady talked about killing people, and she kens about me and who I am and was even going to kill me once but the mon she told to do it couldnae and he left me with Morainn and then she killed him." He looked at Tormand. "And she said ye are my father and some woman named Margaret Macauley was my mother and she was sent to the nunnery where this woman was and the bitch killed my mother and tried to tell her parents that I was her bairn so they would make ye marry her." Walin looked around at all the men. "I think she killed them too. Ye have to get Morainn away from them."

Tormand felt as if he was going to swoon like some lack-witted maiden as what Walin said began to sink into his mind. He staggered back a little and Harcourt caught him by the arm to steady him. It was not that Walin said he was his son that caused the most shock; it was how many times the boy had nearly been killed just because of one madwoman's jealousy. He could have lost his child before he had even learned of his existence.

"I can see it clear now," murmured Harcourt. "It explains why he always made me think I should ken who he is."

"Curse it, I cannae think on this now."

"Nay," agreed a tearful Walin. "Ye have to go and get my Morainn back. Ye cannae let that bad woman hurt her."

Forcing aside all thought on the chance that a madwoman had actually been telling the truth and

Walin was his son, Tormand nodded. "That is what is important now. Do ye ken where they went? Did ye hear anything at all that may help us reach her faster?"

"Nay," Walin said in a small voice. "I was lying there feeling as if I couldnae breathe, ye ken, because I bounced off the bed and landed verra hard on the floor. Morainn told me she loved me as they took her away. Oh, and she said I should tell ye that she will always dream of ye. I dinnae ken why she said that. Why didnae she just say she loved ye, too? Or e'en ask ye to take care of me or the like?"

"Because she was telling me where they were taking her," Tormand said quietly, hope surging in his chest as he crouched down so that he was eye to eye with the boy. "Think verra hard, laddie. Did they say anything about how long they might have to travel or which direction they were going in?"

"Nay, but, if Bonegnasher isnae too badly hurt, ye could have him show ye the way. He bit the giant and the mon was bleeding like a stuck pig." Walin frowned. "The mon did say that they shouldnae be out when it was so light as they might be seen, and if they didnae hurry they wouldnae e'en have the morning mists to hide them as they rode, for they would be burned away by the sun in an hour."

"Bonegnasher is good for a hunt," said Simon.

Uilliam stepped up and lightly brushed his hand over Walin's curls. "I will take the lad back to your home, Tormand, and we will wait there for ye to bring Morainn back."

Walter also stepped up and said, "I will go with them to watch his back unless ye think ye will need me."

Tormand nodded and stood up. "Nay, we face only two people and I would feel better kenning that Uilliam and Walin have someone like ye to watch their backs." He looked down at Walin and then lightly stroked the boy's tearstained cheek. "We will talk later when we have our Morainn safe at home. Aye?"

"Aye."

As Tormand and the others hurried out to where their horses waited, he glanced at the dog and was pleased to see that the animal seemed to be fully recovered. The dog caught the scent quickly and ran around in circles as he waited for the men to mount their horses. It should be an easy trail for Bonegnasher to follow, thought Tormand, as he looked at the blood on the ground. This time there would be no Ide to clean and stitch the bastard's wound.

As they rode, following the dog, Tormand fought his mounting fear for Morainn by thinking of Walin. It was true that, once a relationship was claimed, it was easy to see himself in the boy, but he could not trust only his eyes in such an important matter. Neither did he think it was wise to trust completely in what a scared little boy thought he had heard. The only thing that kept him from immediately denying the possibility that Walin was his son was that he already began to recall a Margaret Macauley and her big blue eyes, eyes just like Walin's. He struggled to pull up every memory of the woman as they rode and found it easier now that he recalled her eyes.

"Do ye remember bedding a woman named Margaret Macauley?" asked Simon, as they slowed for a minute so that Bonegnasher could sniff around to make sure he found the trail they all wanted him to.

"Aye, and the time is right. I spent a week with the lass about seven years ago. I remember that she always thought it amusing how easily she could creep out of her house. One night she e'en had me sneak in, as she wished to make love in her own bed with her parents asleep down the hall." He grimaced. "I left her soon after that for, with a few ales in me, I had thought it funny at the time, but nay when I was sober again. She also had that glint in her eye."

"What glint?"

"The one that says she is trying to think of ways to drag me before the altar. There he goes," he cried when, with a soft yip, Bonegnasher bounded off again.

Tormand put all thoughts of Margaret and blue-eyed sons out of his head and started to plan the many ways he was going to kill the bastards that had taken his Morainn. He used those bloodthirsty thoughts to keep himself from thinking on all the ways they could be hurting Morainn even now. Having seen what these people did to the women they caught, he knew he would become as mad as they were if he allowed such thoughts to prey upon his mind. He kept one thought and one thought only in the fore of his mind—he would find Morainn and he would slaughter the ones who had taken her away from him.

Morainn bit back a groan as she slowly opened her eyes. Only one opened completely and she tensed as she suddenly recalled why her left eye throbbed and would only open a little way. Small had hit her when she had struggled to get away once he had set her down inside of a hovel that smelled strongly of sheep. She had seen the stakes stuck in the dirt floor and, remembering her dream, had fought hard against being tied down to them. Morainn did not have to look to know she had lost that fight.

For a moment a blind panic swelled up inside of her, especially when the feel of the dirt against the skin of her back told her she was naked. Morainn fought against the mindless terror that threatened to steal her wits, but it was several minutes before she began to calm herself. She found anger at what was being done to her and clung to it, using it to give her strength.

She also told herself that Tormand would come for her. In a way, fate had already delivered her one strong hope for rescue, although she thought it odd that that hope had come in the form of a dog called Bonegnasher and a naughty little boy who could not stay where he had been told to. Simon would use his dog to follow the trail left by Small and Ada. Then she recalled that the dog had been hurt and panic tried to stir to life again. She *would* believe that, like her cat William, Bonegnasher would be fine and the dog would lead Tormand and the others right to her. Just as she had to believe that Walin was all right, a little bruised but otherwise fine. All she had to do was stay alive until her rescuers came.

When her tormentors crouched on either side of her Morainn felt her anger sharpen and welcomed it, nurtured it. She glared at both of them even though the knives they each held chilled her to the bone.

Forcing her gaze away from the cold steel that would soon be used on her helpless body, she studied Ada.

Plain was the only word to describe the woman. In fact, Morainn did not think she had ever seen a woman, or man, so lacking in any memorable feature, good or bad. She had dark eyes, but they were not a brown that drew any attention. The woman's hair was that same sort of ordinary brown, not enlivened with a reddish gleam, not too straight, too thin, or too curly. Just plain brown hair. Her skin was clear, her features even, but no more than that. It was the same with her body in that she was neither too tall or too short, too big or too small. If one looked very hard, one could see past the blinding ordinariness of the woman and see that she had a neat, womanly shape, but one had to look very hard and Morainn suspected few bothered. Ada was a woman who did not catch the eye and probably did not stick in a person's memory past a brief greeting.

It explained why Simon had been having difficulty finding anyone who could describe the woman. Ada MacLean had nothing anyone could really describe. Morainn knew that, even though she strongly believed the seeds of this woman's madness had been inside the woman from the moment she was conceived, being a person no one could remember or noticed must have given those seeds some very fertile ground to grow in.

"Are ye ready to be punished, Morainn Ross?" asked Ada.

"For what? Living?" Morainn could see that the anger in her voice surprised the woman. "Och, aye, I suspicion a lot of women didnae mourn the loss of Ladies Isabella and Clara. But Lady Marie? She was an innocent, her only crime being that she was Tormand's friend. For that ye destroyed the heart of a good mon and left two bairns motherless. And Lady Katherine Hay was as near to being a saint as a person can get."

"She took my page away from me!" Ada took several deep breaths and then continued in her usual icy little voice. "The bitch said I was cruel to the boy. I was simply giving the lad the discipline he needed. She told his parents and they took him away. That fat pig I had to marry wouldnae get me another one, either."

"And for that ye butchered her? Ye robbed Sir John of the woman he loved, his angel, and left e'en more children without a loving mother. The punishment doesnae fit the crime."

"She was as bad as all the others, using her beauty and womanly wiles to get what she wanted. She had no right to interfere in my business. No right at all. And, ye, witch, willnae be allowed to either."

The first cut was not deep, but it hurt so bad Morainn nearly screamed. Instead she gritted her teeth and refused to make a sound. She would not give these butchers the pleasure of hearing her plead for mercy.

"I already have," Morainn said, as soon as she felt she could speak without revealing her pain or fear. "They ken who ye are now. They also ken that ye have taken me and, nay matter what happens here, ye will lose this sick game ye play. It willnae be Tormand who dances at the end of a rope, but ye."

"Nay, ye are lying. Ye havenae seen that."

Morainn caught the look of fear in the woman's eyes. "I have seen all of this and I ken how it ends," she lied.

"Ye willnae be a nothing anymore, Lady MacLean. Nay, ye will be a curse on the lips of thousands."

"Make her scream, Small."

A grinning Small slowly ran his knife tip down the inside of one thigh and up the other. Morainn desperately wanted to scream for the pain was even worse than before, but her fury at him and his perverted mistress held it back. As soon as she dared open her mouth again, she cursed them both. It was not long before Morainn was silently praying as hard as she knew how for Tormand to find her before she ran out of curses or blood.

Tormand stood with the others and stared at the hovel the dog had led them to. He wanted to race inside, sword swinging, but a shred of common sense smothered the urge. He did not have any knowledge of the place he would be running into and could easily get himself killed. That would do no one any good. At least he knew Morainn was alive. They had all heard her curses long before they had seen the long deserted cottage.

"Do ye think her father was a sailor?" asked Harcourt, as a particularly vicious insult concerning Small's father and his unnatural love of sheep echoed through the air.

It surprised him that he could do so, but Tormand briefly smiled. "'Tis possible. She does have a unique way with an insult."

"I hadnae wanted to, but I had expected to hear screams of pain."

"The pain is there." Tormand could hear it, almost feel it. "But Morainn has worked herself up into a glorious fury. And, I think, she is determined not to give the bastards e'en a whisper of a plea for mercy."

"Ah, weel, I can understand that but, if she doesnae give them what they want, they could kill her quickly instead of continuing to torment her."

"Aye, they could, but e'en Morainn's stubbornness cannae hold back the pain and fear for verra long, which is why we had best rescue her soon." He looked at Simon. "How do we do this?"

Simon opened his mouth to reply when one of their horses gave a loud challenge to one of the horses grazing in front of the cottage. It came in a brief moment of silence and cut through the air like the blare of a horn. Tormand looked at Simon who nodded and they all started running toward the cottage. A huge man burst out of the cottage nearly carrying a small brown-haired woman. Tormand saw Bennett at his side and, with one sharp move of his hand, sent his brother to the cottage. Tormand then forced all thought of Morainn out of his mind and fixed his attention firmly on the two people trying to escape the justice they so richly deserved.

The big man was just reaching out to grasp the reins of his horse when Tormand hurled himself at the man's back. With an ear-piercing screech the woman stumbled back, deserting the man who had been trying to save her. Tormand got Small pinned to the ground and suddenly saw Simon leap over him. Out of the corner of his eye he saw Simon knock the woman down. The glint of a knife told Tormand that he had been wrong to assume she had been deserting Small. That mistake had nearly earned him a knife buried in his back.

Small suddenly lunged up and threw Tormand off his back. Drawing his sword the man started toward Simon and the woman who was thrashing wildly in Simon's grasp and screaming out curses. Tormand drew his sword, but the sound attracted Small's attention and he abruptly turned back to Tormand, sword in hand. For a moment, Tormand actually wondered if he could win against this man who was so much bigger and stronger than he was. It did not take him long to see that even though Small had more height, more strength, a longer reach, and was surprisingly fast for such a large man, he did not have the skill with a sword that Tormand did. The man was also distracted by the screams of Ada MacLean and that cost him. One bad stumble, one fleeting glance toward Ada, and the man ended his life with Tormand's sword buried in his chest.

After cleaning off his sword and sheathing it, Tormand moved to where Simon stood next to a securely bound Ada. The woman stared at Small's body, her grief a scar upon her plain face. Then she turned to look at Tormand and the hatred in her expression was so fierce he almost took a step back. The madness afflicting the woman began to spill out in a litany of vile curses and gruesome threats that filled the silence until Tormand looked at Simon.

"Please, gag the bitch," he said. "I must see how Morainn fares," Tormand announced, as Simon hurried to silence Ada, and he strode toward the cottage.

* * *

Morainn stared at the door her two tormentors had suddenly, and swiftly, left through. A moment later Ada's screams filled the air and Morainn's relief was so great it almost deadened her pain. When Bennett strode in, however, all she could think of was where was Tormand? Then Bennett tossed a coarse blanket over her and she remembered that she was naked and staked out like some sacrifice to a pagan god. She felt herself blush as he cut the restraints on her wrists and ankles.

"My clothes," she said, and hissed in a breath as pain swept over her when he helped her sit up. "Walin?"

"The boy is fine," replied Bennett, as he collected up her clothing and began to help her get dressed with an efficiency she had to admire. "I am nay sure I should put these on ye until your wounds are cleaned and dressed."

"I will deal with my wounds when I get home." She winced a little as he had to tear a few strips off her petticoat to use to tie the gown on her when it became clear that it had been cut off. "I cannae ride away from here naked." Even though she had done little to help herself get dressed, she felt weak and was breathing hard. Then she heard the clash of swords. "Tormand?"

"Is one of the best swordsmen I have e'er kenned. Now, lean against me if ye must keep sitting up. Ye have more cuts on ye than I wished to count and many are still bleeding."

Morainn did not argue. She fought the need to close her eyes and let unconsciousness ease her pain. Despite Bennett's assurances about Tormand's skill with a sword, she needed to see him. When he finally walked into the cottage, handsome and whole, she almost wept. The look on his face told her that she was not looking very hale herself, however.

"'Tis all right," she said, as he crouched beside her and took her away from Bennett, enfolding her gently in his own arms. "They are all shallow cuts."

"Your gown is soaked in blood," Tormand said. "We need to tend to these wounds."

"Nay here. Please, nay here."

"She insisted on getting dressed," said Bennett. "Said she could tend her wounds at home."

"Aye," Morainn said, clutching at Tormand's arm with one shaky hand. "Nay here. I want to leave this place; I *need* to leave this place. Now." She managed to spit out the last word before the blackness she had been holding back swept over her, taking her away from the pain.

Tormand quickly put his hand over her heart, felt its steady beat, and was able to push back the panic that had seized him when she had gone limp in his arms. She was alive. For now that was all that mattered.

"Caught tight, arenae ye?" murmured Bennett.

"Aye," replied Tormand. "Like running salmon in a weel-cast net. But, first, I must get her healed and strong again."

"And then?"

"Then I pray she doesnae decide to throw this fish back and walk away."

Chapter 18

Pain was the first thing Morainn was aware of as she fought her way out of the clinging web of sleep. Slowly, she opened her eyes and glanced around. Even as she realized she was in Tormand's bedchamber, she recalled everything that had happened to her and fear swept over her. She also wondered why she had a sudden urge to weep like a lost child.

"Morainn?"

Tormand rose from his seat by the bed and moved closer to Morainn. Her hand was clenching the blanket so tightly he feared she would tear it, so he took her hand in his, lightly brushing his thumb over her whitened knuckles. For four long days he had watched over her, cared for her during a thankfully brief and mild bout of fever, and waited for her to come back to him. That she had woken up afraid hurt his heart.

"Ye are safe now, Morainn," he assured her, as he sat down on the edge of the bed. "Small is dead and they hanged Ada MacLean this morning."

She took a deep breath and let it out slowly, pushing the fear out along with the air. Once her fear was greatly eased, Morainn realized that her pain was not really that severe. That implied that she was already healing.

"How long?" she asked, wincing as she forced the words past her painfully dry throat.

"Four days," he replied, as he moved quickly to get her some cider sweetened with honey to soothe her throat.

As he helped her drink, Tormand studied her carefully. The moment they had arrived at his home, he had placed her on his bed and stripped off her bloody clothes. That first sight of her bruised and slashed body had nearly brought him to his knees. He did not think he would ever be able to forget that sight, but seeing that she was looking better and the wounds she had suffered had not festered, lessened the power of it.

"Nora said she and her mother would come round later this morning and help ye bathe, mayhap e'en tend to your hair, if ye were awake and wanted it." He set aside the empty tankard and grasped her hand again, needing to feel it return his grip as proof that she was recovering.

"I want," she said. "I want it verra badly. I need to wash it all away. Did Ada confess everything then?"

"Continuously and loudly. She also had a collection of wee bows made from locks of hair, what we feel sure is hair from her victims. Small was both her lover and her servant." He shook his head. "'Tis hard to believe that such a small, plain woman could have done such things. She was just so—" he hesitated as he tried to think of the right word.

"Ordinary. Verra, verra ordinary," Morainn offered. "There was nothing about her that one would ever remember for verra long."

He nodded. "I suspicion she will be remembered now, if only for all the vile curses she spat out at the crowd that had come to watch her hang."

"Och, aye, they will remember who she was and what she did, but I doubt they will recall what she looked like e'en a week from now. I think the fact that she was always overlooked, always forgotten and ignored, fed a madness she was born with." After a heavy moment of silence while they both thought that over, she asked, "Is Walin weel?"

"Aye, he is fine. I suspicion he will slip in to look at ye before too much longer. He has done so a lot while ye have been sleeping for so long. Simon has decided he was wrong to dismiss the lad's feeling that there was a trap being set. It seems Walin had overheard Ide boasting of how she would soon be rid of ye and that could weel have made us more wary of leaving ye alone and all riding off to meet that mon."

"Walin can be verra good at hearing things and kenning what is important."

He nodded, took a deep breath, and said, "Walin tells me that Ada said he is my son."

Morainn winced because a selfish part of her had wanted to keep that a secret, to keep Walin all to herself. "Did Ada nay tell ye anything about it while she was doing all that confessing?"

"A lot, although she was so crazed, I didnae ken

what to believe. What I do ken is that he might be. A Margaret Macauley was my lover seven years ago and I did hear that she had been sent to a nunnery where she had died. No one had e'er told me that there was a child, however. Yet, there is a look to him, the look of my family."

"Aye, there is." Morainn told him everything Ada had said during the confrontation in the tower house.

Tormand cursed and dragged his hand through his hair. "She has been killing people for a verra long time, hasnae she?"

"Aye. I doubt we will e'er ken just how many she did kill. I think, in the beginning, she was careful to hide what she had done, to make the deaths look, weel, normal."

"Weel, right now we need to talk about Walin and nay that madwoman," Tormand said as he stood up. "Unfortunately, I think Nora and her mother are here and there is nay time for it now. It would be best done when ye are stronger as weel."

He had barely finished speaking when Nora and her mother stepped into the room. Morainn was glad of the reprieve. She feared he was about to tell her that he would be taking Walin away from her and knew she needed to be strong to argue that, to fight for at least a large share of Walin's life.

By the time Nora and her mother had her cleaned up, the bed linen and her nightdress changed, and her hair washed and braided, Morainn doubted she had the strength left to fluff her own pillow. When they left her alone for a while to go and get her something to eat, Morainn simply rested, too tired to even think. She struggled to wake up fully when Nora returned with a tray filled with bread, cheese, fruit, and something that smelled like a well-seasoned broth.

"Did your mother go home?" she asked Nora, as her friend helped her sit up and began to feed her spoonfuls of the thick broth.

"Nay, she is in the kitchen making something for the men to eat and talking Sir Tormand into hiring her cousins Mary and Agnes to keep his house and cook for him. Mary and Agnes lost their wee cottage, ye ken, and have been living with their sons. They would be verra happy to have a room to themselves and a wee bit of coin to spend. They love their sons, but they dinnae love living with them and their growing families."

"I think that, despite what Magda is probably saying, Sir Tormand is a good mon to work for," Morainn said between mouthfuls of food.

"Aye, that is what my mother thinks as weel." Nora handed Morainn a chunk of bread smothered in honey to nibble on. "I wept when I saw what those bastards had done to ye."

"I am alive, Nora. Far too many others were nay as lucky as I was."

"'Tis what I told myself and it helped. That and that ye willnae be left with verra many scars."

Morainn stopped just as she was about to take a bite of bread. She had not considered the possibility of scars and felt dismayed over the thought of being marred. A moment later she inwardly shook her head and took a bite of bread. Vanity was a dangerous thing. She had never thought she possessed any, but she obviously had a little. Whenever it bit again she promised herself she would just keep repeating the words *I am alive.* When a concern about how Tormand might see them started to creep into her mind, she ruthlessly banished it. If the man could not abide a few marks on his lover's body then she was well rid of him.

Which she might be very soon anyway, she realized, and fought the urge to cry. Her heart would undoubtedly break when he left her, but she swore she would not grieve for long. She would always love the rutting fool, but she was not one to bemoan what she could not have. Her life had been filled with could-not-haves. Morainn knew that she would fare better living without him than if she had to spend her life without his love or wondering just how often he left her bed for another's.

"Are ye hurting?" asked Nora.

It was obvious that her friend had seen her darkening mood in her expression and Morainn sent out a little prayer of thanks that Nora had not guessed the true reason behind it. "Nay, not much. I was but struggling with a sudden attack of vanity." She smiled faintly. "I ne'er thought I was vain at all, but there is obviously a wee touch of that sin in my heart."

"Everyone has some. The trick is not to have so much that all ye e'er think about is how ye look. I discovered mine when James once caught me cleaning out the hog pen and I was covered in muck from head to toe. The fool laughed. He was soon covered in muck as weel." She grinned.

Morainn laughed despite how it pinched at her

healing wounds. "I must nay bemoan a few scars. When I gain the courage to look at them, I will just remind myself that I am alive. I also still have all my hair and they didnae have time to cut my face as they did the others."

Nora shuddered. "Hush. I dinnae e'en wish to think about all that might have happened. So, let us speak of something else. Is Walin truly Sir Tormand's son?"

"I am nay sure that talking about that will cheer me much, but, aye, I believe he is. When Ada told me about it she wasnae the crazed woman Simon dragged back here. Och, she was quite mad and nearly lost her tight control on it, but I am certain she kenned what she was saying and I believe it." She told Nora everything Ada had said. "Tormand says the boy has the look of his family and he does. The mother may have given Walin that lovely black hair and those big blue eyes, but everything else about him came straight from Tormand. I could see it the moment she told me the story."

"What are ye going to do about it?"

"I have no idea. He *is* Tormand's son; I am certain of it. I am but the woman who has cared for him for four years."

"Ye are far more than that to Walin. Do ye ken? I am thinking the laddie is the one who will settle all this."

"Mayhap that is just how it should be."

Nora soon left and Morainn was glad of it, something she felt a little guilty about. She was tired, still suffered some pain from her ordeal, and she was heartsore. Reminding herself that she was alive did not, at that precise moment, bring her all that much joy. She told herself she felt so morose, so close to tears, because she was still weak, but did not believe a word of it. The quickest cure for her impending black mood was to let the need for sleep take her away from it all for a little while longer and she closed her eyes. It was a cowardly retreat and she knew it, but she swore to herself that she would be brave and strong later.

"Morainn? Are ye awake?"

It was not really the gentle pat of a small hand on her face that woke Morainn, but that sweet young boy's voice that was as familiar to her as her own. Turning her head even as she opened her eyes, Morainn smiled at Walin. The look of worry on his face vanished abruptly as he smiled back at her. Her heart twisted as she thought of how soon she might lose him to his father, a father who could give Walin a far better life than she ever could.

She reached out to stroke his soft cheek and fought the urge to grab him in her arms and run. It was not only a foolish urge, since she doubted she could even walk very far, but she knew Tormand would find them no matter how far she ran and well she hid. He would undoubtedly have the aid of his very large family as well.

"I am now," she teased. "Have ye behaved whilst I was asleep?"

"Och, aye. They wouldnae let me go to the hanging, but I didnae mind so verra much. I didnae really want to see that woman again. But, Morainn, did ye hear what she said that day? I have a father. Sir Tormand is my father."

"Aye, I heard her and ye are his son. I can see it

now." When Walin frowned, she asked, "Are ye nay pleased? Ye always wished to ken who your father was."

"Aye and I am pleased, but I cannae leave ye and having a father means I have to be with him. His brothers and cousins talk about me meeting with the other Murrays who are now my kin and my clan, but I am nay sure I can do that. I think about it and then I think about how ye wouldnae be with me and I dinnae like it." He sighed and leaned over to rest his head against her chest. "I dinnae want to lose ye. Ever."

"Walin, my love, ye can never lose me. Never. But," she idly stroked his thick black curls, "ye are a growing boy and now have a father willing to teach ye, to train ye, so that ye can have a verra good life."

"I am still a bastard."

"Aye, there is nay changing that, but we both ken that a lot of bastards have gained honor and fortune. All I can give ye is work in the garden and tending the few livestock that we have."

"Dinnae ye want me anymore?"

"Of course I do. Dinnae be foolish. I will always love ye as if ye were my own child and dinnae ye ever doubt it. Howbeit, this is something that must be decided between ye and your father."

Walin stood up straight and nodded. "Aye. Mon to mon."

"Exactly."

Morainn just hoped that somewhere in that man-to-man talk they remembered her. It would kill her to lose Walin, too. Then she would truly be all alone.

* * *

It took three more days before Morainn felt she was strong enough to see to her own personal needs, even to do a little more needlework for Nora's dowry chests. Each task still exhausted her more quickly than she liked, however. It would be, at best, a week or so before she would be able to return to her cottage and her chores.

She did not really want to leave. Tormand visited her several times a day, his kinsmen wandered in and out to talk, or play chess, and everyone took excellent care of her. She was being spoiled and she had to fight the allure of that. She also had to fight the urge to cling to Tormand until he tossed her aside as he had so many other lovers. Morainn knew it would do her heart, and her pride, no good to linger until all that was good between them soured with his rejection and dismissal. It would be best to leave with all of her sweet memories intact, inflicting the pain of loss upon herself before Tormand could do it.

And then there was Walin, she thought as she crawled into bed to rest yet again. The boy was torn between his delight over having a father who welcomed him and a large family who did the same, and her. She and Tormand had agreed to let Walin think it all over for a while, but she knew Tormand wanted the boy. Morainn also knew that no one would take her side over Tormand's, even if Walin was not what most considered a legitimate son.

With each tale told her of the time Walin spent with the Murrays, each time the boy said the word father, Morainn felt sadder. She was losing the boy; she was certain of it. When Nora visited, Morainn could tell by the look on her friend's face whenever they spoke of Walin, that Nora was certain of it too.

There was a soft knock at the door and Morainn told the person to enter. She was at first foolishly delighted to see Tormand, but then she noticed how serious he looked. Had Walin made his choice?

"There is someone here to see you," Tormand said.

"Who could it be that ye feel the need to announce them this way?" she asked. "Someone I dinnae ken?"

"Weel, ye ken who he is, but ye have never really dealt with the mon. He has come round here several times since ye were hurt, but I have held him back. I wanted ye to be stronger ere ye spoke with him."

"Why?"

"Because he feared the news that ye have a brother would be too much for ye to bear."

Morainn stared at the man who stood in the doorway. Even though she had only met him once, briefly, ten years ago, Sir Adam Kerr, laird of Dubhstane, was not a man one easily forgot. He was tall, several inches over six feet, broad-shouldered, yet lean of build and about as breathtakingly handsome as Tormand was. Sir Kerr had blue eyes and thick, long black hair. He also had a beautiful mouth, the lower lip fuller than the top one. The mouth of a skilled seducer, she thought. His face was cut on lines that would make a sculptor weep with joy. Then she looked into his eyes again, heard his startling words race through her mind, and felt all the blood leave her head in a rush. Her last clear thought was—why did Sir Kerr have her eyes?

"I told ye she needed to be stronger," said Tormand, as he rushed to Morainn's side and began to chafe her wrists gently in an attempt to rouse her from her swoon.

"I suspicion she could have been as hale as she always has been and still taken the news hard," said Adam, as he settled himself comfortably in the chair next to the bed.

"Why tell her now?"

"Because she has never been close to dying before," he said quietly. "I suddenly realized she is nearly all the family I have left. Oh, my father scattered a few other bastards about the place, but none of them was verra long-lived. By the time I was able to help in any way, they were long dead and buried. Only Morainn was left." Sir Kerr smiled faintly. "My family has never bred with the proficiency of yours." He looked back at Morainn. "She begins to stir, so, if ye would be so kind, I would like to speak to her alone."

Tormand hesitated a moment, wanting to refuse, but then he left. When Sir Kerr had first arrived at Tormand's door, just after Morainn had had her wounds tended to, he had nearly slammed the door in the man's too handsome face. Jealousy over the man's part in Morainn's life had nearly choked him. Then he had glimpsed the amusement in the man's eyes, eyes exactly like Morainn's, and had wrestled his jealousy into submission. An easy thing to do when he had suddenly admitted to himself that he had liked the fact that Morainn was alone in the world except for Walin, that the family they would make together would never suffer any competition for her affections or her attention. Sir Kerr announcing that he was going to tell Morainn the truth about their kinship had revealed that selfishness in Tormand and he decided it was only fair to resent the man for it.

Although he had finally allowed Sir Kerr to look in on Morainn a few times, he had adamantly refused to allow the man to speak to her. Tormand had felt that finding out that she had a brother would be a hard blow and she needed to be healed before Sir Kerr delivered it. Morainn fainting at the news only proved that he was right. Tormand then decided that it might still be too soon and he sat down at the head of the stairs. He was far enough away for Morainn and Kerr to talk privately without him hearing them, but near enough to hear if things got too heated or Morainn needed some help.

Morainn woke to find Sir Kerr standing by her bed holding out a small tankard. With a murmur of thanks she took it, smelled that it was wine, and gulped it down. The heady brew quickly warmed her insides and she felt calmer as she handed the empty tankard back to Sir Kerr.

"Why?" she asked as she watched him set the tankard down and then sprawl in the chair pulled close to the side of her bed.

"Because my father was a randy old goat," he drawled in reply.

She coughed to hide a sudden urge to laugh. "Nay, I mean why tell me now? Why wait for so long?"

"Ah, weel, whilst my father was alive, he didnae want me to do anything or have anything to do with his other offspring."

"There are more?'

"Sad to say, there were, but ye are the only one who has survived. Once I was old enough to do something, I did, but the few still left didnae last long. Ill-fated lot. I tried to help your mother, but she wanted nothing to do with anyone named Kerr. She had her pride. I still watched over her. Unfortunately, I wasnae here when the people of the town turned on her and cast ye out."

"Pride. Aye, my mother had a lot of that." She frowned. "So that is why ye let me have the use of the cottage and the land."

He nodded. "My father was far too ill by then to ken what I was doing, but aware enough so that I couldnae claim ye outright and bring ye to Dubhstane. And," he winked, "ye do make some verra fine mead."

She smiled even though she felt a little uneasy. It was strange to suddenly have a brother, a blood relation. Morainn could not stop herself from feeling a little suspicious, however. Why would the man suddenly step off the cautious, secretive path he had walked so well until now?

"Ah, and now ye are suspicious," he said, and nodded. "Good. So ye should be, but there is nay need. Aside from a few cousins, mostly distant ones, ye are my only remaining blood kin. That truly didnae strike me until I heard that ye might be dying."

"But your father died years ago, didnae he? Why didnae it occur to ye then?"

"Because ye were doing so weel all on your own. I did consider telling ye then, but I felt ye shouldered enough burdens—what with the child left on your threshold, people whispering that ye are a witch, and every fool for miles believing ye were a lass who was free with her favors, and thus easy game. I also inherited my father's reputation for having too many women too often. Ye didnae need to be tainted by that. When I heard ye had been attacked by those killers, I did entertain the thought of riding to your rescue, but Sir Tormand got there first."

He leaned forward, rested his arms on his knees and studied her very closely. "Just what is Sir Tormand Murray to ye?"

Everything, she thought, but did not say so. "Since ye seem to ken so much about me, I suspicion ye have heard that I have visions." He nodded. "I was having ones concerning these killings and thought they might help in finding out who the murderers were. They also showed me that Tormand was nay the killer. Simon and Tormand agreed that the visions might help. When the killers turned their attentions my way, both men felt I, and Walin, would be much safer if we stayed with them."

"Verra prettily said. The truth, but nay all of it." He held up one long, elegant hand to still her protests. "It doesnae matter now. We can, mayhap, discuss that later."

"Mayhap. I am nay sure why your reputation would hold ye back. I am called a witch, am kenned to be a bastard, and am thought to have had a bastard child. Having a brother who is said to be a lecherous swine wouldnae have done me much added harm."

"I didnae say I had thought the matter out verra carefully." He sat back, crossed his arms over his chest, and scowled at the fireplace. "I hadnae realized how much I counted on ye, weel, to just be there, until I thought ye might die. I didnae want to be alone," he added quietly.

Morainn fought back the urge to hug him, fully understanding what he had been feeling. It was too soon for such closeness, for such signs of sisterly affection. She did not know much about the man except for the good deed he had done for her and his sordid reputation. She needed more before she let go of the wariness she had learned at a very young age.

"What about your harem?" She grinned when he glared at her. "Hard to be alone with a harem."

Adam looked at this woman who was both stranger and sister to him and realized she was teasing him. It felt both odd and good. No one teased him; no one had ever teased him, not even his father. Thinking on what little he had observed of the Murrays each time he had come to try to see Morainn, he realized it must be one of those things families did. It might take some getting used to, he decided.

"I dinnae have one. Ne'er have. One woman at a time is enough trouble for any mon."

"Ouch." The way he looked—as if he did not know what to do with her—amused Morainn for a moment, but she quickly grew serious again. "What do ye expect of me?"

"I am nay sure."

And that, she realized, was not something that afflicted this man very often. "May I continue to stay at the cottage?"

"Ah, of course, but does that mean that ye willnae be staying with Sir Tormand?"

"He hasnae asked me to."

"Should I act the older brother and do something about that?"

"I would rather ye didnae."

"As ye wish."

Morainn could hear the silent *for now* in his deep voice, but decided there was no need to get into an argument over the matter now.

He held out his hand. "So—do we begin to learn how to be kin?"

She smiled and took his hand in hers. "Why not?" She laughed when he hugged her and felt just a little of her heart's pain ease.

Tormand heard her laughter and sighed. He was happy for her, but a brother could prove to be a problem for him. It was past time he sorted out his relationship with Morainn, before her newfound brother stuck his nose into the matter.

Chapter 19

Warm lips touched the hollow of her throat and Morainn sighed. She had not been able to push Tormand out of her dreams, but none of those dreams had felt as real as this one. Lightly calloused hands covered her breasts and she arched up into their warmth. She had thought about making love with Tormand one last time before returning to her cottage, but had not yet decided if that was a particularly wise thing to do. After a week of healing and getting to know her brother, however, plus the four days of sleeping through the worst of her injuries and three days of just trying to stay awake for more than a few hours at a time, she was starved for Tormand's touch.

"Morainn," Tormand whispered in her ear. "Wake up, love. I want ye awake and eager for me as we make love."

That voice was not in her head as a dream-voice ought to be, Morainn decided. It had been whispered against her ear, each word sending a little brush of warm air to caress it. Morainn opened her eyes to find Tormand smiling down at her. They were also both naked. The decision about whether or not to add one more heated memory to the others she had of this man had been made. Now that he was in her arms, she did not have the will to let him go. All too soon her arms would be empty again, and stay empty.

"Ye are a verra sneaky mon," she said.

"More a verra desperate, needy mon," he said, as he nibbled at her lips. "It has been too long."

"Far too long," she agreed and kissed him.

The welcome in her kiss, the hunger lurking there that equaled his own, was all the invitation Tormand needed. He had reined in his need for her as she had healed and he now loosed those reins. He wanted to devour her, to bury himself deep within her again and again. Then he wanted to rest for a while and start the dance all over again. However, this time he would have to sate his hunger for her only once, at least until after they had supped and could share a bed again. There were things he had to do concerning their future together, plans that needed to be made and he could not delay them any longer.

In truth, what he wanted was for her to love him, but he was not willing to wait until she did to claim her as his own. She cared for him. He was certain of it. She also shared his desire. It would be enough for now. And right now, he would make love to her until she cried out her need for him, reminding her of all that they did share.

After kissing her until she was breathless and cling-ing to him, Tormand began to kiss his way down her slender body. He lavished attention on her full breasts until she was panting and arching against him, and then he turned his full attention to her other sweet spot. He lingered over each scar on his way to the prize he sought, determined to show her that they did not matter to him, did not dim her beauty in his eyes at all.

Ever so gently he kissed his way down the scar on the inside of her right thigh and then up the scar on the left thigh. When he kissed the soft curls between her beautiful legs, her whole body jerked. A firm grip on her legs kept her from pulling away. A moment later he felt her tension, her lingering shock over such intimacy, fade away and she opened herself to his greedy attentions. Tormand proceeded to drive her to the heights of pleasure again and again without allowing her to tumble down.

"Tormand," Morainn moaned out his name, "cease this torture."

He grinned against her taut, silken belly despite the fact that his whole body shook with the need to be inside her. "Torture, is it?" he asked, as he slowly kissed his way up her body.

"Tormand," she snapped, and wrapped her legs tightly around him as soon as she felt his hard manhood brush against that place where she so badly ached for it to be. "Now."

"Demanding wench."

He murmured the words against her mouth and caught her gasp of delight as he swiftly joined their bodies. Tormand tried to go slowly, but Morainn's hunger for him snapped what little control he had. With a soft growl, he began to move hard and fast, pushing them both to those delirious heights with an urgency he had never known before.

Morainn glanced at the man sprawled on his back at her side. Her body still hummed with satisfaction and yet she could feel her hunger for him stirring to life again as she looked over his tall, strong body. Tormand Murray had turned her into a complete wanton, she thought, and felt no distress over that fact. She recalled how he had staggered from the bed, fetched a damp cloth, washed them both clean, and then collapsed back onto the bed as if he had used the last of his strength just to do that one little thing. It gave her pride a nice stroking to think that she had put the renowned lover into such a state.

Looking at his manhood nestled limply in the nest of auburn curls between his strong thighs, she idly wondered if she could do something with it that would make him as crazed with desire as his intimate kisses had made her. She turned onto her side and draped her arm around his trim waist. When he opened his eyes, she smiled at him innocently even as she began to plot his downfall.

"We still need to talk about Walin," he said, his voice still husky from the passion they had just shared.

That was the very last thing Morainn wanted to do. She lightly trailed her fingers up and down his hip and thigh. Out of the corner of her eye she could see a twitching of interest between his legs.

Tormand ignored how his body responded to her idle caress. He had to go to court soon and he was determined to get the matter of Walin settled. It was not a good time to discuss all he wanted and needed from her, all his hopes and plans, but in talking about Walin's future he could, perhaps, hint at a future for them. It might be enough to keep her at his side until he could make her fall in love with him.

"I thought we could share the raising of him." He felt the barest hint of faltering in the light, teasing caress she tempted him with. "Walin thinks it a fine plan. He wants both of us in his life."

"And what do ye want?" she asked.

I want that small hand to move a wee bit to the left, he thought, but bit back the words and said, "The lad needs a family."

"Then he shall have one. As much a one as we can give him."

He had to take a deep breath to steady himself when, as if she had read his mind, she moved her hand and curled those long fingers of hers around his rapidly hardening manhood. "I think we could do weel by him."

His words made her think of marriage, of a future, of love and bairns with mismatched eyes. She forced such dreams aside. There had been no proposal of marriage, no words of love. She would not add to her pain by filling her head with foolish hopes and dreams. Worse, if she misunderstood what he was saying, expected more than he was offering, she could easily make a complete fool of herself.

Feeling him harden to soft, silken steel in her hand, she decided she would distract him from talk of Walin and family. Morainn licked his belly and heard him groan. Tormand, she decided, might prove very easy to distract, perhaps even as easy as she was.

Tormand wanted to discuss Walin and their future before he had to go and do his duty to his family by strolling around the court and trying to talk to people who could help his clan either through some sort of alliance or through a profitable venture of some kind. The feel of Morainn's mouth on his skin, her soft hand stroking him, was making it difficult to think clearly, let alone speak. When she kissed the insides of his thighs his whole body tensed in eager and hopeful anticipation. He could not stop himself from jerking in surprise and fierce pleasure when she finally pressed those soft, warm lips against his erection.

"Wrong?" she asked, even as she started to move away.

"Nay," he said as he thrust his fingers into her thick hair and silently urged her back to finish what she had started. "Right. Verra right."

Morainn continued to make love to him with her mouth, judging which touch, which kiss, which stroke of her tongue he liked best by his very vocal appreciation. She discovered that making love to him like this stirred her own passions, making her more daring, more eager to drive him to even greater heights of pleasure. When he asked her to take him into her mouth, she barely hesitated before doing so and discovered that she had as much power over his body as he did over hers.

A squeak of protest and surprise escaped her when he suddenly grabbed her under the arms and dragged her up his body. Dazed by her own tumultuous desires, it took her a moment to understand what he wanted her to do. When she finally began to ease herself down on him, taking him inside of her ever so slowly, she gasped at how good it felt. With his whispered encouragement stroking her ears, she rode him until they grasped the release they both craved and their cries of satisfaction blended like the sweetest of songs.

Memories of her lovemaking with Tormand made Morainn smile as she slowly woke up. She reached out only to find the linen cool and empty where his big warm body had once rested and she sighed. It was for the best, she told herself sternly. There would be no need for any confrontation now. She could simply pack up her belongings and go home.

Forcing herself to get out of bed, she got herself ready to face what she knew would be a very long day. As she went down to the hall to break her fast she tried to decide what to say to Walin. She was not surprised to find him seated at the table, a full plate in front of him. Walin loved to eat and Nora's kinswomen were very good cooks. What did surprise her was that Adam was also there. The man had been to see her many times since the day he had told her he was her brother, but never so early in the morning. She eyed him a little warily as she sat down and filled her plate.

"And what do ye plan to do today, Morainn?" Adam asked, as he served her a tankard of goat's milk.

The way the man watched her made Morainn think he already knew the answer to that question. Now that she thought about it, Adam had never once questioned her claims about her visions and dreams. She began to think her brother had quite a few secrets. She also wondered why he had given her goat's milk. It was not something she often drank and yet she had wanted some the moment she had seen that it was available. Perhaps, she mused as she began to eat, it was not her mother who had gifted her with the ability to have visions.

"I intend to return to the cottage," she replied and saw not one tiny flicker of surprise on his face.

"Then I need to pack my things," said Walin.

Morainn opened her mouth to explain all the choices the boy had, and then quickly filled it with a big spoonful of honey-sweetened porridge. She did not want to discuss his choices. Selfishly, she wanted him to come home with her without question. As she ate, occasionally reminding Walin not to eat too fast, she could feel her brother watching her. It was not until Walin had excused himself and run off to pack his things that Morainn chanced a glance at Adam only to catch him smiling at her.

"Clever lass," he murmured.

"What do ye mean?" she asked.

"Taking the lad with ye is certain to bring Tormand to your door."

"Ye think I would take Walin with me just to use him as bait?" To her shame she had briefly wondered if keeping Walin with her might cause Tormand to pause before separating them again, but she had not really considered the possibility that it might cause Tormand to chase after her.

"Why do ye sound so insulted?"

"Why shouldnae I be? That would be a devious thing to do."

"Aye. As I said—clever. Why dinnae ye just stay here?"

"Because I wish to be the one who chooses when it is time for me to leave." Morainn did not know why she was being so truthful, but something about the way Adam watched her seemed to pull the truth right out of her.

"Pride. It can be a verra cold bedfellow."

"So can a mon who wishes to be in another woman's bed e'en as he holds you." She sighed. "I willnae wait around until he tires of me and sees another he wants. Aye, 'tis pride, and sometimes that is all one has to cling to."

He shrugged. "The mon kens that the boy sees ye as his mother. Mayhap he would marry you and make it legally so. He would be a fine prize for ye."

"Aye, he would be." She had the distinct feeling he was goading her. "So would a big fat salmon." She rolled her eyes when he laughed and then she pushed her empty plate aside so that she could rest her arms on the table. "I love him, Adam."

"I thought ye might. 'Tis why I did naught about his taking ye as his lover. So, why run from the chance to have him?"

Morainn bit back the need to remind him that a brother who had remained unknown to her for three and twenty years had no right to tell her what she should do with her life or her chastity. Some of her annoyance with that came from the fact that she had lived her life as she pleased for too long. "I am nay running." She grimaced when he just cocked one perfect dark brow at her. "Weel, mayhap I am, but only from the hurt I can see coming."

"Why would ye think that he would hurt ye?"

"Because he doesnae love me. E'en men without Tormand's sordid reputation for being a rutting fool will slip into another woman's bed, succumb easily to temptation, if they dinnae love their wives. Aye, I ken that love isnae some impenetrable shield against all temptation, but it helps. Love also means that all the troubles, big and small, that come with marriage dinnae make ye immediately think of seeking out another to hold. I wouldnae survive if I married him and had to spend the rest of my days or nights wondering whose bed he was romping in. It would slowly kill me.

"He hasnae spoken to me of marriage anyway. The mon enjoys his freedom. Right now I hold his interest, but that could change on the morrow."

"And ye dinnae wish to be here when that happens. Fair enough. But, if ye leave, ye lose the chance to make him love you."

Just the way Adam said the word love told Morainn that her brother did not believe in it, but now was not the time to argue that. "Ye cannae make someone love ye. He either does or he doesnae. And, if it takes too long for love to grow, if there are too many other women as I wait for the prize, then how much of my love for him will remain? Aye, I may be fool enough to still love him nay matter what he does to break faith with me, but I willnae trust him, and the hurt, the bitterness, will have twisted everything.

"I need him to love me because I need him to be faithful. Every time he went into another woman's arms, it would cut out another piece of my heart, of my verra soul. 'Twould be a folly to think passion and a little boy are enough to change the ways of a mon like Tormand. There has to be a stronger bond or he will continue to, as Nora says, leap from bed to bed like some demented toad."

Morainn waited patiently for Adam to stop laughing. He looked good when he laughed, she decided. The expression softened some of the harsher lines of his handsome face. Morainn had the feeling that he did not laugh very often and that saddened her.

"Weel, I am nay sure I believe as ye do," he said finally, his voice still a little hoarse from a lingering amusement, "but if that is what ye want."

"It is," she said firmly. "Wheesht, 'tisnae as if I am sailing off to France in the dead of night. I but go to the cottage and Walin comes with me of his own free will. Tormand can find me there if he chooses to. And I think it will do me good to go home for a wee while. A house full of Murray men doesnae allow a lass to think verra clearly."

"Verra weel then. I will help ye. I would offer ye an invitation to come to Dubhstane but I ken ye wouldnae accept it."

"Nay, not now, but I wouldnae mind seeing the place sometime."

"Then ye will." He looked at William who sat on the bench next to Morainn and watched him. "I suspicion helping when ye speak of packing means caging these cats, too."

Morainn stroked William's soft fur. "Aye. They dinnae hurt the one putting them into the cages for all they growl, hiss, and try to wriggle free. And packing willnae take me long as I dinnae have much."

Several hours later Adam stood in front of Tormand's house and watched Morainn drive off in the small pony cart he and Walter had found for her, the cats loudly protesting the travel. He was not sure he believed all her talk of love, but he did know that she was sad, that Tormand had hurt her in some way. It was going to be difficult not to make the man pay dearly for that look of sorrow on Morainn's face, but he would resist the urge to pummel him into the ground. This was Morainn's battle.

"He isnae going to like this," said Walter, scowling after Morainn. "Nay, he willnae be happy. Lassies dinnae walk away from him, ye ken."

"Mayhap this will do him some good then." To Adam's surprise, a big grin split Walter's homely face.

"Aye, that it will. A good knock upside the head often works to knock some sense into a fool."

"Ye think he would be a fool to let my sister go?"

"Biggest one in Christendom. Despite the way the lad has acted the last few years, he is a mon from a strong family, one that is filled with good, strong marriages and healthy bairns. 'Tis as though he has been fighting that, as though he has tried to shake free of all he learned. Weel, he has already had one epiphany."

"Oh? What was it?"

"Had to make a list of all his lovers in this town and

was fair sickened by what he saw, by the proof of the mon he had become."

"Ah, I believe Morainn said her friend called it leaping from bed to bed like a demented toad." He smiled when Walter laughed.

"That says it clear enough. Fool lad was in danger of wearing it out. But I could see that the lass had put the harness on that stallion. He has reached his settling time and that lass is the one he wants to settle with."

"And his family willnae care that she is a poor bastard with no lands or coin?"

Walter made a sharp, derisive noise. "Nay, they willnae care. As for her visions and all that? Wheesht, she will just be another wee lass with a gift. The clan has a lot of them. Source of pride, it is." He looked at Adam as they walked back into the house. "And that has me wondering where she got it from."

"Keep right on wondering, old mon." Adam bit back a grin over Walter's mumbled disgruntlement. "So, ye think Sir Tormand has fallen in love with my sister?"

"Och, aye. Felled like a big old oak. Ye wouldnae e'en be asking if ye had seen him when those bastards took her and cut her. If he hadnae already guessed how he felt about her, I suspicion he had himself another epiphany right then. I had been expecting it. The mon could have any lass he wanted and has done so, especially over the last few years, but nay once in the last three, mayhap four, months or so."

Adam stopped walking and stared at Walter. "Are ye saying that Tormand, the great lover, or the great sinner depending on how righteous ye think ye are, has been celibate for months?"

Walter nodded, a smug look on his face. "He has. Been tucked up in his own bed every night for months and, ere ye ask it, I ken there wasnae a lass tucked up with him. He never brings the lassies into his own home. Told me once that a cousin of his said a mon should never soil his own nest. So, I think his settling time had already come over him. He was just waiting for the right lass."

"And that would be Morainn."

"Nary a doubt in my mind. So, do ye mean to lurk about here until ye can see how the lad reacts when he finds his bird has flown the nest?"

"I believe I will."

"Do ye like to toss the dice?"

"Doesnae any mon? Sure ye have the coin to lose?"

"Boasting, are ye? Weel, settle yourself in the hall whilst I fetch some ale and my dice and we will see which one of us has the skill and the luck. I be thinking ye will soon be wishing the lad comes home soon or ye will have naught left but the clothes ye are wearing."

Adam shook his head and went back into the hall. He had heard of Sir Tormand's squire, of the man's refusal to be knighted. Walter had been called everything from cowardly to stupid, but all those opinions were wrong. Walter was one of those rare men who knew exactly what he wanted and what would make him happy, and would not allow expectations or insults to change his course.

Settling himself at the table, Adam suspected Walter knew the man he served very well. It was going to be interesting to see how Tormand took the news that Morainn had walked away from him. Patting the documents neatly tucked inside his shirt, he decided he would make a small change in his original plan for them. If Tormand felt as Walter said he did, and loved Morainn, then what Adam had planned as a simple brotherly gift to his only sibling would now make a verra fine dowry.

"Where is Morainn? Where is Walin? Where are those cursed cats?"

Each demand got louder until Tormand shouted the last one so loudly Adam was surprised the room did not rock on its foundations. He bit back a grin, held up one hand for silence, and watched Walter throw the dice. Groaning as Walter was yet again the winner and chortled as he raked in even more of Adam's coin, Adam finally turned to look at Tormand.

Tormand looked both furious and frantic. Adam could see the worry, even fear in the man's eyes. This was not the reaction one expected of a man who had simply misplaced one of far too many women. That Tormand might have cursed a little, but quickly gone out to find another. This Tormand looked like he wanted to throttle a few answers out of someone.

"My sister decided it was time to go home," Adam replied, watching in fascination as the color faded from Tormand's face. "Walin went with her."

For a moment it was difficult for Tormand even to catch his breath. He felt a pain cut deep into his heart. How could she walk away after what they had shared this morning? No woman had ever made love to him like that, and he had left thinking to find her still at his house, ready and willing to listen to all he had to say. He had even left court early, handing the chore of staying to promote the interests of the clan to his kinsmen's hands because he could not wait any longer to tell Morainn all he needed to tell her. Yet, the moment he was gone, she packed up and walked away.

Anger surged up inside of him, smothering the hurt. She had not even given him a chance. He had tiptoed around her and wooed her gently because he wanted to show her that he was not simply the man of that reputation he was now so ashamed of. For a brief moment anger had him thinking that, if she could walk away so easily, he should just let her go. After all, he had never had any trouble finding a woman. He easily shook that thought aside. Angry or not, hurt or not, he did not want another woman. He wanted Morainn.

"When did she leave?" he asked, idly thinking that he would like to take the time to pound all that amusement he saw in Adam right out of the man, but beating his future brother by marriage before he had even proposed to the man's sister was probably not a wise thing to do.

"This morning. Mayhap three, four hours ago. Going to go after her?"

"Aye, I am."

"For the laddie?"

"Nay, so I can shake the fool lass until what few wits she has are rattling around inside her head."

"Is that going to be before or after ye ask her to marry ye?"

Although there was still a glint of humor in the man's eyes, there was a hardness in his voice. Adam had thus far said nothing about the relationship between his sister and Tormand, but it was clear that that grace period was over. Tormand was tempted to remind the man that he had only just laid claim to his sister, but bit back the words. The man had had his reasons for that silence and Morainn had accepted them.

"Aye, I am and I dinnae intend to leave the lass alone until she says aye."

"And do ye intend to honor your vows?"

"Aye," Tormand said between tightly gritted teeth. "Now, may I leave so that I may chase the foolish wench down and talk sense to her?"

"One last thing." Adam pulled a sealed pack of documents from inside his shirt. "When ye get her to say aye, open this."

Tormand took the documents, tucked them inside his shirt and hurried out of the house. He would need the ride to the cottage to calm his temper, he decided. It would not do to go storming into her home demanding answers. In a way, he had to accept some blame for her leaving. He should have been clearer in telling her what he wanted, what he felt. This time he would make sure there were no misunderstandings, even if it meant he had to swallow a large portion of his own pride.

Catching sight of Uilliam on his way back from court, he enlisted his brother's help. It would make things a great deal easier if he and Morainn could thrash out their troubles without Walin listening to every word. Tormand was grateful for Uilliam's cooperation, but even more so for his silence as they rode. Never having been in love before, Tormand knew he was going to have to plan every word he would say. It would take some skill to convince Morainn that he was a changed man.

Chapter 20

Morainn stared at her garden and knew it was going to take a long time to feel any joy in it again. The cats were draped over or sprawled in all their favorite spots, Walin kicked a ball around carefully to keep it from rolling into the beds and crushing tender plants, and Nora's cousin had taken such good care of the garden that there was not even any weeding to be done. The garden had always been her pride and joy, but she felt none of those emotions as she looked at it now.

It was all Tormand's fault, she decided crossly, ignoring the little voice in her head that scolded her for her foolishness. Foolish would have been staying with a man like Tormand Murray. He was so far above her touch she could almost hear the loud guffaws of ridicule when she even thought she could have him for her own. He had saved her life, protected her, and given her the greatest pleasure she had ever known. She could ask no more of the man.

A part of her, one she decided was a glutton for

punishment, wanted her to go back to Tormand's house and make a few demands of him. Did he love her? Did he care about her at all? Had he yet overcome his aversion to marriage? Did he ever foresee a day when he could vow fidelity to a woman? She told herself she probably would not like his answers.

And then there was Walin. He was Tormand's son. She really had no right to the child even if she had been caring for him for four years. It was not Tormand's fault that he had never known about Walin. Tormand knew now and he wanted the boy. He would also make a very good father, of that she had no doubt. She did not have any right even to try to deny the child what would be a far better life than she could ever give him. Although Tormand had said they would share the raising of the child, she knew he had meant that sharing to take place beneath his roof.

And once he did not want her in his bed? she asked herself. She would simply become Walin's nursemaid and have to watch the man she loved return to his lecherous ways. Worse, if Walin were to be trained as the son of a knight, a wealthy man, he would not be in need of a nursemaid for long.

She and Tormand could get married, she thought, as she moved to sit on the rough log bench in the shade. She was almost certain that Tormand had been hinting at that, but she had ignored him. Even her brother had thought it would be a good idea.

Morainn sighed. She did not want Tormand to marry her just because neither of them wanted to be separated from Walin. That was not the sort of marriage that kept a man faithful to his wife, especially not a man like Tormand, who was used to having his choice of women. She needed him to be bound to her in heart, mind, and soul, just as she had tried to tell her very cynical brother and just as she was already bound to Tormand. It was the only way she could feel certain that she would not spend the rest of her days wondering whose bed her husband had crawled into now.

True, she had heard Tormand speak of having some sort of epiphany about his lecherous past, but how long would that last before he fell back into his old ways? A man who was used to a constant variety of dishes did not suddenly become content with mutton stew every night. If she were married to him when he fell back into his old habits, she would slowly be crushed under the weight of her own heartache. She knew that as certainly as she knew her own name and no amount of thinking, talking, or persuasion could ever change that cold, hard fact. The more she went through the litany of whys and why nots, the dizzier and the more unhappy she became.

A sudden quiet pulled Morainn out of her dark thoughts and self-pity. She realized she could no longer hear Walin playing with his ball. Just as she was about to get up and look for him, a tall, very familiar figure entered her garden and strode toward her. For a brief moment she considered running, but then sternly told herself not to be such a coward. She had known a confrontation was coming; she had just hoped for more time to prepare for it. The sound of Walin's laughter and a horse riding away told her what had happened and she could almost hear her heart break.

"Ye came to take Walin back," she said, as Tormand stopped to stand in front of her.

"Dinnae be such a complete idiot," he snapped, then cursed and sat down beside her.

She knew she ought to take offense at that remark, but she was too busy trying not to cry. It was not just because of the loss of Walin, either. Tormand was dressed in his plaid and a fine linen shirt. He looked so handsome it almost hurt to look at him, especially knowing that this was a man she could never have.

"I didnae come to take Walin away from ye," he said, after several moments of looking aimlessly around her garden. "I but sent him away with Uilliam so that ye and I could speak. Alone. Without weighing every word we said because a boy of six was near and listening. And so we could talk without interruptions."

That sounded ominous and Morainn tensed, clenching her hands tightly together in her lap. "Talk about what?"

"Why dinnae we start with why ye left?"

There was a touch of anger in his voice and Morainn wondered if she had bruised his pride. "I am healed, we found the killers, and ye are now safe. There wasnae really any other reason for me to stay, was there?"

"I see. So ye took your fill of me and then walked away. Is that it?"

Tormand nearly grimaced. He sounded like some outraged maiden or, worse, like some of the women he had been with, the ones who thought themselves so skilled, so beautiful, that they could entrap him with such shallow bait. He would feel guilty about that, but he sincerely doubted any of them had felt the pain he did right now. He had always been careful to avoid any women with tender hearts or high expectations.

"Weel, nay, of course not. And, if I recall right, ye came to my bed. I didnae seek ye out. And if I took what I wanted of something freely offered, who are ye to act so outraged? Isnae that what ye have been doing for years?"

That stung, but she was right. Yet, he could not completely banish that outrage. Morainn was supposed to be different from all the other women he had known. In his heart he knew she was. He was saying everything wrong and it was angering her, maybe even hurting her. He knew her well enough now to know that those two emotions put a very sharp edge on her tongue. Somehow he would have to keep his own temper and fear under control and weigh his words very carefully. Nothing would be accomplished if they just kept snapping and snarling at each other. He had intended to do that, but seeing her had stirred up all his anger and hurt again.

It was not going to be easy, he decided as he stood up and began to pace back and forth in front of her. He was terrified of offering her all he had only to discover that she did not want it. It was true that he had wooed her, but he could not be sure that he had won her. For once in his life he cared how a woman felt about him and he did not know which way to step next. Turning to look at her, he found her watching him a little warily. He was probably acting like some madman.

"I thought we could marry and raise Walin together." A look passed quickly over her face and he realized he had hurt her with those words. Strangely enough that gave him hope. He could not hurt her if she did not care for him.

"Walin is like my own child. Aye, when he was left upon my threshold I tried to find his mother or his father, any kin at all, but I wasnae terribly disappointed that no one kenned where he had come from." She sighed and stared down at her hands. "I was so verra alone and then, there was Walin. He was like some precious gift. I wasnae alone anymore. I had someone who loved me and needed me, someone I could love back, and someone who didnae care if I had visions. We have ne'er been apart since the day I picked him up off my threshold, save for a few hours here and there, but I willnae marry a mon just for his sake."

"Why not?"

"Because that is a verra weak foundation for a marriage."

Tormand grabbed her by her hands, pulled her into his arms, and then kissed her until she was clinging to him. "And what about that? What about the fire that burns between us?"

She pushed him away. "Ye have warmed yourself against far too many fires and ne'er once married. Ye would try to ensnare me with passion? Ye who have been dodging just such a snare for many years?"

"Passion is a strong bond within a marriage and is no

trap if I step into it willingly. What are ye asking of me? Tell me so that I cease stepping on my cursed tongue."

Morainn stared at him, her mouth still warm from his kiss. He truly meant it. He would marry her to make a family for Walin and because they desired each other. It was a lot, more than too many wives ever had, but it was not enough.

"And will ye be faithful?"

Tormand tried not to look or act as offended as he was by that question. She knew nothing of the beliefs his family held so dear, of the beliefs he had learned he could not shake free of and no longer wished to. He had also earned her doubt. His reputation was well earned and she had seen that obscenely long list of his lovers.

"I believe in honoring vows taken," he said, hoping he did not sound as pompous to her as he did to himself. When she just frowned at him, he asked, "Why dinnae ye believe me? Because of my past?"

"Your past certainly doesnae make a lass feel verra confident in any vow of fidelity that ye make. But, nay, I just wondered why ye are so affronted that I dinnae immediately believe ye. Most men dinnae honor vows of marriage. I suspicion ye can think of a lot of men who speak their vows before God and family and forget them ere the words have left their mouths. Men who would willingly fight to the death over a few slighting words, claiming they need to defend their honor, yet think nothing of breaking vows made to their wives before a priest."

"I am nay one of those men. Morainn, I am determined to stay right here until we sort this out. I want

ye to be my wife, I want ye to help me raise Walin, and
I have sworn to be faithful, yet ye still hesitate. Why? I
swear it, I will badger ye all night until I feel certain ye
have told me the truth."

Telling him the truth meant she had to set aside
her shield, leave herself open for what could prove to
be fatal wounds to her heart. She would be letting this
man know exactly how much power he held over her.
And, yet, she could not fight this battle with only
half-truths. She had spoken freely of her feelings to
her brother whom she had only known for a week. It
should not be so hard to speak freely with the man
who had shared her bed, the man who would forever
be in her heart. And there was always the chance,
however small, that speaking her heart would cause
him to feel free to speak of his feelings for her, instead
of just rambling on about passion and how Walin
needed a family. She would be a fool not to take it.
In the end, she really had nothing to lose except a
little piece of her pride.

"Then I will tell ye the truth. I love you." She held
out her hand to halt his attempt to pull her into his
arms, where she knew he could kiss her into agreeing
to almost anything, but she was pleased to see that her
news had not displeased him or made him uncomfortable. In fact, he looked delighted. "'Tis because I
love ye that I say I willnae marry you."

"That makes no sense."

"It will if ye let me finish. I love ye and, so, if I wed
ye for naught but passion and Walin, I leave myself
open for more pain than I care to think about. Ye
would have all of my heart, my mind, e'en my soul,

but I would have only your passion for as long as it lasted and your sense of responsibility. Ye are a mon who has probably ne'er stayed with a woman e'en as long as ye have stayed with me and I doubt ye were ever faithful to one. Aye, the desire ye feel for me is strong now, but what happens when it fades? What do ye think it will do to me when ye start to turn to other women to satisfy your needs?

"It will eat at me, Tormand. It will slowly destroy me and whatever good we might share. And what will I have left in the end but a shattered heart, mayhap a deep bitterness inside of me that darkens my every thought and sharpens my every word. I can see it as clearly as the strongest of my visions. I love ye and I love Walin, but I could end up making us all so verra unhappy."

Tormand stared at her as she sat down and buried her face in her hands. For a moment all he could think about was that she loved him. Then the sound of her weeping broke him free of the spell of those words. He sat down beside her, ignoring how tense she was as he pulled her into his arms, and kissed the top of her head.

"All ye say is true, lass," he said quietly. "I have seen far too many marriages such as ye have just described to argue it. But this time your vision is all wrong."

"Tormand," she began to protest even as she began to relax in his arms.

"Nay, now ye will hear me out. Ye didnae have one verra important fact when ye thought this all out so verra carefully. I love ye. That is why ye will marry me."

He smiled when she lifted her head from his chest

to look at him. Her beautiful eyes were puffy and her nose was red from weeping, but he still thought her the loveliest woman he had ever seen. She also looked dazed. He felt that it was an appropriate reaction to the words he had never spoken to another woman.

"Ye love me? Are ye sure?" she asked, even as a still sane part of her declared that that was a foolish question.

Tormand brushed his lips over hers. "Verra sure."

"Oh, then, aye, I will marry ye."

"I am pleased that ye have finally come to your senses."

Before she could scold him for that remark, he kissed her. Morainn was quickly swept away, the fierce hunger of his kiss rousing her own greed for him. She barely noticed when he picked her up in his arms and strode toward the cottage. Her mind was too full of those three little words that put everything in her world to rights. It was not until she was on her bed, naked, and she was watching Tormand rapidly shed his clothes that she regained a few of her scattered wits.

"Walin?" she asked even as she welcomed Tormand into her arms.

"Will be staying at my house until I return a betrothed mon. And, now, I believe we will take some time to celebrate our betrothal."

Her laughter was swiftly ended by his kiss that proved to be only the beginning of his sensual assault. He caressed and kissed her everywhere, making her feel both beautiful and treasured in a way he had never done before. Morainn did not shy away from any of his attentions, but reveled in them. His vow of love had loosened the last restraints upon her modesty in the bedchamber. The freedom she now felt to fully express her passion for him only heightened her desire.

When he shifted his body in preparation of uniting them, she pushed him onto his back and began to return the homage he had done her in full measure. Tormand made no secret of the pleasure he felt with her every kiss, her every caress. Morainn felt almost light-headed from the freedom he allowed her to do whatever she wanted with him and from the knowledge that she had the touch needed to make a man like Tormand squirm.

She started to kiss and lick her way back up his body when he suddenly turned, pushing her onto her back. He eased himself inside her so slowly that she was nearly ready to scream out her frustration by the time he was lodged deep inside her. When he did not move, she looked at him and saw how bright with love his beautiful mismatched eyes were. He held her gaze as he began to move inside of her and Morainn watched his eyes grow soft and cloudy as he neared his time of release. As her own passions rose toward that pinnacle, she finally closed her eyes. Wrapping her legs more tightly around him, Morainn clung to Tormand as she joined him on that wild tumble into bliss.

Still deep inside of Morainn, Tormand had to struggle to find the strength to turn onto his back. He pulled Morainn along with him, smiling faintly at the way she sprawled on top of him, boneless in her satisfaction. Idly smoothing his hand up and down her slim back, he had to wonder how he would have survived if she had said that she did not love him and that that was why she could not marry him. He thanked God he had not had to know how that would have felt.

Morainn felt her breathing even out just as Tormand's manhood softened and slipped out of her. She almost grinned. She was sated with the pleasure he had gifted her with and so dazed with love, she could barely move and yet she wanted him back inside her. Since that would require some movement on her part, she decided to let him rest.

"When did ye first ken that ye loved me?" she asked him as she nuzzled her cheek against his chest.

"Ah, weel, do ye want to ken just when I suspicioned it or when I was certain of it?" He grinned when she gave a soft grunt of annoyance.

"I never just *suspicioned*; I kenned it and verra quickly too."

"Weel, ye are a woman and women are always more certain about such things. I also felt I was too young to settle yet. I fought it hard. Despite having been celibate for four months—"

Morainn rapidly lifted her head off his chest and stared at him. "Were ye truly celibate for four months?"

"Do ye have to make that sound as if it is akin to the second coming?" he grumbled and then sighed. "Aye, I just stopped. Told myself that I just needed a rest and ignored the voice in my heart that told me I was sick of the game, even a little sick of myself. That didnae mean I was ready to find a wife and all of that though."

"Of course not," she murmured, propping her head up on her hand and watching him.

"I had a lot of reasons for why I felt what I did when

I first looked into your eyes. Had a lot more for why I couldnae seem to go a day without trying to see ye again. I think ye can see how that game was played."

"Aye, I did a wee bit of it myself when I first started to feel, weel, something for ye."

"I kept thinking I should get as far away from ye as possible, but I couldnae. Then I didnae even think of it anymore. Then I started calling ye my woman in my head. Still kept fighting it, however."

"Stubborn."

"Verra. But when those bastards took ye, intending to hurt ye and kill ye, I kenned it. Nay, I admitted it to myself. The way I felt when I thought I might nay be able to save ye from them—" he took a deep breath and briefly hugged her tightly.

"I suffered much the same, just kenned what I was afraid of earlier than ye did. Why did ye think I let ye into my bed? Me who has held off so many over the years either with a knife, an ability to run verra fast, or a vicious cat?"

He laughed softly. "I did think on why ye would have gifted me with your innocence, weel, once I got over the urge to preen some like cock on a hill."

"I suppose we should return to your house and tell everyone what has been decided. I have the feeling they are all waiting for that news."

"Without a doubt."

Tormand kissed her and then rose from the bed to get his shirt. As he picked it up he saw the packet Adam had given him and sat down on the bed next to Morainn, who was taking her time getting up. Silently he held it out to her, curious but knowing that it was really hers to open.

Morainn sat up and took the packet from him. "What is this?"

"Your brother said that once we were betrothed I was to give that to ye."

Wondering if Adam had gifted her with a small dowry, she opened the packet. Her eyes widening so much they actually stung, she looked over the documents—twice. Even then she found it hard to believe.

"He has given me the cottage," she said. "And some land."

Tormand took the papers she held out to him. "Weel, ye ken that I would have taken ye if ye had naught but a shift, but this is good of him." His words choked to a halt as he read the documents. "*Some* land? *Jesu*, Morainn, did ye ken how many acres came with this cottage?"

"Nay." She looked down at the paper she had kept, unfolded it and read her brother's message. "He says this was the dowry his mother brought to her marriage and he had intended to give it to me, but then decided it was best given as a dowry." She read the last two sentences her brother had written before slashing his signature at the end and blushed. She had been right to think Adam had a few secrets, for he had obviously had a little peek into the future. "He says that, if ye have lands of your own, this will be a good holding to pass on to one of your sons."

"One of my sons? Weel, I suppose we may have a son and there is also Walin to consider, but, to be honest, I have coin, but I am land poor. But, if ye are uncomfortable in taking such a gift, we dinnae need it."

"Nay, I will take it if only because he already planned to give it to me and I believe he has enough that I will nay be depriving any children he may have. But what of your house in town?"

"'Tis my family's, nay mine. We have one in every town the court spends any time in." He put his arm around her and looked into her face, seeing that she looked a little uneasy. "If ye have no trouble accepting this then why do ye look so, weel, uncomfortable?"

"Because I think I may have gotten my ability to see things in some part from Adam's father." She held out the letter. "Read his last sentence."

Tormand read it and gaped. "Twins? Eight months from now?" He looked at her. "Are ye with child?"

"Nay that I ken yet, but it is certainly possible. So, do we name the firstborn Adam as he asks?"

Tormand laughed and pushed her back down on the bed. "We celebrate and, mayhap, do our best to make sure he is right in what he sees ahead for us."

"Sinful mon," she murmured.

"Aye, but only yours. All my sinning will now be done only with ye."

"Weel, I am verra glad ye said that, for I had a fear that ye might have become completely reformed."

"Never. I have just discovered that love makes a little sinning so much more exciting," he whispered against her lips.

"Aye, my love, it does indeed."

Morainn held him close, but she was smiling in her

mind. She would tell him later that her brother did indeed have a gift. His prophecy for them matched a dream she had had. As she fell beneath the spell of the pleasure he gave her, she decided she would wait before she told him that the soon-to-be-born twins would just be the first of eight boys. The man did not need to be put into a panic yet.

Greetings Readers:

For those of you who have been faithfully reading my Highland tales and the never-ending travails of the prolific Murray clan, the bad news is—I'm taking a little break from the braw Highlanders. For those of you who may be upset by this news, the good news is—I'll be back with more Murray stories in a little while. After ten years of writing about the Murrays and their extended family, I wanted a breather to do something just a little different. And for those of you who might be tensed for some great dramatic change—breathe. It's still me and I'm still doing historicals, but for just a little while I'm traveling to England and the Late Georgian period.

This trilogy will concern two connected families: the Wherlockes and the Vaughns. Their families are riddled with people with strong psychic gifts. You name it— they've got it. Considering how people with such gifts were often treated, it's no surprise that they're a reclusive and troubled lot. In the three stories, I will introduce you to three cousins in these families: Chloe Wherlocke, Penelope Wherlocke, and Alethea Vaughn Channing. I hope you enjoy them as much as I enjoyed writing about them.

Best,
Hannah Howell

Please turn the page
for an exciting sneak peek of
Hannah Howell's
IF HE'S WICKED,
coming in June 2009!

Prologue

England—Fall 1785

"Damn it, Tom, the woman is dying."

Tom scowled down at the pale woman lying so still on the tiny bed. "She is still breathing."

"Barely."

"Just worn thin from birthing is all, Jack." Tom picked up the swaddled child that rested in the woman's limp arm. "Poor wee mite. Throttled by the cord, it looks like. Well, come on then, Jack, set that lad in this one's place."

"I hate this, Tom." Jack gently settled the peacefully sleeping newborn he held next to the woman. "'Tain't right. "'Tain't right at all. The poor lass has no strength to care for the mite. He will be dying right along with her. Mayhap we could—"

"You just stop right there, Jack Potter," Tom snapped. "You be forgetting what happened to Old Melvin when he tried to say no to that bitch? You want your bones tangled up with his in that pit? 'Course this ain't right, but we got no choice. No choice at all. Better the wee lad dies, than gets reared up by that woman, I says. Or e'en murdered by his own mam."

"His lordship'd take good care of the lad."

"His lordship is blind to what that woman is and you be knowing that. Now, let us be gone from here. The bitch wants this poor dead babe in her arms ere his lordship returns and that could be soon, as he sent word that his wife had been brought to the birthing bed hours ago. The fool who did that will be fair sorry, I can tell ye," Tom muttered and shook his head.

Jack started to follow Tom out of the tiny, crude cottage, but then hesitated. "I will come with you in a blinking, Tom. I just—"

"Just what? We *have* to go now!"

"I just want to make 'em warm and comfortable, give 'em a fighting chance, or I will ne'er rest easy."

"Hurry then or soon we be both resting easy right alongside Old Melvin."

After making a fire and covering the woman and child with another thin blanket, Jack looked around to make certain Tom was not watching him. He took a sheath of papers from inside his old coat and hastily tucked them beneath the blankets. When he looked at the woman again, he started in surprise. She was watching him.

"Your babe will have a fine resting place," he whispered. "I hate doing this, I surely do, but I got me a wife and five wee ones. Aye, and I be a coward when all be said and done. That vile woman would ne'er hesitate to kill me if I ruined her evil plans. If ye can, take them papers and hide them well. If his lordship survives all his wife's plots, he will be wanting his son and them papers will be all the proof he will be aneeding from you. 'Tis as much as I and a few others dared to do, sorry poor help that it is. I will pray for you, missy. You and the lad here. Aye, and I will pray for meself as well, for I have surely blackened my soul this day." He hurried out of the cottage.

After waiting a few moments to be certain the men were gone, Chloe Wherlocke crept out of the niche by the fireplace where she had hidden herself when the men had ridden up to the door. She moved to kneel by her sister Laurel's bed and stared at the child she held, the living, breathing child. Touching the baby's soft, warm cheek, she looked at her sister, grief forming a tight knot in her throat. Laurel was dying. They both knew it. Yet, her sister smiled at her.

"'Tis just as you foresaw it, Chloe," Laurel whispered, weakness and not a need for secrecy robbing her of her voice. "Life appearing in the midst of death is what you said."

Chloe nodded, not at all happy to be proven right. "I am so sorry about your child."

"Do not be. I will join him soon."

"Oh, Laurel," Chloe began, her voice thick with tears.

"Do not weep for me. I am ready. In truth, I ache to be with my love and our child. My soul cries out for them." Laurel lifted one trembling, pale hand and brushed a tear from Chloe's cheek. "This is why I lingered on this earth, why I did not die soon after my dear Henry did. This child needed us to be here, needed my son's body to be here. I recovered from that deadly fever because fate required it of me. My little Charles Henry will have a proper burial. A blessing, too, mayhap."

"He should not be placed in the wrong grave."

"It matters little, Chloe. He is already with his father, waiting for me. Now, remember, you must make it look as if this child died. Be sure to mark the cross with both names. Wrap the bones we collected most carefully. Ah, do not look so aggrieved, sister. Instead of being tossed upon a pile, as so many others dug out of the London graveyards are, that poor child we gathered will have a fine resting place, too. Here in the country we are not so callous with our dead, do not have to keep moving the old out of the ground to make room for the new 'Tis a fine gift we give that long dead babe."

"I know. Yet, throughout all our careful preparations I kept praying that we were wrong."

"I always knew we were right, that this was a fate that could not be changed by any amount of forewarning. I will miss you, but, truly, do not grieve o'er me. I will be happy."

"How could a mother do this to her only child?" Chloe lightly touched the baby's surprisingly abundant hair.

"She cannot bear his lordship a healthy heir, can she? That would ruin all of her plans."

When Laurel said nothing more for several moments, Chloe murmured, "Rest now. There is no need to speak now."

"There is every need," whispered Laurel. "My time

draws nigh. As soon as I am gone, see to the burial, and then go straight to our cousin Leopold. He will be waiting, ready to begin the game. He will help you watch over this child and his father, and he will help you know when the time is right to act against that evil woman and her lover." Laurel turned her head and pressed a kiss upon the baby's head. "This child needs you. He and his poor love-blind father. We both know that this boy will do great things some day. It gives me peace to know that my sorrows are not completely in vain, that some good will come out of all this grief."

Chloe kissed her sister's ice cold cheek and then wept as she felt the last flicker of life flee Laurel's bone-thin body. Pushing aside the grief weighing upon her heart like a stone, she prepared Laurel for burial. The sun was barely rising on a new day when she stood by her sister's grave, her sturdy little mare packed with her meager belongings, a goat tethered to the patient mount, and the baby settled snugly against her chest in a crude blanket sling. One wind-contorted tree was all that marked Laurel's grave upon the desolate moors. Chloe doubted the wooden cross she had made would last long and the rocks she had piled upon Laurel's grave to deter scavengers would soon be indistinguishable from many another one dotted about the moors.

"I *will* come back for you, Laurel," Chloe swore. "I *will* see you and little Charles Henry buried properly. And this wee pauper child you hold will also have a proper burial right beside you. It deserves such an honor." She said a silent prayer for her sister and then turned away, fixing her mind upon the long journey ahead of her.

When, a few hours later, Chloe had to pause in her journey to tend to the baby's needs, she looked across the rutted road at the huge stone pillars that marked the road to Collinsmoor, the home of the child she held. She was tempted to go there to try to find out exactly what was happening. The village had been rife with rumors. Chloe knew it would be foolish, however, and remained where she was, sheltered among the thick grove of trees on the opposite side of the road which would lead her to London and her cousin Leopold.

Just as she was ready to resume her journey, she heard the sound of a horse rapidly approaching. She watched as a man recklessly galloped down the London road and then turned up the road to Collinsmoor to continue his headlong race. He made quite a show, she mused. Tall and lean, dressed all in black, and riding a huge black gelding, he was an imposing sight. The only color showing was that of his long, golden brown hair, his queue having obviously come undone during his wild ride. His lean aristocratic face had been pale, his features set in the harsh lines of deep concern. He was the perfect portrait of the doting husband rushing to join his wife and welcome their child. Chloe thought of the grief the man would soon suffer, believing that his child was dead, and the grief yet to come when he discovered the ugly truth about the woman he loved. And wondered how it might change the man.

She looked down at the infant in her arms. "That was your papa, laddie. He looked to be a fine man.

And up the road lies your heritage. Soon you will be able to lay claim to both. On that I do swear."

With one last look toward Collinsmoor, she mounted her horse and started to ride toward London. She fought the strange compelling urge to follow that man and save him from the pain he faced. That, she knew, would be utter folly. Fate demanded that the man go through this trial. Until his lordship saw the truth, until he saw his lady wife for exactly what she was, Chloe knew that her duty, her *only* duty, was to keep this child alive.

A fortnight later she knocked upon the door of her cousin Leopold's elegant London home, not really surprised when he opened the door himself. He looked down at the baby in her arms.

"Welcome, Anthony," he said.

"A good name," Chloe murmured.

"'Tis but one of many. The notice of his death was in the papers."

Chloe sighed and entered the house. "And so it begins."

"Aye, child. And so it begins."

Chapter 1

London—Three Years Later

Struggling to remain upright, Julian Anthony Charles Kenwood, ninth earl of Collinsmoor, walked out of the brothel into the damp, foul London night. Reminding himself of who he was was not having its usual stabilizing effect, however. His consequence did not stiffen his spine, steady his legs, or clear the thick fog of too much drink from his mind. He prayed he could make it to his carriage parked a discreet distance away. While it was true that he had been too drunk to indulge himself with any of Mrs. Button's fillies, he had felt that he could at least manage the walk to his carriage. He was not so confident of that anymore.

Step by careful step he began to walk toward where his carriage awaited him. A noise to his right drew his attention but, even as he turned to peer into the shadows, he felt a sharp pain in his side. Blindly, he struck out, gratified to hear a cry of pain and a curse. Julian struggled to pull his pistol from his pocket as he caught sight of a hulking shadowy form moving toward him. He saw the glint of a blade sweeping down toward his chest and stumbled to the left, crying out as the knife cut deep into his right shoulder. A stack of rotting barrels that smelled strongly of fish painfully halted his fall backward.

Just as he thought that this time whoever sought to kill him would actually succeed, another shadowy form appeared. This one was much smaller. It leapt out of the thick dark to land squarely upon his attacker's back. As Julian felt himself grow weaker, he finally got his pistol out of his pocket, only to realize that he could not see clearly enough to shoot the man who had stabbed him. Even now the pistol was proving too heavy for him to hold. If this was a rescue, he feared it had come too late.

Chloe held on tight as the man who had stabbed the earl did his best to shake her off his back. She punched him in the head again and again, ignoring his attempts to grab hold of her, as she waited for Todd and Wynn to catch up with her. The moment they arrived she flung herself from the man's back and let Leo's burly men take over the fight. She winced at the sounds of fists hitting flesh, something that sounded a lot more painful than her fist hitting a very hard head, and hurried to the earl's side.

He did not look much like the elegant gentleman she had seen from time to time over the last three years. Not only were his fine clothes a mess, but also he stank of cheap liquor, cheap women, fish, and blood. Chloe took his pistol from his limp hand, set it aside, and then, with strips torn from her petticoats and his cravat, bound his wounds as best she could. She prayed she could slow his bleeding until she could get him to Leo's house and tend to his injuries properly.

"Need him alive," Julian said, his voice weak and hoarse with pain. "Need to ask questions."

Glancing behind her, Chloe saw the man sprawled on the ground, Todd and Wynn looking satisfied as they idly rubbed their knuckles. "Did you kill him?"

"Nay, lass, just put him in a deep sleep," replied Wynn.

"Good. His lordship wants to ask him a few questions."

"Well enough then. We will tie him up and take him with us."

"My carriage—" began Julian.

"Gone, m'lord," replied Chloe. "Your coachman still lives and we have him safe."

"Wynn's got the other man," said Todd, as he stepped up to Chloe. "I will be toting his lordship."

Julian tried to protest as he was picked up and carried like a child by the big man, but no one heeded him. He looked at the small figure leading them out of the alley and suddenly realized that one of his rescuers was a woman. This has to be some delusion brought on by too much drink, he thought.

When he was settled on a plush carriage seat, he looked across at his coachman. Danny's head was bloody, but his chest rose and fell evenly proving that he still lived. The small woman climbed into the carriage and knelt on the floor between the seats, placing a hand on him and the other on Danny to hold them steady as the carriage began to move.

"Who are you?" he asked, struggling to remain conscious and wondering why he even bothered.

"Hold your questions for now, m'lord," she replied. "Best they wait until we can sew you up and some of that foul brew you wallowed in tonight is cleared out of your head and belly."

His rescuer obviously had little respect for his consequence, Julian thought, as he finally gave in to the blackness that had been pulling at him.

Chloe sat in a chair by the bed and sipped her coffee as she studied the earl of Collinsmoor. He smelled better now that he had been cleaned up, but his elegant features held signs of the deep dissipation he had sunk himself in for the last year. She had been disappointed in him and a little disgusted when he had begun to wallow in drink and whores, but Leopold had told her that men tended to do such things when they had suffered betrayal at a woman's hands. Chloe supposed that, if her heart had been shattered so brutally, she too might have done something foolish. Yet, rutting like a goat and drinking oneself blind seemed a little excessive.

Even so, she had to wonder if the earl was lacking in wits. Three times before this he had nearly been killed, yet he had continued to do things that left him vulnerable, just as he had done two nights ago. Did he think he was simply a very unlucky man? She had hoped he knew he was marked for death, and at least had some idea of the who and the why. Chloe did not look forward to trying to get the man to heed her warnings, but Leopold felt they could no longer just keep watch over the man, that it was time to act.

For little Anthony's sake she had agreed. The boy saw her and Leo as his family. The longer that was allowed to continue, the harder it would be to reunite him with his father. Her heart would break when that happened, but she was determined to see that Anthony did not suffer unduly. The boy also needed his father alive to help him claim his heritage and hold fast to it. Between the earl's increasingly dissipated ways and his mother's greed, Anthony would not have much heritage left to claim unless this game was ended very soon. That was unacceptable to her. Anthony was innocent in all of this and did not deserve to suffer for the follies of his parents.

She smiled at her cousin Leopold when he ambled into the room. Leopold never seemed to move fast, appearing permanently languid in his every action, but it suited his tall, almost lanky, body. Those who did not know him well thought him an amiable but useless fellow living off the wealth of his forefathers. Appearances could be deceptive, however. Leopold had been indefatigable in his surveillance of the Kenwoods, had gathered up reams of information, had assembled a large group of associates who were all dedicated to keeping the earl alive and getting proof of who was trying to kill him, and was himself responsible for saving the man's life three times. England also benefited from dear Leopold's many skills, for he was one of their most dedicated and successful agents. Chloe wondered at times if there was something about the earl's enemies that made Leopold think they might be a threat to England as well, but she never asked. Leopold held fast to the country's secrets.

"He will live," Leopold said, after carefully examining Lord Kenwood's wounds.

"Again. The man has more lives than a cat," Chloe drawled.

"His enemies are certainly persistent." Leopold lounged at the end of the bed, his back against the thick ornately carved post. "Clever, too. If not for us they would have won this game long ago, even after his lordship discovered the ugly truth about his wife."

"Ah, but not *all* the ugly truth."

"I think he suspects most of it. He already strongly suspects that that babe was not his get. And that his wife was never faithful to him, never much cared for him at all."

"How do you know all that?"

"His best friend has become mine. Do not look so uneasy, love. I truly like the fellow. Met him the first time I saved this poor sot's hide. Thought he could be useful, but quickly saw that he was a man I could call friend. Even more important—he was a man I could trust."

Chloe nodded and set aside her empty cup. "How much does this friend know?"

"Nearly all. Guessed most of it himself. Since I was already disinclined to lie to the man, I *implied* that I had begun to look into the business after the second attempt on the earl's life. He told me that was exactly when Lord Kenwood himself had begun to believe that his wife wanted him dead, that she was no longer happy just cuckolding him."

"Who is this friend?"

"The honorable Sir Edgar Dramfield."

"Oh, I know him. I have met him at Lady Millicent's on occasion. She is his godmother. A very good fellow. He is kinder to Lady Millicent than her own daughter is."

"He *is* a good man and he is very concerned about his friend. That is why I sent word to him this morning about Lord Kenwood's injuries, asking him to keep it quiet. Very quiet. He will undoubtedly arrive soon."

"Are you sure that is wise? Lord Kenwood may not wish others to hear what we have to tell him."

Leopold sighed. "It was a hard decision. Yet, the earl does not know us at all, does he? He has, however, known Edgar all his life, trusts him, and has bared his soul to the man on a few occasions."

"Whilst deep in his cups, I suspect."

"That is usually when a man bares his soul," Leopold drawled and then smiled at Chloe when she rolled her eyes. "I felt the earl would need a friend, Chloe, and Edgar is the only close one he has. We will be telling his lordship some very ugly truths and he needs to believe us."

"You said he already has his own suspicions," Chloe began.

"Suspicions do not carry the same weight, or wield the same blow to one's heart. We will be filling in a lot of holes he may have concerning his suspicions and giving him proof. There is also one hard, cold fact we must present to him, one that would bring many a man to his knees. It would certainly cut me more deeply than I care to think about. We may also need Edgar to help us keep this fool from going off half-cocked and to convince him to allow us to stay in the game."

"What game?"

Chloe joined Leopold in staring at Lord Kenwood in surprise. There had been no warning that he was about to wake up, no movements, not even a faint sound. When he attempted to sit up he gasped with pain and grew alarmingly pale. Chloe quickly moved to plump up the pillows behind him even as Leopold helped the man sit up and drink some cider doctored with herbs meant to stave off infection and strengthen the blood.

"I know you," Julian said after taking several slow, deep breaths to push aside his pain. "Lord Sir Leopold Wherlocke of Starkley." He looked at Chloe. "I do not know you."

"Chloe Wherlocke. Leo's cousin," Chloe said.

There was definitely a similarity in looks, Julian decided. Chloe was also slender, although a great deal shorter than her cousin. Julian doubted Chloe stood much higher than five feet, if that. She had the same color hair, a brown so dark it was nearly black, but her hair appeared to be bone straight whereas Leopold's was an unruly mass of thick curls and waves. Chloe was also cute more than pretty, with her wide inky blue eyes. Julian nearly started in surprise when he suddenly realized where he had heard that low, faintly lilting voice before.

"You were there," he said. "When I was attacked."

"Ah, aye, I was." Chloe decided it would be best not to tell the man just how she had known he needed her help. People often found her visions a little difficult to understand, or tolerate. "Me and Leo's men, Todd and Wynn."

With his left hand Julian touched the bandages at his waist and shoulder. "How bad?"

"You will live. The wounds were deep enough to need stitching, but are not mortal. They also cleaned up well, the bleeding was stopped fair quickly, and you continue to reveal no sign of a fever or an infection. You have also slept most peacefully for nearly two full days. All good."

He nodded faintly. "I should go home. I can have my man care for me and relieve you of this burden."

"That might not be wise," said Leopold. "This is the fourth time someone has tried to murder you, m'lord. The ones who want you dead nearly succeeded this time. Indeed, they came closer than ever before. I think you might wish to consider letting them think that they *have* succeeded. The rumors of your sad fate have already begun to slip through the ranks of the ton."

Before Julian could ask just how Lord Sir Leopold knew this was the fourth attack on him he was surprised by the arrival of Edgar Dramfield. He watched his old friend greet Lord Leopold with obvious warmth and wondered when the two men had become such good friends. It surprised Julian even more when Edgar greeted Miss Wherlocke as though he had known her for quite a while as well. Finally

Edgar stepped up to the side of the bed and studied him.

"Either the ones trying to kill you are completely inept or you are one very lucky man, Julian," said Edgar.

"'Tis a bit of both, I think," replied Julian. "Have you come to take me home?" He frowned when Edgar looked at Leopold before answering and that man slowly shook his head.

"Nay," replied Edgar.

"What is going on here?"

Edgar sat in the chair Leopold brought to the edge of the bed. "We have decided that it is time this deadly game was ended, Julian. You have been attacked four times. Four times someone has tried to kill you. Your luck simply cannot hold. Do you really wish to continue to give them the chance to succeed? To win?"

Julian closed his eyes and softly cursed. He was in pain, although he wondered what had been in that drink he had been given, for his pain was definitely less sharp than it had been when he had first woken up. Nevertheless, he was not in the mood to discuss this matter. And, yet, Edgar was right. He had been lucky so far, but this time, if not for the Wherlockes, he would be lying dead in a foul alley outside a brothel. And what the Wherlockes had to do with his troubles he did not know. He looked at Edgar again.

"No, I do not want them to win, whoever they are," he said.

"I think you know exactly who is behind it all, Julian," Edgar said quietly, his eyes soft with sympathy.

Not ready to say the name, Julian turned his attention

to the Wherlockes and frowned. "Just what do you have to do with all of this?"

Chloe felt a pang of sympathy for the man. She knew the pain in his jade green eyes was not all due to his injuries. Even if he had lost all love for his wife, the betrayal still had to cut deep and she was soon to add to his wounds. As her cousin retook his seat at the foot of the bed, she clasped her hands in her lap and tried to think of just what to say and how best to say it.

"I believe we can leave the explanations as to *how* we stumbled into this until later," Leopold said.

"That might be best," Chloe agreed and then smiled faintly at Julian. "We have been involved in your difficulties for quite some time, m'lord."

Edgar nodded. "Leopold was the one who brought you to my house the last time you were attacked."

"But did not stay until I could offer my gratitude for his aid?" Julian asked.

"Nay," Leopold replied. "You were not as sorely injured as you were this time and I felt we still had time."

"Time for what?"

"To gather the proof you will need to end this deadly game." Leopold cursed softly. "It is time to be blunt, m'lord. You know who wants you dead. Edgar knows. We know. I can understand your reluctance to speak the ugly truth aloud."

"Can you?"

"Oh, aye, most assuredly. Our family is no stranger to betrayal."

"Fine," Julian said between tightly gritted teeth. "My wife wants me dead."

"Your wife and her lover."

"Which one?" The bitterness in his voice was so sharp Julian nearly winced, embarrassed by the display of emotion.

"The only one who could possibly gain from your death—your uncle Arthur Kenton."

Chloe clenched her hands together tightly as she fought the urge to touch Lord Julian, to try to soothe the anger and hurt he felt. She was relieved when Wynn arrived with tea and food, including a bowl of hearty broth for his lordship. It was best if the harsh truth was allowed to settle in a little before they continued. She proceeded to feed Lord Julian the broth, oddly relieved by the way he grimaced over such weak fare in the normal manner of most patients. Edgar and Leopold moved to the table set near the fireplace to sip tea, eat a little food, and talk quietly while she tended to Lord Julian.

"What are they talking about?" Julian asked between mouthfuls of the surprisingly tasty broth.

"You, I suppose," Chloe replied. "They are probably making plans to keep you alive and bring down your enemies."

"Edgar's interest I can understand, but I still have to wonder what you and your cousin have to do with this."

"What sort of people would we be if, upon knowing someone was in danger, we just turned our backs simply because we did not know him?"

"Quite normal people."

"Ah, well, very few people have ever accused the Wherlockes of being normal." After feeding him the last of the broth, Chloe set the bowl aside and retook her seat by the bed. "Perhaps we just feel that one cannot allow people to dispose of the gentry whenever the mood takes them. Tsk, think of the chaos that would result."

"Enough of your sauce," said Leopold, as he and Edgar rejoined them. "Shall we plot our plots, m'lord?" he asked Lord Julian as he sat down at the end of the bed again. "Unless, of course, you enjoy indulging in a slow, catch-me-if-you-can sort of suicide."

"And you reprimand *me* for sauce," Chloe muttered, but everyone ignored her.

"No, curse you, I do not enjoy this game," snapped Lord Julian, and then he sighed. "I but wished to ignore the harsh truth staring me in the face. It is bad enough knowing one's wife is cuckolding one—repeatedly. To think one's own uncle is not only doing the cuckolding, but that he and said wife want one dead is a bitter draught to swallow. I am not a complete idiot, however. You are all right. They nearly succeeded this time. I am just not certain what can be done about it. Did the man you caught say anything useful?"

"Nay, I fear not," Leopold replied. "He says the man who hired him was well hidden in a large coat, a hat, and a scarf. All he is certain of is that the man was gentry. Fine clothes, fine speech, smelled clean. All the usual clues. He also said that he was paid a crown to follow you about until an opportunity to kill you arose and then to grasp that opportunity."

"A crown? Is that all?" Julian felt strangely insulted by that. "An earl's life ought to be worth more than that."

"To that man a crown is a small fortune and he was promised more if he could prove that you were dead. And, nay, there is no hope of catching anyone red-handed. A very convoluted way was set up to deliver the extra payment. One that easily allows your enemy every chance to slip free of any trap set for him. Also, proof of your death must be shown and we cannot feign that. I am assuming that you are rather fond of your right hand."

"You could say that." Julian frowned at his right hand, at the scar that ran raggedly over the back of it. "It was a near miracle that I did not lose it to this wound. A duel," he said when he noticed the curiosity the Wherlockes could not hide. "The first and last I fought in the name of my wife's honor."

Julian was beginning to feel very tired and he knew it was not just because of his wounds. It was his own emotional turmoil that stole his strength, a heaviness of the spirit and the heart. Not only had his pride been lacerated by his wife's betrayal, but also his confidence in himself and his own judgment. However, he had wallowed in self-pity long enough. Painful though it was to face the truth, he could no longer try to ignore it, not if he wished to stay alive. Soaking himself in drink and whores might have looked like a slow suicide to others, but that had never been his intent. He was certainly miserable, but not so much that he was ready to welcome the cold oblivion of the grave.

"Edgar and I think you should play dead for a while," said Leopold. "Aside from us, the only one who knows you are alive is the man who attacked you. He will very soon be too far away to tell anyone the truth."

"Your servants—"

"Will keep the secret." Leopold smiled faintly at Julian's look of doubt. "You must accept my word on that, m'lord. Our family and our cousins the Vaughns have servants whose loyalty and silence is absolute."

"Something many would pay a fortune for. So, I remain dead. Do I hide here then?"

"Do you trust *your* servants to be silent?"

"Not all of them, no." Julian sighed. "I still do not understand how you became involved in this mess."

"We have been involved from the beginning, m'lord," said Chloe. "From the night your wife gave birth—"

"To someone else's child," he snapped. "That was *not* my child."

"I know, m'lord. It was my sister's."

Julian was shocked speechless. As he slowly recovered his wits enough to start asking a few questions, he became acutely aware of a new, very pressing need. He tried to will it away, but reluctantly accepted that his body was not willing to wait until he got the answers he needed.

"Damnation," he muttered. "We need to talk about that, but, right now—" He hesitated then said, "I need some privacy."

"Ah, I understand." Chloe stood up, quickly guessing what he needed and moved toward the door. "I will have the answers to your questions when I return."

"How can she know what my questions will even be?" he asked Leopold the moment Chloe was gone and Edgar quickly moved to help him tend to his personal needs.

"Oh, she can only guess," replied Leopold.

Julian fought down a sense of humiliation as the two men helped him, washed him down, and put him in a clean nightshirt. He hated being so weak and helpless, but had to accept that he was both at the moment and that he needed all the help he could get. Once settled back in his bed, he needed a few moments to still the trembling in his body and will his pain to recede. When he finally opened his eyes again, he gave the two men watching him with concern a weak smile. Then he recalled what Chloe had said and frowned. Julian decided he must have misheard her.

"Did she really say that the child was her sister's?" he asked. "That I have interred her sister's child in my family crypt?"

Leopold sighed and nodded. "Her sister Laurel's child. Laurel married a poor man who died whilst out fishing. She knew she would not survive the birth of her child, that she was too weakened by a recurring fever and grief. Two men came whilst Laurel lay dying on her childbed, her babe born dead, and they took the child away."

"But why? Was Beatrice feigning that she was with child? Was it *all* a lie?"

"Oh, nay, not all," said Chloe, as she entered the room and walked to the side of his bed, allowing little Anthony to remain hidden behind her skirts for the moment. "Your wife was indeed with child. She and Laurel took to their birthing beds at the same time, something your wife was well aware of as she held the midwife in her power. S'truth, I think the midwife made certain that both women birthed their children at the same moment."

"That makes no sense," Julian muttered. "If Beatrice *was* with child, what happened to it? Where is it buried?"

"It is not buried, m'lord, although Laurel and I worked very hard to make your wife believe the child lies in a grave with Laurel. A trade was made. Lady Beatrice's live child for my sister's dead one."

"Again—why? To what purpose?"

"Why? Because the very last thing your wife and uncle wanted was for you to have an heir."

"If the child was even mine. That woman was never faithful."

Chloe stared at him for a moment and then smiled. "Then it seems you won the luck of the draw, m'lord. The child *is* yours."

"You have seen the child? You know what happened to the baby?"

"The baby has been well cared for." Chloe tugged Anthony out from behind her until he stood in front of her. "The child is the very image of his father. My lord, meet Anthony Peter Chadwick Kenton—your son and heir."

Julian stared into eyes the same verdant green as his own. Thick golden curls topped the boy's head, sharply reminding Julian of his own boyish curls. Julian looked at the three adults all watching him intently and then looked into those eyes that marked the child as his own. Even as he opened his mouth to speak, he felt himself tumble into blackness.

About the Author

Hannah Howell is an award-winning author who lives with her family in Massachusetts. She is the author of twenty-nine Zebra historical romances and is currently working on a new historical romance, *If He's Wicked*, coming in June 2009! Hannah loves hearing from readers and you may visit her Web site: *www.hannahhowell.com*.